PINEAL

All rights reserved. No part of this publication may be reproduced, distributed, or transmitted in any form or by any means, including photocopying, recording, or other electronic or mechanical methods, without the prior written permission of the author, except in the case of brief quotations embodied in critical reviews and certain other non-commercial uses permitted by copyright law.

First Edition: 2025

Publication Month: June
Copyright © Sujay Das

PINEAL

SUJAY DAS

*This page was not part of the original manuscript.
It was recovered under unexplained circumstances and later
inserted during the final stages of editing.
Its origin remains unknown. The symbols match descriptions in the
book — though none were made public during writing.*

*Those who tried to remove it reported strange activity. So, we
kept it in.*

Found After Submission

What you saw was not part of the original manuscript.

It was discovered months after the final chapter was written, sealed inside a courier envelope addressed to no one, with no postmark, no return address. The image was included in this edition only after several editors insisted it *"somehow completes the book."*

Shortly after including the page:

- ***One editor fell sick while proofreading Chapter 13 — with no diagnosis.***
- ***A junior typesetter reported hearing tapping sounds each time she opened this file.***
- ***Another team member quit, claiming he saw his name hidden in the page's smudges.***

When asked, the author claimed he had never seen the page before.

Yet, the symbols scrawled on it match elements described in the novel — symbols that were never publicly released during writing.

The publisher debated removing it.
But every test print without the page resulted in data corruption during export.

No explanation. No pattern.

The image now remains in every version.
Not by choice.

AUTHOR'S NOTE

This book contains disturbing horror, twisted truths, and sexual content.

(You're welcome)

It involves child brutality.

(My favorite part—don't judge me)

It might make you question reality, lose sleep, or avoid going to the washroom alone.

(I'm not even sorry)

There's blood. There's madness. And there's no happy ending to hold your hand.

If you came here for a cozy ghost story—you might want to run. **Now.**

But if you're the kind who smiles at the dark and whispers ***"bring it on"***...

Welcome to **PINEAL**.

— **Sujay Das**

(Hell, I might even do it again)

CONTENTS

Chapter 1 Bound in Fear 1
Chapter 2 Homebound Horizons 13
Chapter 3 Serenity Grove 25
Chapter 4 Beneath the Surface 37
Chapter 5 An Ominous Morning 49
Chapter 6 Shadows in the Light 65
Chapter 7 Fractured Trust 79
Chapter 8 Healing Wounds 93
Chapter 9 Shadows of Doubt 102
Chapter 10 Seeking Answers 115
Chapter 11 The Investigation Begins 127
Chapter 12   Shape-Shifter 140
Chapter 13 Need Help 152
Chapter 14 Vanishing Fear 162
Chapter 15 The Familiar 179
Chapter 16 Lingering Shadows 191
Chapter 17 A Call to Action 204
Chapter 18 The Hidden Truth 216
Chapter 19 August 12, 2005 – Before the Reckoning 229
Chapter 20 The Thin Veil Between Worlds 245
Chapter 21 A Shrouded Pact 258
Chapter 22 Tiptoe Through the Tulips 279
Chapter 23 The Garden of the Damned 293

Chapter 24 The Breach 306
Chapter 25 He Who Recites 325
Chapter 26 The Cost of Salvation................................. 349
Chapter 27 Ashes and Echoes....................................... 369

CHAPTER 1
BOUND IN FEAR

The thunderstorm raged outside St. Augustine's Hospital, sheets of rain battering the windows and lightning illuminating the darkened sky in brief, eerie flashes. Inside, the fluorescent lights flickered, casting unsettling shadows on the peeling walls. In his small office, Dr. Richard Mallory sat hunched over a set of brain scans, the furrows in his brow deepening with each passing second.

The clock on the wall ticked loudly, each movement of its hands echoing in the silent room. Dr. Mallory's fingers traced the outline of an abnormal pattern on the scan, a sense of dread tightening his chest. "This... doesn't make any sense," he whispered, shaking his head. The patterns on the brain were unlike anything he'd ever seen, an enigma wrapped in a nightmare. He rubbed his temples, trying to quell the rising tide of unease.

Just as he began to reach for another report, the door to his office flew open with a deafening crash, making him jump. Nurse Clara burst in, her face ashen and eyes wide with terror. Blood trickled down from a gash on her forehead, staining her white uniform. She was shaking, her breaths coming in panicked gasps.

"Dr. Mallory! It's started," she cried, her voice cracking. "And it's... it's very violent. We can't control it anymore!"

Mallory's heart skipped a beat. "What? Clara, what's going on?" He rushed to her, his eyes widening at the sight of her wound. "Who did this to you?"

She shook her head, a haunted look in her eyes. "Not who, Doctor... what. It's... it's here. And it's getting stronger."

Before he could press her for details, a chilling scream echoed down the hallway, a sound so filled with terror that it sent shivers down his spine. Clara flinched, clutching at her wound as if the scream itself had caused her pain.

"We need to get you treated," Mallory insisted, guiding her toward the chair. "You're bleeding badly."

"No!" Clara shrieked, pulling away from him. "There's no time! It's already loose. It's hurting everyone. You have to see it for yourself!" Her voice was frantic, and her eyes darted toward the dark corridor beyond the open door.

Mallory felt a cold sweat break out on his forehead. "What do you mean, it's loose? What's hurting people?"

Clara's voice dropped to a whisper, her gaze fixed on something unseen. "It's in the west wing. We tried to lock it in, but... but it's not... it's not something that can be contained."

Another crash, closer this time, made them both jump. The sound of shattering glass followed, and the lights flickered violently before plunging the room into a momentary darkness. Mallory's pulse quickened as he grabbed a flashlight and turned it on, the beam cutting through the shadows.

"Clara, you need to stay here and—" he began, but she cut him off, her voice trembling.

"No, Doctor. You don't understand. It's already here. It's been here all along." She backed away, her eyes wide with fear as she looked at the darkened corridor. "Please, come with me. We have to try to stop it."

Mallory hesitated, the dread in his stomach growing. He followed Clara into the hallway, his flashlight casting eerie shadows on the walls. The hospital, normally a place of sterile safety, now felt like a tomb, every corner hiding unspeakable horrors. The storm outside seemed to mirror the chaos within, each clap of thunder shaking the building to its foundations.

As they neared the west wing, the atmosphere grew thicker, the air cold and oppressive. The walls seemed to close in, the shadows growing darker and more malevolent. Mallory could hear the faint murmur of voices, distorted and unsettling, as if coming from far away or another realm entirely.

A door ahead hung off its hinges, and beyond it, the darkness seemed almost alive. Mallory's flashlight beam revealed overturned beds, shattered equipment, and, in the midst of the chaos, a single figure standing motionless. Its back was turned to them, but even from a distance, Mallory could see the tension in its posture, the unnatural stillness.

Clara grabbed his arm, her grip like a vice. "It's there, Doctor. Do you see? It's... it's watching us."

Mallory's throat tightened as he stared at the figure. It moved suddenly, a slow, deliberate turn that revealed a face contorted with an expression of pure malice. The figure's eyes, hollow and lifeless, seemed to bore into his soul.

"Run," Clara whispered, her voice barely audible. "Please, Doctor, we have to run."

But Mallory couldn't move, his feet rooted to the spot by a terror he couldn't understand. The figure began to advance, its movements unnaturally fluid, almost as if it were gliding.

Another scream, more desperate than the last, echoed through the hospital, and Mallory knew, in that moment, that they were facing something far beyond human comprehension. The storm outside raged on, but it was nothing compared to the storm of fear that now consumed St. Augustine's Hospital.

Dr. Mallory's heart hammered in his chest as the figure glided closer, its eyes reflecting a malevolence that chilled him to the core. Clara's grip tightened around his arm, her nails digging into his skin as if anchoring herself to reality. The corridor seemed to stretch endlessly behind them, offering no escape, no sanctuary from the approaching terror.

"We need to move, Doctor," Clara whispered urgently, her voice quivering with fear. "Now."

Mallory forced himself to take a step back, his flashlight trembling in his hand. The figure's eyes never left his, and a twisted grin spread across its face, revealing teeth that were unnaturally sharp. The air around them grew colder, the chill seeping into his bones, making every movement sluggish and labored.

As they turned to flee, the lights flickered once more, casting grotesque shadows that seemed to mock their fear. The hospital's normal hum of machinery and distant chatter was replaced by a suffocating silence, broken only by the echo of their hurried footsteps.

"This way!" Clara hissed, pulling him toward a side door that led to the stairwell. "We can't go through the main corridor. It's... it's watching us."

Mallory didn't need any further convincing. He followed her through the narrow door, the flashlight beam bouncing erratically as they descended the stairs. Each step echoed like a drumbeat, marking their progress—or their doom. The air in the stairwell was damp and cold, smelling faintly of mold and decay.

"Where are we going?" he panted, trying to keep his voice steady. "What is this thing?"

Clara shook her head, her face a mask of terror. "I don't know, Doctor. It started a few days ago, but... but it's getting worse. It's like... it's feeding off our fear."

They reached the basement level, a dark, labyrinthine space that was rarely used. The walls were lined with old equipment, covered in dust and cobwebs. The fluorescent lights buzzed and flickered overhead, casting eerie, intermittent light that only added to the sense of impending doom.

Clara led him to a small room at the end of the corridor, its door marked with a faded "Maintenance" sign. She fumbled with a key, her hands shaking, before finally managing to unlock it. "We can hide here, at least for a moment," she said, pushing the door open. "We need to think. We need to figure out what to do."

Mallory stepped inside, his eyes scanning the cramped room filled with shelves of cleaning supplies and tools. The flickering light from the corridor cast long, distorted shadows that seemed to move on their own. He closed the door behind them, leaning against it as if trying to keep the darkness at bay.

"What happened, Clara? You need to tell me everything," he demanded, his voice low and urgent.

Clara sank onto an old chair, her face pale and drawn. "It started with the new patient. The one in Room 13. They brought him in after he was found wandering the woods, mumbling about... about seeing things. Things that weren't there."

Mallory frowned. "Room 13? But that room's been empty for years. We don't use it anymore."

"We didn't have a choice," Clara replied, her eyes wide. "The ER was full, and... and no one wanted to take him. There was something about him... something wrong."

Mallory's mind raced. Room 13 was in the oldest part of the hospital, a place where the walls seemed to hold onto the past, whispering forgotten secrets to those who would listen. "What happened to him?"

Clara shuddered. "He started talking about the shadows. Said they were alive, that they were following him. No one believed him at first, but then... strange things started happening. Objects moving on their own, voices whispering in the dark. And then he... he disappeared."

Mallory's blood ran cold. "Disappeared? How?"

"Just vanished. One moment he was there, the next he was gone. And then... people started seeing things. The shadows, they... they began to move. To watch us. It's like... like they're alive."

A sudden loud bang from the corridor made them both jump, their eyes darting to the door. The sound of footsteps—slow, deliberate—echoed through the basement, each step a grim reminder of the terror lurking just outside. The doorknob rattled, and Mallory held his breath, his heart pounding in his ears.

Clara's eyes widened in fear, and she clutched his arm. "It's here. It knows we're here."

The door creaked open slowly, the darkness beyond it impenetrable. The footsteps grew louder, closer, and a cold, malevolent presence filled the room, pressing down on them like a physical weight. Mallory's flashlight flickered and then died, plunging them into total darkness.

In the pitch black, he felt the air grow colder still, the presence looming over them. A low, guttural whisper filled the room, a sound that seemed to come from everywhere and nowhere.

"Run," Clara breathed, her voice barely audible. "Run, before it's too late."

But Mallory knew they had nowhere to run. The darkness was alive, and it had already claimed them. As the oppressive silence closed in, he could feel the cold tendrils of fear wrapping around his heart, and he realized, with a sinking dread, that there was no escape from the terror.

The oppressive silence was shattered by the distant wail of sirens, growing louder as a team of police officers stormed the basement, their flashlights cutting through the darkness like blades. Clara and Dr. Mallory blinked in the harsh light, relief flooding through them at the sight of the uniformed figures.

"Over here!" Clara called, her voice trembling with a mixture of fear and hope. "It's... it's right behind us!"

The officers, led by Detective Harris, fanned out, their faces set with grim determination. Harris, a grizzled veteran with a scar running down his cheek, approached Clara and Mallory. "Are you two okay? We got a call about some kind of disturbance. What the hell is going on here?"

"It's... it's not human," Mallory stammered, his eyes darting to the dark corridor. "Whatever it is, it's incredibly strong. You have to help us contain it."

Harris nodded, his face hardening. "All right, men, be ready for anything. We don't know what we're dealing with." He motioned for his team to advance, their guns drawn and flashlights trained on the corridor.

The air grew colder as they approached the door, a palpable sense of malevolence pressing down on them. The shadows seemed to pulse with life, whispering dark secrets that clawed at the edges of sanity. Harris glanced at his men, his jaw set. "Stay sharp. We're not leaving here until this thing is neutralized."

Suddenly, the door burst open, and the figure lunged at the nearest officer, its eyes glowing with unholy light. The officer screamed as he was thrown against the wall, the sound of breaking bones echoing through the basement. Harris fired his gun, the shot deafening in the confined space, but the bullets seemed to have no effect. The figure turned its gaze on him, a cruel smile twisting its features.

"Fall back!" Harris shouted, his voice cracking with urgency. "Fall back and regroup!"

The officers retreated, their faces pale with terror. The figure advanced slowly, its movements fluid and unnatural, as if it were gliding on air. Clara clutched Mallory's arm, her eyes wide with fear. "We have to do something, Doctor. It's going to kill us all!"

Mallory nodded, his mind racing. "We need to get it into the chair. It's the only way we might have a chance to contain it."

With a surge of desperate courage, Mallory grabbed a nearby metal chair and swung it at the figure, knocking it off balance. "Now, Clara!" he yelled. "Help me restrain it!"

The figure hissed, its eyes burning with rage, but Clara and Mallory managed to wrestle it into the chair, securing it with heavy leather straps. The police officers joined them, holding the figure down as it thrashed violently, its strength nearly overwhelming them.

"Get the sedative!" Mallory shouted, his voice strained. "We need to sedate it before it breaks free!"

Clara ran to the medical cart, her hands shaking as she prepared the syringe. The figure's eyes locked onto hers, a look of pure malevolence that made her blood run cold. She hesitated for a moment, but then steeled herself and plunged the needle into its arm, injecting the sedative.

The figure's struggles slowed, its movements growing sluggish as the drug took effect. Its head lolled to the side, and its eyes flickered, the unholy light fading. But even as it seemed to succumb to the sedative, an eerie, guttural whisper escaped its lips, sending chills down the spines of everyone in the room.

"It's... it's working," Clara said, her voice barely more than a whisper. "I think it's finally calming down."

Harris, his face drawn and haggard, stepped forward, his gun still trained on the figure. "We need to make sure it stays that way. If this thing wakes up again, we're all in serious trouble." He glanced at Mallory, his eyes hard. "I say we end this now. Let's shoot it before it has a chance to break free."

Mallory held up a hand, his face resolute. "No. We can't just kill it. I need to understand what it is. There's something... something more going on here. It's not just a threat; it's a puzzle that needs solving."

Harris scowled, his finger tightening on the trigger. "Doctor, with all due respect, that thing isn't a puzzle. It's a goddamn monster. And if we don't take care of it now, it's going to kill us all."

Clara, her face pale, looked between Harris and Mallory. "Doctor, are you sure? What if... what if it gets loose again?"

Mallory shook his head. "I'm not saying it isn't dangerous. But killing it might not solve the problem. There could be others like it. We need to find out where it came from and how to stop it for good."

Harris gritted his teeth, lowering his gun slightly. "Fine. But if that thing so much as twitches, I'm putting a bullet in its head. Understand?"

Mallory nodded, stepping closer to the restrained figure. Its eyes were closed, its breathing shallow and labored. He could feel the cold emanating from its body, a chilling presence that seemed to reach into his very soul.

"Clara, I need you to monitor its vital signs," Mallory said, his voice steady. "We need to keep it sedated and contained until we can figure out what to do next."

Clara nodded, her hands still trembling as she adjusted the IV drip. "Okay, Doctor. But what if it doesn't stay asleep? What if... what if it's just waiting?"

Mallory glanced at the figure, his heart pounding in his chest. "We'll cross that bridge when we come to it. For now, we need to stay calm and focused. Whatever this thing is, we can't let fear control us."

The figure stirred slightly, a low growl rumbling from its throat. Harris raised his gun again, his eyes narrowing. "Doctor, I don't like this. I've seen enough horror movies to know this doesn't end well. Are you absolutely sure you want to keep this thing alive?"

Mallory took a deep breath, his eyes locked on the creature. "I don't know what this is, but I do know that killing it won't give us the answers we need. We have to try to understand it. That's the only way we can protect ourselves and everyone else."

Harris sighed, lowering his gun reluctantly. "All right. But this is on you, Doctor. If this thing breaks loose again, you'd better have a damn good plan."

Mallory nodded, feeling the weight of responsibility pressing down on him. He knew that whatever happened next, it would change everything. The creature in the chair was a harbinger of something far darker, a glimpse into a world of nightmares that they had only just begun to uncover.

As the storm raged on outside, the basement of St. Augustine's Hospital seemed to close in around them, the darkness filled with unseen eyes and whispered threats. Mallory stared at the restrained figure, his mind racing with questions and fears. He knew that they were standing on the edge of an abyss, and that the horrors they had faced so far were only the beginning.

CHAPTER 2
HOMEBOUND HORIZONS

The first light of Sunday morning slipped through the curtains, casting long, golden shadows across the room. The digital clock on the bedside table blinked lazily, showing 7:00 a.m. In the bed, the young couple lay wrapped in the remnants of their dreams, her head resting on his chest, the rise and fall of his breathing lulling her into a deeper sleep.

Suddenly, the sharp ring of the doorbell cut through the silence, its persistent call pulling the girl from the warmth of her slumber. She groaned softly, her eyelids fluttering open. She glanced at the clock, confusion and annoyance clouding her sleepy eyes.

"Who on earth is ringing the doorbell at this hour?" she muttered, her voice still thick with sleep. Her partner stirred beside her but remained blissfully unaware of the intrusion, lost in his dreams.

The girl, only half awake, stretched languidly, her white shirt riding up to reveal a glimpse of her smooth, toned midriff. She swung her legs out of bed, her movements slow and deliberate, the shirt falling just shy of her thighs. The top three buttons of the shirt were undone, exposing a tantalizing hint of her collarbone and the soft curve of her cleavage. Her bare feet made no sound as she crossed the room, her long legs catching the morning light, skin glowing with youthful allure.

As she reached the door, she smoothed her hair with one hand, trying to bring some semblance of order to her disheveled appearance. She opened the door, blinking against the sudden brightness, and found herself face to face with their landlord, a burly man whose eyes widened slightly at the sight of her.

"Good morning," he said, his voice rough, eyes lingering appreciatively on her. "It's the third of the month. The rent is two days late."

She could feel his gaze trailing over her body, taking in every detail of her appearance—the tousled hair, the shirt barely clinging to her curves, the bare skin of her legs. Her irritation flared, but she forced a polite smile.

"Yes, I know," she replied, trying to keep her voice steady. "I'm really sorry about that. I'll get it for you right away."

The landlord's gaze didn't waver, a smirk curling at the corners of his mouth. "You should really keep better track of these things," he said, his tone dripping with condescension. "You wouldn't want to fall behind on your payments, now, would you?"

She bristled at his words, her cheeks flushing with a mix of embarrassment and anger. "I'm aware of that," she snapped, the forced politeness slipping from her voice. "Just give me a moment."

She turned on her heel, feeling his eyes boring into her back, and walked to the small dresser in the corner of the room. She bent over slightly, rummaging through the drawer, aware of how the movement made her shirt tighten across her hips. She grabbed the envelope with the rent money, straightened up, and walked back to the door.

"Here it is," she said, thrusting the envelope into his hand. "All taken care of."

The landlord's fingers brushed against hers as he took the money, his touch lingering a moment longer than necessary. His smirk widened, his eyes never leaving her face. "Thank you," he said, his voice low. "You know, if you ever need any help with anything, don't hesitate to ask."

Her jaw tightened, and she forced a tight smile. "I'll keep that in mind," she said through gritted teeth. "Now, if you'll excuse me, I'd like to get back to my morning."

The landlord nodded, but his gaze remained fixed on her, a look of smug satisfaction on his face. "Of course," he said. "Enjoy the rest of your day."

She shut the door firmly, her hand trembling with anger and disgust. Leaning against the door, she let out a heavy sigh, muttering under her breath. "Asswipe," she hissed, shaking her head. She felt a shiver run down her spine, the unease from the encounter clinging to her like a shadow.

She stood there for a moment, trying to shake off the discomfort that lingered in the air. The morning that had started so peacefully now carried a weight she couldn't quite identify, a shadow creeping into the edges of her mind.

With a deep breath, she pushed away from the door and walked back to the bed, where her partner still lay sleeping. She climbed in beside him, seeking the comfort of his warmth.

She gave him a gentle shake, her voice soft but urgent. "David, wake up."

David stirred, his eyes fluttering open. He glanced at her, blinking away the remnants of sleep. "What is it? What's wrong?" he asked, his voice groggy.

"It's that sleazy landlord again," she said, her frustration evident. "I'm fed up with him and this whole place. We really need to find somewhere else to live."

David sighed, rubbing his eyes as he sat up. "What happened this time?" he asked, concern mingling with fatigue in his voice.

"He came by for the rent again," she replied, her voice trembling with anger. "He was practically leering at me the entire time. I felt like he was undressing me with his eyes. It's disgusting!"

David's brow furrowed, anger flashing in his eyes. "That creep! I'm sorry you had to deal with that. He's such a piece of shit."

She nodded, her eyes filling with frustration. "I know, right? I'm just so tired of it. It's not just this morning, either. He's always finding excuses to come by and stare at me. I can't stand it anymore."

David wrapped an arm around her, pulling her close. "We'll figure something out. I promise. But you know how hard it is to find a decent place in New York. The rents are insane, and good apartments get snatched up so quickly."

"I know," she said, resting her head on his shoulder. "But we have to try. I can't keep living here, not with him around. It's making me miserable."

David kissed the top of her head, his voice soothing. "We'll start looking today, okay? We'll find something better, I promise."

She sighed, feeling a bit of the tension ease from her shoulders. "Thanks, David. I just want to feel safe and comfortable in our home, you know?"

"I understand," he said softly. "And we'll make it happen. We'll find a place where we can be happy and not have to worry about that asshole."

She nodded, a small smile breaking through her frustration. "You always know how to make me feel better," she said, leaning in to kiss him gently.

David smiled, his expression warm and reassuring. "That's because I love you," he said. "And I hate seeing you upset. We'll get through this, together."

She hugged him tightly, feeling a sense of relief. "I love you too," she said. "And I'm glad we're in this together."

David nodded, his expression determined. "First things first, though," he said, glancing at the clock. "Let's get some breakfast and then we'll start looking for a new place. We'll find somewhere that's perfect for us, no matter how long it takes."

She smiled, feeling a renewed sense of hope. "That sounds like a plan," she said. "I'll make some coffee while you get ready."

David kissed her again, a quick, affectionate peck. "Deal," he said, climbing out of bed. "And don't worry about that jerk. We're going to find something better, and he'll be nothing but a bad memory soon."

As David headed to the bathroom, she made her way to the kitchen, feeling lighter and more optimistic. The morning had started off horribly, but with David's support, she felt ready to take on the challenge of finding a new home.

In the small, cozy kitchen, the scent of fresh coffee began to fill the air as Claire, now more awake and determined, started brewing a pot. The soft hum of the coffee maker was a comforting sound, a small routine that brought a sense of normalcy to the otherwise unsettling morning.

As she reached for a frying pan to start breakfast, she heard the sound of tiny feet pattering on the wooden floor behind her. She turned to see her twin daughters, Lily and Emma, standing in the doorway, their identical faces lit up with sleepy smiles.

Lily, the more adventurous of the two, was the first to speak, her voice a sweet, high-pitched melody. "Mommy, we waked up early! We want breakfast!"

Emma, always slightly shyer, clung to her sister's hand, nodding enthusiastically. "Yes, Mommy, we hungwy."

Claire's heart melted at the sight of her daughters, their curly brown hair tousled from sleep, their big blue eyes sparkling with innocence. They wore matching pajamas decorated with tiny stars, their little feet bare against the cool floor.

"Good morning, my angels," Claire said, a smile spreading across her face despite the earlier tension. She crouched down to their level, opening her arms wide. "Come here, give Mommy a hug."

The twins rushed forward, giggling as they threw their small arms around her neck, their warm bodies pressing against hers. Claire held them close, feeling the pure, uncomplicated love that only children could give. It was moments like these that made all the struggles worthwhile.

"Are my little munchkins hungry?" she asked, pulling back slightly to look at their cherubic faces.

"Yes, yes!" Lily exclaimed, bouncing on her toes. "We want pancakes! With stawbewwies!"

"Pwitty pwease, Mommy?" Emma added, her big eyes pleading, her voice soft and earnest.

Claire laughed, unable to resist their adorable requests. "Alright, pancakes with strawberries it is. But you two have to help me, okay?"

"Okay!" they chorused, their excitement bubbling over as they followed Claire to the counter.

Claire handed them each a small bowl of washed strawberries. "Can you two cut these up for me?" she asked, guiding them to a safe spot on the counter. "Be careful with the knife, remember how we practiced?"

The twins nodded seriously, taking their tasks to heart. Lily, with her tongue poking out in concentration, carefully sliced the strawberries, while Emma, with a furrowed brow, mimicked her sister's movements. Claire watched them with a fond smile, feeling a swell of pride for her little girls.

As the kitchen filled with the sound of happy chatter and the sizzle of pancakes on the griddle, Claire couldn't help but feel a sense of peace. Despite the tension with the landlord and the uncertainty of their future living arrangements, moments like these reminded her of what truly mattered. Her family, their happiness, and the love that bound them together.

"Mommy, can we have extra syrup?" Lily asked, her eyes twinkling mischievously as she held up a perfectly cut strawberry.

"Yes, pwetty pwease, extra sywup!" Emma echoed, her face lighting up at the thought.

Claire chuckled, shaking her head. "Alright, alright, extra syrup for my two little chefs. But you have to promise not to make a mess, okay?"

"We pwomise!" they said in unison, their faces beaming with delight.

As the pancakes cooked to a golden brown, Claire glanced out the kitchen window, her mind briefly drifting to the landlord and the earlier conversation with David. The road ahead might be uncertain, but with her family by her side, she felt ready to face whatever challenges came their way.

Just as she was plating the pancakes, David walked into the kitchen, looking more awake and ready to face the day. He smiled at the sight of his daughters, their faces smeared with strawberry juice, and at Claire, who seemed to radiate calm despite the morning's earlier chaos.

"Smells good in here," he said, leaning in to kiss Claire on the cheek. "Are we having a pancake party?"

Claire laughed, handing him a plate piled high with pancakes and fresh strawberries. "Something like that," she said. "Lily and Emma decided we needed a special breakfast today."

David grinned, ruffling Lily's hair. "You two are the best chefs in New York," he said, making the girls giggle with pride.

As they sat down to eat, the mood was light and full of warmth. The twins chatted excitedly about their plans for the day, their innocent joy a bright contrast to the tension that had hung over the morning.

As the family sat around the small kitchen table, the sweet aroma of freshly made pancakes filled the air, mingling with the cheerful chatter of Lily and Emma. The twins were engrossed in a playful argument about who had the best pancake toppings, their giggles echoing through the room. Claire watched them with a smile, savoring the moment of peace and happiness.

David, ever the doting father, added more syrup to the twins' plates, eliciting squeals of delight. "Alright, you two, don't make too big of a mess," he said, chuckling as Lily tried to catch a dripping glob of syrup with her fork.

"Mommy, look! I made a pancake tower!" Emma announced proudly, stacking three pancakes on top of each other, her eyes wide with excitement.

Claire laughed, nodding approvingly. "That's an impressive tower, sweetie. Just make sure it doesn't topple over, okay?"

Emma nodded vigorously, her little hands working to keep the pancakes balanced. "I'm gonna eat it all up, Mommy!"

While the twins continued their pancake adventures, Claire casually scrolled through her Facebook feed on her phone, taking a sip of her coffee. Among the usual updates from friends and family, a particular post caught her eye. It was an advertisement for a property—an old house with a large, lush yard. The headline read: ***"Spacious Historic Home for Sale: Incredible Deal!"***

Intrigued, Claire tapped on the ad to read more. The post was accompanied by several photos of a grand, two-story house with a charming, if slightly weathered, exterior. It had a wraparound porch, tall windows, and a beautiful, albeit overgrown, garden. The asking price was surprisingly low, especially given the size of the property.

"David, look at this," Claire said, her voice tinged with excitement. She turned her phone towards him, showing him the pictures.

David leaned over, his eyebrows raising in interest. "Wow, that's a big place. And for that price? In New York? Are they serious?"

Claire nodded, scrolling through the photos. "It looks like it's been on the market for a while. Maybe they're desperate to sell. It's in Hudson Valley, not too far from here."

David looked thoughtful, his mind already working through the possibilities. "It could be a great opportunity," he said slowly. "I mean, we've been talking about finding a new place. This could be perfect for us."

"I think so too," Claire said, her excitement growing. "It's got plenty of space for the girls to play, and we wouldn't have to deal with any more landlords leering at us."

David chuckled, nodding. "Yeah, that would be a big plus. But we should definitely check it out before getting too excited. There's got to be a reason it's so cheap."

"Can we go see the new house, Mommy?" Lily piped up, her face smeared with syrup. She had been listening intently to their conversation, her eyes wide with curiosity.

"Yes, Mommy, pwease!" Emma added, her pancake tower now a distant memory as she focused on the prospect of a new adventure.

Claire smiled at her daughters, their enthusiasm infectious. "Of course, sweeties. We'll all go take a look. It could be our new home."

David nodded in agreement, already planning out their day. "How about we finish breakfast, clean up, and then head out to check it out? I'll give the real estate agent a call to set up a viewing."

Claire's eyes sparkled with anticipation. "That sounds perfect. Let's do it."

As they finished their breakfast, the conversation buzzed with excitement and curiosity about the house. Claire couldn't help but feel a thrill of hope as they discussed the possibilities.

"It could be really nice to have a big yard," she mused, picturing the girls playing outside on sunny afternoons. "And we'd have so much more space for everything."

David nodded, his mind already racing with ideas. "I bet we could fix it up a bit, make it really homey. And no more dealing with annoying landlords."

"Do you think it will have a big kitchen?" Claire asked, her eyes lighting up at the thought. "I've always wanted a big kitchen where I can cook and bake with the girls."

"I hope so," David said, smiling at her excitement. "And maybe we'll even have room for a little workshop or office space for you."

Claire's heart swelled with the possibilities. "That would be amazing. I can't wait to see it."

As they wrapped up their breakfast, Claire felt a renewed sense of optimism. The prospect of a new home, a fresh start, filled her with hope. She glanced at her daughters, their faces still smeared with syrup, and felt a surge of determination. They would find a place where they could all be happy and secure, away from the shadows of the past.

David wiped the syrup off Lily's cheek with a damp cloth, his expression tender. "Alright, girls, let's get you cleaned up and ready for our adventure."

"Yay! We're going to see the new house!" Emma cheered, clapping her sticky hands together.

Claire laughed, shaking her head. "Yes, but first, let's get you both cleaned up. We can't have you meeting the real estate agent covered in syrup."

With their breakfast finished and their spirits lifted, the family set about tidying up the kitchen. Claire's thoughts were filled with visions of their potential new home, a place where they could create new memories and build a life together. The shadows of the past seemed to fade as they prepared for their journey, replaced by the bright promise of the future.

CHAPTER 3
SERENITY GROVE

The morning sun filtered through the dense canopy of trees as David navigated the winding road, Claire beside him with her phone pressed to her ear. Lily and Emma, strapped securely in their car seats in the back, peered out the windows with wide-eyed wonder. The air was crisp, carrying the earthy scent of pine and damp leaves, a stark contrast to the hustle and bustle of city life they were leaving behind.

"Hello? Yes, hi, this is Claire. We're on our way to see the house," Claire spoke into the phone, her voice filled with anticipation. She glanced at David, who flashed her a reassuring smile before focusing back on the road.

The gravel crunched under the tires as they drove deeper into the forest. Tall trees towered overhead, their branches creating a natural canopy that filtered the sunlight into dappled patterns on the road. Shafts of golden light broke through, illuminating patches of wildflowers and ferns that lined the roadside.

"So, how far out are we, Claire?" David asked, his eyes scanning the road ahead as he steered around a gentle curve.

Claire listened intently to the real estate agent on the other end of the line. "Okay, got it. Yes, we're looking forward to seeing it. Thank you," she said, ending the call and slipping her phone back into her purse. "She said it's just a few more miles. The house is tucked away in a secluded area, surrounded by woods."

David nodded thoughtfully. "Secluded sounds nice. Away from the noise and crowds," he said, glancing in the rearview mirror at Lily and Emma, who were pointing excitedly at a deer darting across the road.

"Yeah, and plenty of space for them to run around," Claire replied, her eyes following their daughters' animated gestures. "I can already imagine them exploring the woods, finding secret hideouts."

David smiled, a hint of adventure in his voice. "Maybe even build a treehouse," he suggested, his gaze drifting to the towering trees that stretched endlessly into the horizon.

The road began to wind more steeply uphill, the trees closing in around them. Shafts of sunlight danced across the windshield, casting fleeting patterns of light and shadow. The air grew cooler, carrying a hint of pine and earth.

"It's getting pretty remote out here," David remarked, his tone thoughtful as he navigated a narrow stretch of road. "I hope the house is worth the drive."

"I think it will be," Claire replied optimistically, leaning forward to catch a glimpse of the road ahead. "The pictures looked promising, and the price seems too good to pass up."

The family's excitement bubbled over as they drove through the winding forest road. Claire sat beside David, her eyes scanning the road ahead while David occasionally glanced back to check on Lily and Emma, who were babbling happily in the back seat.

"Daddy, wook! Birdie!" Emma exclaimed, pointing out the window with chubby fingers.

Lily clapped her hands, her face lighting up with joy. "Birdie fly high!"

David smiled warmly, his heart melting at their innocent excitement. "Yes, sweeties, that's a birdie," he replied, glancing at Claire with a grin.

Suddenly, Claire's voice pierced the air, sharp with urgency. "David, look out!"

Startled, David snapped his attention back to the road just in time to see a deer darting out from the trees directly in front of them. He slammed on the brakes, but it was too late to avoid a collision. The car struck the deer with a sickening thud, sending it flying into the roadside bushes. The impact jolted the car and caused Lily and Emma to shriek in fear.

"Mama! Dada!" Lily cried out, her tiny voice trembling with fright.

Emma clung to her plush toy, tears welling up in her eyes. "Wha' happened, Daddy? Birdie okay?"

Claire hugged Emma close, trying to soothe her. "It's okay, honey. We hit a deer, but we're all safe," she reassured, her heart racing with adrenaline.

David quickly checked on Claire and the girls, his hands shaking slightly as he tried to calm his own nerves. "Is everyone alright?" he asked urgently, his voice strained with concern.

"I-I think so," Claire replied, her voice shaky as she stroked Emma's hair. "Just... just a little shaken up."

Lily peeked out from behind her hands, tears streaming down her cheeks. "Is the birdie okay, Daddy?"

David sighed heavily, his gaze flickering to the roadside where the deer lay motionless. "I don't think so, sweetheart," he said softly, his heart heavy with regret.

As they sat in stunned silence, the reality of the situation began to sink in. The deer, once a fleeting glimpse of wildlife in their journey, now lay still and lifeless by the roadside. The forest around them seemed eerily quiet, as if holding its breath in the aftermath of the sudden collision.

Claire took a deep breath, trying to steady herself. "What do we do now?" she asked, her voice trembling slightly.

David glanced at the damage to the front of the car, assessing their options. "We should check the car first," he replied, his tone practical despite the lingering shock. "Make sure it's safe to continue."

With cautious movements, David stepped out of the car and inspected the front bumper and grille. The damage appeared minimal, mostly cosmetic, but the car was still driveable.

"It looks okay," David called back to Claire, relief evident in his voice. "I think we can still make it to the house."

Claire nodded, her hands still trembling slightly. "Okay," she said quietly, her thoughts racing with the close call they had just experienced.

David returned to the driver's seat and started the car again, the engine rumbling to life. He glanced at Claire, his expression filled with concern. "Are you alright?" he asked gently, reaching out to take her hand.

Claire nodded, tears welling up in her eyes. "I-I think so," she admitted, her voice wavering. "Just... that was so sudden."

David squeezed her hand reassuringly. "I know, I know," he murmured, his own emotions raw from the scare. "But we're okay. That's what matters."

They sat in silence for a moment, the weight of the near-miss heavy in the air. Lily and Emma sniffled softly in the backseat, their fear gradually easing as their parents reassured them.

"Let's get going," David finally said, his voice steady as he shifted the car into gear. "We're almost there."

With a deep breath, Claire nodded, wiping away her tears. "Right," she agreed, steeling herself for the continuation of their journey. "Let's see this house."

"We'll be there soon," David said softly, glancing at Claire with a reassuring smile. "And then we can put this behind us."

Claire nodded, her heart still racing with adrenaline. "Yeah," she agreed, her voice stronger now.

The gravel road wound through the forest, eventually opening up to reveal a picturesque clearing where the sunlight played upon the expansive property before them. Claire and David exchanged a relieved glance, their hearts still racing from the earlier scare with the deer. Lily and Emma, now more composed after the incident, gazed wide-eyed at the scene unfolding before them.

The house stood at the edge of a vast lawn dotted with wildflowers, its two stories adorned with a charming wraparound porch that invited exploration. Mature trees bordered the property, their branches swaying gently in the breeze, and beyond the lawn lay a serene lake that shimmered under the midday sun.

"There it is," Claire breathed, a sense of awe coloring her voice as she took in the sight. "It's beautiful."

David nodded in agreement, a small smile tugging at his lips. "It's even better than the pictures," he remarked, his eyes scanning the surroundings with approval.

As they approached the house, a figure emerged from the shadows of the porch—a woman with a warm smile and a clipboard in hand. She waved as they parked the car, welcoming them with a friendly demeanor.

"Hello, I'm Rachel," the agent introduced herself, extending a hand to Claire and David. "Welcome to Serenity Grove. I'm so glad you could make it."

Claire shook Rachel's hand warmly, returning her smile. "Thank you, Rachel. We're excited to see the place."

Rachel nodded, her gaze shifting to Lily and Emma who peeked shyly from behind their parents. "And who do we have here?" she asked kindly, crouching down to their level.

"I'm Lily!" one of the twins announced proudly, her eyes twinkling with curiosity.

Emma followed suit, clutching her plush toy tightly. "And I'm Emma," she added, her voice quieter but no less eager.

Rachel chuckled warmly, her eyes crinkling at the corners. "Well, Lily and Emma, it's a pleasure to meet you both. Are you excited to see your potential new home?"

Lily nodded vigorously, her curls bouncing. "Yes! Is there a tree house?"

Emma looked up at Sarah with wide eyes. "And birds?"

Rachel laughed softly, her demeanor reassuring. "There's plenty to explore here, I promise. Let's go inside and take a look around, shall we?"

With Rachel leading the way, the family crossed the porch and entered the house through a set of double doors that opened into a spacious foyer. The interior was bathed in natural light filtering through large windows, casting a warm glow over the hardwood floors and high ceilings adorned with intricate moldings.

"The previous owners took great care of the place," Rachel explained as she led them through the foyer into a cozy living room with a stone fireplace and plush furniture. "It's got four bedrooms, three bathrooms, and a renovated kitchen with all new appliances."

Claire nodded appreciatively, envisioning their belongings in the space. "And the garden outside is lovely," she remarked, peering through the windows at the expanse of greenery and colorful blooms.

David followed Rachel into the kitchen, his eyes scanning the countertops and cabinets. "Plenty of room for cooking," he observed, picturing family meals and holiday gatherings in the inviting space.

As they explored the rest of the house—a sunlit dining room overlooking the lake, a spacious master bedroom with a balcony offering stunning views, and a cozy study tucked away on the second floor—Claire and David exchanged excited whispers about the possibilities.

"I can see us living here," Claire admitted quietly to David as they stood together on the balcony, taking in the tranquil view of the lake and surrounding woods.

David nodded, a smile spreading across his face. "It feels like home already."

Lily and Emma, their initial shyness melting away, giggled as they explored their potential new bedrooms and peeked into closets. They chattered excitedly about where they would put their toys and books, their imaginations sparked by the new surroundings.

Rachel watched the family with a knowing smile, sensing their growing attachment to the house. "It's a special place," she remarked, her voice filled with genuine warmth. "And there's even more to discover outside."

With Rachel's guidance, they ventured out to explore the sprawling backyard. The garden bloomed with roses and daisies, and a stone path led them to the edge of the lake where ducks paddled lazily in the water.

"This is amazing," Claire breathed, her heart swelling with a mix of joy and relief. "It's everything we've been looking for."

As they walked back towards the house, the sun began to set, casting a golden glow over the property. Lily and Emma skipped ahead, their laughter mingling with the rustling of leaves and the distant calls of birds.

Rachel smiled at Claire and David, her eyes twinkling with satisfaction. "So, what do you think?" she asked gently, knowing their hearts were already entwined with the place. Claire's eyes sparkled with excitement as she looked around at the picturesque property. "Rachel, it's absolutely wonderful," she exclaimed, her voice filled with enthusiasm. "I think this could be the perfect place for us."

David nodded thoughtfully, his brow furrowing slightly. "It's beautiful," he admitted, his gaze scanning the tranquil landscape. "But it's quite a distance from the city. Commuting could be challenging."

Rachel nodded understandingly, accustomed to such concerns. "Many families find the peace and quiet worth the commute," she reassured him. "And the community here is very supportive."

David hesitated, glancing at Claire. "But what about amenities?" he asked, voicing another worry. "Schools, hospitals..."

Claire stepped closer to David, placing a reassuring hand on his arm. "There are good schools nearby, and the hospital isn't too far," she said calmly. "We'll make it work, David. We always do."

David sighed, his shoulders tense with uncertainty. "But buying this place would wipe out all our savings," he murmured, his concern evident.

Claire met his gaze with unwavering confidence. "It's an investment in our family's future," she insisted. "We've been saving for this opportunity, and Serenity Grove feels like the right place for us."

David pondered her words, weighing the pros and cons in his mind. He looked around at the expansive property, imagining their future there. "I know," he said finally, his voice tinged with reluctance. "But it's a big decision."

Claire nodded sympathetically, understanding his hesitation. "I understand," she said softly. "But think about the girls, David. They would love it here. And we could create so many wonderful memories."

David sighed again, torn between his practical concerns and Claire's unwavering optimism. He looked at Rachel, seeking reassurance. "What do you think?" he asked, turning to the real estate agent.

Rachel smiled warmly, sensing their dilemma. "I think Serenity Grove has great potential," she replied sincerely. "And with a little love and care, it could become your dream home."

David nodded slowly, his mind racing with thoughts of their future. "Okay," he said finally, his voice resigned but tinged with hope. "Let's do it."

Claire's face lit up with joy, and she hugged David tightly. "You won't regret this," she promised earnestly.

Rachel beamed at them both. "Congratulations," she said warmly. "I'll start preparing the paperwork." With the decision made to move forward with purchasing Serenity Grove, Rachel smiled warmly and began gathering her paperwork. David, however, had one lingering question on his mind as they stood on the porch overlooking the expansive property.

"Rachel," David began, his brow furrowed with curiosity, "can I ask why the owners are selling this property? It seems like such a gem, and at this price point, I would have expected it to be highly sought after."

Rachel nodded understandingly, her expression thoughtful as she considered how to explain. "It's true that Serenity Grove is a special place," she began, choosing her words carefully. "But the main reason the owners decided to sell is because the house itself is quite old. It needs some updating and maintenance, which can be a deterrent for some buyers."

David nodded thoughtfully, considering her words. "I see," he said slowly, processing the information. "And is the location a factor as well? It's a bit further out from the city."

Rachel nodded again, her professionalism evident as she continued to provide insight. "Yes, that's another consideration. Some people prefer to be closer to urban amenities and workplaces, which can make commuting from here less convenient for some."

Claire stepped closer to David, offering him a reassuring smile. "But think about the positives, David," she interjected gently. "We'll have more space, peace, and privacy here. And with a bit of work, we can make this house truly our own."

David nodded, feeling a sense of reassurance from Claire's optimism. "You're right," he admitted, a small smile tugging at his lips. "We've always wanted a place where the girls can have room to grow and explore."

Rachel smiled warmly at the couple, sensing their growing excitement despite their initial concerns. "And Serenity Grove offers exactly that," she said warmly. "It's a place where you can create lasting memories and build your future together."

David glanced around at the sprawling property once more, imagining their life there. "Okay," he said finally, his voice filled with determination. "Let's make it happen."

Claire squeezed his hand affectionately, her heart swelling with gratitude and anticipation. "You won't regret this, David," she promised earnestly.

Rachel nodded in agreement, already mentally preparing to finalize the sale. "Congratulations," she said sincerely. "I'll get started on the paperwork right away."

As they turned to head back inside, the sun dipped lower on the horizon, casting a golden glow over Serenity Grove. David and Claire exchanged a glance filled with hope and excitement for their future in their new home.

CHAPTER 4
BENEATH THE SURFACE

The sun hung low in the sky as the moving truck rumbled up the long gravel driveway, the tires crunching rhythmically over the stones. Serenity Grove stood ahead, a beacon of promise against the backdrop of the forest. Claire and David, brimming with a mix of excitement and nervous energy, led the way in their car. The twins, Lily and Emma, sat in the backseat, their wide eyes filled with wonder as they glimpsed their new home peeking through the trees.

"Look, Mommy!" Emma pointed out the window, her tiny finger trembling with excitement. "It's our new house!"

Claire turned to smile at her daughters, her heart swelling with love and anticipation. "That's right, sweetie. It's our new adventure."

David pulled the car to a stop in front of the house, the tires crunching over the gravel. He shut off the engine and took a deep breath, feeling the weight of their decision settle in. "We made it," he said, turning to Claire with a tentative smile.

Claire nodded, her eyes glistening with unshed tears. "We did," she whispered, squeezing his hand.

The moving truck parked behind them, and the driver jumped out, stretching after the long drive. He walked up to David with a clipboard in hand. "Mr. Thompson, where would you like us to start?"

David glanced at the house, then back at the truck, filled to the brim with their belongings. "Let's start with the living room furniture," he said, handing the man the keys. "We'll figure out the rest as we go."

Claire unbuckled the twins and helped them out of their car seats. They stood on the gravel driveway. "Can we see our new rooms now?" Lily asked, bouncing on her toes.

"Of course," Claire said, smiling down at her. "Let's go see where you'll be sleeping."

They made their way up the porch steps, and Claire fumbled with the keys before unlocking the front door. The house greeted them with the scent of fresh paint and polished wood, the air filled with the promise of new beginnings. They stepped inside, the sunlight streaming through the windows and casting warm, inviting pools of light across the floor.

"Wow," Emma whispered, her eyes wide as she took in the large, airy foyer. "It's so big!"

David chuckled, his nerves easing as he saw the girls' excitement. "It is, isn't it? Come on, let's explore a bit while the movers get started."

They wandered through the house, the girls' laughter echoing off the walls as they ran from room to room, their footsteps tapping lightly on the hardwood floors. Claire watched them with a smile, her heart swelling with happiness. This was the fresh start they had been yearning for.

Meanwhile, the movers began unloading the truck, carrying in boxes and furniture, their faces determined as they maneuvered through the front door. David helped direct them, ensuring that everything was placed in the correct rooms. He worked alongside them, sweat beading on his forehead as they carefully carried in the heavier items.

"Where do you want this couch, Mr. Thompson?" one of the movers called out, struggling to balance the large, plush piece of furniture.

"Right over there, against that wall," David replied, pointing to the spacious living room. "We'll set up the TV on the opposite side."

Claire, carrying a smaller box marked "Kitchen," made her way into the heart of the house. She began unpacking, arranging dishes and utensils in the cabinets, her movements purposeful and efficient. She glanced out the window occasionally, watching the movers as they worked, a smile playing on her lips as she thought of the memories they would create here.

In the backyard, Lily and Emma discovered the garden, their eyes lighting up as they saw the wildflowers and the gentle slope leading down to the lake. They chased each other, giggling and shouting in delight, their voices mingling with the chirping of birds and the rustling of leaves in the breeze.

"Mommy, look!" Lily called out, her face glowing with excitement. "There's a ducky in the pond!"

Claire stepped out onto the porch, her heart warming at the sight of her daughters exploring their new home. "Isn't it beautiful?" she asked, smiling at them. "You can play out here every day."

As the sun began to set, casting a golden glow over the property, the movers finally finished their work. The house was now filled with boxes and furniture, a chaotic jumble that promised to be sorted and organized in the days to come. David wiped his brow, looking around with satisfaction.

"Thank you, guys," he said, shaking hands with the movers. "We couldn't have done it without you."

The driver nodded, a friendly grin on his face. "No problem, Mr. Thompson. Enjoy your new home."

With the movers gone and the house now quiet, David and Claire stood in the living room, their arms around each other as they surveyed the work that lay ahead. Lily and Emma, exhausted from their excitement, had fallen asleep on a makeshift bed of pillows and blankets.

"We did it," Claire whispered, leaning her head on David's shoulder. "We're finally here."

David nodded, his heart swelling with pride and relief. "We sure are," he said, kissing her gently on the forehead. "Welcome home, Claire."

As they stood together in the fading light, the promise of new beginnings filled the air, wrapping them in a warm embrace. Serenity Grove was more than just a house; it was the start of a new chapter, a place where their dreams could take root and grow.

Night had fallen on Serenity Grove, wrapping the house in a thick shroud of darkness. Inside, Claire was knee-deep in boxes, her brow furrowed in concentration as she tried to organize their new life. The dim glow of a single bulb cast eerie shadows that flickered and danced on the walls, adding an unsettling ambiance to the room.

In the dining room, Lily and Emma sat at the table, their tiny feet swinging in rhythm as they enjoyed their dinner. Macaroni and cheese, a simple comfort food, seemed to lift their spirits as they giggled and chattered.

"Mommy," Emma chirped, her voice bright against the gloomy backdrop, "why is this house so big?"

Claire glanced at her daughters, her fatigue momentarily melting away at their innocent joy. "Because it's our new adventure, sweetie," she replied, mustering a smile.

Lily, with her cheeks smeared with cheese, giggled. "I want to find treasure!"

Claire laughed softly, though a shiver ran down her spine at the thought of the many hidden nooks and crannies of the old house. "Maybe you will, honey. Maybe you will."

Meanwhile, David, determined to explore every corner of their new home, was on a mission. He roamed the house, mapping out the rooms in his mind and considering how they might best utilize the space. As he wandered through the hallway, his flashlight's beam illuminated a small, inconspicuous door under the stairs.

"Claire, did you know there's a door here?" he called out, his voice echoing slightly in the quiet house.

Claire, arms full of linens, looked up. "A door? No, I didn't notice. What's behind it?"

David shrugged, fiddling with the ring of keys. "Only one way to find out."

"Be careful," Claire advised, her tone a mix of curiosity and caution. "Who knows what's down there?"

With a mixture of excitement and apprehension, David unlocked the door. It swung open with a creak, revealing a narrow staircase descending into pitch darkness. He flicked on his flashlight, the beam slicing through the blackness to reveal cobwebs and the faint outline of a damp, stone-walled corridor.

"Looks like a basement," he muttered, more to himself than Claire. "I'm going down to check it out."

"Just be careful," Claire repeated, her voice trailing off as she resumed her unpacking.

The steps groaned under David's weight as he descended, each creak echoing ominously. The air grew colder, heavy with the scent of mildew and forgotten things. The flashlight's beam wavered as he reached the bottom, revealing a large, cavernous space cluttered with relics from the past.

"Wow," he breathed, his voice swallowed by the shadows. "This place is like a time capsule."

Boxes and old furniture lay scattered about, draped in dusty sheets. A spinning wheel, its wood worn and cracked with age, stood in one corner. Nearby, a grand, though neglected, piano loomed, its presence both commanding and eerie.

He moved cautiously, the flashlight picking out details in the gloom: an old rocking chair, its seat threadbare; a shelf of yellowed books; and in the corner, the piano, its keys like a row of crooked teeth. Tentatively, he pressed one of the keys. A low, haunting note resonated, echoing through the cold air.

"Well, would you look at that," David muttered, intrigued. "Still in working condition."

Suddenly, a rustling sound froze him in place. His heart skipped a beat, the blood pounding in his ears.

"Hello?" he called out, his voice trembling. "Is someone there?"

Silence answered him, oppressive and thick. He took a cautious step forward, the beam of his flashlight jittering across the floor. "Claire, you need to see this!" he shouted, hoping the sound of his own voice would ward off the encroaching fear. "There's some really old stuff down here!"

"Like what?" Claire's voice was faint and distant, almost drowned by the oppressive quiet.

"A bunch of old furniture and... there's a piano," he replied, trying to keep his voice steady. "But I heard something. Might be rats."

"Rats?" Claire's voice carried a mixture of concern and annoyance. "Great. Just what we need."

As David took another step, the rustling noise came again, louder this time, from a dark corner of the basement. His flashlight flicked across the space, catching glimpses of old tools and a shattered mirror. His breath caught in his throat, and he turned towards the sound.

"Who's there?" he demanded, trying to sound braver than he felt. "Show yourself!"

Suddenly, a series of rapid, scurrying sounds erupted from the darkness. His heart leapt into his throat, and he spun around, the flashlight beam cutting through the blackness. For a moment, he saw nothing, only the clutter of the basement and the dancing shadows.

Then, the piano emitted a sudden, discordant note, as if struck by an invisible hand. He whipped around, the beam of his flashlight landing on the instrument. The keys moved slightly, as if played by unseen fingers.

"Claire!" he shouted, his voice cracking. "Something's down here!"

"David?" Claire's voice was now tinged with genuine fear. "What's happening?"

He approached the piano, the flashlight trembling in his grasp. As he neared, he caught a glimpse of movement—something small and dark darted across the keys, striking another discordant note. He jumped, the beam of the flashlight faltering as he stumbled back.

A rat. It was just a rat. He let out a shaky laugh, relief washing over him. "It's just a rat," he called up, trying to sound more confident than he felt. "Nothing to worry about."

"Are you sure?" Claire's voice was still edged with concern.

"Yeah, I'm coming back up," he replied, casting one last look around the basement. The flashlight beam swept across the old, abandoned items, lingering on the dusty piano. "Just rats."

As he turned to ascend the stairs, another sound—a soft, almost imperceptible whisper—brushed against his ears. He froze, the flashlight slipping from his grasp and clattering to the floor. He bent down to retrieve it, his heart pounding in his chest.

"David?" Claire's voice called out again, now closer and more urgent. "Are you okay?"

He picked up the flashlight and hurried up the stairs, his pulse racing. "Yeah, I'm fine. Just... let's lock that door."

He shut the basement door firmly, the reassuring warmth of the house wrapping around him as he stepped back into the light. As he secured the lock, a chill ran down his spine, and he couldn't shake the feeling that the basement held more secrets than he cared to uncover.

"Let's not go down there again," he muttered to himself, turning away from the door. "At least, not alone."

The night was draped in a thick, velvety darkness, cloaking Serenity Grove in a quiet stillness that seemed to amplify every creak and groan of the old house. Inside, the atmosphere was warm and intimate as Claire and David sat at the kitchen table, sharing a late dinner under the dim, flickering light of a solitary bulb.

The children, exhausted from the excitement of the day, were already asleep in their new room. Their tiny forms, barely visible under their blankets, gave the house a sense of quiet serenity.

"Finally, some peace," Claire said, stretching her arms and letting out a deep sigh. "It's been such a long day."

David nodded, chewing on a slice of cold pizza, his eyes heavy with fatigue. "Yeah, I didn't realize how much stuff we had until we had to move it all. This place is bigger than it seemed."

Claire leaned back, a small smile playing on her lips. "It's big, but it feels cozy, in a way. Like it's been waiting for a family to bring it back to life."

David chuckled softly, though his eyes held a trace of worry. "It's definitely got character. But that basement, Claire… it gives me the creeps. I think we need to get someone to check it out."

Claire's eyes twinkled with a mix of amusement and concern. "I know what you mean. It feels like it hasn't been touched in years. Did you find anything interesting down there?"

David shook his head, leaning back in his chair. "Just a lot of old furniture and a piano. Oh, and a lot of rats. It's going to need some serious cleaning."

Claire nodded thoughtfully, taking a sip of her tea. "We'll get it sorted. It's just going to take some time. But look at the rest of the house. It's beautiful, isn't it?"

David's gaze softened as he looked around the kitchen, his eyes lingering on the high ceilings and the intricate woodwork. "Yeah, it is. It's just… it's pretty remote. I worry about being so far from the city."

Claire's eyes met his, full of determination. "It's a big change, but that's what we wanted, right? A fresh start, away from all the noise and stress. This place is perfect for the girls. They'll have so much space to play and grow."

David sighed, running a hand through his hair. "You're right. I just need to get used to the idea. And the commute is going to be tough."

"I know it's a bit of a drive," Claire said gently, reaching across the table to take his hand. "But think of it as a new start. We're creating a new life here, one that's going to be amazing for all of us."

David squeezed her hand, a smile tugging at the corners of his mouth. "I guess I can handle a longer drive if it means we get to live in a place like this. But you're in charge of coffee duty in the mornings."

Claire laughed softly, the sound echoing in the quiet kitchen. "Deal. And I promise to make it extra strong for you."

They finished their meal in a comfortable silence, the house around them settling into a quiet lull. The only sound was the gentle ticking of a clock and the distant chirping of crickets outside.

"Come on," David said, pushing back his chair. "Let's get to bed. Tomorrow's going to be another long day."

Claire stood up, stifling a yawn. "You're right. I'm exhausted."

They headed to the bedroom, their steps slow and heavy with the weariness of the day. The house creaked softly in the cool night air, the old wooden floors whispering secrets of times long past. The moonlight streamed through the windows, casting eerie, shifting shadows that seemed to follow them as they walked.

As they climbed into bed, David turned to Claire, his voice a soft murmur in the darkness. "Do you really think this was the right choice?"

Claire's eyes met his, full of a quiet confidence. "I do. It's a new beginning, a place where we can build a life together. It's not going to be easy, but it's going to be worth it."

David smiled, leaning over to kiss her forehead. "You always know how to make me feel better. Goodnight, Claire."

"Goodnight, David," she replied, snuggling into her pillow. "Sweet dreams."

They drifted into a deep, dreamless sleep, the exhaustion of the day finally catching up with them. The house seemed to breathe around them, settling into its new role as their home.

Outside, the house stood in stark contrast to the serene night. The tall trees loomed over it, their branches swaying gently in the breeze, casting long, sinister shadows that danced across the lawn. The garden, tangled and overgrown, whispered secrets to the wind, its dark foliage rustling softly.

A thick mist began to roll in from the lake, curling around the base of the house like ghostly fingers. The old structure, with its weathered facade and cracked windows, took on an eerie, almost sinister quality under the pale light of the moon.

The night was silent, save for the occasional rustle of leaves or the distant call of an owl. The house stood as a lone sentinel in the darkness, its secrets hidden beneath layers of dust and history. From the outside, it appeared peaceful, almost serene, but a closer look revealed the cracks and fissures that hinted at the mysteries within.

As the mist thickened, swirling around the house, a faint, almost imperceptible sound could be heard—a soft, rhythmic tapping, like the echo of footsteps long forgotten. The sound grew louder, a persistent reminder that Serenity Grove was not as tranquil as it seemed.

CHAPTER 5
AN OMINOUS MORNING

The morning sun filtered through the sheer curtains, casting a soft, golden glow over the kitchen. Claire was bustling around, her movements efficient and practiced as she prepared breakfast. The aroma of freshly brewed coffee mingled with the scent of frying bacon, creating a comforting ambiance.

"Mommy, can I have more banana?" Lily called out from the dining area, her voice high and sweet, echoing through the house.

"Me too! Me too!" echoed her twin sister, Emma, waving her tiny hand eagerly.

"Alright, alright," Claire replied with a smile, slicing another banana and placing it on their plates. "But no running around the house, okay? We don't want any accidents."

The girls nodded, their eyes wide with innocence as they munched on their bananas. Their tiny feet, however, seemed to have a mind of their own, already itching to dart around the house in a playful frenzy.

David, meanwhile, was upstairs in the bedroom, struggling to tie his tie as he balanced his phone between his shoulder and ear. "Yes, I know it's a long drive, but I'll be there on time," he assured his boss, glancing at his watch and frowning at the time.

Claire called up the stairs, her voice carrying a hint of urgency. "David, breakfast is ready! You'd better hurry or you'll be late."

"I'm coming, I'm coming," David muttered, finally getting his tie in place. He grabbed his briefcase and made his way out of the bedroom, his phone still glued to his ear.

Downstairs, Lily and Emma had finished their bananas and were now gleefully chasing each other around the living room, their laughter filling the air. In their excitement, Lily dropped her banana peel on the staircase, which neither of them noticed in their haste.

Claire, coming in from the kitchen with a tray of breakfast items, caught sight of the running girls and sighed. "Girls, I told you to stop running. It's not safe," she admonished gently, setting the tray down on the dining table.

"Sorry, Mommy," Lily said, her cheeks flushed from the exertion.

"We're just playing," Emma added, her eyes wide with innocence.

"Okay, but no more running," Claire said, ruffling their hair affectionately. "Go sit down and finish your breakfast. Daddy's coming down soon."

David, now heading downstairs while still checking his phone, glanced up briefly to greet his daughters. "Good morning, my little munchkins. Ready for another day?"

"Yes, Daddy!" the girls chorused, their faces lighting up with joy.

Claire gave David a warm smile as she entered the kitchen to prepare his coffee. "You're going to be late if you don't hurry," she teased, pouring the dark, steaming liquid into a mug.

"I'm on it," David replied, slipping his phone into his pocket as he stepped onto the stairs. He didn't notice the banana peel lying innocuously in his path, its yellow skin blending almost seamlessly with the wooden steps.

"Claire, can you—" David began, but his words were cut short as his foot landed squarely on the slippery peel. In an instant, his world tilted as he lost his balance, his arms flailing wildly in a desperate attempt to grab onto something.

"David!" Claire screamed, dropping the mug in shock as she watched him tumble down the stairs. The girls gasped, their eyes in horror as their father's body crashed against the steps, his head hitting the edge with a sickening thud.

David's vision blurred as pain exploded in his forehead, a sharp, blinding agony that made the room spin. He landed at the foot of the stairs, his body sprawled awkwardly, and a dark bruise already forming in the center of his forehead.

"Daddy! Daddy!" the girls cried, rushing over to him, their tiny faces pale with fear.

"David, are you okay?" Claire asked, her voice trembling as she knelt beside him, her hands hovering uncertainly over his body, afraid to touch him and cause more harm.

David groaned, his eyes fluttering open as he struggled to focus. "I'm... I'm okay," he said, though his voice was shaky and weak. "Just... just need a moment."

Claire's heart pounded in her chest, her mind racing with worry. "We need to get you to a doctor. That hit looked pretty bad."

"No, no, I'm fine," David insisted, trying to sit up but wincing as a wave of dizziness washed over him. "I just need to rest for a minute."

"Daddy!" Emma cried, her little hands clutching at his sleeve. "You're hurt!"

Lily's eyes were wide with tears, her lower lip trembling. "Please don't be hurt, Daddy."

Claire's face softened as she looked at her daughters, their concern evident in their innocent faces. "It's okay, girls. Daddy's just a little banged up. He's going to be alright."

David managed a weak smile, reaching out to pat their heads reassuringly. "I'm okay, my brave little girls. Just a bit of a bump, that's all."

Claire helped him to his feet, her arm around his waist for support. "Let's get you to the couch. You need to sit down and take it easy for a bit."

David nodded, leaning heavily on her as they made their way to the living room. He sank onto the couch with a groan, his head throbbing with every beat of his heart.

"Stay here and rest," Claire said firmly, brushing a strand of hair from his forehead. "I'll call the doctor just to be safe."

David sighed, closing his eyes. "Alright, but I really think I'll be okay. Just need to catch my breath."

Claire shot him a worried look but nodded, turning to the girls who were watching anxiously. "Let's clean up the mess, okay? We don't want anyone else getting hurt."

Lily and Emma nodded, their faces still etched with concern as they picked up the banana peel and helped Claire tidy up the dining area.

As they worked, the house seemed to settle into an uneasy quiet. The morning light, once bright and cheerful, now cast long, eerie shadows that danced across the walls, as if whispering secrets of a darkness lurking just beneath the surface.

The morning sunlight filtered softly through the curtains, casting a gentle glow over the bedroom where David lay, his head resting heavily on the pillow. The throbbing in his forehead was a constant reminder of his fall, a dull, insistent pain that made it difficult to concentrate on anything else.

Claire, standing by the bed, looked down at him with a mixture of worry and relief. The doctor had just left, reassuring her that David's injury was minor and that he simply needed rest to recover.

"Baby, are you comfortable?" Clair asked softly, smoothing the blankets around him.

David opened his eyes, giving her a tired smile. "Yeah, I'm okay. Just a bit of a headache, that's all."

Claire nodded, her fingers brushing lightly against his forehead. "I'm just glad it wasn't worse. You gave us all quite a scare."

David reached up, squeezing her hand. "I'm sorry, Claire. I didn't mean to. I just wasn't paying attention."

"It's not your fault," Claire replied, sitting on the edge of the bed. "Accidents happen. Just focus on getting better, okay? I'll handle everything else."

David nodded, his eyes fluttering closed again as fatigue overtook him. "Thanks, love. I think I'll just rest for a while."

Claire watched him for a moment longer, her heart aching with a mixture of love and concern. Then, she stood up, pulling the door closed softly behind her as she left the room.

She made her way back to the kitchen, her mind already turning to the tasks that needed to be done. The girls needed lunch, and there was still so much to do to get the house in order. But for now, all that mattered was that David was safe and resting, and that they were together.

Claire prepared a light lunch for the girls, her mind still on David as she moved through the kitchen. She knew he needed rest.

The girls ate their lunch with a quiet seriousness, their earlier playfulness subdued by the morning's events. Claire watched them with a smile, her heart warming at their innocence and resilience.

"Is Daddy going to be okay?" Lily asked, her eyes wide with concern.

"Yes, sweetie," Claire replied, brushing a strand of hair from Lily's forehead. "Daddy just needs to rest for a few days, and he'll be all better."

Emma nodded, her expression serious. "Can we bring him something to make him feel better?"

Claire smiled, her heart swelling with love for her daughters. "That's a great idea. Why don't you draw him some pictures? I'm sure he'd love that."

The girls nodded eagerly, their faces brightening as they ran off to find their crayons and paper. Claire watched them go, her heart filled with a deep sense of love and gratitude for her family.

She finished her own lunch quickly, her mind already on the tasks ahead. There was still so much to do, but for now, she would focus on taking care of David and making sure he got the rest he needed.

David lay in bed, the room dim and quiet around him. The headache was still there, a dull, persistent throb that made it hard to think clearly.

He closed his eyes, letting the silence wash over him. The events of the morning played through his mind, the sudden fall, the pain, and the fear in Claire's eyes. He knew he had scared her, and he hated the thought of causing her any more worry.

But for now, all he could do was rest and let his body heal. The house was quiet, the only sound the soft rustle of the wind outside and the distant laughter of his daughters playing in the next room. He let the peace of the moment soothe him, his thoughts drifting as he slipped into a deep, healing sleep.

As the day drew to a close, the house settled into a quiet calm. The afternoon light cast long shadows across the lawn, the trees swaying gently in the breeze. .

David lay in bed. Claire was finally free from her household duties, and she relished the chance to retreat into her sanctuary—a room she had designated for her art.

The house was bathed in a dim, golden light, the sun casting long, eerie shadows that stretched across the walls. Claire sat in front of her easel, her brush gliding across the canvas, lost in the serenity of her work. She was painting something special for David, something to lift his spirits when he woke up. The colors on the canvas blended into a serene landscape, a peaceful escape from the stresses of their new home.

As she concentrated, the sound of light, tinkling laughter echoed through the hallway outside her studio. Claire's hand paused, her brush hovering mid-stroke. It was a child's laughter, soft and innocent, yet it sent a shiver down her spine.

"Girls," she called out, her voice cutting through the silence. "No running around the house, you hear? You could hurt yourselves!"

She waited for a response, but none came. The laughter faded into an unsettling quiet. Shaking her head, she tried to focus on her painting again, but the tranquility was broken. She dipped her brush into a deep shade of blue, blending it carefully with the lighter hues of the sky. Just as she began to find her rhythm, the laughter came again, closer this time, echoing down the corridor.

"Girls, I'm serious!" Claire's voice was sharper now, tinged with frustration. "Stop running around and making noise!"

The laughter persisted, light and playful, almost taunting. Claire set her brush down with a sigh, wiping her hands on her apron. She stepped out of her studio and into the hallway, her heart beating with a mix of irritation and unease.

The corridor was empty, the light from the setting sun casting long shadows that flickered with the movement of the trees outside. Claire's pulse quickened as she walked toward the girls' room, her footsteps echoing in the silence. She glanced into each room as she passed, each one empty and dark, shadows playing tricks on her eyes.

Reaching the end of the hall, she hesitated before the door to her daughters' room. It was slightly ajar, a soft, warm light spilling out into the dim hallway. She pushed it open gently, peering inside. To her surprise, Lily and Emma were sitting quietly at their little table, crayons scattered around them, their faces focused intently on their drawings.

"Mommy!" Emma looked up with a beaming smile, her eyes sparkling with excitement. "We're making pictures for Daddy! Look!"

Claire felt a wave of relief wash over her, her frustration melting away at the sight of their innocence. "That's wonderful, sweethearts. But were you running around just now? I told you to be careful."

Lily shook her head, her pigtails bouncing with the motion. "No, Mommy. We've been here the whole time."

Claire glanced around the room, her confusion deepening. "Are you sure? I heard laughing in the hallway just now."

Emma giggled, a sound so pure and innocent it brought a smile to Claire's lips. "It wasn't us, Mommy. We've been here, drawing."

A chill ran down Claire's spine as she looked back at the empty hallway, shadows lengthening in the fading light. "Alright then. Just remember, no running in the house, okay? You don't want to end up like Daddy."

The girls nodded, their attention already back on their drawings. Claire watched them for a moment longer, a feeling of unease lingering. She gently closed the door behind her, the unsettling laughter still echoing faintly in her mind.

As she walked back to her studio, the house seemed unusually silent, the shadows deepening as the sun dipped below the horizon. She tried to shake off the eerie feeling, convincing herself it was just the stress of moving into a new home, the unfamiliar sounds playing tricks on her.

Back in her studio, she picked up her brush again, but the magic was gone. The laughter, the empty hallway, the strange feeling that something was watching her—it was all too much. She forced herself to focus on the canvas, trying to find solace in the familiar strokes of her brush.

"Just a new house," she whispered to herself. "New sounds, new creaks. Nothing to worry about."

As Claire returned to her art room, a shiver ran down her spine. She sat in her chair, staring at the door, replaying the laughter in her mind. It had been so clear, so tangible.

She took a deep breath, her eyes on the door a moment longer before she turned back to her painting. The brush lay where she had left it, ready to resume its dance across the canvas. But as she reached for it, the brush slipped from her fingers, clattering to the floor. She sighed, bending down to pick it up.

When she straightened, her heart skipped a beat. Standing in the doorway was a child, a small figure bathed in the soft glow of the setting sun. The child's face was pale, almost ethereal, with eyes that gleamed with a mischievous light. The child smiled, a slow, unsettling grin that sent a chill down Claire's spine.

"What the...?" Claire's voice trailed off, her breath catching in her throat.

Before she could say more, the child turned and ran down the hall, laughter echoing through the quiet house. Claire's heart pounded in her chest as she dropped the brush and hurried to the door. She stepped into the hallway, but it was empty, the shadows stretching long in the fading light.

"Who's there?" she called, her voice trembling. "This isn't funny!"

There was no answer, just the faint echo of laughter that seemed to dance on the edge of her hearing. Claire's eyes darted around, her breath quickening as she scanned the empty corridor. She took a tentative step forward, her mind racing.

"Lily? Emma?" she called again, though she knew it wasn't her daughters. The laughter had been different, not their innocent giggles but something more haunting, more unsettling.

She walked down the hall, her footsteps echoing loudly in the silence. As she reached the staircase, she glanced up and froze. Standing at the top of the stairs was the same child, a shadowy figure in the dim light, laughing softly. Claire's heart raced as the child turned and ran, disappearing around the corner.

"Hey, wait!" Claire called, her voice cracking. She dashed up the stairs, her pulse pounding in her ears. When she reached the landing, she looked around frantically, but the hallway was empty, the doors to the rooms closed and silent.

She walked slowly down the hall, her eyes darting from door to door. "Where are you?" she whispered, fear creeping into her voice.

As she reached the end of the hallway, she heard the laughter again, this time from below. It was a light, airy sound that seemed to float up the stairs, taunting her. Claire turned, her heart racing as she hurried back down the stairs. She peered into each room as she passed, but they were all empty.

"Please, just stop," Claire muttered, her voice trembling. She reached the bottom of the stairs, her breath coming in short gasps. The laughter echoed around her, seeming to come from everywhere and nowhere all at once.

She turned towards the living room, her eyes wide with fear. The room was dark, the only light coming from the faint glow of the street lamps outside. She took a step forward, her heart pounding in her chest. As she reached the center of the room, she heard the laughter again, this time directly behind her.

Claire whirled around, her breath catching in her throat. The room was empty, the shadows flickering in the dim light. She took a step back, her eyes darting around the room, searching for any sign of movement.

"Who are you?" she whispered, her voice barely audible over the pounding of her heart. "What do you want?"

There was no answer, just the oppressive silence of the empty house. Claire stood there for a moment, her mind racing. She felt a chill run down her spine as she realized she was alone in the dark.

She took a deep breath, trying to steady herself. "It's just an old house," she muttered to herself. "Old houses make strange noises."

Claire stood in the living room, her breath shallow and ragged. The laughter had finally ceased, leaving a creepy silence that seemed to press in on her from all sides.

Just then, she felt it—a cold, clammy hand, small and unnaturally frigid, wrapping around her own from behind. The touch was icy, sending a jolt of terror through her veins. She gasped, a scream catching in her throat, and turned sharply, her eyes wide with fear.

But there was nothing. The room was empty, the only movement the fluttering of curtains in the faint breeze. She staggered back, clutching her chest, her breath coming in short, panicked bursts. "What the hell?" she whispered, her voice trembling.

She spun around, half-expecting to see the child standing there, but the house was silent, the shadows deep and unyielding. The memory of that cold touch lingered, her skin still tingling with the sensation. Without thinking, she bolted towards the hallway, her mind racing with fear.

"Lily! Emma!" she cried, her voice echoing through the house. "Come here, now!"

She reached the girls' room. The door was slightly ajar, a soft light spilling out into the dim hallway. Claire burst into the room, her eyes wide with terror.

"Mommy" Lily looked up from her drawing, her eyes wide with concern.

Claire rushed over and scooped them both into her arms, her hands shaking. "Come with me, now," she said, her voice trembling. "We have to go to Daddy."

The girls clung to her, their small arms wrapping around her neck as she hurried down the hallway, her mind racing. She could still feel the cold touch of that hand, the fear gnawing at her.

"Mommy, why are we going to Daddy's room?" Emma asked, her voice muffled against Claire's shoulder.

"Because...because something's not right," Claire replied, her voice barely above a whisper. "We need to stay together."

She reached David's room and flung open the door. David lay on the bed, his eyes closed, his face pale and still. Claire hurried in and set the girls down, her hands shaking as she locked the door behind them.

"David, wake up!" she cried, rushing to his side. She shook him gently, then harder when he didn't respond. "David, please, wake up!"

But David didn't stir, his body limp and unresponsive. Claire's heart raced as she checked his breathing—shallow but steady. She shook him again, harder this time, her fear mounting with each passing second.

"Daddy, wake up!" Lily shouted, climbing onto the bed and shaking his arm. "Please, Daddy, wake up!"

"Daddy, wake up!" Emma echoed, her voice breaking with fear.

Claire's mind raced. She shook David again, her voice rising in desperation. "David, please! Wake up! Something's wrong!"

But David remained still, his eyes closed, his face expressionless. It was as if he were trapped in a deep, unyielding sleep, one he couldn't wake from. Claire's mind racing with fear and confusion.

She glanced at the girls, their faces pale with fear. "It's okay," she said, trying to keep her voice steady. "Daddy's just...he's just very tired. We'll get him to wake up, okay?"

The girls nodded, their eyes wide with terror. Claire turned back to David, her hands shaking as she shook him again. "David, please! You have to wake up!"

She leaned over him, her ear close to his mouth, listening for any sign of movement. His breath was shallow, barely audible, but he was alive. Claire felt a wave of relief wash over her, but it was quickly replaced by fear.

"What's happening?" she whispered, her voice trembling. "Why won't you wake up?"

The room was silent, the only sound the faint, rhythmic breathing of her husband. Claire looked around, her eyes scanning the dark corners, half-expecting to see the child standing there, watching. But the room was empty, the shadows deep and unyielding.

"Mommy, I'm scared," Lily whispered, her voice breaking.

"It's okay, sweetheart," Claire replied, trying to keep her voice steady. "Daddy's just very tired."

She shook David again, harder this time, her hands trembling with fear. "David, please! You have to wake up! The girls are scared!"

But there was no response, his eyes still closed, his face pale and still. Claire's heart raced as she looked at the girls, their eyes wide with fear.

"Mommy, why won't Daddy wake up?" Emma asked, her voice trembling.

"I...I don't know, sweetheart," Claire replied, her voice breaking.

She leaned over David again, her hand on his chest, feeling the faint rise and fall of his breathing. "David, please," she whispered, her voice trembling. "Wake up. We need you."

She shook David again, her voice rising in desperation. "David, please! Wake up! The girls need you!"

And then, suddenly, David's eyes snapped open, wide with shock. Claire screamed, her heart leaping into her throat, the girls clutching at her, their cries echoing through the room.

CHAPTER 6
SHADOWS IN THE LIGHT

The morning sun filtered through the heavy drapes, casting long shadows across the room. Claire sat by David's side, her hand gently resting on his, her mind still reeling from the events of the previous night. David lay there, his eyes closed, breathing steadily now, but the memory of his sudden awakening, his eyes wide with fear, lingered in her mind.

Downstairs, the girls were playing in the living room, their laughter a welcome sound in the otherwise tense atmosphere. Claire took a deep breath, trying to steady herself. She knew she had to keep it together, for the girls' sake if nothing else.

"Mommy, can we go outside and play?" Emma's voice broke through her thoughts, bringing her back to the present.

Claire smiled, though it felt forced. "Of course, sweetie. Just stay in the garden, okay?"

"Okay, Mommy!" Emma replied, her face lighting up with excitement.

As the girls ran off, Claire turned back to David, her expression softening. She reached out, brushing a lock of hair from his forehead, her heart aching with worry.

The room was silent, the only sound the distant laughter of their daughters playing outside. Claire sat there for a moment longer, then stood up, her resolve hardening. She needed answers, and she wasn't going to find them sitting here.

Claire headed downstairs, her mind racing with determination. She couldn't shake the feeling that something was terribly wrong with the house, something that went beyond the usual creaks and groans of an old building. The laughter, the cold touch, David's sudden collapse—it all pointed to something sinister lurking just out of sight.

She made her way to the kitchen, her eyes scanning the room for anything out of place. The breakfast dishes still lay on the table, a reminder of the chaos of the morning. Claire started to tidy up, her mind working through the events of the previous night.

As she washed the dishes, she heard a soft knock on the door. She turned, her heart racing. "Who could that be?" she muttered to herself.

Claire dried her hands and walked to the door, her steps hesitant. She opened it to find Rachel, the real estate agent, standing on the porch, a concerned look on her face.

"Rachel?" Claire said, her voice a mix of surprise and relief. "What are you doing here?"

"I heard about David," Rachel replied, her expression cautious. "I wanted to see if everything's okay."

Claire stepped aside, allowing Rachel to enter. "Thank you. It's been...it's been a rough morning."

"I can imagine," Rachel said, her eyes taking in the kitchen. "Is there anything I can do to help?"

Claire shook her head, her mind racing. "I don't know. Everything's just...it's all so strange."

"Strange how?" Rachel asked, raising an eyebrow.

Claire hesitated, then decided to tell her everything. "Last night, I heard laughter—children laughing. But it wasn't my girls. And then I felt something, like a cold hand, grab me. David, he...he wouldn't wake up. It was like he was trapped in some kind of deep sleep."

Rachel's expression remained neutral. "Claire, you know how old houses can be. They creak, they groan. Sometimes we imagine things, especially in a new, unfamiliar place."

Claire's heart skipped a beat. "But it felt so real. And David, he's never been like this before."

Rachel sighed, a hint of impatience creeping into her voice. "Look, Claire, these kinds of stories are common with old houses. It's why you got this place for such a good price. People make up ghost stories and rumors, but that doesn't mean there's anything to it."

Claire felt a chill run down her spine. "You're saying this house is just...creaky?"

Rachel nodded. "Exactly. Old houses have a way of playing tricks on your mind. Just give it some time. You'll get used to it."

Claire nodded, her mind racing. "I don't know what to think anymore. Everything's been so strange since we moved in."

Rachel's expression softened slightly, but her tone remained professional. "Look, if it helps, I can stay for a bit and help you look around. Maybe it will ease your mind."

Claire felt a surge of relief. "Thank you, Rachel. That would mean a lot."

As they headed to the living room, Claire's mind was filled with a sense of unease. She couldn't shake the feeling that something is wrong, something that went beyond creaks and groans.

Rachel sat down on the couch, her eyes scanning the room. "So, tell me more about what happened last night."

Claire took a deep breath, recounting the events in as much detail as she could remember. As she spoke, she noticed Rachel's eyes narrowing, a hint of skepticism clear.

"I've heard similar stories before," Rachel said when Claire finished. "People have claimed to see things, hear things. But it's always just been stories."

"Do you believe any of it?" Claire asked, her voice trembling.

Rachel shrugged. "I don't really put much stock in ghost stories. Old houses make noises. People have vivid imaginations. It's just part of living in a place like this."

Claire felt a knot of frustration in her stomach. "But it felt so real. The laughter, the cold touch..."

"Claire," Rachel interrupted, her tone firm. "I'm sure it's nothing. Just give it some time. You'll see that there's nothing to worry about."

They spent the rest of the morning going through the house, checking every room, every corner for anything unusual. But the house was silent, the shadows still and unyielding. It was as if whatever had been there the night before had vanished, leaving only the echo of its presence behind.

As the sun began to set, casting long shadows across the room, Claire felt a sense of unease settle over her. She couldn't shake the feeling that something was watching them, something that lurked just out of sight, waiting for the right moment to strike.

"Do you feel that?" she asked Rachel, her voice barely above a whisper.

Rachel glanced around, her expression still skeptical. "Feel what?"

Claire's heart raced as she glanced towards the stairs, half-expecting to see the shadowy figure of a child standing there, watching them. "Like we're not alone."

Rachel sighed, standing up. "Claire, I think you're just letting your imagination get the better of you. This house is old, yes, but it's not haunted. You'll see, everything will be fine."

Claire nodded. She knew they had to do something, but she didn't know what.

As the evening settled over the old house, a warm glow filled the kitchen where Claire and Rachel sat talking, sipping on cups of tea. David, having woken up and reassured Claire that he was feeling better, joined them, looking visibly relieved though still a bit weary.

"Thanks for checking in, Rachel," David said, his voice still carrying a hint of the fatigue he felt. "I really appreciate it."

"No problem at all," Rachel replied with a professional smile, her eyes flicking towards Claire. "I'm glad to hear you're feeling better. It's good to see you up and about."

David nodded, rubbing the back of his neck. "Yeah, the headache's mostly gone. Just feels like there's a weight on me, you know? Like I've been carrying a load of bricks around."

Claire placed a comforting hand on his arm. "Maybe it's just the stress of the move. It's a big change, and you've been working so hard."

"Could be," David agreed, his eyes distant as if lost in thought.

In the living room, the twins, Emma and Olivia, were playing hide and seek, their giggles echoing through the house. Their joyful sounds were a stark contrast to the eerie silence that had filled the house earlier.

"Mommy, Daddy, look at us!" Emma called out, peeking from behind the sofa. Her little face was flushed with excitement.

"Are you hiding, sweetie?" David asked, a smile tugging at the corners of his mouth.

"Got you!" Lily shouted, jumping out from her hiding spot behind the curtains.

Rachel glanced at her watch and stood up. "I should get going. It's getting late, and you all need to rest. Moving into a new house is exhausting."

"Thanks again for stopping by," Claire said, walking her to the door. "It means a lot to have someone check in on us."

Rachel smiled, but it didn't quite reach her eyes. "Of course. It's all part of the service. Just remember, if you have any more concerns about the house, feel free to call."

David, who had walked over to join them, gave a nod. "We will. Thanks, Rachel."

Rachel opened the door and stepped outside, the cool evening air rushing in. "Take care, you two. And try not to worry too much about the noises. Old houses like this have a lot of character, but they're harmless."

As she walked down the path towards her car, the last rays of the setting sun cast long shadows across the garden, giving the house an almost surreal, haunted look. Claire watched her go, a sense of unease creeping over her.

"Do you think she's right?" Claire asked, closing the door and turning to David. "About the house just being...quirky?"

David shrugged, his expression thoughtful. "I don't know. I mean, it's an old house, right? It's bound to make some noise"

Claire sighed, her mind replaying the events over and over. "I just want us to be safe, that's all."

"We will be," David said, pulling her into a reassuring hug. "We'll figure it out together."

Just then, the twins ran up, their faces glowing with the excitement of their game. "Mommy, Daddy, we were hiding so good! You couldn't find us!"

"We sure couldn't," Claire said, her voice filled with a forced cheerfulness. "You two are the best hiders ever."

David ruffled Emma's hair. "Time to say goodbye to Auntie Rachel, girls."

"Bye, Auntie Rachel!" the twins called out, waving energetically towards the door, unaware that Rachel had already left.

As the evening wore on, Claire and David tried to settle back into a semblance of normalcy. They had dinner, sharing stories and laughter, but the underlying tension was palpable

After dinner, David helped Claire clear the table. "I'm glad you're feeling better," she said softly, glancing at him. "I was really worried."

"I'm sorry I scared you," David replied, his eyes filled with regret. "I don't know what came over me."

Claire shook her head. "It's not your fault. I just want to make sure you're okay."

David smiled, pulling her into a hug. "I am, thanks to you."

As they finished cleaning up, Claire couldn't shake the feeling that they were being watched. The shadows seemed to loom larger, and the house felt colder, more foreboding.

When the twins were finally tucked into bed, their tired eyes closing almost immediately, Claire and David headed to their own room. The events of the day had left them exhausted, but sleep seemed like a distant hope.

"I've got to be up early tomorrow," David said, lying down on the bed. "Big day at work."

"I know," Claire replied, lying next to him. "Just promise me you'll take it easy, okay?"

"I will," David said, closing his eyes. "Goodnight, Claire."

"Goodnight, David," she whispered, turning off the light.

As the house settled into the quiet of the night, Claire lay awake, staring at the ceiling. The shadows seemed to shift and move, and the air felt thick with an unseen presence. She took a deep breath, trying to calm her racing heart, but the fear lingered.

The old house lay shrouded in the stillness of midnight, its corridors filled with shadows that seemed to dance and flicker under the dim light. The only sounds were the soft breaths of its sleeping inhabitants and the occasional creak of aging wood settling into the night.

In the twin's room, Lily shifted in her bed, her small body twisting in search of comfort. Her throat felt parched, dry like the desert she had seen in her picture books. Groggily, she sat up, rubbing her eyes with tiny fists. The room was a wash of moonlight and shadow, a gentle play of light filtering through the curtains.

She reached for the bottle of water on her nightstand, lifting it with a sleepy sigh, only to find it empty. Disappointed, she shook it, hoping for just a drop, but it was dry. Lily glanced over at Emma, who was still peacefully dreaming, and decided not to wake her sister.

With a soft sigh, she climbed out of bed, her bare feet making light tapping sounds on the wooden floor. She pulled her small blanket around her shoulders and tiptoed towards the door, opening it slowly so it wouldn't creak and wake anyone. The hallway stretched out before her like a dark, mysterious tunnel, the shadows deeper and more menacing in the stillness of the night.

The air was cold against her skin as she made her way down the hall, the silence around her so complete it was almost deafening. Each step she took seemed to echo in her ears, amplifying her heartbeat. The house, usually so full of life and warmth during the day, now felt like a different place, a place where the unknown lurked just beyond the edge of vision.

As she reached the top of the stairs, she hesitated, looking down the long flight to the ground floor. The staircase seemed to stretch out longer than she remembered, the darkness at the bottom a yawning abyss that sent a shiver down her spine. But her thirst pushed her on, and she carefully descended, one small foot after the other, gripping the railing tightly.

Every creak of the wooden steps felt like a loud, booming noise in the quiet house. Shadows moved in the corners of her vision, and she thought she saw something dart across the floor below. She froze, heart pounding, but when she squinted into the darkness, there was nothing there.

She reached the bottom of the stairs and stepped into the kitchen, the room illuminated only by the faint glow of the moon filtering through the window. The kitchen seemed so large and intimidating in the dark, the familiar shapes of furniture and appliances now casting eerie, elongated shadows.

She approached the sink, dragging a stool over to reach the faucet. The metal felt cold against her small hands as she turned it, filling her bottle with water. As the water gurgled into the bottle, she heard a faint, almost imperceptible whisper. It was a child's laughter, echoing through the silence, sending a chill down her spine.

Lily's heart pounded in her chest as she spun around, her eyes darting to every corner of the kitchen. The laughter had come from behind her, but now the room was silent and empty. She tightened her grip on the bottle, her small knuckles turning white.

She hurriedly finished filling the bottle and hopped off the stool, eager to get back to the safety of her bed. But as she turned to leave, she froze, her breath catching in her throat. There, at the edge of the kitchen, just at the border of shadow and light, stood a figure. It was a child, about her age, with eyes that gleamed with a strange, eerie light.

The figure smiled, a slow, creeping grin that made Lily's blood run cold. It laughed again, a sound that seemed to echo from the depths of the house, chilling her to the bone. She wanted to scream, but her voice was stuck in her throat, her body frozen in fear.

The figure took a step forward, and the shadows around it seemed to writhe and twist, like dark tendrils reaching out to engulf her. Lily's heart was beating so loudly in her chest she thought it might burst. She squeezed her eyes shut, praying it would be gone when she opened them.

With a trembling breath, she forced her eyes open, and the figure was gone. The kitchen was empty once more, but the fear remained, pressing down on her like a weight.

She turned and fled, her feet barely touching the floor as she ran back towards her room, the child's laughter echoing in her ears.

As she raced down the hallway, her breath coming in ragged gasps, she stopped dead in her tracks. At the far end of the hallway stood another figure, an adult woman with a twisted, grotesque appearance. Her face was a mask of malevolence, her eyes glowing with a sickly yellow light.

Lily's heart felt like it might explode from fear as she stood rooted to the spot, unable to tear her gaze away from the figure. The woman didn't move, just stared at her with those piercing eyes. The hallway light flickered and went out, plunging the corridor into complete darkness. Lily's breath hitched as the shadows seemed to press in around her, the silence broken only by the pounding of her heart.

When the light flickered back on, the woman was closer, her twisted smile even more menacing. Lily's stomach churned with fear. The light flickered off again, and when it came back on, the woman was closer still, her skeletal hand reaching out as if to grab Lily.

Suddenly, the lights went out completely, and the darkness seemed to swallow Lily whole. She felt something cold and clammy wrap around her hand, and a high-pitched, eerie laughter filled the air. She screamed, yanking her hand away and turning to flee. She glanced back, and her blood ran cold as she saw the woman scuttling across the ceiling, her limbs moving in unnatural, jerky motions.

Lily's scream echoed through the house as she bolted down the hallway, the sound of the woman's laughter ringing in her ears. She ran as fast as her little legs could carry her, not daring to look back.

Lily let out a terrified scream and turned to run, the woman's eerie laughter echoing behind her. Her small feet pounded against the floor as she fled down the hallway, desperate to escape the nightmarish figure.

David and Claire, jolted awake by the scream, raced toward the sound. They found Lily in the hallway, her face pale and eyes wide with terror, her tiny body trembling uncontrollably.

"Lily, what happened?" Claire cried, scooping her daughter into her arms, her voice tinged with panic.

David knelt beside them, his heart thudding with worry. "Are you okay, sweetie? What happened?"

Lily opened her mouth to speak, but no words came out. Her eyes were wide with fear, her small hands clutching at her mother's shirt. She turned her gaze toward the ceiling, trying to point at the place where the woman had been, but her hand trembled too much to form a coherent gesture. Her voice was caught in her throat, the terror rendering her speechless.

"Lily, please, tell us," Claire urged gently, her own fear growing with each passing second. "What did you see? Was it a bad dream?"

But Lily could only shake her head, her eyes pleading with them to understand. She pointed again at the ceiling, her breath coming in shallow gasps, but no words would come. The horror of what she had seen had stolen her voice, leaving her mute with fear.

David and Claire exchanged a worried glance, their hearts heavy with dread. David took a deep breath, trying to sound reassuring despite the fear gnawing at his insides. "It's okay, baby. We're here. You're safe now. Whatever it was, it can't hurt you."

But as they held their trembling daughter, the shadows in the house seemed to grow darker and more oppressive, the sense of unease settling over them like a suffocating shroud. The image of the terrified little girl, unable to speak, haunted them, leaving an indelible mark of fear that would linger in their hearts.

CHAPTER 7
FRACTURED TRUST

The morning light filtered through the old, dusty curtains, casting a pale glow across the room. The air was thick with worry as David and Claire hovered near Lily's bed, their faces etched with concern. Lily lay there, her eyes wide and staring, her tiny body curled up tightly under the covers. She hadn't spoken a word since the terrifying events of the previous night.

Claire clutched her phone in her trembling hands, pacing back and forth. "The doctor should be here any minute," she said, her voice tinged with anxiety. "I called him first thing this morning. I can't believe she's still not talking."

David nodded, his expression grim. "I know. I just... I don't understand. What could have scared her so badly?" He ran a hand through his hair, his mind racing with worry and confusion.

A few moments later, the doorbell rang. Claire hurried to answer it, letting in Dr. Reynolds, an elderly man with kind eyes and a reassuring demeanor. He carried a black leather bag, the kind that seemed to belong to another era, filled with various medical tools.

"Thank you for coming so quickly, Dr. Reynolds," Claire said, her voice shaky with gratitude.

"Of course," Dr. Reynolds replied with a gentle smile. "Let's see what's going on with your little one."

They led him to Lily's room, where she lay still and silent. Dr. Reynolds sat on the edge of the bed, his eyes soft and kind as he looked at her. "Hello, Lily," he said warmly. "My name is Dr. Reynolds. I'm here to make sure you're feeling okay. Can you tell me what's wrong?"

Lily stared at him, her eyes wide and frightened. She didn't move, didn't speak, just watched him with an expression that broke her parents' hearts.

Dr. Reynolds gently examined her, checking her pulse, looking into her eyes and ears, and listening to her heartbeat. He took his time, careful not to startle her. "There's no sign of any physical injury," he said finally, looking up at David and Claire. "No bruises, no cuts, nothing that suggests she's been hurt in any way."

"But she won't talk," Claire said, her voice trembling. "She's just... silent. Like she's too scared to say anything."

Dr. Reynolds nodded thoughtfully. "It's not uncommon for children to be so frightened by something that they temporarily stop speaking. It's called selective mutism. It happens when a child experiences something that scares them so much, they feel unable to talk about it."

David frowned, his brow furrowed with worry. "But what could have scared her that much? She's only two years old. How could something frighten her so badly that she can't even speak?"

"It's hard to say," Dr. Reynolds replied gently. "Children have vivid imaginations, and sometimes the things they see or hear can seem very real to them. It could have been a nightmare, or perhaps she saw something that startled her."

Claire's eyes filled with tears as she looked down at her daughter. "Is there anything we can do to help her?"

"The most important thing is to give her time and support," Dr. Reynolds said. "Reassure her that she's safe and that you're here for her. Sometimes, just knowing that they're loved and protected can help children find their voices again."

David nodded, his jaw set with determination. "We'll do whatever it takes. We just want her to be okay."

Dr. Reynolds stood and placed a reassuring hand on David's shoulder. "I'm sure she will be. It might take some time, but with your love and support, she'll come through this."

As Dr. Reynolds packed up his bag, Claire walked him to the door. "Thank you so much for coming," she said, her voice heavy with gratitude.

"Anytime," he replied with a kind smile. "Call me if you need anything, and I'll check in on her in a few days."

With that, Dr. Reynolds left, and Claire returned to the bedroom, where David sat on the edge of the bed, holding Lily's small hand in his. The room was filled with a heavy silence, the weight of their worry pressing down on them like a dark cloud.

The passing months weighed heavily on the old house, each day stretching into the next with an uneasy calm. Winter had come and gone, and spring now breathed life into the surrounding forest, but inside the house, a different kind of silence persisted. Lily had not spoken a single word since that terrifying night, and the once joyful sound of her laughter had been replaced by an unsettling quiet.

In the kitchen, the aroma of breakfast filled the air as Claire flipped pancakes on the stove. The morning sunlight streamed through the windows, casting a warm glow across the room. David sat at the table, sipping his coffee and glancing at the newspaper, his brow furrowed in thought.

Lily and Emma sat across from him, their tiny hands busy with crayons and coloring books. Lily's eyes flicked up occasionally, watching her parents with a cautious curiosity. She had adapted to her silence, learning to communicate through gestures and the few signs her parents had painstakingly taught her. Emma, ever the chatterbox, filled the room with her cheerful prattle, oblivious to the shadows that lingered over her sister.

"Do you like blue or red, Lily?" Emma asked, holding up two crayons. "I'm gonna make a big sun, but I can't decide which color to use for the sky."

Lily pointed to the blue crayon, her eyes lighting up with a hint of a smile.

"Blue it is!" Emma declared, starting to color with enthusiasm. "You're the best at picking colors."

Claire set a plate of pancakes on the table and smiled at her daughters. "Breakfast is ready, girls. Eat up before it gets cold."

David folded his newspaper and reached out to pat Lily's hand. "How's my little artist today?" he asked, his voice gentle. Lily responded with a shy smile, her eyes meeting his with a silent warmth.

As they ate, the conversation turned to the mundane matters of daily life. "Did you finish that report for work?" Claire asked, glancing at David over her coffee cup.

"Almost," David replied, cutting into his pancakes. "I've got a few more things to wrap up, but it should be ready by tomorrow. How about you? Any new paintings?"

Claire's face brightened at the mention of her art. "Yes, I've been working on a new series. I think it's coming along nicely. Maybe I'll show you tonight."

"That sounds great," David said with a nod, then turned to Lily. "And what about you, Lily? How's your drawing going?"

Lily held up her coloring book, pointing to the brightly colored pictures she had been working on. Her eyes shone with pride as she showed off her work.

"Beautiful, as always," Claire said, smiling at her daughter. "You've got such a talent, sweetie."

Emma, not to be outdone, held up her own drawing. "Look, Mommy! I made a picture of our house, with all of us in it."

"That's lovely, Emma," Claire said, admiring her daughter's work. "You're both such talented girls."

The morning continued in its quiet routine, but beneath the surface, the tension remained. David and Claire exchanged worried glances over their coffee cups, the unspoken concern for Lily hanging heavy between them.

"Lily," Claire said gently, reaching out to touch her daughter's hand. "Is there anything you want to tell us? Anything you're thinking about?"

Lily shook her head, her eyes downcast. She lifted her hands and made a few tentative signs, spelling out a message they had come to understand: **"No, Mama. I'm okay."**

David leaned forward, his expression earnest. "You know you can tell us anything, right? We're here for you, no matter what."

Lily nodded, her eyes flicking between her parents. She lifted her hands again, signing another message: **"I love you."**

"We love you too, sweetie," Claire said, her voice catching in her throat. She squeezed Lily's hand, her eyes bright with unshed tears.

Emma, asked. "Can we play outside after breakfast? I want to show Lily my new dance."

David smiled, grateful for the distraction. "Of course. Finish your breakfast first, and then we'll all go outside."

As they finished their meal, the house seemed to breathe a little easier, the weight of worry lifting just a bit. The sun outside promised a beautiful day, and for a moment, the world felt almost normal.

As the morning sun climbed higher into the sky, casting long shadows across the old house, David readied himself for work. He kissed Claire and the girls goodbye, promising to be home early. Claire watched him leave with a mixture of concern and hope, the recent months having weighed heavily on her mind. She turned to her daughters, Lily and Emma, who were playing in the garden, their laughter a small comfort against the eerie silence that had settled over their home.

Determined to make the most of the day, Claire decided to retreat to her studio to continue working on her paintings. The studio, with its large windows and bright, natural light, had become her sanctuary. She set up her easel, arranged her paints, and immersed herself in her work. The world outside faded away as she lost herself in the strokes of her brush, the colors blending together to create something beautiful.

Hours seemed to pass in a blur, the house settling into a quiet rhythm. But then, in the periphery of her vision, Claire caught sight of movement near the door. Her heart skipped a beat. She glanced up, expecting to see one of the girls, but instead, she saw a shadowy figure slip past the doorway. The figure was tall, unnaturally so, and moved with a disturbing fluidity.

Claire's breath caught in her throat, her brush frozen mid-stroke. "Who's there?" she called out, her voice trembling with uncertainty. Silence answered her. She set down her brush and moved cautiously toward the door, her pulse quickening. The hallway was empty, the house eerily still. Claire's eyes darted around, searching for any sign of an intruder, but there was no one there.

Her mind raced, a thousand thoughts colliding at once. Had she imagined it? Was it just her eyes playing tricks on her? She shook her head, trying to dispel the uneasy feeling that had settled in her chest. She turned back toward the studio, determined to return to her painting and forget about the shadow. But as she passed by the window, she paused, something catching her eye.

Claire stepped back, peering out through the glass. Her daughters were playing near the edge of the lake, their small forms a contrast against the dark, still water. But they were not alone. Standing a short distance away was a man, or at least something resembling one. He was tall, impossibly tall, with limbs that seemed too long and a face that was hidden in shadow. The man's presence exuded a cold malevolence, an aura of danger that set Claire's heart racing.

Panic surged through her veins as she saw him take a step toward her daughters, his gaze fixed on them with an unsettling intensity. "Hey! Get away from them!" Claire shouted, her voice trembling with fear. The man turned his head slowly, his eyes meeting hers through the window. His lips curled into a grotesque smile, a smile that spoke of malice and darkness.

Without thinking, Claire bolted from the studio, her feet barely touching the ground as she ran toward the door. She burst outside, her heart pounding in her chest, her mind a whirl of fear and adrenaline. " Lily! Emma! Get away from the lake!" she screamed, her voice breaking with desperation.

The man moved then, his long legs covering the ground in a few unnaturally quick strides. He seemed to glide rather than run, his movements too smooth, too inhuman. The girls turned at the sound of their mother's voice, their faces lighting up with innocent smiles. They hadn't noticed the man yet, hadn't felt the icy tendrils of fear that gripped Claire's heart.

As Claire sprinted toward her daughters, the man was already closing in. He reached out a long, spindly arm, his fingers curling toward the girls with a sickening intent.

Claire's breath came in ragged gasps as she pushed herself harder, her legs burning with the effort. She could see the man's face now, twisted into a mask of pure evil, his eyes glinting with a hunger that made her blood run cold.

"No! Get away from them!" Claire screamed again, her voice echoing across the water. The man turned to face her fully, his smile widening, revealing teeth that were sharp and unnaturally white. His eyes were empty, voids that seemed to swallow the light.

Just as he reached out to touch Lily, Claire reached her daughters, grabbing them both and pulling them close. The man stopped, his expression turning into one of cold amusement. He tilted his head, as if considering his next move, then stepped back, melting into the shadows of the trees with a speed that was both terrifying and surreal.

Claire's heart pounded in her chest as she held her daughters tight, her eyes rolling around, trying to track the man's movements. But he was gone, vanished into the dark forest as if he had never been there. She knelt down, clutching Lily and Emma to her, her breath coming in ragged gasps.

"It's okay, it's okay," she whispered, her voice shaking. "Mommy's here. Mommy's got you."

The girls clung to her, their small bodies trembling with fear. Claire glanced back toward the house, her mind racing. Who was that man? And what did he want with her daughters? The questions swirled in her mind, but no answers came. All she knew was that they were not safe, not anymore.

With a last, fearful glance at the trees, Claire scooped up her daughters and hurried back into the house, locking the door behind her. She knew she had to protect them, whatever it took. The shadows had come too close this time.

As the day slowly turned to evening, the golden light through the windows dimmed to a dusky grey, casting long shadows across the living room. Claire sat on the couch, her arms wrapped protectively around Lily and Emma. The girls were unusually quiet, their eyes wide with fear.

The front door creaked open, and David stepped inside, looking weary from a long day at work. He placed his briefcase by the door and loosened his tie, noticing the tense atmosphere in the room. "Hey, everyone. What's going on?" he asked, trying to muster a smile despite the tiredness etched on his face.

Claire stood up, her expression a mix of relief and frustration. "David, we need to talk. Something happened today" she said, her voice trembling slightly.

David frowned, concern flickering across his features. "What do you mean, Claire? What happened?" he asked, walking over to her.

Claire took a deep breath, trying to steady herself. "There was a man, or something like a man. He was watching the girls from the edge of the forest. I saw him. He was so close to them, and when I yelled, he ran toward them. It was terrifying, David. He had this... this horrible smile. I've never seen anything like it," she said, her voice rising with anxiety.

David's brow furrowed as he listened. He looked at Lily and Emma, who were now clinging to Claire, their faces pale and scared. "Are you sure, Claire? It could have been a trick of the light or maybe a neighbor just passing by," he said, trying to sound reassuring.

Claire's eyes widened in disbelief. "A neighbor? David, I'm telling you, this was no neighbor. He was tall and had this... unnatural look about him. He vanished into the trees like he wasn't even human," she insisted, her voice shaking.

David sighed, running a hand through his hair. "Look, Claire, I know you're upset, but you've been under a lot of stress lately. Maybe you just imagined it or misinterpreted what you saw. We live near a forest; it's easy to mistake shadows and shapes," he said, trying to sound rational.

Claire's frustration grew, her face flushing with anger. "Imagined it? David, our daughters were in danger! I know what I saw. You weren't here, you didn't see him. This is serious," she snapped, her voice cracking with emotion.

David rubbed his temples, clearly exhausted. "Claire, I'm not saying you're lying or that you didn't see something, but you have to understand that moving here has been stressful for all of us. Maybe you're just overreacting," he said, his tone weary.

Claire clenched her fists, her nails digging into her palms. "Overreacting? David, I'm scared for our girls! We need to do something. We need to call the police or... or move out of here. This place isn't safe," she said, her voice breaking with desperation.

David shook his head, his patience wearing thin. "We can't just pack up and leave, Claire. We've invested everything into this house. And the police? What are we going to tell them, that a scary man was watching our kids? They'll think we're crazy," he said, his voice rising with frustration.

Claire's eyes filled with tears. "I don't care what they think! I just want to keep our family safe. Why can't you see how serious this is?" she pleaded, her voice choked with emotion.

David sighed deeply, his shoulders slumping. "Claire, I get that you're scared, but we have to be rational about this. Maybe we can put up some security cameras or talk to the neighbors. But we can't make rash decisions based on fear," he said, trying to sound reasonable.

Claire shook her head, her heart sinking. "You don't understand. This isn't just fear. It's real. I saw him, and I know he meant harm," she said, her voice barely above a whisper.

David looked at her, his face softening with a hint of regret. "I'm sorry, Claire. I really am. I just need you to trust that we'll figure this out. But right now, we need to stay calm and not let fear take over," he said, reaching out to gently touch her arm.

Claire pulled away, her eyes filled with disappointment. "I just wish you would believe me," she said, her voice heavy with sadness.

David sighed, looking at her with a mix of frustration and concern. "I do believe you, Claire. I just think we need to handle this differently. Let's take a step back, okay? We'll talk about it more in the morning," he said, his tone softening.

Claire's frustration reached a boiling point. "You're not taking this seriously because they're not your daughters! If they were, you'd be just as terrified as I am," she burst out, her voice trembling with a mixture of fear and anger.

David's face went pale, his eyes flashing with hurt and anger. "Don't bring that up, Claire! I've been doing my best for this family, for you and the girls. You can't just throw that in my face whenever we disagree," he snapped, his voice rising in anger.

Claire's eyes filled with tears, but she stood her ground. "I'm just saying, if you really cared, you'd understand why I'm so scared. You'd be just as worried as I am," she said, her voice breaking with emotion.

David shook his head, his face hardening. "That's not fair, Claire. I care about you and the girls more than anything. But we can't live our lives in fear. We need to find a solution, not just run away," he said, his voice firm but laced with pain.

Claire's heart ached with frustration and fear. "I'm not asking us to run away. I'm asking you to take this seriously. I'm asking you to help me protect our family," she said, her voice trembling.

David took a deep breath, trying to calm himself. "I get it, Claire. I do. But we need to be practical. We need to find a way to deal with this that doesn't involve uprooting our entire lives," he said, his voice softening.

Claire wiped away her tears, feeling a mix of anger and sadness. "I just wish you'd understand how scared I am. How scared we all are," she said, her voice barely above a whisper.

David nodded, his eyes filled with regret. "I'm sorry, Claire. I'll try to do better. I'll try to be more understanding. But please, let's not make any decisions we'll regret," he said, his voice gentle.

As they stood there, the tension between them slowly easing, the house seemed to settle into a heavy silence, the air thick with unspoken fears and unresolved questions

And as they went to bed that night, the sense of unease lingered, the darkness outside pressing in on the windows, whispering of things unseen and dangers yet to come.

CHAPTER 8
HEALING WOUNDS

The morning sun filtered through the curtains. David blinked awake, his head throbbing slightly. He instinctively reached out to the side of the bed where Claire usually slept, but found it empty.

He sat up slowly, rubbing his eyes, and took a deep breath. The house was unusually quiet. Slipping out of bed, he made his way downstairs, his mind replaying fragments of the argument from the night before.

In the kitchen, Claire was moving around with deliberate, mechanical motions. The clinking of dishes and the sizzle of something on the stove were the only sounds breaking the silence. David paused at the entrance, taking in the sight of her back turned towards him.

"Claire," he began softly, hesitant. "Good morning."

Claire didn't turn around. She continued her task, her silence a cold barrier between them. David sighed, feeling the weight of her unspoken words pressing on his chest.

"I'm sorry about last night," he said, his voice barely above a whisper. "I just..."

Claire's shoulders tensed, but she didn't respond. David swallowed hard, knowing it would take more than a few words to mend the rift between them.

With a heavy heart, he turned and headed towards the girls' room. As he reached the doorway, he paused, a faint smile touching his lips. Emma and Lily were sitting on the floor, their faces lit up with the innocent joy of play. They were surrounded by crayons and paper, their little hands busy creating colorful masterpieces.

"Hey, my little artists," David said, his voice breaking the silence.

The girls looked up, their faces lighting up at the sight of their father. "Daddy!" Emma exclaimed, her voices filled with pure delight.

David sat down beside them, his heart swelling with love. "What are you two working on?"

Emma held up her drawing, a colorful depiction of their family. "We're drawing our family, Daddy! Look, this is you, and Mommy, and me, and Lily!"

David's eyes filled with tears as he looked at the drawing. He pulled both girls into his arms, hugging them tightly. "I love you both so much," he whispered, his voice choked with emotion. "You mean everything to me."

Emma and Lily smiled, their small arms wrapping around his neck. "We love you too, Daddy!" Emma said, her voice muffled against his shoulder.

Claire stood in the doorway, watching the scene unfold. Her heart ached as she saw the tears streaming down David's face, the genuine love he had for their daughters evident in every word and gesture. She could feel her own resolve starting to crack.

David kissed the tops of their heads, his tears falling freely now. "I'm so sorry for everything," he said, his voice trembling. "I'll do better. I promise."

Emma looked up at him with wide eyes. "Why are you crying, Daddy?" she asked, her voice filled with concern.

David chuckled through his tears. "Sometimes grown-ups cry when they're really happy," he explained, his voice soft and reassuring. "I'm just so happy to have you both in my life."

The evening had cast a soft glow over the room as David sat with his glass of scotch, the amber liquid reflecting the turmoil within him. His thoughts were clouded by the strain in his relationship with Claire. The door creaked open, and Claire entered, bringing with her a wave of change that was impossible to ignore.

Claire's dress was both alluring and bold. It was a deep, rich crimson that seemed to flow like liquid silk over her body. The fabric clung to her curves, accentuating the softness of her breasts and the gentle curve of her waist. The dress was cut daringly low, revealing a hint of the delicate swell of her cleavage. The hem of the dress fell just above her thighs, offering glimpses of her long, smooth legs with each step she took. Her bare shoulders were adorned with a subtle sheen of moisturizer, adding a touch of radiance to her already captivating presence.

David's eyes widened as Claire closed the door behind her, the click of the latch sealing their private moment. He looked up, his expression a mix of surprise and longing. Claire approached him with a purposeful grace, her gaze locked onto his, conveying a desperate need that transcended words.

David tried to speak, to voice the concerns that had been weighing on him, but Claire silenced him with a kiss. Her lips were soft and insistent, carrying a passion that was both urgent and tender. David's hands instinctively moved to her waist, pulling her closer as he deepened the kiss. The heat between them was undeniable, a physical manifestation of the emotions that had been simmering beneath the surface.

Claire's fingers deftly worked at the buttons of David's shirt, her movements quick and determined. Each button that came undone revealed more of his chest, the fabric falling away to expose the taut muscles beneath. David's hands roamed over her body, his touch a mixture of reverence and desire. He gripped the hem of her dress, lifting it over her head in one swift motion. The dress fell to the floor in a pool of red silk, leaving her standing before him in nothing but her lace panties and a pair of high heels.

David's breath caught in his throat as he took in the sight of her. Her skin was smooth and flawless, her curves perfectly accentuated by the dim light. He could feel his own arousal growing, fueled by the sight of Claire's body and the intensity of their shared desire. In a sudden burst of passion, David's hands grasped at Claire's remaining clothing, his movements rough yet driven by an overwhelming need.

Claire's panties were swiftly discarded, and her body was now bare against his. David's hands roamed over her skin with a mix of urgency and tenderness, his touch igniting a fire within her. She responded in kind, her fingers exploring his chest and shoulders, her kisses trailing along his neck and jawline.

"I need you," Claire whispered breathlessly, her voice a seductive murmur. "I need to feel you."

David's response was a low growl of agreement. He guided Claire gently to the bed, their bodies pressed together with an intensity that was both wild and intimate. Their movements were a dance of passion, their breaths mingling as they lost themselves in each other. The room filled with the sounds of their pleasure, the heat of their connection palpable in every touch and kiss.

David's hands moved to Claire's back, unhooking her lace bra and tossing it aside. His lips traced a path from her neck down to her collarbone, planting kisses that sent shivers down her spine. Claire arched her back, her body responding eagerly to his touch. She could feel the warmth of his breath against her skin, heightening her senses.

Claire's fingers found the waistband of David's pants, tugging them down with a sense of urgency. She threw them into the corner, her hands moving to grasp his arousal. She started with a gentle caress, her touch sending waves of pleasure through him. David's breath hitched, his hands tightening on her hips.

"Claire," he murmured, his voice thick with desire.

Claire met his gaze, her eyes filled with a mixture of love and need. She lowered herself, her lips brushing against his most sensitive area. She took him into her mouth, her movements slow and deliberate. David's hands tangled in her hair, his body trembling with the intensity of her ministrations.

Claire's skillful movements drove him wild, her tongue teasing and caressing. She took him deeper, her pace increasing as she felt his reaction. David's groans filled the room, his body arching towards her. The pleasure was almost overwhelming, each stroke bringing him closer to the edge.

Just as David was about to reach his peak, Claire pulled away, a mischievous smile playing on her lips. She pushed him back onto the bed, climbing on top of him with a sense of purpose. David looked up at her, his eyes dark with desire. Claire positioned herself over him, lowering herself slowly until they were completely joined.

The sensation was electrifying, their bodies moving in perfect harmony. David's hands found her breasts, kneading them gently as Claire began to ride him. Her movements were fluid and rhythmic, each motion driving them both closer to ecstasy.

"David," Claire moaned, her voice a symphony of pleasure. "Don't stop."

David's grip on her tightened, his hips meeting hers with each thrust. The room seemed to disappear around them, their world reduced to the exquisite pleasure they were sharing. Claire's pace quickened, her movements becoming more urgent as she felt the peak of her climax approaching.

"Claire, I'm so close," David gasped, his body tensing.

Just as they were nearing their climax, a sharp knock on the door jolted them from their intimate moment.

David's breath faltered, and he tried to pull away, his eyes wide with a mix of surprise and frustration. "Someone's knocking," he said, his voice strained.

Claire, however, was overcome by the intensity of their connection. With a determined look, she pressed her body closer to his and whispered urgently, "Shut the fuck up and keep fucking me." Her voice was filled with a desperate need that drove David to push aside his concern.

He resumed their passionate rhythm, his movements becoming more fervent. Yet the knock came again, more insistent this time. David's concentration was broken, and he reluctantly pulled away.

"Who is it?" he called out, trying to mask the frustration in his voice.

"It's us, Daddy," came the muffled response from the other side of the door—his daughters' voices filled with worry.

David's heart sank as he realized it was his daughters. "It's the girls," he said urgently, breaking away from Claire. He scrambled to put on his pants, his movements frantic and disoriented. Claire, still breathless and disheveled, watched him with a mix of frustration and embarrassment.

David dashed to the door, yanking it open with a deep breath, trying to compose himself. He was met with the sight of his daughters standing in the hallway, their faces lit up with excitement. Behind them, his wife Claire stood, holding a beautifully decorated cake. The cake was adorned with colorful frosting and candles, the words "Happy Birthday, David" elegantly scripted across it.

David's heart raced as he faced the sight of his daughters and Claire, holding a birthday cake. The happy atmosphere of the celebration clashed violently with the fear surging through him. "If they were knocking on the door, then who was I with in the bed?" he thought, panic gripping him.

He spun around abruptly, rushing back to the bedroom. His steps were heavy, almost deafening in the stillness. The room was unnervingly silent. The bed was impeccably made, the sheets smooth and undisturbed. David's breath caught in his throat. The passionate scene he had just experienced had vanished without a trace. The faint scent of perfume that had lingered moments ago was now gone, leaving only the sterile smell of the room.

"What the f—" David muttered, his voice trembling. His eyes darted around the room, searching for any sign of the woman he had been with. His gaze fell on a dark, cold spot on the bed where a shadow had seemed to linger. The room felt oddly chill, despite the warmth outside.

As he stood there, the door creaked open slightly, the birthday song from the other room becoming a distorted echo in his ears. David's hands were clammy as he turned back to the living room. Claire was standing there, her face a mixture of concern and confusion, her eyes searching his for answers.

"David, what's wrong?" Claire's voice was sharp with worry, her eyes flitted nervously towards the bedroom.

David struggled to find words, his mind a whirlwind of confusion and dread. "I—there was someone here," he stammered. "I thought I was with someone, but now..."

Claire's expression shifted to one of deeper concern. "What are you talking about? There's no one here but us."

David looked back at the empty room, the disquieting realization sinking in. "But I felt her," he said, his voice barely above a whisper. "I saw her. It was so real."

A sudden cold draft swept through the room, causing the birthday candles to flicker ominously. David's pulse quickened as he glanced nervously around, the celebratory mood now tainted by an inexplicable sense of dread.

Claire stepped closer, her concern evident, but there was something unsettling in her eyes—a flicker of something he couldn't quite place. "Maybe you're just stressed," she suggested, though her voice held a note of uncertainty.

David shook his head, trying to steady himself. "I don't know," he said, his voice trembling. "Something's wrong. This isn't just in my head."

The air seemed to grow colder as if something unseen was pressing in on them. David could almost hear a faint whispering, a haunting echo that seemed to come from nowhere and everywhere at once. The happy noise from the other room seemed miles away, and the room around him felt more like a trap than a sanctuary.

CHAPTER 9
SHADOWS OF DOUBT

The next morning, the sun cast a warm glow over the kitchen, but the atmosphere inside was anything but warm. David sat at the dining table, staring blankly at his untouched breakfast. His mind was still reeling from the strange events of the previous night. Emma and Lily were happily munching on their cereal.

Claire moved around the kitchen, her movements efficient and precise. She placed a fresh pot of coffee on the table and took a seat across from David. She noticed the dark circles under his eyes and the tension etched into his features. He hadn't said much since waking up, and she could see the weight of last night's incident still pressing heavily on him.

"David," she called softly, her voice cutting through his thoughts.

He didn't respond. His eyes were fixed on a distant point, his mind replaying the surreal events over and over.

"David," Claire repeated, a bit louder this time.

David jolted, his fork clattering against his plate. "What? Oh, sorry, Claire. I was just..."

Claire's brow furrowed with concern. "You haven't touched your breakfast. What's on your mind?"

David sighed deeply, rubbing his temples. "It's just... last night. It felt so real, Claire. I don't understand what happened."

Claire reached across the table, placing a reassuring hand on his. "Maybe it was just a bad dream, David. We've all been under a lot of stress lately."

David shook his head, his expression troubled. "No, it wasn't a dream. I know what I saw, what I felt. It was so vivid, so... real."

Emma and Lily looked up from their breakfast, sensing the tension in their parents' voices. "Daddy, are you okay?" Emma asked, her big eyes filled with worry.

David forced a smile, trying to mask his anxiety. "I'm okay, sweetheart. Just a little..."

Claire squeezed his hand, trying to offer some comfort. "David, maybe you just need some rest."

David looked at her, his eyes searching for answers. "Claire, I felt her, I saw her. And then, she was gone. Like she was never there."

Claire nodded slowly, trying to find the right words. "I believe you, David. But right now, we need to focus on the present."

David sighed again, the tension in his shoulders refusing to ease. "You're right. I'm sorry. I just can't shake this feeling that something's not right."

Claire glanced at the girls, then back at David. "Let's talk more about it later, okay? Right now, we need to keep things as normal as possible."

David nodded, reluctantly agreeing. "Okay. But we can't ignore this forever, Claire."

Claire gave him a reassuring smile, though worry still lingered in her eyes. "We'll figure it out, together."

As they finished their meal, David cleared the table, his movements slow and deliberate. Claire watched him, her heart aching with concern. She wished she could offer more comfort, but she knew that only time and understanding could truly help him.

David looked at her, his eyes filled with determination. "I just hope we're strong enough to face whatever's coming."

"David, we need some private time. It's been too long since we went out, just the two of us," Claire said softly, breaking the silence.

David looked at her, his brow furrowing. "What about the girls? We can't just leave them alone."

Claire smiled gently, brushing a stray lock of hair behind her ear. "We can call a babysitter. Just for a few hours. An evening out might help us clear our minds and recharge. We need to be strong, and for that, we need to be together."

David hesitated, his mind racing with worries. "Are you sure? With everything that's been happening..."

Claire nodded firmly. "Yes, I'm sure. We need this. The girls will be safe, and we can be back before they even realize we're gone."

David sighed, running a hand through his hair. "I suppose you're right. A little time away might help us think more clearly."

Claire's smile widened, relief evident in her eyes. "Exactly. We need to remember why we're together, why we're a family. We need to be strong for them and for each other."

David took a deep breath, feeling the tension in his shoulders ease slightly. "Alright, let's do it. Who do we call for a babysitter?"

Claire stood up, her movements more relaxed now. "I'll handle it. There's a reliable babysitter in the neighborhood, Emily. The girls know her & will love her as a companion, and she's available on short notice."

David nodded, a small smile playing on his lips. "Okay. When do you want to go?"

Claire glanced at the clock on the wall. "How about this evening? We can go to that little Italian place downtown. It's quiet, and the food is great."

David's smile grew. "That sounds perfect. I'll make the reservation."

Claire kissed his cheek, her touch warm and reassuring. "Thank you love. This will be good for us. I can feel it."

David watched her as she picked up the phone and dialed Emily's number. As Claire spoke with the babysitter, he felt a glimmer of hope. Maybe a few hours away from the house would help them regain some perspective, to see things more clearly and find the strength they needed to face whatever was lurking in the shadows.

After a few minutes, Claire hung up the phone and turned back to David. "Emily is available and will be here by six. That gives us plenty of time to get ready and head out."

David stood up, wrapping his arms around Claire. "Thank you, Claire. I really needed this."

Claire hugged him back tightly, her voice filled with warmth. "We both did. Now let's plan and make the most of our evening."

As they prepared for their night out, the sense of unease that had settled over the house seemed to lift slightly. The anticipation of spending time together, away from the worries and fears, brought a sense of normalcy and comfort

At six o'clock sharp, Emily arrived, her cheerful demeanor immediately putting the girls at ease. Emma and Lily were excited to see her, their earlier worries forgotten in the excitement of having Emily.

"Hi, Emily! We missed you!" Emma exclaimed, running up to hug her.

Emily laughed, hugging both girls back. "I missed you too! We're going to have so much fun tonight."

Claire and David exchanged grateful smiles as they watched the girls interact with Emily. Claire gave Emily a quick rundown of the evening's plans and any important instructions.

"Thank you so much for coming on such short notice, Emily," Claire said, her voice sincere.

Emily waved her hand dismissively. "It's no problem at all. You two go and have a great time. The girls and I will be just fine."

David and Claire kissed their daughters goodbye and stepped out of the house, hand in hand. As they walked to the car, the evening air felt refreshing, a welcome change from the oppressive atmosphere that had been hanging over them.

Claire looked at David, her eyes sparkling with anticipation. "Ready for our evening out?"

David smiled, feeling a lightness he hadn't felt in days. "Absolutely. Let's make the most of it."

As they drove towards the restaurant, the city lights twinkled around them, casting a warm glow over the streets. For the first time in what felt like ages, David and Claire allowed themselves to relax, to enjoy each other's company without the weight of their fears pressing down on them.

After David and Claire left for their night out, Emily turned to Emma and Lily with a warm smile. "How about a game of hide-and-seek?" she suggested.

Emma's face lit up with excitement, and Lily clapped her hands in agreement. "Yes! But you have to count first, Emily!" Emma declared, pulling Lily by the hand.

Emily laughed, covering her eyes with her hands. "Alright, I'm counting! One... two... three..."

Giggling, Emma and Lily ran off to find hiding spots. When Emily reached ten, she uncovered her eyes and called out, "Ready or not, here I come!"

As she began searching, the house seemed to grow quieter. Too quiet.

Little did she know, something else was playing the game with them.

Emily climbed the stairs, her footsteps echoing softly in the quiet house. The hallway was dimly lit, the shadows long and eerie. She was about to check one of the bedrooms when she caught a glimpse of a small figure darting into another room. Emily chuckled to herself, thinking it was one of the girls.

"Oh, you think you can trick me, huh?" she called out, a playful edge in her voice.

She followed the fleeting figure into the room, but when she entered, it was empty. The room was still, the air heavy and cold. The only sound was the soft hum of the air conditioner. Emily's brow furrowed in confusion. She was sure she had seen someone.

"Okay, you little rascals, come out, come out wherever you are," she called, her voice tinged with uncertainty.

As she stepped out of the room, she saw the figure again, this time darting into another part of the house. Her pulse quickened, a strange sense of unease settling in her stomach. Just as she was about to follow, she heard the Emma's voice echoing from downstairs.

"You can't find us!" Emma giggled.

Emily froze, her heart pounding. If the girls were downstairs, then who was up here? She felt a chill run down her spine. Swallowing her fear, she decided to investigate, her movements cautious and deliberate.

She approached the room where she had seen the figure run. The door creaked open slowly under her hand, revealing a darkened space. Her breath hitched as she stepped inside, the wooden floorboards creaking under her weight.

"Hello?" she called out softly, her voice trembling.

The room was eerily quiet. Emily's eyes scanned the darkness, trying to make out shapes. Suddenly, the door slammed shut behind her with a loud bang. She jumped, her heart racing, and spun around to face the door.

"Who's there?" she demanded, her voice barely above a whisper.

A cold breeze seemed to pass through the room, and the hairs on the back of her neck stood up. Emily could hear her own heartbeat thundering in her ears as she reached for the doorknob. It felt icy to the touch, but it turned easily, and she pushed the door open.

As she stepped out into the hallway, she saw the figure again—this time more clearly. It was a little girl, but not Emma or Lily. This girl had long, dark hair and wore a tattered white dress. Her face was turned away, but Emily could feel the weight of her presence.

The girl suddenly turned her head, and Emily caught a glimpse of her face—pale, with hollow eyes that seemed to stare right through her. Emily's breath caught in her throat, and she stumbled back, a wave of cold fear washing over her.

The girl turned and ran down the hall, disappearing around a corner. Emily's legs felt like lead, but she forced herself to follow. Each step she took was filled with dread, the shadows around her seeming to grow darker.

"Come play with me," a faint, whispery voice called out, sending a shiver down Emily's spine.

She turned the corner, only to find herself facing a dead end. The hallway was empty, and the silence was oppressive. Emily's fear mounted as she realized there was no place for the girl to have gone.

Suddenly, a loud thud echoed from behind her, and she whipped around to see the girl standing at the far end of the hallway. Her eyes were fixed on Emily, and she began to walk slowly towards her.

Emily's instinct was to run, but her feet felt glued to the floor. She backed away slowly, her breath coming in short, panicked gasps. The girl kept advancing, her hollow eyes never leaving Emily's.

Just when it seemed like the girl would reach her, Emily heard Emma and Lily's voices again, louder this time.

"You can't find us, Emily!"

The voices snapped her out of her terror. Emily turned and bolted down the stairs. She reached the living room, where Emma and Lily were, oblivious to the horror she had just experienced.

Emily took a moment to catch her breath, her hands shaking. "You girls are really good at hiding," she said, trying to keep her voice steady.

Emma peeked out from behind the couch, her face lit up with delight. "Did we scare you, Emily?"

Emily forced a smile. "You definitely did. But the game isn't over yet."

As she glanced back up the stairs, a cold, unsettling feeling lingered in the pit of her stomach. She couldn't shake the image of the pale girl with hollow eyes.

Emily decided it was time to end the game. "Alright, girls, let's get you to your room," she said, her voice tinged with a mix of forced cheerfulness and underlying fear.

Emma and Lily followed her up the stairs, their playful giggles contrasting sharply with the tension Emily felt. She ushered them into their bedroom and locked the door. She glanced around the room, her mind racing with thoughts of the strange girl she had seen earlier.

"Stay here, okay?" Emily said, trying to keep her voice steady. "I need to make a call."

She pulled out her phone and dialed Claire's number, her fingers trembling. The phone rang for what felt like an eternity before Claire answered.

"Hey, Emily, how's everything?" Claire asked, her voice warm and cheerful.

"Claire, you need to come home. Something's wrong," Emily said urgently, her voice shaking.

There was a brief pause on the other end of the line. "What do you mean? What's happening?" Claire's tone turned serious.

"I don't know. I just—there's something in the house. I saw a girl, but it wasn't Emma or Lily. Please, come quickly," Emily pleaded.

"Alright, we're on our way. We'll be there in ten minutes," Claire assured her.

As Emily hung up the phone, she heard a faint noise coming from the wardrobe. Her blood ran cold. It was a soft, almost imperceptible sound—like a whispering giggle. She turned to face the wardrobe, her heart pounding in her ears.

"Stay here," she told the girls, who were now watching her with wide, fearful eyes.

Emily approached the wardrobe slowly, each step feeling heavier than the last. She could clearly hear the giggling now, an eerie, childlike sound that made her skin crawl. She reached out, her hand shaking, and flung open the wardrobe door.

It was empty.

She turned back to the girls, trying to mask her fear with a reassuring smile. "See? Nothing to worry about," she said, her voice strained.

But before she could move, something yanked her from behind. She screamed as she was pulled into the wardrobe, the door slamming shut behind her. Emily pounded on the door, her screams muffled by the thick wood.

"Help me! Girls, help!" she cried, her voice filled with desperation.

Emma and Lily rushed to the wardrobe, their small hands pulling at the door handle, but it wouldn't budge. Emily's screams echoed inside the wardrobe, mingling with the eerie giggling.

"We can't open it!" Emma yelled, her voice trembling with fear.

Inside the wardrobe, Emily felt a cold hand grasp her wrist. She tried to pull away, but the grip was too strong. The giggling grew louder, and she heard a voice whisper in her ear, "The game isn't over yet."

Emily's screams turned into a gut-wrenching wail as the wardrobe seemed to vibrate with an unseen force. The sound of her screams carried through the house, making the girls' blood run cold. They backed away from the wardrobe, tears streaming down their faces, too terrified to move.

The room felt charged with a sinister energy, the air thick with fear. The girls huddled together, their small bodies shaking as Emily's screams continued, a haunting reminder that something dark and malevolent had taken hold of their home.

Suddenly, the wardrobe door flew open with a deafening creak, and Emily tumbled out, her face pale and eyes wide with terror. Her breaths came in ragged gasps, and she scrambled to her feet, grabbing the girls without a second thought.

"We need to go! Now!" Emily's voice was frantic as she hoisted Emma onto one hip and grabbed Lily's hand.

The girls clung to her, their small bodies trembling with fear. Emily darted down the hallway, her heart pounding in her chest as she headed towards the front door. The house seemed to close in around her, the shadows lengthening and the air growing colder with each step.

"Emily, what's happening?" Emma asked, her voice tiny and scared.

"Just hold on tight, sweetie," Emily replied, her voice strained. "We're getting out of here."

As she reached the front door, it swung open, and Claire and David stepped inside, their faces etched with concern. Emily nearly collided with them in her haste, her eyes wild with fear.

"Emily, what's going on?" Claire asked, reaching out to steady her.

Emily shoved the girls into Claire and David's arms, her voice shaking. "Take them! Get out of this house! Now!"

"Emily, wait!" David called after her as she bolted past them, not even pausing to grab her things.

"Just leave the house!" Emily screamed over her shoulder, her footsteps echoing as she fled into the night.

Claire looked down at the girls, who were clutching her tightly, their faces buried in her shoulder.

"What did she mean? What happened?"

CHAPTER 10
SEEKING ANSWERS

The children sat huddled in the middle of the hallway, their faces pale with fear and confusion. Their parents, David and Claire, stood before them, trying to make sense of the frantic story.

David's face was a mask of frustration and disbelief. He paced back and forth, his steps echoing in the tense silence. "This is ridiculous," he muttered under his breath, glancing sharply at the girls. "What kind of nonsense are you talking about?"

Emma and Lily clung to each other, their eyes wide with terror. Emma, the older of the two, tried to find her voice. "Daddy, we... we were playing hide and seek with Emily, and then—"

"Enough!" David's voice thundered through the hallway, making the girls flinch. "I've had enough of these silly stories. There are no ghosts, no monsters, nothing of the sort. You two need to stop this nonsense right now."

Claire, who had been standing silently, her face etched with worry, stepped forward. "David, please, they're just children. They're scared. We need to listen to them."

David rounded on her, his eyes blazing. "Listen to what, Claire? To more wild tales? This is insane. They're just trying to get attention."

Emma's lip quivered, and she began to cry softly. "But Daddy, it's true. We heard something in the wardrobe, and Emily—"

"Stop it, Emma!" David snapped, his tone harsh. "I'm tired of these games. Do you realize how much trouble you've caused? Emily ran out of here like she'd seen a ghost. We're lucky she didn't call the police!"

Claire's face flushed with anger. "David, that's enough. Can't you see they're scared out of their minds? Something happened tonight, and we need to figure out what."

David scoffed, his frustration boiling over. "Oh, so now you believe in ghosts, too? What next, Claire? Are we going to call a priest to exorcise the house?"

Claire stepped closer to him, her eyes blazing with fury. "This isn't about ghosts. This is about our daughters. They experienced something that terrified them, and we need to be there for them, not dismiss their fears."

David's face contorted with anger. "Oh, really? And what exactly do you suggest we do? Sit around and listen to their bedtime stories?"

Claire took a deep breath, trying to steady herself. "No, I suggest we take this seriously and try to understand what happened. We owe them that much."

David threw up his hands in exasperation. "Fine! You deal with this. I've had enough of this madness." He turned on his heel and stormed down the hallway, leaving Claire standing there, trembling with a mix of anger and worry.

She turned back to the girls, kneeling down to their level. "It's okay, my loves. Mommy's here. We're going to figure this out together, okay?"

Emma nodded, tears streaming down her face. Lily clung to her sister, her small body shaking with sobs. Claire gathered them into her arms, holding them close. "Shh, it's going to be alright," she whispered, though her own heart was pounding with fear.

As she held her daughters, Claire's mind raced. What had happened tonight? Was it really just a figment of their imagination, or was there something more sinister lurking in their home? She needed to find answers, and she needed to protect her family.

David's heavy footsteps echoed through the house as he disappeared into the study, slamming the door behind him. The sound reverberated through the hall, underscoring the tension that now hung thick in the air.

Claire stood, keeping a protective arm around Emma and Lily. "Come on, let's get you to bed," she said softly. "We'll figure this out in the morning."

The girls nodded, their faces still pale with fear. Claire led them down the hallway, her mind whirling with questions and doubts. As they passed by the wardrobe where Emily had experienced her terrifying ordeal, Claire felt a chill run down her spine.

She stopped, staring at the wooden doors. "Mommy?" Emma's voice was a tremulous whisper. "Is there something in there?"

Claire forced a reassuring smile. "No, sweetheart. It's just a wardrobe. But if it makes you feel better, we'll check it together." She opened the doors slowly, her breath held.

The wardrobe was empty, just as she expected. But the cold feeling remained.

"See? Nothing to worry about," she said, though she wasn't entirely convinced herself. She closed the doors firmly and led the girls to their room. Once they were tucked in, she sat by their bedside, stroking their hair until they finally drifted off to sleep.

As she sat in the dimly lit room. She needed to talk to David, to make him understand that this wasn't just childish imagination.

But for now, she stayed with her daughters, her presence a silent promise of protection. She listened to their soft breathing, her heart aching with the need to keep them safe.

The morning light filtered softly through the curtains of Claire's art room, casting a gentle glow over her easels and paints. Claire sat in a chair, her eyes heavy with exhaustion. She hadn't slept at all, her mind racing with the events of the previous night. She stared blankly at a half-finished painting, her thoughts a whirlwind of fear and confusion.

Claire sighed deeply and stood up, pushing her hair back from her face. "I need to find answers," she muttered to herself. Determined, she walked over to her desk and opened her laptop. She needed to find someone who could help, someone who understood what was happening in their home.

She began typing into the search bar, her fingers trembling slightly. "Paranormal investigator," she whispered, hitting enter. The screen filled with results, but most seemed either too far away or too dubious to be of any real help. She scrolled through the list, frustration growing with each passing moment.

Then, a particular entry caught her eye: "Specialist in Supernatural Phenomena and Unexplained Activities." The description seemed promising, and the website had a professional look to it. Claire clicked on the link and began reading about the investigator, a man named Dr. Hawthorne. His credentials were impressive, and he had numerous testimonials from clients who had experienced similar situations.

Claire felt a glimmer of hope. She noted down his address and phone number, then closed the laptop. She needed to go see this Dr. Hawthorne. Maybe he could provide the answers they desperately needed.

Before leaving the house, Claire decided to check on David and the girls. She walked downstairs, her footsteps silent on the wooden floor. As she approached the back door, she saw David outside in the yard, breaking wood for the fireplace. His movements were jerky and mechanical, as if he were a puppet being controlled by invisible strings.

Claire frowned, watching him. Something about David seemed off. His face was unusually pale, and his expression was vacant, almost lifeless. She shivered, the memory of last night's argument still fresh in her mind.

"David?" she called softly, stepping outside. "David, are you alright?"

David didn't respond immediately. He continued to chop the wood, the axe rising and falling with unsettling precision. Finally, he paused and turned to look at her, his eyes unfocused. "I'm fine," he said flatly, his voice devoid of its usual warmth.

Claire's concern deepened. She walked closer, trying to catch his gaze. "Are you sure? You seem... different."

David's eyes flickered with a strange intensity. "I said I'm fine," he repeated, his tone sharper. "Just... leave me to my work."

Claire hesitated, then nodded slowly. "Okay, but if you need anything, please let me know." She turned away, a knot of worry tightening in her chest. Something was very wrong with David, but she didn't have time to figure it out right now.

She went back inside and grabbed her keys and purse. As she walked out the front door, she glanced back one more time, watching David as he resumed his mechanical chopping. His pale face and vacant expression haunted her as she got into the car and drove away.

Claire navigated the streets with a sense of urgency, the address of Dr. Hawthorne firmly in her mind. The drive felt longer than it actually was, her thoughts racing with what she would say and how she would explain their situation.

Finally, she arrived at the address, a modest but well-kept house in a quiet neighborhood. Claire parked the car and took a deep breath, trying to steady her nerves. She hoped this man could provide the help they needed. With a determined step, she walked up to the front door and rang the bell, her heart pounding with a mixture of hope and fear

The door creaked open, revealing an elderly man with a kind but weathered face. His white hair was neatly combed, and he wore round glasses that perched on his nose, giving him a scholarly appearance. His eyes, though tired, held a spark of curiosity and wisdom.

"Good morning," Claire began, feeling a bit nervous. "Are you Dr. Hawthorne?"

The man nodded slowly, his expression gentle. "Yes, I am. And you must be Claire. Please, come inside."

Claire stepped through the threshold into a beautifully kept home. The interior was cozy and inviting, filled with rich, wooden furniture and shelves lined with books. The walls were adorned with various artifacts and framed photographs, each telling a story of a life well-lived. The house exuded an air of timeless charm and quiet elegance.

"Your home is lovely," Claire remarked, trying to ease the tension she felt.

"Thank you," Dr. Hawthorne replied with a smile. "It's been my sanctuary for many years. Please, have a seat in the hall."

Claire followed him into a spacious hall where an assortment of comfortable chairs and a plush sofa surrounded a coffee table. The room was bathed in soft, natural light from large windows, which offered a view of a meticulously maintained garden outside.

Dr. Hawthorne gestured to a chair, and Claire sat down, her hands fidgeting slightly in her lap. "I'll bring us some coffee," he said before disappearing into the kitchen.

As Claire waited, she took in her surroundings. The room was filled with a sense of history and personal significance. A large fireplace dominated one wall, and above it hung a portrait of a woman with kind eyes and a warm smile. Claire guessed this was Dr. Hawthorne's late wife.

He returned with a tray holding two steaming mugs of coffee. He placed it on the table and handed one to Claire before sitting down opposite her. "Here you go," he said warmly. "I hope you like it black. It's how I always make it."

"That's perfect, thank you," Claire replied, taking a sip and finding the rich, bitter taste surprisingly comforting.

Hawthorne settled into his chair, looking at her with a mix of curiosity and concern. "So, Claire, what brings you to my door today?"

Claire hesitated, unsure where to start. "I... I was searching for someone who could help with, well, supernatural issues. Your name came up, and I read about your work. I hope you don't mind me intruding."

"Not at all," Hawthorne assured her. "Though, as you might know, I retired from active investigations a few years ago. My wife passed away two years ago, and since then, I've led a quiet life here."

"I'm so sorry for your loss," Claire said softly. "It must have been difficult."

Hawthorne nodded, a shadow passing over his face. "It was. She was my partner in everything. After she died, I lost the will to continue. But enough about me. You seem troubled, Claire. Please, tell me what's happening."

Claire took a deep breath and began to recount the events that had led her to his doorstep. "We moved into a new house a few months ago. At first, everything was normal, but strange things started happening. My husband, David, seems to be changing, and our daughters have been experiencing terrifying events. Last night, our babysitter was so scared she ran out of the house without taking her money."

Hawthorne listened intently, his expression serious. "And you believe these events are of a supernatural nature?"

Claire nodded. "I do. It feels like something is wrong with our house, something we can't explain or control. David doesn't believe it, and it's causing a lot of tension between us. I don't know what to do.

Hawthorne leaned back in his chair, his fingers steepled thoughtfully. "It sounds like you're dealing with a very serious situation, Claire. Despite my retirement, I can offer you guidance and perhaps even take a look at your house if necessary."

Claire felt a wave of relief wash over her. "Thank you, sir. I didn't know where else to turn."

He gave her a reassuring smile. "You're not alone in this. Let's start by understanding more about your house and its history. Often, these occurrences have roots in the past. Do you have any information about the previous owners or any unusual events that happened there?"

Claire shook her head. "No, we moved in without much knowledge of its past. We were just excited to have a home of our own."

"That's where we'll begin then," Hawthorne said, his tone decisive. "I'll do some research, and I'll need you to keep a detailed record of any events that occur from now on. It will help us identify patterns and understand what we're dealing with."

Claire nodded, feeling a renewed sense of hope. "I'll do whatever it takes. Thank you again for agreeing to help us."

Hawthorne smiled warmly. "It's my pleasure, Claire. We'll get to the bottom of this, together."

With a plan in place, Claire felt a little more prepared to face the challenges ahead. She finished her coffee, thanked Dr. Hawthorne again, and promised to stay in touch.

On her way back home, Claire's thoughts turned to David. She needed to get through to him, to make him understand the seriousness of their situation. And with Dr. Hawthorne's help, she hoped they could find the answers they needed before it was too late.

Claire arrived back at their house, her mind buzzing with the conversation she'd had with Dr. Hawthorne. As she entered the front door, she noticed an eerie quietness in the air, a stillness that made her uneasy. Walking through the hallway, she found David sitting at the dining table, his face partially illuminated by the flickering flame of a lighter he was turning on and off.

"Where have you been?" David's voice was sharp, almost accusatory.

Claire took a deep breath, steeling herself for the conversation that was bound to escalate. "I went to see someone who can help us," she said, trying to keep her tone calm. "A specialist in paranormal activities."

David's expression darkened instantly, and his grip on the lighter tightened. "What? You went behind my back to some crackpot who claims to deal with ghosts? Are you out of your mind, Claire?"

His words cut through the air like a knife. Claire felt a surge of anger but tried to maintain her composure. "David, listen to me. We need help. You know what's been happening in this house. You can't deny it anymore."

David slammed his fist on the table, causing the lighter to fall to the floor with a clatter. "This is bullshit, Claire! You're letting your imagination run wild, and now you're bringing strangers into our home? I won't have it!"

Claire's eyes flashed with determination. "Our daughters are terrified, David. They've seen things no child should see. I can't sit by and do nothing while they're suffering."

David stood up, his face contorted with rage. "And you think letting some fraud poke around our house is going to solve anything? You're pathetic, Claire. You always have been."

The insult stung, but Claire held her ground. "This isn't just about you, David. This is about our family. And if you won't do anything to protect them, then I will."

David took a step towards her, his eyes cold and unyielding. "Our family? You mean your family, don't you? Maybe that's why you're seeing things. Maybe you're the problem, Claire."

Claire felt a mix of fear and anger. "No, David. The problem is you refusing to see what's right in front of you. Our daughters need us, and I won't let your stubbornness put them in danger. I've already arranged for Dr. Hawthorne to come and assess the situation."

"Over my dead body!" David shouted, his voice echoing through the house. "I won't have anyone coming here to stir up more trouble. This is my house, and I make the decisions."

Claire's eyes hardened, and she stepped closer to David, her voice low but firm. "This isn't just your house. And those girls are my responsibility as much as yours. If you can't see that, then maybe you're the one who needs help."

David sneered, his face inches from hers. "You think you're so smart, Claire. Always thinking you know better. But you're just a scared little girl, hiding behind your fantasies. Grow up."

Claire's hands were trembling, but she refused to back down. "You're wrong. I'm not hiding. I'm facing the truth, and I'm doing what's necessary to keep our daughters safe. If you can't support that, then maybe you're the one who needs to grow up."

David's face twisted in fury. "I don't need this crap, Claire. Do whatever you want, but don't expect me to be part of your ridiculous plan. You're on your own."

Claire watched as he stormed out of the room, the door slamming behind him. She stood there for a moment, her heart pounding in her chest. The argument had left her shaken, but also more determined than ever. She knew she had to protect her daughters, no matter what it took.

David's behavior was becoming increasingly erratic, and the darkness that seemed to envelop their home was growing thicker by the day.

Claire only hoped that Dr. Hawthorne could help them before it was too late.

CHAPTER 11
THE INVESTIGATION BEGINS

The evening shadows lengthened as Claire waited anxiously for the investigator to arrive. David had been furious since her return the previous night, and to avoid another confrontation, he had taken himself outside, chopping wood with relentless fury. The children were in their room, the door closed, their voices occasionally breaking through the silence with muffled giggles.

Claire paced nervously in the living room, glancing at the clock every few minutes. Finally, the doorbell rang, and she jumped up, her heart pounding. She hurried to the door and opened it to find the investigator standing there, a suitcase in hand. He looked the same as before: tall and imposing, with silver hair and sharp, perceptive eyes. His presence was commanding yet comforting.

"Good evening, Mrs. Turner," he said, tipping his hat slightly. "I trust you've been well."

"Please, call me Claire," she replied, stepping aside to let him in. "Thank you for coming on such short notice, Mr. Hawthorne."

"It's no trouble at all," he said, stepping into the house and glancing around. "I find that these things can't wait."

Claire offered a weak smile and closed the door behind him. "Would you like some coffee?"

"Thank you, but I'd rather get to work first," he said, setting his suitcase down and opening it to reveal an array of strange instruments and devices.

He took out a small device that emitted a low hum and began to move around the living room, his eyes scanning every corner. Claire watched him intently, a mixture of hope and fear in her heart.

"Tell me, Claire," he said, his voice calm and steady, "what exactly has been happening here?"

Claire took a deep breath and began to recount the events that had led them to this point. She started with the strange sensations and noises, the feeling of being watched, and the unsettling dreams that plagued her sleep. She described David's increasingly erratic behavior and the frightening encounter by the lake.

The investigator listened attentively, nodding occasionally as he moved from room to room. They started in the living room, where Claire pointed out the spot where the mysterious cold draft had often been felt. He took notes, his eyes narrowing as he focused on the details.

Next, they moved to the kitchen, where Claire described the morning David had seemed out of sorts, his mind elsewhere as he struggled to eat breakfast. The investigator took more notes, his fingers tracing invisible lines along the countertops and cabinets.

"Let's check the children's room," he suggested, and Claire led the way upstairs.

As they entered the girls' room, Claire's voice trembled slightly. "This is where Emily, the babysitter, had that terrifying experience. She thought she saw one of the girls upstairs, but they were actually hiding downstairs. And then there was the wardrobe..."

Mr. Hawthorne walked over to the wardrobe, his expression serious. "Did Emily describe exactly what she saw?"

"She said over the phone that, she saw a girl, but it couldn't have been one of ours. When she opened the wardrobe, something pulled her inside. She was terrified," Claire explained, her voice barely above a whisper.

The investigator opened the wardrobe door slowly, revealing nothing but clothes hanging neatly inside. He took out a small flashlight and shone it around the interior, looking for any signs of disturbance. After a few moments, he closed the door and turned to Claire.

"Let's move on," he said, leading her back downstairs.

They made their way through the hallway and into the master bedroom, where Claire pointed out the spot where she had seen the apparition by the lake. The investigator nodded thoughtfully, jotting down more notes.

"Now, let's go outside," he suggested. "I want to see this lake."

Claire led him through the back door and across the yard to the edge of the lake. The water was still and dark, reflecting the fading light of the evening. Mr. Hawthorne stood silently for a moment, his eyes scanning the surface.

"It was right here," Claire said, her voice shaking. "I saw something... someone... standing by the water."

The investigator crouched down and examined the ground, looking for any signs of disturbance. He stood up and faced Claire, his expression serious.

"This is more than just a haunting, Claire," he said quietly. "There is something deeply wrong with this place. I will need to conduct a thorough investigation to get to the bottom of it."

Claire nodded, her eyes wide with fear. "What do we do now?"

"Stay close to your family," he advised. "And be vigilant. I will begin my work immediately. We need to uncover the truth about what is happening here."

When they re-entered the house, Claire offered Mr. Hawthorne the coffee she had promised. They sat at the dining table, the tension in the air palpable.

"Let's focus on your situation now. I have a feeling this is more than just a restless spirit."

As he sipped his coffee, his eyes wandered around the room, eventually landing on a door at the far end of the hallway. "What is that door?"

"Oh, that's the basement," Claire replied, her voice trembling slightly. "We don't go down there much."

Mr. Hawthorne's eyes sharpened. "I'd like to take a look. Basements often hold secrets."

Claire nodded, feeling a chill run down her spine. She led him to the basement door. Mr. Hawthorne took out one of his instruments and a flashlight, preparing to descend into the darkness below.

With a deep breath, he opened the door and started down the stairs, Claire following close behind, her mind racing with fear and anticipation.

As Claire and Mr. Hawthorne descended the creaking wooden steps into the basement, the darkness seemed to close in around them. The only light came from Mr. Hawthorne's flashlight, casting eerie shadows on the stone walls. The air was damp and heavy, with a faint musty odor that spoke of years of neglect.

The basement was a large, open space cluttered with old furniture and forgotten belongings. In one corner, an antique piano stood silently, its keys covered in a thick layer of dust. Claire shivered as she remembered the stories she had heard about haunted pianos playing by themselves. She dismissed the thought, focusing on the present.

Mr. Hawthorne's eyes scanned the room with a practiced intensity. He moved the flashlight slowly, illuminating shelves filled with dusty jars, old tools hanging on the walls, and cobwebs stretching across the ceiling. The investigator took in every detail, his expression grave.

"Tell me, Claire," he said, his voice low, "has anything unusual happened down here?"

Claire shook her head, her voice barely a whisper. "No, we rarely come down here. It's just storage."

Mr. Hawthorne nodded, his attention shifting to the device in his hand. It was a small, box-like instrument with a screen that displayed a grid. He adjusted a few knobs and held it up, watching the display intently.

"What is that device?" Claire asked, her curiosity piqued.

"This is an EMF detector," he explained. "It recognizes unusual energy patterns. If it detects a significant fluctuation, a red dot will appear on the screen.

If there are multiple sources of energy, it will show that as well."

Claire watched as he moved the device slowly around the room, his eyes never leaving the screen. The basement was silent except for the faint hum of the EMF detector. The tension in the air was palpable, each creak and groan of the house above adding to the sense of unease.

They moved through the basement methodically, Mr. Hawthorne leading the way with Claire close behind. They passed by the old piano, its presence looming ominously in the darkness.

The investigator stopped at an old workbench, the surface covered in rusty tools and bits of metal. He held the EMF detector over it, but the screen remained blank. He moved on, shining the flashlight into the corners and recesses of the basement.

As they approached a large wooden wardrobe, Claire felt a chill run down her spine. The temperature seemed to drop even further, the cold seeping into her bones. Mr. Hawthorne noticed the change as well and turned to her.

"The temperature is extremely cold here," he remarked, his breath visible in the frigid air. "Are you sure nothing has happened down here?"

Claire shook her head again. "Nothing that I know of. We've always felt uneasy down here, but we thought it was just because it's old and creepy."

Mr. Hawthorne nodded, his expression thoughtful. He directed the EMF detector towards the wardrobe and watched the screen. For a moment, nothing happened. Then, a single red dot appeared, blinking ominously. Claire gasped, her heart racing.

"What's happening?" she asked, her voice trembling.

The investigator's face was tense. "It's detecting an energy source. Something is here."

He moved the device closer to the wardrobe, and the red dot grew brighter. He slowly reached out and opened the wardrobe door, the hinges creaking loudly in the silence. Inside, it was empty except for a few old coats hanging limply from rusty hooks.

Claire let out a shaky breath, but Mr. Hawthorne wasn't finished. He moved the detector around the inside of the wardrobe, his brow furrowed in concentration. The red dot flickered and then disappeared. He stepped back, his eyes scanning the room once more.

"We need to keep looking," he said, his voice steady. "There's something here, I can feel it."

They continued their search, moving to the far end of the basement. As they passed by a stack of old crates, Claire thought she heard a faint whisper. She froze, her eyes wide with fear.

"Did you hear that?" she asked, her voice barely audible.

Mr. Hawthorne turned to her, his expression serious. "What did you hear?"

"A whisper," she said, her voice shaking. "It sounded like a child's voice."

The investigator nodded, his grip tightening on the EMF detector. "Stay close to me," he instructed. "We're getting closer."

They moved slowly, the flashlight beam cutting through the darkness. The tension was almost unbearable, each step bringing them closer to the source of the disturbance. The basement seemed to close in around them.

Finally, they reached a small, cluttered corner. Mr. Hawthorne pointed the EMF detector at the ground, and the red dot appeared again, blinking rapidly. Claire felt a surge of fear, her mind racing with possibilities.

Mr. Hawthorne turned to Claire to say something, but as he did, the device blinked with two red dots pointed towards her. He froze, his eyes wide with shock.

"What...?" Claire started, but before she could finish, Mr. Hawthorne turned back around and the screen now showed four dots.

"Stay behind me," Mr. Hawthorne said, his voice a tight whisper. "Something isn't right."

He moved the device in a slow circle, the flashlight beam sweeping the basement. With each turn, more red dots appeared on the screen. Five, then ten, then more. The dots multiplied rapidly, spreading across the grid until the entire screen was a sea of red.

Claire's breath hitched, her eyes darting around the room as if expecting to see the sources of these energy readings. "What does it mean?" she whispered, clutching the back of Mr. Hawthorne's jacket.

"It means," Mr. Hawthorne said slowly, "that there are a lot of them. Spirits, entities, whatever they are, they're here. And there are too many to count."

The basement grew colder, the temperature dropping sharply. Claire could see her breath in the dim light. The walls seemed to pulse with a dark energy, and the faint sound of whispers filled the air, growing louder and more insistent.

"Claire," Mr. Hawthorne said urgently, "we need to leave. Now."

As they turned to head back up the stairs, the old piano suddenly let out a discordant note, as if struck by an unseen hand. Claire screamed, her hand flying to her mouth.

"Go!" Mr. Hawthorne shouted, pushing her towards the stairs. "Get out of here!"

They scrambled up the steps, the EMF detector clutched tightly in Mr. Hawthorne's hand, its screen still glowing red. The basement door seemed to slam shut behind them of its own accord, the sound echoing through the house like a gunshot.

They burst into the kitchen, breathing heavily, the oppressive darkness of the basement finally behind them. Claire's mind raced, the sheer number of entities below their feet overwhelming her.

Mr. Hawthorne set the EMF detector down on the table, its screen now dark. He looked at Claire, his expression grave.

"We have a serious problem," he said quietly. "This house is more than just haunted. It's a focal point for something far more sinister."

Claire nodded, her body trembling. "What do we do now?"

"We prepare," Mr. Hawthorne replied, his eyes narrowing with determination. "This isn't over yet."

They sat at the table, the weight of their discovery pressing down on them. As they drank their coffee in silence, Mr. Hawthorne's eyes drifted to the basement door, still closed and foreboding. He knew that whatever they were dealing with, it was powerful, and it wouldn't be easily defeated.

Claire's mind was racing, trying to process the enormity of their situation when the front door creaked open.

David walked in, his face still pale and drawn from the previous night's events. He looked at Claire and Mr. Hawthorne with a mixture of irritation and curiosity. His eyes briefly lingered on the EMF detector before he turned to head upstairs.

"David," Claire called out, her voice firm. "We need to talk."

David stopped, his shoulders stiffening. He turned slowly to face them, his expression dark. "What now?" he snapped. "More ghost stories?"

Mr. Hawthorne stood up, extending a hand. "Mr. Turner, I'm Dr. George Hawthorne. Claire asked me to come and investigate the strange occurrences in your home."

David glanced at the extended hand but didn't take it. "Investigate, huh? And what have you found? More nonsense to scare my wife and kids?"

Mr. Hawthorne remained calm, lowering his hand. "We found significant energy readings in the basement. It's more than just a haunting; it's a focal point for something much darker. I believe we need to take immediate action to protect your family."

David laughed bitterly. "Protect my family? From what? Ghosts? You expect me to believe in this supernatural crap?"

Claire interjected, her voice shaking with frustration. "David, please. You saw what happened last night. Emily was terrified, and the girls are scared. We need to do something."

David's eyes narrowed, his anger boiling over. "And you think bringing this charlatan into our home is the solution? This is all nonsense, Claire!"

Mr. Hawthorne stepped closer, his gaze intense. "David, I'm not a charlatan. I've been doing this for decades. There's something very real and very dangerous in your home. Denying it won't make it go away."

David scoffed, turning to head upstairs again. "I've had enough of this. I'm going to bed."

As he turned, Mr. Hawthorne's eyes locked onto David's face, a flicker of recognition crossing his features. "David, have we met before?" he asked, his voice curious.

David paused, his back to them. "No, we haven't. And I have no interest in getting to know you."

"It's just that your face seems familiar," Mr. Hawthorne continued, a hint of suspicion creeping into his voice. "Like I've seen you somewhere before."

David's body tensed, but he didn't turn around. "You're mistaken," he said coldly. "Now leave me alone."

With that, David stormed up the stairs, leaving Claire and Mr. Hawthorne standing in the kitchen, the tension thick enough to cut with a knife.

Claire sighed, her shoulders slumping. "I'm sorry about him," she said quietly. "He's been acting so strange lately."

Mr. Hawthorne nodded, his expression thoughtful. "It's alright, Claire. This isn't uncommon in situations like this. The entities we're dealing with could be influencing his behavior."

Claire's eyes widened in fear. "You think they're controlling him?"

"I can't say for sure," Mr. Hawthorne replied, his voice grave. "But it's a possibility we need to consider. We have to be careful and watch for any signs of further changes."

Claire asked. "What do we do now?"

Mr. Hawthorne looked towards the stairs where David had disappeared. "For now, we prepare. I'll set up some equipment to monitor the house overnight. We need to gather as much information as possible."

Claire agreed, her resolve hardening. "Alright. Whatever it takes to protect my family."

As they began setting up the equipment, the house seemed to grow colder, the shadows lengthening as the evening turned to night.

Upstairs, David sat on the edge of the bed, his mind swirling with anger and confusion. He glanced at his reflection in the mirror, his own eyes staring back at him with a cold, unfamiliar intensity. A chill ran down his spine, and for a moment, he thought he saw a shadow move behind him.

He shook his head, trying to dismiss the creeping sense of dread. Deep down, he didn't know that something was very, very wrong.

CHAPTER 12
SHAPE-SHIFTER

The next morning, the sun had just begun to peek over the horizon when a large white van pulled up in front of Claire's house. Three people—two men and a woman—stepped out, each carrying various pieces of equipment. The woman, with short auburn hair and a cheerful demeanor, led the way up the path to the front door, her two male companions following closely behind.

Claire, still feeling the weight of yesterday's unsettling discoveries, was in the kitchen when the doorbell rang. She approached the door cautiously, peering through the peephole. Seeing three unfamiliar faces, she hesitated for a moment before opening the door a crack.

"Yes?" Claire asked, her voice tinged with curiosity and caution.

"Good morning! We're here with Mr. Hawthorne," the woman said brightly. "I'm Sarah, and these are my colleagues, Mike and Tom. We're his assistants."

Claire relaxed slightly, opening the door wider. "Oh, I see. He didn't mention anyone else was coming. Please, come in."

The trio entered, each offering a polite greeting. Sarah was in her late twenties, with a friendly, open face and an air of competence. Mike was tall and lean, with a mop of curly hair and a perpetual grin, while Tom, shorter and more serious, carried a notebook and a digital recorder.

As they stepped inside, Claire noticed the van parked outside, packed with various pieces of equipment. "That's quite a lot of gear you've got there," she remarked.

Sarah chuckled. "Yeah, we like to come prepared. You never know what you might need in these situations."

Mike chimed in, his grin widening. "Last time we were called out, we ended up using half of it just to figure out it was a raccoon causing all the trouble. Not exactly paranormal, but hey, you never know!"

Tom rolled his eyes good-naturedly. "Mike loves telling that story. We do more serious work than just chasing raccoons, I promise."

Claire couldn't help but smile at their banter, feeling a bit of her tension ease. "Well, I hope whatever's happening here isn't caused by a raccoon."

Sarah laughed. "We'll do our best to get to the bottom of it. Where should we start setting up?"

Claire led them to the living room, where they began unpacking their equipment. There were EMF detectors, cameras, audio recorders, and various other devices that Claire couldn't identify.

As they worked, Mike kept up a steady stream of chatter. "So, Claire, how did you end up with Hawthorne on the case? He's like the Sherlock Holmes of the paranormal world, you know."

Claire nodded, appreciating the light-heartedness. "I found him online after everything that's been happening here. He seemed like the right person to help us."

Tom looked up from setting up a camera. "You've definitely got the right team. Hawthorne's the best, and we're here to back him up."

Just then, the front door opened, and Hawthorne himself walked in, carrying his own set of instruments. He nodded at his team and smiled at Claire. "Morning, Claire. I see you've met my assistants."

Claire nodded. "Yes, they're setting up now."

Hawthorne clapped his hands together. "Excellent. Let's get started, shall we?"

The team continued to set up their equipment, the air buzzing with activity and anticipation. Despite the seriousness of their task, the light-hearted conversations and occasional jokes made the atmosphere a little less tense. Claire felt a small spark of hope. Maybe, just maybe, they would finally get to the bottom of the mysteries that had been haunting her family.

As they finished setting up, Sarah looked around and asked, "So, Claire, any chance we can get a cup of that coffee you offered earlier? It's going to be a long day."

Claire laughed and nodded. "Of course. I'll get right on it."

With the equipment in place and the team ready to start their investigation, Claire headed to the kitchen, feeling more prepared for whatever the day might bring.

As the team was busy setting up their equipment, a voice from the doorway caught their attention. "Need help?"

It was David, looking much more composed and normal than the previous night. His presence added a surprising but welcome energy to the room.

Claire looked at him, a mixture of relief and wariness in her eyes. "David, you're up early."

David nodded, walking over to where the team was arranging their instruments. "Thought I'd lend a hand. What's all this setup about?"

Sarah smiled warmly and extended her hand. "Hi, I'm Sarah. This is Mike, and that's Tom. We're Hawthorne's assistants."

David shook each of their hands in turn. "Nice to meet you all. I'm David."

Mike, ever the talker, jumped in first. "We're setting up a variety of instruments to monitor for any unusual activity in the house. For instance, this," he said, holding up a small handheld device, "is an EMF detector. It measures electromagnetic fields. Sometimes, spikes in EMF readings can indicate paranormal activity."

David raised an eyebrow, clearly intrigued. "And what about that one?" he asked, pointing to a camera mounted on a tripod in the corner.

Tom, adjusting the camera's angle, explained, "This is an infrared camera. It can capture images in complete darkness by detecting heat signatures. If there's any movement or changes in temperature, we'll be able to see it on the screen."

Sarah picked up another device, a small box with several blinking lights. "This is an EVP recorder. It stands for Electronic Voice Phenomenon. It picks up sounds that the human ear can't always hear. We're hoping to catch any unusual voices or noises."

David nodded, clearly impressed. "So you've got all the bases covered. How do these things work together?"

Mike grinned, clearly enjoying David's interest. "Well, while the EMF detector scans for changes in electromagnetic fields, the infrared camera keeps an eye on any visual anomalies in the dark. The EVP recorder listens for any strange sounds, and we have motion sensors set up in key areas to detect any physical movements. All this data gets collected and analyzed together to see if we can pinpoint the source of the disturbances."

David looked thoughtful, then glanced at Hawthorne. "Sounds like quite the setup. How long does this usually take?"

Hawthorne, who had been listening quietly, finally spoke up. "It varies. Sometimes we get results quickly, other times it takes longer. The important thing is to be thorough and patient. Every house is different."

David nodded. "Makes sense. So, where do you need me?"

Sarah handed him a bundle of cables. "If you could help me with these, we need to connect the motion sensors to the central monitor."

As David and Sarah worked together, Mike and Tom continued their setup, each explaining their equipment in more detail.

Mike, setting up another infrared camera, said, "This one will cover the hallway. We've had cases where activity is confined to specific areas, so it's good to have multiple angles."

Tom, adjusting a set of motion sensors near the basement door, added, "And these sensors will alert us to any movement in and out of the basement. Given what you experienced down there, it's a key area to monitor."

David glanced at the basement door, his face darkening slightly. "Yeah, that place gives me the creeps. Good call."

Claire watched as David interacted with the team, his earlier anger seemingly replaced with curiosity and a willingness to help. It was a relief to see him so engaged, even if the circumstances were far from normal.

As they finished setting up, Hawthorne gathered everyone in the living room. "Alright, we're ready to start. We'll begin with a baseline sweep to get a sense of the normal readings in the house. Then, we'll conduct more focused investigations in the areas with the most activity."

David nodded, looking around at the array of equipment. "Sounds good."

Claire handed out cups of coffee as the team took their positions, the atmosphere a mix of anticipation and determination. With everyone ready, the investigation was about to begin in earnest.

As evening descended, the house was a hive of quiet activity. The girls were in their room, playing with their toys and occasionally glancing nervously at the door. Claire busied herself in the kitchen, her hands moving methodically as she prepared dinner, though her mind was elsewhere, filled with unease and hope.

In the living room, David and Hawthorne sat on opposite ends of the couch. The television was on but muted, casting flickering shadows across the room. David was flipping through a magazine, though he wasn't really reading it.

Hawthorne broke the silence, "How are you holding up, David?"

David glanced up, his eyes weary. "I've had better days. Just want all this to be over."

Hawthorne nodded sympathetically.

"Understandable. But these things take time. We need to be patient."

Nearby, Sarah sat in front of a monitor, watching the live feeds from the cameras and sensors they had placed around the house. The screen displayed various rooms, including the basement, the hallway, and the girls' room, in eerie green night vision.

Tom, moving silently from room to room with an EMF detector, checked for any spikes or unusual readings. The device remained stubbornly quiet, showing nothing out of the ordinary.

Outside, Mike patrolled the perimeter of the house, a flashlight in one hand and a handheld camera in the other. He paused every now and then, listening for any sounds beyond the usual night noises, but everything was still.

As the minutes ticked by, a growing sense of frustration began to settle over the team. Sarah sighed, leaning back in her chair. "I'm not seeing anything unusual on the monitors."

Tom's voice crackled over the walkie-talkie, "All clear inside. No EMF spikes, no strange sounds, nothing."

Mike chimed in from outside, "Everything's quiet out here too. No movement, no disturbances."

Hawthorne listened, his brow furrowed. He turned to David. "We need to wait. Sometimes these things take time to manifest. The spirits, if they are here, may not always be active on our schedule."

David clenched his jaw, frustration evident. "How long do we wait? This is driving us all crazy."

Hawthorne's voice was calm but firm. "As long as it takes. We can't rush this. If there's something here, it will reveal itself eventually."

Claire walked into the living room, wiping her hands on a towel. "Any updates?"

Sarah shook her head. "Nothing so far. Everything looks normal."

Claire sighed, sitting down next to David. "I just want our lives back to normal."

David put an arm around her shoulders. "We all do."

Tom came back into the living room, his footsteps soft on the carpet. "Maybe it's just not the right time. These things can be unpredictable."

Hawthorne nodded. "We need to stay vigilant. Keep an eye on the monitors, and we'll continue to sweep the house periodically."

Mike entered from the back door, shaking his head. "It's like a ghost town out there. No pun intended."

Sarah turned back to the monitor, adjusting the settings to enhance the sensitivity of the cameras. "We'll keep watching. If there's anything here, we'll find it."

As the evening wore on, the team settled into a rhythm, each person performing their assigned tasks with a mix of diligence and anticipation. The suspense grew with every passing minute, the tension winding tighter and tighter as they waited for any sign of the paranormal activity that had disrupted their lives.

Suddenly, a faint sound crackled over the EVP recorder, causing Sarah to sit up straighter. She adjusted the volume, her eyes narrowing as she tried to discern the source. "Did anyone hear that?"

Tom paused in his pacing. "Hear what?"

Sarah leaned closer to the monitor, her face illuminated by the green glow. "I thought I heard...something. A faint whisper or a sigh."

David and Claire exchanged nervous glances. Hawthorne stood, his expression serious. "Let's check the playback."

As they replayed the recording, the room fell silent, everyone straining to hear the faint, ghostly noise that had briefly broken the silence. The suspense was almost unbearable, each second stretching out as they waited to hear what the recorder had captured.

When the faint whisper played again, barely audible but unmistakable, a chill ran down everyone's spine. Sarah looked up, her face pale. "There it is again. Did you hear it?"

David nodded slowly, his anger replaced by a cold dread. "Yeah, I heard it."

Hawthorne's eyes were sharp, his voice low. "This is just the beginning. Whatever is here, it's starting to make itself known."

As evening turned to night, the team gathered in the dining room with the family for a quick dinner. The mood was somber, and conversations were hushed. Plates clinked and silverware scraped as everyone tried to make the best of the tense situation. Claire moved about, serving everyone with a forced smile.

In the makeshift command center, Sarah sat in front of the monitor, her eyes heavy with fatigue. She watched the camera feeds intently, not wanting to miss a single moment. The basement, the hallways, the girls' room—each screen displayed a different angle of the house. She yawned, rubbing her eyes, but the footage remained uneventful.

On one of the screens, Claire was seen entering the girls' room to feed them. Sarah's eyes grew heavier, and she struggled to keep them open. The repetitive nature of the surveillance was lulling her into a trance. She blinked slowly, her eyelids drooping until they finally closed.

Suddenly, a soft voice called her name. "Sarah?"

She jolted awake, her heart racing. Claire stood next to her, holding a plate of dinner. "I brought you some food. You need to keep your strength up."

Sarah blinked in confusion, her mind racing. She glanced back at the monitor, her pulse quickening. The camera feed still showed Claire in the girls' room, bending over the bed to tuck them in. She looked back at Claire, standing right in front of her. "But... you're here. I just saw you in the girls' room on the camera."

Claire's face drained of color. "What do you mean? I've been in the kitchen this whole time."

A cold chill ran down Sarah's spine. She turned back to the monitor, staring at the footage of Claire in the girls' room. The figure in the video turned slowly, as if sensing they were being watched, and the screen flickered, the image distorting momentarily before going black. When it came back on, the room was empty.

Claire's voice trembled. "What did you see?"

Sarah's voice was barely above a whisper. "It was you. Or... someone that looked exactly like you. But now it's gone."

Claire set the plate down, her hands shaking. "This isn't possible. I haven't been up there."

Hawthorne entered the room, sensing the tension. "What's going on?"

Sarah quickly explained what she had seen. Hawthorne's eyes narrowed, and he looked at Claire. "Are you sure you haven't been in the girls' room in the past few minutes?"

Claire nodded emphatically. "I swear, I haven't."

Hawthorne turned to Sarah. "Show me the footage."

Sarah rewound the tape, playing the eerie scene again. Everyone watched in silence as the figure resembling Claire moved about the room, and then disappeared when the screen flickered. The air in the room seemed to grow colder, and the shadows on the walls deepened.

Hawthorne spoke quietly but firmly. "We're dealing with a shape-shifter. Something that can mimic people in the house. We need to be very careful."

David entered the room, having overheard part of the conversation. "What do you mean, mimic? You're saying there's something here that can look like us?"

Hawthorne nodded grimly. "It seems so. This complicates things. We need to stay vigilant and keep track of everyone's movements. No one goes anywhere alone."

The tension in the room was palpable, each person feeling the weight of the unknown presence among them. Sarah's eyes flicked back to the monitor, scanning each feed with renewed urgency. Claire stood close to David, her fear evident.

As they resumed their dinner, the atmosphere was thick with unease.

Mike, who had been outside, came in and noticed the strained faces. "What happened?"

David filled him in, and Mike's expression hardened. "We need to up our game. This thing is playing tricks on us."

Hawthorne agreed. "From now on, we double-check everything. We don't take anything at face value."

Sarah, though tired, felt a new surge of determination. "I'll keep watching the monitors. If it shows up again, I'll catch it."

Claire put a reassuring hand on her shoulder. "Thank you, Sarah. Be careful."

Sarah nodded, her eyes back on the screen, her senses on high alert. The night was far from over, and the true nature of their spectral adversary was just beginning to reveal itself.

CHAPTER 13
NEED HELP

The air in the house felt thicker that night, as if the walls themselves were holding their breath, waiting. Outside, the wind howled through the trees, its eerie whistle finding its way through the cracks in the windows, adding a haunting soundtrack to the tense atmosphere inside. The team gathered in the living room, surrounded by an assortment of high-tech equipment that beeped and blinked intermittently, a stark contrast to the unsettling silence that had settled over the house.

David sat in his usual chair, one foot tapping nervously against the floor. His eyes kept darting to the stairs as if expecting something—or someone—to appear at any moment. Across from him, Hawthorne leaned back, hands steepled, watching David with an intensity that made even Claire uncomfortable. She stood by the doorway, her hands wringing together as if she were trying to squeeze out her anxiety.

One of the assistants, Mike, was pacing around the room, his eyes never leaving the monitor he was holding. "I'm getting nothing, Hawthorne," he muttered, shaking his head. "No spikes, no temperature drops, nothing. It's like this place is...normal."

Tom, who was stationed outside, chimed in over the radio. "Same here. I've swept the perimeter twice now, and there's no sign of anything unusual. No EMF readings, no movement. Nada."

"Maybe it's a good thing," Claire offered weakly, trying to inject some optimism into the thick tension. "Maybe whatever was here is gone now."

Hawthorne glanced at her, his expression unreadable. "Maybe," he replied, though his tone suggested otherwise. "Or maybe it's waiting."

The wind outside seemed to pick up in response, rattling the windows violently. Everyone jumped slightly, even David, whose nerves were clearly frayed. The storm was moving in, but it felt like more than just a change in the weather. It felt like the house was responding to them.

Hawthorne finally stood, the creak of the old floorboards loud in the quiet room. "We need to stay vigilant," he said, his voice low and commanding. "Whatever's here, if it's here, will reveal itself when it's ready. We need to be ready for that moment."

David scoffed, trying to mask his unease with bravado. "What exactly are we waiting for, Hawthorne? Some ghost to come out of the walls and say boo? This is ridiculous."

Claire shot him a sharp look. "David, please. We agreed to this. We need to know what's happening in our home. For the girls."

David opened his mouth to retort, but Hawthorne cut him off. "It's not just about knowing, David. It's about understanding. This house, this presence—it's not playing by our rules. And the moment we think it is, that's when we're most vulnerable."

A heavy silence followed his words, everyone exchanging uneasy glances. The wind outside was now accompanied by the soft patter of rain, the first drops heralding the coming storm.

Upstairs, the girls were in their room, oblivious to the tense atmosphere downstairs. Or so they thought. Emma had insisted on keeping the lights on, and Lily hadn't argued, though she usually would have. Something about the night felt off to her too, even if she couldn't put her finger on it.

Meanwhile, back in the living room, the tension was palpable. Mike was now positioned by the basement door, his hand on the knob as if expecting it to suddenly burst open. "I don't like this," he muttered. "It's too quiet. Too calm."

Hawthorne nodded, his gaze shifting to the door. "Calm before the storm," he said softly. "It's always the way with these things. You think everything's fine, and then—"

His sentence was cut off by a sudden, loud bang from the girls' room. It reverberated through the house, freezing everyone in their tracks. Claire was the first to move, bolting towards the stairs. "The girls!" she cried out, her voice tinged with panic.

David was right behind her, his earlier bravado gone. "What the hell was that?" he demanded as they raced up the stairs, with Hawthorne and the others close behind.

When they reached the girls' room, they found Emma and Lily huddled together on the bed, wide-eyed and terrified. The room was in disarray—books had fallen from the shelves, the curtains were swaying as if a strong breeze had blown through, though the windows were firmly shut.

Claire rushed to her daughters, pulling them into her arms. "What happened? Are you okay?"

Emma pointed to the corner of the room, her voice shaking. "It was there. A shadow. It was there"

David looked around the room, his anger returning as a way to mask his fear. "There's nothing here! It's just your imagination, Emma. There's no shadow, no ghost—nothing!"

But Hawthorne was already moving towards the corner Emma had pointed out, his eyes narrowed in concentration. He pulled out a small device from his pocket, holding it up as he scanned the area. The device let out a soft beep, the screen flickering to life with red dots—first one, then two, then four, then countless, until the screen was a solid red mass.

"It's here," Hawthorne said quietly, his voice carrying an ominous weight. "It's here with us, right now."

The tension in the room was suffocating. Claire's heart pounded in her chest as she looked between Hawthorne, David, and her daughters. The storm outside raged on, the rain now hammering against the windows as if trying to break through.

Suddenly, Sarah's voice crackled over the radio, her tone frantic. "Guys, you need to see this. There's...there's something on the monitor. It's not picking up where it should be. It's like...it's in the house, but not. I don't know how to explain it."

Hawthorne turned to Mike. "Go. Now."

Mike nodded and sprinted out of the room, leaving the rest of them in a tense silence. The girls clung to

Claire, their eyes wide with fear, while David stood there, unsure of what to do or believe.

Downstairs, Mike skidded to a halt in front of Sarah's monitor. "What is it?" he asked, out of breath.

Sarah pointed to the screen, her face pale. "Look. It's...it's everywhere. All at once. Like the entire house is...is being watched."

Mike stared at the screen, his stomach turning. "This...this isn't right. It's like the house itself is alive."

Back upstairs, Hawthorne's gaze shifted to the door. "We need to get out of here," he said quietly. "This isn't just a haunting. It's something much worse."

David scoffed, though there was no real conviction behind it. "You're overreacting, Hawthorne. It's just some glitch in your equipment. This isn't real."

But deep down, even David wasn't sure if he believed his own words anymore. The house had always felt different, strange, but now it was something else entirely. Something malevolent.

As they all made their way back downstairs, the oppressive atmosphere seemed to thicken, the darkness of the house closing in around them. The storm outside roared, the wind slamming against the walls like a beast trying to get in. Or was it already inside?

Hawthorne glanced at Claire as they reached the bottom of the stairs. "We need to leave. Now."

Claire hesitated, looking at her daughters, who were clinging to her tightly. "But where would we go? This is our home."

"This isn't a home anymore," Hawthorne said, his voice grim. "It's something else now. Something dangerous."

David opened his mouth to argue, but the words died in his throat as a cold, eerie whisper echoed through the house. It was a voice, faint but unmistakable, and it sent chills down everyone's spine.

"Need help?"

A whisper came, close, as if it were right next to them. The lights flickered, plunging the house into darkness for a brief moment before they came back on, dimmer than before.

Claire's grip tightened on her daughters. "We need to leave," she said, her voice trembling. "We need to leave now."

As they hurried towards the front door, the house seemed to come alive around them, the walls groaning, the floorboards creaking as if something was moving beneath them. Hawthorne ushered them out first, his eyes scanning the darkness for any sign of movement.

But the house wasn't done with them yet.

As they reached the door, it slammed shut on its own, the force rattling the entire frame. They tried to pull it open, but it wouldn't budge. The temperature in the house plummeted, their breath visible in the air as the oppressive presence closed in around them.

David finally gave in to the fear that had been gnawing at him. "What the hell is happening?" he shouted, banging on the door in a desperate attempt to open it.

Hawthorne didn't answer, his focus on the darkness surrounding them. The red dots on his device were multiplying, spreading out across the entire screen until there was no more room left. Whatever was in the house, it was everywhere now, closing in on them.

And it wasn't going to let them leave.

Next day morning light filtered weakly through the drawn curtains, casting long, eerie shadows across the hallway where everyone had sought refuge during the night. The house was silent, unnervingly so, as if it had settled back into a false sense of normalcy after the previous night's chaos. Claire was the first to awaken, her body stiff from sleeping on the hard floor. She blinked, trying to shake off the fog of exhaustion, and slowly began to take in her surroundings.

Her daughters were curled up beside her, their small bodies still nestled in the makeshift bedding. David was sprawled out on his back, his mouth slightly open as he slept, the tension from the night still etched on his face. A few feet away, Hawthorne lay on his side, his face contorted in discomfort. Even in sleep, he seemed troubled.

Claire's attention was drawn to Hawthorne as he shifted restlessly, his brows knitting together as if he were deep in thought—or in pain. The memory of the previous night's events hung heavy in the air, and for a moment, she wondered if it had all been a collective nightmare. But as she watched Hawthorne, she knew that wasn't the case. Something had happened—something real and terrifying.

Without warning, Hawthorne's eyes snapped open, his body jerking upright as if he had been shocked awake. His breath came in short, panicked bursts, and a cold sweat glistened on his forehead. The sudden movement startled everyone else awake, their eyes widening in confusion and fear.

Claire reached out to him, her voice filled with concern. "Hawthorne, are you okay?"

Hawthorne blinked rapidly, trying to orient himself. "I—I heard something," he stammered, his voice hoarse. "It was that whisper again. 'Need help.' It was so clear, like it was right next to me."

David groaned as he pushed himself up from the floor, rubbing his eyes as if trying to erase the remnants of sleep. "Again? What the hell is happening in this place?"

Hawthorne ran a trembling hand through his hair, his eyes darting around the hallway as if expecting to see something lurking in the shadows. "It's more than just a sound. It's like...a memory, something I should know but can't quite grasp."

Claire's gaze softened as she watched him struggle to make sense of the situation. "A memory? Did you hear that before?"

Hawthorne shook his head, frustration evident in his furrowed brow. "I don't know. It's familiar, but it's like it's just out of reach, like a word on the tip of your tongue that you can't quite remember."

Sarah and Mike, who had been sleeping near the monitors, scrambled to their feet and rushed to check the footage.

Sarah's fingers flew over the keyboard, her heart pounding in her chest. "There's...nothing," she said, her voice trembling. "No disturbances, no anomalies. Just us, moving around the house."

Mike leaned in closer, his face drawn with frustration. "It's like the cameras didn't pick up anything from last night. Everything looks...normal."

Claire felt a chill run down her spine at the word "Normal." There was nothing normal about what they had experienced, and yet the footage seemed to mock them, presenting a reality that was starkly different from their own.

Hawthorne remained where he was, his head in his hands, trying to rub away the headache that was forming. The whispers from his dream—or memory—echoed in his mind, growing louder with each passing second. He couldn't shake the feeling that he was missing something crucial, something that could explain the strange occurrences in the house.

Claire approached him cautiously, kneeling beside him. "Do you remember anything?"

He looked up at her, his eyes bloodshot and filled with uncertainty. "I don't know, Claire. It's like the whisper is trying to tell me something, but I can't figure out what. 'Need help'—it's so simple, but it feels like it has a deeper meaning. I just...I just don't know where I've heard it before."

David, who had been pacing the hallway, finally stopped and turned to them. "So what now? We've got nothing to show for last night. Do we just sit around and wait for something else to happen?"

Hawthorne straightened up, forcing himself to focus despite the lingering headache. "No, we can't just sit back.

We have to keep pushing forward, analyzing every detail, every bit of information we have."

Claire nodded in agreement, her resolve hardening. "Whatever it takes to protect our family. Just tell us what we can do to help."

Hawthorne took a deep breath, steeling himself for the task ahead. "First, we need to go over everything again—review the footage, examine the evidence, look for patterns or inconsistencies. We need to understand what we're dealing with here, and we need to stay vigilant."

As they all began to prepare for the day, the weight of the previous night's events lingered heavily over them. The house, with its deceptive calmness, seemed to hold its breath, waiting for the next move. Every creak of the floorboards, every sigh of the wind outside, felt charged with hidden menace, as if the very walls were watching them.

The day ahead promised more questions than answers, and an uneasy feeling settled in the pit of Claire's stomach. They were no closer to understanding the presence that haunted their home, but one thing was certain: whatever it was, it was far from done with them.

CHAPTER 14
VANISHING FEAR

Claire sat at the edge of the couch, her eyes weary and bloodshot from the lack of sleep. The tension in the room was palpable, everyone on edge from the night's unexplained events. David, standing by the window, rubbed his temples, clearly exhausted. The rest of the team huddled together, sipping on hastily prepared coffee, their faces reflecting the same unease.

"We need to leave," Claire finally broke the silence, her voice trembling slightly. "This house... it's not safe. We can't stay here any longer."

David looked at her, clearly caught off guard by her suggestion. "Claire, are you serious? After all we've been through, you want to leave now?"

"Yes," Claire insisted, her voice gaining strength. "We've tried everything, and it's only getting worse. We need to get the girls out of here."

Hawthorne, who had been sitting quietly, deep in thought, suddenly looked up. "Leaving isn't the solution," he said, his voice calm but firm. Everyone turned to him, waiting for an explanation.

"No point in leaving," Hawthorne continued, glancing around the room. "I'm afraid it's not just the house that's the problem. There's something else... something I'm not catching, but I can feel it. We leave now, and it might follow us. Or worse, we might leave the source of it here, unchecked."

Claire's brow furrowed in confusion. "What do you mean?"

Hawthorne sighed, clearly struggling to find the right words. "It's hard to explain, but... this isn't just a haunting. It's something deeper. Something connected to all of us. I can't shake the feeling that if we don't confront it here, now, we may never be rid of it. We have to wait until nightfall. That's when we'll get our answers."

David shook his head, skeptical. "And what if you're wrong? What if staying here just makes things worse?"

"Then we'll deal with it," Hawthorne replied, his gaze steady. "But I don't think I am. Not this time. Last night, I heard something—something familiar. I need to hear it again. We need to face this head-on, or it'll never end."

The room fell into a heavy silence as everyone absorbed Hawthorne's words. Claire bit her lip, torn between her instincts to protect her children and the uncertainty of what they were dealing with.

"Maybe he's right," one of the assistants spoke up, breaking the tension. "I mean, we've been through a lot, but if this is more than just a haunting, maybe we need to see it through."

David sighed, running a hand through his hair. "I hate this. I hate that we're even in this situation. But if you're saying we have no choice, then... I guess we have to stay."

Claire looked at her husband, then back at Hawthorne, who was watching them with an unreadable expression. "Alright," she finally said, her voice soft but resolved. "We'll stay. But this better end tonight. I can't take much more of this."

Hawthorne nodded, a flicker of relief passing over his face. "Thank you. We'll stay vigilant, and tonight... tonight we'll find out what this is. One way or another."

The group dispersed, each person lost in their thoughts as they prepared for another night in the house. The sun continued to rise outside, but the shadows in the house seemed darker, more menacing. The calm before the storm, as they awaited whatever horrors the night would bring.

As the evening descended, an unsettling stillness enveloped the house, casting long shadows that seemed to stretch and twist in unnatural ways.

Claire, unable to stay still, moved to the kitchen, trying to busy herself with mundane tasks to calm her nerves. As she washed dishes, she noticed the water in the sink turning a murky red. Her breath caught in her throat. She blinked and shook her head, hoping it was just her imagination, but when she looked again, the water was blood-red. Her hands trembled as she turned off the tap, and the water continued to pool in the sink. Suddenly, the faucet started to drip slowly, each drop echoing in the quiet kitchen.

Drip... drip... drip... Claire felt her heart race.

"David?" she called out, her voice shaky as she backed away from the sink. But there was no answer. The kitchen seemed to grow darker as the sound of the dripping intensified. She whipped around, sensing someone behind her, but the kitchen was empty. Then she heard it—a faint whisper. "Need help?"

Claire's skin prickled with fear as the whisper grew louder and more insistent. She spun around, trying to locate the source, only to find the refrigerator door slowly creaking open. She stepped closer, cautiously peering inside, expecting the worst. But as she opened the door fully, a shadow darted past her peripheral vision. She screamed and dropped the dish she was holding, shattering it on the floor. When she turned back to the refrigerator, it was empty, the whisper gone.

Meanwhile, in the living room, Hawthorne sat alone, scribbling notes and trying to make sense of the strange occurrences. His head throbbed with the memory of the whisper from his dream, a sound that seemed to echo from deep within his past, but he couldn't quite place it. As he flipped through his notes, the words on the page began to blur and shift, rearranging themselves into a single phrase: "Need help?"

He blinked, rubbed his eyes, and stared at the paper again, but the words continued to rearrange themselves no matter how much he tried to focus. Then, without warning, his notebook flew off the table, crashing into the wall with a loud thud. Hawthorne stood abruptly, his chair toppling over behind him. He heard footsteps, quick and light, echoing in the hallway. His breath caught as he realized they were coming closer.

"H-Hello?" he stammered, his voice betraying the fear he was trying to suppress. The footsteps stopped suddenly, and the silence that followed was deafening. He grabbed a flashlight from his bag, his hands shaking as he turned it on, the beam cutting through the darkness. He pointed it down the hallway but saw nothing. Just as he began to relax, a figure darted across the beam of light. Hawthorne's heart pounded in his chest as he tried to follow the figure with his flashlight, but it was gone.

"David! Claire! Did you see that?" he called out, but the house remained eerily silent.

David, who had been pacing the hallway upstairs, heard Hawthorne's call and moved toward the stairs, but something felt wrong. The temperature in the hallway had dropped drastically, and his breath came out in visible puffs of cold air. His heart raced as the hallway lights flickered, casting strange shadows on the walls. Suddenly, the lights went out completely, plunging him into darkness.

"Dammit!" he cursed under his breath as he fumbled for his lighter. He struck it once, twice, but the flame wouldn't catch. Panic started to rise as the lighter refused to cooperate. Finally, on the third strike, the flame flickered to life, casting a dim light in the pitch-black hallway. As the flame steadied, David saw something that made his blood run cold—his own reflection staring back at him from the hallway mirror, but twisted and distorted. The reflection grinned at him with an unnatural, malevolent smile, its eyes glowing with a sinister red light.

"What the—" David stumbled backward, the lighter slipping from his fingers and extinguishing as it hit the floor. In the brief moment of darkness, he felt a cold, clammy hand grip his shoulder. He whipped around, expecting to confront whatever was behind him, but there was nothing there. The hallway was empty, and the lights flickered back on as if nothing had happened.

Downstairs, Sarah, was monitoring the equipment, her eyes glued to the screen. She hadn't moved from her spot since the previous night, determined not to miss a single anomaly. But exhaustion was beginning to take its toll on her. Her eyelids drooped as she struggled to stay awake. Suddenly, the monitor flickered, and for a brief moment, she saw something—a dark figure standing in the corner of the room.

Her heart leapt as she leaned closer to the screen, trying to make sense of what she saw. But the figure was gone as quickly as it appeared. "What the fuck…?" she muttered, rubbing her eyes and trying to shake off the fatigue. Then the monitor flickered again, and this time, she saw a figure standing directly behind her in the reflection of the screen. She gasped and spun around, but the room was empty.

Her breathing quickened as she slowly turned back to the monitor. The screen was black, the camera feeds all dead. Then, in the darkness of the screen, two red eyes appeared, staring directly at her. Sarah screamed, jumping out of her chair and backing away from the monitor. The screen suddenly flickered back to life, showing nothing out of the ordinary.

She rushed out of the room, almost bumping into Claire, who was on her way to check on her. "Sarah, are you okay?" Claire asked, concerned.

"I—I don't know," Sarah stammered, her voice trembling. "There was something on the monitor, something not human…"

Claire's face paled. "Let's find Hawthorne," she said, leading Sarah down the hallway, the unsettling feeling growing stronger with every step.

As they reached the living room, they found Hawthorne pacing, his face pale and his expression troubled. "What's happening?" Claire asked, her voice barely above a whisper.

Hawthorne shook his head, his hand still pressed to his temple as if trying to soothe the persistent headache. "I don't know, Claire. But whatever it is, it's not bound by the rules of the living. This house… it's just a vessel. The real horror is something else, something that's targeting each of us… individually."

A cold silence fell over the room as everyone exchanged fearful glances. The sense of dread in the air was palpable, suffocating, as if the very walls of the house were closing in on them.

As the evening wore on, the stillness in the house became almost oppressive.

Hawthorne, who had been anxiously scanning every corner of the living room, finally spoke up, breaking the uncomfortable quiet. "It's too quiet," he murmured, more to himself than anyone else. His eyes were dark with exhaustion, but his mind was still racing. "This doesn't feel right."

David, sitting stiffly on the couch, nodded in agreement. "Yeah, it's like the calm before the storm," he said, his voice low and tense. "But it doesn't make any sense. Why would it just stop like that?"

"It's playing with us, waiting for the right moment to strike again." Hawthorne replied, rubbing his temples as if trying to ease a headache.

Claire, who had been hovering near the doorway, looked over at Hawthorne with concern. "Do you really think it's going to start again? What if it was just… I don't know, a fluke?"

Hawthorne shook his head. "No, this isn't over. I can feel it. It's not going to let us go that easily."

Claire sighed, her nerves frayed from the night's events. "Then what do we do? Just sit here and wait for it to start again?"

"That's all we can do for now," Hawthorne said, his voice resigned. "We have to stay vigilant. Whatever it is, it's going to try to catch us off guard."

The hours ticked by with agonizing slowness. Midnight came and went, but the house remained eerily calm. The team, who had been prepared for another night of paranormal activity, began to relax, though the tension never fully left the room. The earlier sense of impending doom had faded, leaving behind an uneasy calm.

Sarah, who had been glued to her monitors for what felt like an eternity, finally allowed herself to lean back in her chair. Her eyes were red from lack of sleep, and her head throbbed with fatigue. She tried to focus on the screens, but her vision was blurring, and she could barely keep her eyes open.

Hawthorne noticed her struggling and walked over, placing a hand on her shoulder. "Sarah, you need to get some rest," he said gently. "You've been up all night. Go lie down for a few hours."

Sarah blinked, trying to shake off the drowsiness. "But what if something happens?" she asked, her voice tinged with worry.

"We'll handle it," Hawthorne assured her. "You've done more than enough for tonight. Get some sleep, and we'll wake you if anything comes up."

Sarah hesitated, glancing back at the screens. She didn't want to leave her post, but she knew she was running on empty. "Okay," she finally agreed, her voice heavy with exhaustion. "But only for a little while."

Claire, who had been listening to the conversation, stepped forward. "I'll show you to a room where you can rest," she offered with a warm smile. "It's quiet, and you should be able to get a few hours of sleep there."

"Thanks, Claire," Sarah said, managing a tired smile. She stood up, wobbling slightly on her feet as the fatigue hit her all at once.

Claire led Sarah down the hallway, the sound of their footsteps muffled on the carpet. "I know it's been a rough night," Claire said softly, trying to offer some comfort. "But hopefully, you'll be able to get some rest now."

"I hope so," Sarah replied, her voice barely above a whisper. She was too tired to even think about what might happen next.

They reached a cozy guest room at the far end of the house. The room was small but comfortable, with a soft bed covered in a quilted blanket and a nightstand with a lamp that cast a warm, soothing light. "Here we are," Claire said, opening the door and gesturing for Sarah to enter. "You'll be safe here."

Sarah stepped inside, the room's warmth immediately lulling her into a sense of safety. She slipped off her shoes and sank into the bed, the mattress soft and inviting. The exhaustion weighed her down like a heavy blanket, and she could feel herself drifting off almost as soon as her head hit the pillow.

Claire lingered in the doorway for a moment, watching as Sarah's breathing slowed and deepened. "If you need anything, just call," she said softly. "I'll leave the door slightly open so you can hear us."

Sarah nodded weakly, already half-asleep. "Thank you, Claire," she murmured, her voice trailing off as she slipped into unconsciousness.

Claire closed the door gently, leaving it ajar as promised. She turned back down the hallway, her mind racing with the events of the night. As she rejoined the others in the living room, the uneasy calm settled over the house once more. The team was scattered around, trying to make sense of the situation. Hawthorne sat in silence, his mind clearly elsewhere, while David paced back and forth, his nerves frayed.

"How's Sarah?" David asked as Claire entered the room.

"She's exhausted," Claire replied, sitting down next to him. "But she'll be okay. She just needs to sleep."

"Good," David muttered, though his eyes were still darting around the room, as if expecting something to leap out at them.

Hawthorne, who had been silent for several minutes, suddenly spoke up, his voice tinged with confusion. "That whisper… 'Need help,'" he said, rubbing his temples as if trying to remember something important. "It's familiar. I've heard it before, but I can't place where."

Claire looked at him, concern etched on her face. "What do you mean?"

"I don't know," Hawthorne admitted, his brows furrowed in concentration. "It's like a memory I can't quite reach. But there's something about it… something important."

David frowned. "Maybe it's just your mind playing tricks on you," he suggested, though he didn't sound entirely convinced himself.

"Maybe," Hawthorne replied, though his tone suggested otherwise. "But I need to figure it out. There's something we're missing."

The group fell silent, each lost in their own thoughts. The house was still, the earlier chaos replaced by an eerie calm that was almost worse.

And as they waited, the words "Need help" echoed in Hawthorne's mind, growing louder and more insistent with each passing minute.

The clock struck midnight, and an eerie stillness settled over the house. The earlier tension had finally dissipated, and one by one, everyone succumbed to exhaustion, their bodies giving in to the need for rest. The silence that filled the house was unnaturally deep, as if the very walls were holding their breath.

Sarah had eventually fallen into a fitful sleep in the small guest room. Her breathing was slow and steady, the events of the day drifting away in the haze of sleep. The room was dark, the only light coming from the faint glow of the moon filtering through the curtains & a small light in the room.

But then, something changed. The door to Sarah's room, which had been left slightly ajar, began to creak open ever so slowly. The sound was barely audible, a soft groan of wood on wood. Yet Sarah remained asleep, unaware of the subtle shift in the atmosphere. The door opened wider, and a shadow moved quickly past the doorway, accompanied by the faint, sinister sound of laughter—a young woman's laugh, light and almost playful, but with an edge of something dark beneath it.

Suddenly, the light in the room flickered and then went out completely, plunging the room into total darkness. Sarah stirred, her eyes fluttering open as she awoke with a start. The darkness was disorienting, and she blinked, trying to adjust her vision, but there was nothing to see—just an inky blackness that seemed to press in on her from all sides.

Panic flared in her chest, but she forced herself to stay calm. With trembling hands, she fumbled for her phone on the nightstand, the small device feeling like her only lifeline in the suffocating darkness. She found it and quickly turned on the flashlight, the beam of light slicing through the dark like a knife.

She didn't move from the bed, too frightened to leave the relative safety of the mattress. Her heart raced as she slowly moved the flashlight around the room, the beam of light illuminating the familiar furniture and walls, now cast in harsh, stark shadows.

As she scanned the room, she tried to convince herself that everything was fine, that it was just her imagination playing tricks on her. But then the light caught on something that made her blood run cold—a pair of feet, pale and twisted, standing just outside the doorway.

The feet were bare, the skin an unnatural, sickly color, as if the blood had drained from them long ago. The toes were gnarled and bent at odd angles, and the nails were cracked and blackened. Sarah's breath caught in her throat as she stared at the feet. She couldn't see anything else—

just those horrible, misshapen feet standing in the hallway.

Her hand shook as she slowly moved the flashlight beam upward, desperately needing to see who—or what—was standing there. But as the light climbed, revealing the empty space above the feet, she saw nothing. The body that should have been attached to those feet wasn't there. It was as if the feet were floating, disembodied in the darkness.

Sarah's heart beating louder in her ears, drowning out the silence. She quickly jerked the light back down to where the feet had been, only to find the doorway empty. The feet were gone. The hallway was completely dark, nothing out of place—except the door was still slightly open.

Before she could even process what she had seen, a sudden rustling noise came from the floor beneath her bed, accompanied by a quick, shuffling movement. The sound was faint, like something sliding across the floor, but it sent a bolt of fear through her.

Sarah gasped, her body frozen with terror. She barely had time to react as something darted out from the doorway and scuttled beneath her bed, moving so fast that it was nothing more than a blur in the corner of her vision. Whatever it was had crawled under her bed with a speed and agility that was unnervingly inhuman.

Sarah's breath hitched in her throat, and she dared not move a muscle. The air in the room felt heavy and oppressive, and every instinct in her screamed to get off the bed, to run, but she couldn't bring herself to move. She felt utterly paralyzed, as if something was holding her down, keeping her from fleeing.

She aimed her phone's flashlight at the floor, pointing it over the edge of the bed, her hand shaking violently. The beam illuminated the bare wooden floorboards, casting long shadows in the small space beneath the bed. But there was nothing there—just an empty, dark void.

For a moment, she almost convinced herself that she had imagined it all, that the darkness and her fear had played tricks on her. But then she heard it—a faint, almost imperceptible sound. Breathing. Slow, steady breathing, coming from directly beneath her.

Sarah's eyes widened in terror, her heart slamming against her ribs. She didn't dare move, didn't dare make a sound. The breathing continued, quiet but unmistakable, just inches below where she lay on the bed. The thing beneath the bed was waiting, lurking in the shadows, just out of sight.

And then, the breathing stopped, replaced by an unnatural silence. The air grew colder, and the darkness seemed to deepen, pressing in on her from all sides. The flashlight flickered, the beam weakening as the battery began to die. Sarah's grip tightened on the phone, her knuckles white with fear.

She didn't know what to do, where to go. The thing under the bed was there, hiding in the darkness, waiting for her to make a move. She could feel it, could sense its malevolent presence, even though she couldn't see it.

The seconds stretched into what felt like an eternity, the silence unbearable. Sarah's breath was shallow, her body trembling as she fought to stay still. She couldn't stay there, couldn't just wait for whatever was under the bed to make its move. But she didn't know how to escape, didn't know how to get out of the room without provoking whatever it was.

Then, just as she thought she couldn't bear it any longer, the light in the room suddenly flickered back on, flooding the space with harsh, artificial brightness. The warmth of the light brought her a small measure of relief, but it was fleeting. She immediately pointed the flashlight under the bed, expecting to see something, anything.

But there was nothing. The space under the bed was completely empty. The room was as it had been before—normal, undisturbed. The only thing that remained was the residual cold that lingered in the air.

Sarah let out a shaky breath, her heart still pounding in her chest. She couldn't comprehend what had just happened, couldn't understand how the thing under the bed could have disappeared so completely, so silently.

Sarah carefully slid out of bed, her feet hitting the cold floor. The terror she had just experienced still gripped her, but she knew she couldn't stay in that room any longer. The light was back on, but she had no idea how long it would last. She needed to get out, now.

With trembling hands, she reached for the door, her breath quick and shallow. Each step felt like it took an eternity, her legs shaky and weak from fear. She kept her phone's flashlight aimed ahead, lighting her path as she moved toward the exit. The room was eerily quiet, the only sound being the soft pad of her feet on the floor.

She was almost at the door, her fingers brushing against the cool metal of the doorknob, when the light suddenly went out again. Darkness swallowed the room whole, and the oppressive blackness closed in around her like a vice. Panic surged through her, her breath hitching in her throat.

Before she could react, something cold and clammy wrapped around her ankle with a vice-like grip. It was a hand—rough, bony fingers digging into her flesh with unnatural strength. Sarah let out a bloodcurdling scream, the sound piercing through the silence of the house. The grip on her ankle tightened, pulling her backward with a force that sent her sprawling to the floor.

She clawed at the ground, trying to free herself, but the hand wouldn't let go. She kicked out with her other leg, desperate to break free, but it was like kicking into the void—there was nothing there, just that unyielding grip dragging her back into the darkness.

Her screams echoed through the house, jolting everyone awake. Claire and the others bolted from their makeshift sleeping spots in the hallway, their hearts pounding with fear as they raced toward Sarah's room.

But as Hawthorne sprinted down the hallway, something caught his eye—a figure standing still as a statue at the basement door. The dim light barely illuminated the figure, leaving its features obscured in darkness, but there was something unmistakably familiar about it. His breath caught in his throat, and he slowed his pace, unable to tear his eyes away from the shadowy figure.

He quickly pulled out his flashlight and aimed it at the basement door, the beam slicing through the darkness. His blood ran cold as the light revealed what was standing there—a person, or at least something that resembled a person. Its face was pale and gaunt, its eyes hollow, and its body draped in tattered clothing that looked like it had been unearthed from a grave.

Hawthorne's heart skipped a beat, and a chill ran down his spine as the recognition hit him like a freight train.

His mouth went dry, and he whispered in disbelief, "You! Oh my god!"

CHAPTER 15
THE FAMILIAR

The hallway was eerily quiet as the others rushed towards Sarah's room, their footsteps echoing off the walls. Hawthorne stood rooted to the spot, his flashlight trembling in his hand as he stared at the basement door. The figure that had been there was gone now, leaving only a lingering chill in the air. His heart pounded as he whispered, "Oh my God…"

Claire, Mike, and Tom burst into Sarah's room, their faces painted with concern. Sarah was pale, trembling, as she sat on the edge of her bed, trying to catch her breath. The room was filled with an unsettling silence, broken only by the faint sound of Claire's worried voice.

"What happened, Sarah?" Claire asked, her voice barely above a whisper as she knelt beside the bed, placing a comforting hand on Sarah's knee.

Sarah's eyes were wide, darting nervously around the room as if she expected something to leap out at her at any moment. "I—I don't know. Something was in here with me. I saw… I saw feet outside the door, but when I looked again, there was nothing there. And then…" she stammered, her voice trembling, "something crawled under the bed, and then it grabbed my leg when I tried to leave."

Mike and Tom exchanged a worried glance, their expressions turning from concern to fear. Mike moved to check under the bed, but there was nothing there—just an empty, dark space that somehow felt more menacing now.

"Are you sure it wasn't just a bad dream?" Tom asked, trying to sound calm, but his voice betrayed his unease.

"No, it wasn't a dream," Sarah insisted, her voice rising in panic. "It was real. I felt it—its grip on my ankle. It was cold…so cold."

Before anyone could respond, Hawthorne appeared in the doorway, his face ashen and his hands trembling slightly. He looked as if he had seen a ghost, and in a way, he had.

"Hawthorne," Claire said, her voice filled with both relief and concern, "what's going on?"

Hawthorne stood there for a moment, silent and lost in thought, before finally speaking. "Maybe I…I know why everything here felt so familiar," he said, his voice barely above a whisper. His eyes were distant, as though he was reliving an old, painful memory.

Mike stepped forward, concern etched on his face. "What do you mean? Familiar how?"

Hawthorne took a deep breath, trying to steady himself. "I saw someone…no, something, standing by the basement door. For a moment, I thought it was a person, but then…I realized it couldn't be. It was as if it wasn't really there, yet it was."

"Who did you see?" Sarah asked, her voice still trembling.

"I don't know who it was, but it felt like I'd seen that figure before. Something about this place… It's like a memory that I can't quite grasp," Hawthorne replied, his voice shaking with a mix of fear and confusion.

Claire felt a chill run down her spine. "Hawthorne, what are you talking about?"

Hawthorne rubbed his temples as if trying to push the thoughts away, but they clung to him, refusing to be ignored. "I think… I think this house is more than just haunted. It's connected to something—someone—from my past. And whatever it is, it's dangerous."

A tense silence fell over the room as everyone absorbed Hawthorne's words. The reality of their situation seemed to grow heavier with each passing moment.

"What do we do now?" Tom finally asked, breaking the silence.

Hawthorne looked at each of them, his expression one of grim determination. "We have to find out why it's here, and what it wants. But whatever we do, we have to be prepared. This is no ordinary haunting."

Sarah's eyes widened with fear, and Claire's heart raced with a mix of dread and anticipation.

Hawthorne's voice was low, almost a whisper. "This isn't just about the house anymore. It's about something much deeper…and much darker."

As the night stretched on and the faint light of dawn began to seep through the curtains, the house remained unnervingly quiet. Everyone had gathered in Sarah's room, crowded around her bed, their nerves still on edge from the night's terrifying events. The only ones who had found any rest were Claire's daughters, who slept soundly in her arms, unaware of the dark shadows looming over the household.

Claire's eyes drifted to Hawthorne, who stood near the window, staring out into the dim morning light. His face was etched with worry, deep lines of concentration furrowing his brow. His silence only added to the tension in the room, making everyone else more uneasy.

Suddenly, Hawthorne spoke, breaking the heavy silence. "I remember now," he said, his voice low and burdened with realization. Everyone turned to look at him, their attention fully captured.

Tom, always the one to probe for answers, asked, "What is it? What do you remember?"

Hawthorne didn't meet anyone's gaze. He seemed lost in his own thoughts, his mind racing through memories from years ago. "It's... it's something I encountered when I was much younger, just starting out in this line of work," he began slowly, as if piecing the puzzle together in real-time. "I was involved in a case... a haunting that had similarities to what we're experiencing now. But I can't figure out how, after all these years, it's happening again... and here of all places."

The room was thick with suspense. Claire, holding her daughters close, asked, "What was the case? What happened?"

Hawthorne shook his head, still not fully grasping the situation himself. "It was a long time ago. I thought... I thought it was over, dealt with. But now, seeing what's happening here... I have to be sure. I need to find someone—an old colleague who helped me back then. He might have answers."

Sarah, still shaken from her encounter, asked, "So what do we do? Do we stay here?"

Hawthorne nodded firmly. "Yes, you stay here. I'll go alone. Whatever this is, it's dangerous, and I need to know more before we can act. I'll be back soon, and hopefully, I'll have the answers we need."

Mike, usually calm and collected, looked uneasy. "Are you sure about going alone? What if something happens while you're away?"

"I'm sure," Hawthorne replied, his tone leaving no room for argument. "I need to move quickly, and I can't risk anyone else. Just... keep the house secure. I'll be back as soon as I can."

The tension in the room was palpable. No one liked the idea of Hawthorne leaving, but they all knew it might be their only chance at understanding the horrors that plagued the house.

"Just be careful," Claire finally said, her voice soft but laced with concern.

Hawthorne gave a tight nod, his mind already focused on the task ahead. "I will."

As the first light of day fully broke, illuminating the room in a soft, eerie glow, Hawthorne gathered his things, ready to embark on a journey that might hold the key to saving them all.

Hawthorne glanced up at Claire, his expression a mix of relief and anxiety. "Claire, may I use your laptop? I need to find an address before I leave."

"Of course," Claire replied, nodding quickly. She fetched the laptop from the other side of the room, her hands slightly trembling as she handed it over.

Hawthorne settled into the chair, the soft glow of the screen reflecting in his eyes. His fingers moved quickly over the keys, searching with a purpose that was almost frantic. The others watched him in silence, the tension in the room thickening with each passing moment.

Claire stood nearby, arms crossed, worry etched on her face. "Are you sure you'll be okay alone?" she asked, her voice laced with concern.

"I'll be fine," Hawthorne replied without looking up, his focus still on the screen. "This…this thing, whatever it is, ties back to an old case. I need to confirm something, and I know just the person who can help me. But it's something I have to do on my own."

Tom, standing near the doorway, exchanged a glance with Mike. "We can go with you, you know. You don't have to do this alone."

Hawthorne paused, his fingers hovering over the keyboard for a brief moment before he resumed typing. "I appreciate the offer, Tom, but this is something I need to do myself. I don't want to risk anyone else getting caught up in this…whatever it is."

Mike frowned, clearly uncomfortable with the idea of splitting up. "Just be careful, alright? We don't know what we're dealing with here."

After a few more moments of tense silence, Hawthorne's eyes brightened. "I got it," he murmured, jotting down the address on a piece of paper. He closed the laptop and stood up, turning to Claire with a determined look. "I'll be back soon. Tell everyone to stay inside and be safe."

Claire nodded, though her eyes betrayed her lingering fears. "We will. Just…be careful, Hawthorne."

With that, Hawthorne pocketed the slip of paper, nodded to the group, and headed toward the door. The sound of the door closing behind him seemed to echo through the house, leaving the rest of them in a tense, uneasy silence.

No one had eaten since the previous night, and it was starting to take its toll. The children, who had been silent for hours, finally began to stir. The youngest one whimpered, and soon, both girls were crying, their small voices piercing the silence.

Claire, exhausted but determined to keep things as normal as possible, knelt by them, trying to comfort them. "Shh, sweethearts, it's okay. Mommy will make breakfast soon. Everything will be alright," she said, her voice wavering as she smoothed their hair.

But the children were inconsolable, their cries growing louder and more insistent. David, who had been pacing back and forth, his face a mask of frustration, suddenly snapped.

"Enough!" he bellowed, turning sharply towards them. His eyes, usually kind, were now wild with anger. "These kids are a damn nuisance!"

Claire shot up, her protective instincts flaring. "David, they're just hungry! They haven't eaten since yesterday."

But David wasn't listening. He pointed an accusing finger at the children, his voice rising. "No, Claire, they're always the problem! You spoil them too much! This house would be peaceful if they weren't always whining and crying about something!"

Claire clenched her fists as David's voice grew louder, venom seeping into every word. "You think I wanted this? You think I wanted two screaming kids around all the time, messing everything up?" He paced back and forth, his face twisted in anger. "They're the reason everything's going wrong! Maybe if they weren't here, none of this would be happening!"

Claire's eyes narrowed, her heart pounding with a mix of anger and disbelief. "David, they're just children! Our children! How can you even say that?"

David's eyes flashed with a mix of rage and frustration. "Your children, Claire! You were pregnant before we even met! I took on that responsibility, but maybe that was the biggest mistake of my life!" His voice cracked, filled with a bitterness that shocked Claire to her core.

Claire felt a wave of cold anger wash over her. "How dare you? How dare you throw that in my face now, after everything we've been through?" Her voice trembled with a mixture of hurt and fury. "You knew about my past, about the girls. You chose to be a part of this family, and now you're blaming them for everything?"

David scoffed, his face contorted with contempt. "Blame? They're the cause, Claire! I can't stand it anymore. Their whining, their constant neediness... it's driving me insane! And now, with everything going on, it's like they're a curse!" He spat the last word, his voice rising with each sentence.

Claire's voice shook as she stepped closer, her anger boiling over. "You don't get to talk about them like that! They're not a curse; they're my daughters! You're the one who's been changing, not them!"

David's eyes burned with rage as he stepped forward, his voice dropping to a dangerous whisper. "You think you're so perfect, don't you? But you're the one who brought them into this mess, who brought them into my life. Maybe you should've stayed single, Claire. Maybe then, you wouldn't be dragging everyone down with you."

Claire's breath caught in her throat, the cruelty of his words hitting her like a physical blow. "You... you're not the man I married," she whispered, tears brimming in her eyes. "What happened to you, David? Where's the man who loved me and the girls?"

David's face twisted into a sneer. "He's gone, Claire. Maybe he never even existed."

The tension in the room was suffocating, the air thick with unspoken emotions. Mike, Sarah, and Tom exchanged uneasy glances, feeling the weight of the argument but unsure whether to intervene. Mike's hand twitched, as if he wanted to step in, but he held back, respecting the family's space despite the heated exchange.

David's words cut through the silence again, harsher than before. "Maybe I was wrong to ever get involved with someone like you. With your baggage, your kids, your messed-up life!"

Claire's voice cracked as she tried to maintain her composure. "If that's how you really feel, then why are you still here? Why haven't you left?"

David's face hardened, his eyes cold and distant. "Maybe I should."

Claire's heart pounded in her chest, fear and anger swirling within her. "Then go, David! Go if that's what you want! But don't you dare put this on them, or on me! This is on you!"

David glared at her, the anger simmering beneath the surface. Without another word, he turned on his heel and stormed out of the room, slamming the door behind him. The sound echoed through the house, leaving a heavy silence in its wake.

Claire stood there, trembling with a mixture of rage and despair, her breath coming in short, shallow gasps. The tears she had been holding back finally spilled over, streaming down her cheeks as she sank into a chair, feeling utterly drained.

The team remained quiet, the tension in the air palpable. Sarah glanced at Tom and Mike, unsure of what to say or do. The argument had been brutal, and they knew this wasn't the time to interfere.

Finally, Tom spoke up, his voice gentle. "Claire, we're here if you need anything. We'll give you some space, but just know we're here."

Claire nodded, wiping away her tears with the back of her hand. "Thank you," she whispered, her voice barely audible.

The team slowly retreated, leaving Claire alone with her thoughts. The weight of David's words hung heavy in the air, a reminder of how fragile everything had become.

Hawthorne drove through the winding roads of the forest, the thick canopy of trees casting long, flickering shadows across the path. The morning light filtered through the branches, but the further he drove, the more the day seemed to darken, as if the very air around him was growing heavy with the weight of old memories. His mind drifted back to a case from many years ago, a case that had haunted him but had since faded into the background of his career. Yet, something about the current events had brought it all rushing back, though the details were still blurry, like a half-remembered dream.

The journey was long, and the monotonous hum of the engine did little to distract him from the unsettling thoughts circling in his mind. He had started early, hoping to arrive before the day grew too late, but the forest seemed endless, stretching on in a way that made time feel slow and distorted. By the time he finally saw the break in the trees that signaled the end of his drive, the sun was already high in the sky, casting harsh midday light on the world around him.

Hawthorne pulled up to a secluded house at the edge of the woods. The house was old but well-kept, with a rustic charm that seemed to stand in stark contrast to the eerie memories tugging at the edges of Hawthorne's consciousness. He parked the car, took a deep breath, and stepped out. His boots crunched on the gravel path as he approached the front door, his mind racing through the fragmented recollections of the past.

He rang the bell and waited, his heartbeat quickening in the silence that followed. After what felt like an eternity, the door creaked open, and a man appeared. The man was older, perhaps in his late sixties, but his posture was straight, and his physique was surprisingly fit for his age. His eyes, sharp and probing, scanned Hawthorne up and down.

"Can I help you?" the man asked, his voice carrying the authority of someone who had seen a lot in his life.

Hawthorne took a moment, studying the man's face, the lines of experience etched deeply into his skin. He swallowed, his own voice feeling heavy in his throat.

"Hello, Harris. I'm Hawthorne. Do you remember me?"

The old man's eyes narrowed slightly, as if searching through the catalog of faces and names stored in his memory. A flicker of recognition passed over his features, followed by a cautious curiosity.

"Hawthorne...," Harris murmured, the name rolling off his tongue as if testing its familiarity. "Yes, I remember you now. You were just starting out back then, weren't you?"

Hawthorne nodded, feeling a strange mixture of relief and apprehension. "It's been a long time."

"It has," Harris said, his tone neutral, but there was a glint in his eyes that suggested he was already trying to piece together why Hawthorne had come after all these years. "What brings you here?"

Hawthorne hesitated for a moment, the words struggling to form in his mind. "I... I need your help. It's about a case—one from a long time ago. Something's happening again, something connected to that case. I think you're the only one who might be able to help me figure it out."

Harris studied Hawthorne for a long moment, his expression unreadable. Then, with a nod, he stepped aside and gestured for Hawthorne to enter.

"Come in," Harris said. "Let's talk."

CHAPTER 16
LINGERING SHADOWS

The afternoon sun dipped low, casting long shadows through the windows of the house. As evening approached, an uneasy silence hung over the household. Claire sat in the living room, her daughters nestled beside her, their eyes fixed on a children's book she was reading. Sarah and Tom sat nearby, both trying to keep their anxiety at bay.

"I can't believe how quiet it's been," Sarah remarked, glancing around the room. "It's like the house is holding its breath."

Tom, fidgeting with a small object on the coffee table, tried to lighten the mood. "Maybe it's just the calm before the storm. You know, like when everything goes still before something big happens."

Claire looked up from the book, her eyes tired but determined. "I'm going to make some coffee. Does anyone else want a cup?"

Sarah nodded gratefully. "Yes, please. I could use something to wake me up. It's been a long day."

Tom chimed in, "Same here. Coffee sounds perfect right now."

Claire headed to the kitchen; her mind preoccupied with the day's events.

Claire tried to focus on the comforting routine of making coffee, but her thoughts kept drifting back to

Hawthorne. She glanced at the clock—another hour had passed since she last checked.

As she stirred the coffee, she called out, "Has anyone seen Mike? I haven't noticed him around this evening."

Tom, who had been pacing near the hallway, looked up. "Mike's just doing a sweep of the house. With Hawthorne gone, he doesn't want to leave any stone unturned. He's been checking every room and every corner."

"That's good," Claire said, though her tone betrayed her worry. "I hope he's okay. We've had enough stress already."

Sarah, rubbing her eyes wearily, added, "It feels like something's off. The house seems... different. Since yesterday, it's like it's holding onto a secret."

Claire set the coffee on the table and sat down, trying to relax. "I know exactly what you mean. It's like the house is waiting for something to happen."

Tom took a sip of his coffee, then said, "Maybe it's just the stress making us feel this way. But with everything that's happened, who knows what's next?"

Claire nodded, trying to stay positive. "Let's try to stay calm. We don't know anything for sure yet. Let's just hope Mike comes back soon and we can get some answers."

The coffee maker beeped, signaling that the coffee was ready. Claire poured cups for Sarah and Tom and carried them into the living room. As she handed them out, she glanced at the door to David's room, which had remained shut since morning. David hadn't emerged at all since their argument earlier.

"Has David said anything to you two?" Claire asked, trying to steer the conversation away from their collective unease.

Sarah shook her head. "No, he hasn't come out since you had that argument. I'm worried about him too."

Tom frowned. "I think he's just overwhelmed. It's been a rough few days. Maybe he needs some time alone to process everything."

"Maybe," Claire agreed. "But we need to keep an eye on him. The last thing we need is more tension in the house."

As they talked, the house seemed to settle into an eerie quiet, the only sounds being their murmured conversations and the occasional sip of coffee. The minutes stretched on, each one adding to the oppressive atmosphere.

"Did you hear anything from Mike?" Claire asked, trying to break the silence.

Tom shook his head. "No, he's been out of touch for a while now. I hope he's okay."

Sarah, clearly anxious, said, "This silence is unsettling. It feels like we're waiting for something to happen, but we don't know what."

Claire tried to reassure them. "We'll get through this. Hawthorne will be back soon, and hopefully, he'll have some answers. In the meantime, we should try to stay calm and support each other."

The three of them fell into a tense silence, the quiet of the house amplifying their unease. Claire's eyes occasionally darted towards the door, hoping to hear some sign of Mike's return or any update from Hawthorne.

As the evening turned into night, the atmosphere in the house remained thick with tension. The shadows lengthened, and the once-comforting aroma of coffee seemed to do little to ease the growing sense of foreboding.

The warm glow of the living room lamp cast a soft light over Detective Harris's study. The room was lined with old bookshelves filled with faded volumes and framed photos of Harris's career. A large leather couch sat in the middle of the room where Hawthorne had taken a seat, his face etched with concern. Harris, now slightly older but still physically fit, paced around the room, a glass of red wine in hand.

Harris took a sip of his wine and looked at Hawthorne, his expression one of skepticism mixed with curiosity. "You're telling me this all comes back to the case from twenty years ago? I've heard about a lot of strange things in my time, but this... this doesn't make any sense."

Hawthorne leaned forward, his hands clasped together. "I know it sounds strange, but there are details in this case that match exactly with what I encountered back then. It's almost as if the same entity is involved."

Harris raised an eyebrow, leaning against the edge of his desk. "But how? What's making you think that this case is connected to that old one? I mean, that was a different time, a different place."

Hawthorne took a deep breath, trying to articulate the nagging feeling that had been bothering him. "I remember the case vividly. The entity we dealt with back then had specific traits, behaviors. The whispers, the appearance, even the feelings it evoked—they're the same."

Harris took another sip of his wine, his gaze shifting to a framed photograph on the wall. "I've seen a lot over the years, but connecting this to an old case... it's a stretch. What exactly did you see that made you think of the old case?"

Hawthorne's eyes narrowed as he recalled the eerie details. "Last night, at the house, I heard whispers that seemed familiar. It was a phrase—a voice saying 'Need help.' It was almost identical to the voice we encountered years ago. And then there's the behavior of the entity, the way it manipulates the environment. It all matches."

Harris set his wine glass down on the desk and took a seat opposite Hawthorne. "Alright, let's break this down. What do you remember from that old case? Maybe we can find some connections that make sense."

Hawthorne leaned back, trying to piece together the fragmented memories. "The old case involved a similar pattern of haunting. We had reports of strange noises, disappearances, and unexplained phenomena. It all seemed to revolve around an entity that fed on fear and manipulated people's perceptions."

Harris's face grew serious. "And you're saying this entity might be the same one causing trouble now?"

Hawthorne nodded, frustration evident in his voice. "Yes. It's not just the similarities in the phenomena; it's the feeling of malevolence, the way it targets individuals' fears. I've seen this before, and I'm certain there's a connection."

Harris stood up, walking to the window and looking out at the darkening sky. "You're asking me to believe that a case we closed twenty years ago is somehow reopening itself in a new location. It's a lot to take in, Hawthorne."

Hawthorne stood as well, moving closer to Harris. "I understand it sounds far-fetched, but the evidence is piling up. The descriptions from the current case match the old case too closely to be coincidental. And the entity's behavior—it's almost like it's following a pattern."

Harris sighed, turning back to face Hawthorne. "Alright, if we're going to pursue this, we need to be methodical. What do you propose we do next?"

Hawthorne's expression was resolute. "We need to dig into the old case files, look for any overlooked details or patterns. I want to see if there's something we missed back then that could shed light on why this is happening again."

Harris nodded, a hint of intrigue in his eyes. "Okay, let's start by reviewing the old case documents. I still have them archived. If there's anything to find, it's there."

Hawthorne let out a breath he didn't realize he was holding. "Thank you, Harris. I know it's a lot to ask, but I believe this is the only way to understand what's really going on."

Harris poured himself another glass of wine, his demeanor shifting to one of cautious optimism. "We'll give it a shot. If there's a connection, we'll find it. But I hope you're right about this, because if not, we might be chasing ghosts."

Hawthorne smiled faintly, feeling a glimmer of hope amidst the tension. "We'll find the answers. I'm sure of it."

The two men began their search through old case files, the weight of their investigation pressing down on them. The room was filled with the quiet rustling of papers and the occasional murmur of discussion, both men deeply engrossed in their task.

The scene was set, the old case files were being scrutinized, and the search for answers continued, with the shadows of the past lurking just out of sight.

Claire, Sarah, and Tom were gathered in the kitchen, their voices low and strained from the previous night's events. The smell of freshly brewed coffee lingered in the air, providing a semblance of normalcy.

Claire glanced around the room and then looked at her watch. "Mike should have been back by now. It's getting late."

Tom, his brow furrowed in concern, responded, "That's strange. He left a while ago to check the house and the grounds."

Sarah, still visibly shaken from the night's events, nodded in agreement. "We should look for him. It's not safe to be wandering around here on his own this late."

Just as Sarah finished speaking, Mike appeared at the top of the stairs, his face a mixture of relief and fatigue. He descended slowly, his movements purposeful. "Did you guys miss me?"

Everyone's faces lit up with a mix of surprise and relief. Claire quickly put down her coffee cup and walked over to Mike. "Mike! We were starting to get worried. Where have you been?"

Mike shrugged off his jacket and took a seat at the kitchen table. "I was just doing a thorough check of the house. I had already scanned the outside but figured I'd check the inside again. Nothing unusual outside, so I thought I'd focus on the interior."

Sarah, her eyes wide with concern, asked, "You didn't find anything at all?"

Mike shook his head. "Nope, not a thing. I went through every room, checked all the closets, and even went into the basement again. Everything seems clear."

Tom leaned forward, his skepticism evident. "Are you sure? The house has been acting up a lot lately. Maybe you missed something."

Mike gave a reassuring smile. "I'm sure. I used all the equipment we have. If there was anything off, we would've picked it up."

Claire, trying to ease the tension, said, "It's good to have you back. We could use a break from all this tension."

Mike nodded and poured himself a cup of coffee. "I agree. I could use a coffee break myself. It's been a long day."

Sarah forced a weak smile and added, "We all could use a break. It's been non-stop since last night."

Mike joined the group at the table, sipping his coffee. "So, what's the plan now? Hawthorne is still not back, right?"

Claire sighed, her gaze shifting to the door. "Yes, he's still out with someone named Harris. They're going through old case files, trying to find any connection to what's happening here."

Tom, flipping through some documents on the table, said, "We should keep an eye on things until they return. We can't afford to be caught off guard."

Mike nodded in agreement. "Agreed. I'll keep the scanners running and do another round of checks later. Hopefully, we'll get some answers soon."

As they continued to chat, the atmosphere in the room remained tense but slightly more relaxed. The team members took solace in the small moments of normalcy, hoping that the worst was behind them.

However, as the night wore on, a sense of unease lingered. The house, which had seemed quiet for the moment, held its breath, waiting for the next unsettling event to unfold.

At Harris's house, the two men sifted through the old case files. The room was dimly lit, with only a single desk lamp casting shadows on the scattered documents. Harris took a long sip of his wine before speaking.

"This really doesn't make any sense, Hawthorne. The old case was about a boy, and there were no reports of a haunted house. The situations seem entirely different."

Hawthorne, eyes scanning the papers intently, shook his head. "I know it seems disconnected, but I can't shake the feeling that there's a connection. When I saw those elements in the current case, it triggered something in my memory. It's almost like déjà vu."

Harris leaned back in his chair, tapping his fingers on the armrest. "You're saying you remember something similar from the old case?"

"Yes," Hawthorne replied, his voice tense. "I remember the boy had a strange, almost unexplainable link to something supernatural. It wasn't clear at the time, but something feels eerily familiar now. The haunting, the whispers, the manifestations—they all seem to echo what I saw back then."

Harris raised an eyebrow. "But how can we connect this to the current situation? The old case involved just one person, and this is a family with multiple occurrences."

"That's exactly it," Hawthorne said, frustration evident in his tone. "We might be missing a critical link. In the old case, Dr. Richard Mallory was involved later on, but he wasn't the primary investigator. You were. I need to understand how it all started from your perspective."

Harris frowned, sipping his wine thoughtfully. "Mallory was the one who delved deeper into the psychological aspects. I only handled the initial investigation. If we need to find a connection, we might need to speak to Mallory himself."

Hawthorne nodded vigorously. "That's exactly what I was thinking. We need to talk to him. He might have insights that could help us see the bigger picture."

Harris looked skeptical but nodded. "Alright, I'll get in touch with Mallory. But if this leads us nowhere, we'll have to consider other angles."

Hawthorne exhaled, a mix of relief and anxiety visible on his face. "Thank you, Harris. I just feel that Mallory might hold the key to this mystery."

The evening shadows lengthened as Claire, Sarah, and the kids sat together in the living room, their conversation punctuated by the occasional nervous glance toward the clock.

Mike was also present, quietly observing the situation. Tom, clearly feeling the weight of the night's events, turned to Mike.

"I'm going to step outside for a smoke," Tom said. "I need a minute to clear my head."

Mike nodded, his expression unreadable. "Just make sure you stay alert. We're not out of the woods yet."

Tom walked to the door, giving a nod to Claire. "I'll be back in a few."

The air outside was crisp and cool, and the lake nearby glistened under the fading light. Tom walked towards the wooden dock that extended over the lake's edge, enjoying the solitude and the quiet. He lit his cigarette and took long, slow drags, letting the smoke swirl around him as he gazed out over the water.

The lake was serene, a stark contrast to the tension he felt inside. After finishing his cigarette, he flicked the ember into the water and watched it sink beneath the surface. As he turned to head back towards the house, something caught his eye.

He glanced back at the water, noticing a peculiar object floating where he had thrown his cigarette. It was a dark, muddy shape. Curiosity piqued, Tom crouched down for a closer look. The object was a shoe, its once-white surface now stained and grimy, drifting slowly with the ripples.

Tom's heart raced as he squinted, trying to make sense of the sight. His breath caught in his throat as the shoe was joined by something more sinister. The water began to bubble and churn, and with a grotesque slowness, a body began to emerge.

It was Mike, or what was left of him. The body was in a horrific state, barely recognizable. The face was bloated and discolored, eyes open in a ghastly stare. The once-clear features were now obscured by decomposition and murk. The clothes were tattered and sodden, clinging to the lifeless form. As the body floated face-up, the expression was hauntingly vacant, adding to the chilling effect of the scene.

Tom recoiled in terror, stumbling backward as the realization of what he was witnessing sank in. He scrambled to his feet, his heart pounding as he looked around, trying to steady himself. The calmness of the lake was now overshadowed by the grim discovery.

Panicking, Tom sprinted back towards the house, his steps heavy and hurried. He burst through the front door, panting heavily, his face pale with shock. Claire, Sarah, and the kids looked up in alarm as he stumbled into the living room.

"Oh my God!" Tom gasped, his voice trembling.

Sarah jumped up from her seat, her eyes wide with concern. "What's wrong? What happened?"

Tom, breathless and terrified, struggled to speak. "I saw Mike's body... in the lake. It's not him inside. He's already dead... We need to be ready. It's starting."

The room fell silent, the gravity of Tom's words sinking in. Claire's face went white, and Sarah's expression turned from concern to horror. The kids, sensing the tension, clung to their mother, their innocent faces reflecting the fear that had suddenly gripped the house.

Claire took a deep breath, trying to maintain composure. "What? Mike was here just a moment ago."

Tom nodded vigorously. "Yes, I'm sure. Whatever's happening, it's getting worse."

Harris was pacing back and forth in his study, phone pressed to his ear. The room was dimly lit, casting shadows across the walls. His face was etched with concern as he listened intently to the person on the other end of the line.

"What? How? Are you sure about this?" Harris's voice was tinged with disbelief.

After a few moments of intense conversation, Harris's expression turned grim. He hung up the call and turned to face Hawthorne, who was sitting nearby, eyes filled with anticipation.

Hawthorne's voice was low but urgent. "What happened? Did you get any useful information?"

Harris rubbed his temples, the weight of the news settling heavily on him. "Dr. Mallory... he's dead. He drowned in his pool this evening."

CHAPTER 17
A CALL TO ACTION

The morning light filtered softly through the curtains of Detective Harris's living room. Hawthorne, who had stayed the night, was seated at the table, staring at a cup of coffee, deep in thought. The weight of the previous night's revelations hung heavily in the air.

His phone vibrated on the table, snapping him out of his reverie. It was Sarah. He hesitated for a moment, his instincts bracing for the worst. Finally, he answered.

"Sarah?" Hawthorne said, his voice carrying a note of concern.

"Hawthorne... something terrible happened last night," Sarah's voice trembled on the other end. "Mike... he... we found his body in the lake this morning. Tom saw it first. We don't know how long he's been dead, but... it wasn't him who was with us last night."

Hawthorne felt a chill creep up his spine. The room seemed to close in around him, the coffee cup suddenly forgotten. "What... what do you mean, it wasn't him?"

"Tom went out for a smoke, and when he got near the lake, he saw Mike's body, floating there. But the Mike who was with us last night, it wasn't him. It couldn't have been. It's... it's like something took his place."

Hawthorne's mind raced. The eerie familiarity of the events, the connection to the old case, everything was starting to form a twisted picture in his mind. But before he could speak, Sarah's voice came through again, more urgent now.

"What should we do? It's not safe here anymore, Hawthorne."

Hawthorne took a deep breath, trying to steady himself. "Sarah, listen to me. Keep everyone together, and don't let anyone else near the lake. I'll be there as soon as I can."

He ended the call and looked at Harris, who had been silently watching him, the older man's keen eyes studying Hawthorne's every reaction.

"I have to go back," Hawthorne said, his voice firm but laced with tension. "Mike's dead, but something… something's still there."

Harris nodded, his expression grave. "I figured it was only a matter of time before things escalated. But before you go, Hawthorne, there's something you should know."

Hawthorne looked at him, waiting.

"I've been trying to reach Clara," Harris continued. "She was the nurse who worked closely with Mallory during the old case. If anyone knows what really happened back then, it's her."

Hawthorne nodded, piecing together the fragments of information. "And? Did you get through to her?"

Harris sighed, a deep, weary sound. "Not yet, but I'm not giving up. If Mallory's gone, Clara's our last link to that case. I'll find her and see what she knows. You just focus on keeping everyone safe at the house."

Hawthorne stood, the weight of responsibility pressing down on him. "You know where to find her?"

Harris gave a slight nod. "I'll track her down. You just get back to that house and figure out what the hell is going on."

"Thank you, Harris," Hawthorne said, genuinely relieved to have the old detective's support.

As Hawthorne made his way to the door, Harris called after him. "Hawthorne, be careful. Whatever this is, it's not going to go down easily."

Hawthorne turned back, a grim determination in his eyes. "I know. But I won't let it take anyone else."

With that, Hawthorne left, the door closing behind him with a quiet finality. He had to get back to Claire's house, back to where the horrors of the past and present were converging. As he drove, his thoughts were filled with the image of Mike's lifeless body in the lake and the ominous sense that whatever was haunting this family had only just begun its twisted game.

After Hawthorne left, the house settled into a tense silence. Harris remained in the living room, his mind racing as he went over the details of the old case. The room was dimly lit, with shadows creeping across the walls as the day outside began to turn into early afternoon. He knew he had to find Clara—she was the only one left who could shed light on what was happening.

Harris reached for his phone, scrolling through his contacts. There was one person he hadn't called in years, an old informant who had a knack for tracking down people who didn't want to be found. Harris hesitated for a moment, then dialed the number. It rang twice before a gruff voice answered.

"Harris? It's been a while," the voice on the other end said.

"I need a favor," Harris said, skipping the pleasantries. "I need to find someone, a nurse named Clara. She worked with Dr. Richard Mallory years ago on a case. I've hit a wall, and she's the only lead I've got left."

There was a brief pause, then the voice replied, "Clara, huh? Give me a second." The sound of typing filled the line, followed by a low whistle. "Found her. She's been off the grid for a while, but I've got an address. Last known residence in a small town about an hour from you. Sending it over now."

Harris heard his phone ping as the address came through. "Got it. Thanks. I owe you one."

"You always do, Harris. Good luck."

Harris ended the call and stared at the address on his screen. The town wasn't far, but getting there meant navigating through winding back roads and dense forest—typical of the remote places people like Clara tended to disappear into. He had no idea what state she would be in or if she would even remember the case, but he had to try.

He moved to his study, where he kept a small safe tucked away in a corner. Entering the combination, he opened it to reveal his service revolver. Harris hadn't had to use it in years, but something about this situation made him uneasy. The nightmares of the old case were returning, and now with Mallory dead and the strange events surrounding the family, he couldn't shake the feeling that he was walking back into something dark and dangerous.

Harris loaded the revolver with practiced ease, the familiar weight of it in his hand bringing a sense of grim reassurance. He tucked the gun into the holster inside his jacket, then gathered the files and documents he had on the old case, slipping them into a leather satchel. He knew that if Clara had any answers, he needed all the evidence at hand to jog her memory.

Before leaving, Harris stood in the doorway of his study, looking around the room as if saying goodbye to an old friend. He had spent countless hours in there, going over cases, solving mysteries, and piecing together puzzles. But this time felt different—like he was on the edge of something he wasn't sure he wanted to uncover.

He shook off the unease and headed to the front door. As he stepped out, the cool air hit him, and the reality of what he was about to do settled in. The sun was beginning to dip lower in the sky, casting long shadows across the yard. He climbed into his car, started the engine, and set off toward the address he had just received.

The drive was quiet, the only sound the hum of the tires on the road and the occasional rustling of trees as the wind picked up.

As the roads became narrower and the trees thicker, Harris checked the address again, confirming that he was close. The town was small, barely more than a few scattered houses and a gas station. It was the kind of place people went to disappear, to be left alone. He followed the directions to a small, isolated house at the end of a gravel road.

He parked his car and stepped out, taking in the sight of the house. It was old, the paint peeling, and the windows covered with thick curtains. A single light burned in the front window, casting a dim glow over the front porch.

Harris walked up to the door, his hand hovering over the revolver tucked inside his jacket. He rang the bell and waited, his senses on high alert. There was no sound from inside, no movement. He rang the bell again, more insistently this time.

Finally, the door creaked open, and a woman appeared in the doorway. She was older than he remembered, her hair streaked with gray and her face lined with age. But her eyes—sharp, wary—hadn't changed.

"Clara?" Harris asked, keeping his tone composed.

She didn't respond immediately, studying him with a mix of suspicion and recognition. "Detective Harris," she finally said, her voice raspy. "It's been a long time."

"It has," Harris replied. "I need to talk to you about the old case, Clara. The one with Dr. Mallory."

Clara's expression hardened, and she shook her head. "I left that life behind, Harris. Whatever's going on now, I want no part of it."

"I understand," Harris said gently. "But this isn't just about the past. People are in danger, Clara. The things we thought were over… they're happening again."

Clara's grip tightened on the doorframe. "You don't understand, Harris. There are things we weren't meant to know. Things that should have stayed buried."

Harris stepped closer, lowering his voice. "That's why I'm here. I need your help to stop it. Please."

For a moment, Clara seemed to hesitate, her eyes flicking to the files Harris held. Then, with a sigh, she stepped back and opened the door wider. "Come in, Detective. But I warn you, what you're asking for… it might be more than you're ready to handle."

Harris nodded and entered the house, the door closing behind him with a quiet click. As Clara led him into the dimly lit living room, he couldn't shake the feeling that they were both about to unearth something dark and dangerous, something that had been waiting in the shadows for far too long.

As Hawthorne reached Claire's house, he was met with a heavy atmosphere. The room was thick with tension and sorrow; the air felt suffocating. Sarah was sitting in a corner, her eyes red from crying, while Claire held her daughters close, their faces pale with fear and confusion. The grief and dread in the room were palpable.

Hawthorne's voice cut through the silence, heavy with urgency. "Where is it?" he asked, his tone direct but filled with underlying sorrow.

Tom, his face ashen and his demeanor subdued, stepped forward. "In the lake," he said quietly, his voice barely above a whisper.

Without another word, they all headed outside. The group moved in a somber procession toward the lake, the tension growing with every step. As they neared the water, the putrid smell of decay hit them first, sharp and overwhelming. Sarah, who had been holding it together, suddenly gagged and turned away, unable to hold back the bile rising in her throat. Claire, trying to be strong for her daughters, pressed a hand to her mouth, her eyes filled with horror as she fought the urge to vomit.

Tom led the way, his steps heavy. As they approached the dock, the smell hit them first—a pungent, decaying odor that made them instinctively cover their noses. The water was tranquil, but at the edge of the dock, a figure bobbed gently against the ripples. Mike's body, lifeless and bloated, floated face-up in the water, his skin pale and swollen from hours spent submerged. His once vibrant eyes were dull, and his mouth was slightly ajar, as if frozen mid-scream. His clothes clung to his frame, waterlogged and dirty, while his limbs floated unnaturally, tethered only by the weight of his body.

Hawthorne's heart sank. Mike had been the youngest member of his team, full of energy and optimism. Seeing him like this, reduced to a lifeless husk, filled him with a deep sadness. He knelt down beside the dock, reaching out a hand to gently touch Mike's arm. The coldness of the skin sent a shiver through him.

"We need to get him out," Hawthorne said, his voice strained with emotion.

Tom nodded, his hands shaking slightly as they both moved to the edge of the lake. The body was heavier than they expected, waterlogged and limp. They struggled with the weight, the mud at the lake's edge making it difficult to get a good grip. The smell was overpowering now, and Sarah turned away completely, tears streaming down her face as she choked back sobs.

Just as they managed to pull the body halfway out, a voice came from behind them, clear and gentle, startling them all. "Need help?"

Hawthorne whipped around, his heart skipping a beat. Standing there, looking eerily, was David. He seemed almost...different. There was something in his eyes, something off, a strange look that didn't match the horror around them.

David didn't wait for a response. He stepped closer, his movements fluid, almost too smooth. "I can help," he said again, his voice carrying an unsettling quietness.

Hawthorne, his instincts screaming that something was wrong, nevertheless nodded slowly. "Sure, David...we could use a hand."

David joined them, grabbing onto Mike's body with an unsettling ease. Tom shot Hawthorne a quick, worried glance, but together, they managed to pull the body fully onto the shore. The three of them stood there, staring down at the remains of their friend, the silence heavy with grief and unease.

As they did, Claire approached cautiously, holding her daughters back. Her eyes met Hawthorne's, wide with fear and uncertainty. "What do we do now?" she asked, her voice trembling.

Hawthorne was about to respond when he noticed David still staring at the body, his expression unreadable, almost detached. The hairs on the back of his neck stood up as a chill ran down his spine. David finally looked up, his gaze locking with Hawthorne's, a small, almost imperceptible smile curling at the corner of his mouth.

"There's more to this," David said quietly, his tone chilling. "Isn't there?"

Hawthorne, unnerved by David's sudden change, nodded slowly. "Yes...yes, there is."

Sarah, now trying to regain her composure, stepped closer, her voice shaky. "What are we going to do, Hawthorne? We can't stay here with...with this," she said, gesturing helplessly at Mike's body.

"We'll take care of it," Hawthorne said firmly, trying to take control of the situation. "We need to keep cool and stick together. No one goes anywhere alone."

As they stood there, the group's unease was palpable, the horror of the situation sinking in deeper with every passing moment. And through it all, David watched them, his expression mellow and eerily composed, as if the events unfolding before him were nothing out of the ordinary.

As David turned away, his steps slow and deliberate, he announced, "I'm going to call the police. They'll handle the body." His voice was strange, lacking any of the emotional turbulence that one might expect in such a grim situation. David walked back toward the house, his pace unhurried, as if he had all the time in the world.

Hawthorne watched him go, his instincts telling him something was very wrong. Tom, still reeling from the shock of finding Mike's body, turned to Hawthorne with a troubled expression. "What's wrong with David?" he asked, his voice low and edged with concern. "He's acting really strange."

Sarah, who had finally managed to compose herself, nodded in agreement. "Yeah, David's behavior has been off ever since we found Mike," she said. "He's barely spoken, and now he's just wandering around like he's in a daze."

Claire, still visibly shaken, chimed in. "He was locked away in his room for almost a day, not coming out at all. The first time he's left that room in hours, and it's to do this..."

Hawthorne's face tightened as he considered their words. "I noticed it too," he said, his voice low. "David's quietness... it's unsettling. It's almost as if he's detached from the reality of what's happening."

Tom glanced back toward the house, where David had disappeared from view. "You think something's wrong with him?"

"I don't know," Hawthorne admitted, rubbing the back of his neck. "But it's certainly worth looking into. There's something off about his demeanor, something that doesn't add up."

Sarah shivered slightly, looking from Hawthorne to Claire. "Do you think he might be involved in all of this somehow? With Mike dead, it feels like everything's spiraling out of control."

Claire shook her head, trying to stay despite her obvious distress. "I don't know, but something's definitely not right. We need to stay alert and keep an eye on him. If he's acting like this, we can't rule anything out."

As they spoke, the tension among them grew. The peaceful lake, once a serene backdrop, now seemed to cast a dark shadow over their thoughts. The body of Mike, now covered by a tarp, lay on the shore, a grim reminder of the danger they faced.

Hawthorne nodded, his mind racing. "Let's not jump to conclusions. For now, we need to focus on getting the police here and securing the scene. We'll deal with David later, once we have more information."

As they waited for David to return, the feeling of dread intensified. The quiet of the early morning seemed to press in on them, amplifying their fears.

Minutes ticked by slowly. Claire, Sarah, and Tom stood together, their eyes constantly darting toward the house, awaiting David's return and the arrival of the authorities. The air was thick with unspoken fears and the uneasy feeling that something darker was unfolding just beyond their understanding.

David finally reappeared, his face a mask of unreadable calm. "The police are on their way," he announced, his tone flat. "They should be here soon."

Hawthorne looked at him, scrutinizing his expression. "Thanks, David. I'll need to speak with them once they arrive."

David merely nodded, not offering any further details. He turned and walked back toward the house, leaving the others to process their mounting unease.

As they stood by the lake, the reality of the situation weighed heavily on them. The sense of impending doom was palpable, the tranquil morning now a backdrop for a mystery that seemed to grow more sinister with each passing moment.

CHAPTER 18
THE HIDDEN TRUTH

The evening sun cast long shadows across Clara's modest living room. The room was furnished with an old, worn couch, an antique coffee table, and a few framed photographs of family memories scattered on the walls. Clara, a woman in her early forties with a kind face that belied the horrors she had witnessed, sat across from Detective Harris. Harris, now older but still sharp, sat in a comfortable armchair, his eyes focused on Clara.

"Thank you for meeting me, Clara," Harris said, pouring tea into two cups. "It's been twenty years, but the details of that night are as vivid as ever."

Clara took a sip of her tea, her hands trembling slightly. "I never thought I'd have to revisit those memories. It was a night that changed everything."

Harris leaned forward, his expression serious. "I need to understand what happened in St. Augustine Hospital. Specifically, the night you and Dr. Mallory encountered that boy. What do you remember about him? Why was he in the hospital?"

Clara's eyes grew distant as she searched for the words. "The boy... he was found in a derelict house. I don't know how he ended up there, but he was in a state of shock. They brought him to us, hoping we could help him. But something was wrong. It was as if he wasn't alone. There was something else with him."

Harris nodded, urging her to continue. "What do you mean by 'something else'?"

Clara took a deep breath, preparing herself to recount the chilling events from twenty years ago.

"After the boy was taken to the hospital," Clara began, her voice trembling slightly, "he seemed calm at first. We did our best to treat him, but as days went by, he started to change."

Harris leaned forward, his interest piqued. "Change how?"

Clara took a sip of her tea before continuing. "He began to say there were voices in his head. He claimed they were talking to him, whispering things only he could hear. It wasn't just that. He had an unnatural ability to hear even the smallest sounds from far away. He'd tell us what was happening in the kitchen before the food was even served. It was like he could perceive things that were beyond normal human capability."

Harris nodded slowly, absorbing the details. "That's troubling. What else?"

Clara's eyes grew distant as she recalled the events. "The boy also suffered from severe headaches every night. They were so intense that he'd be in agony. We tried various treatments, but nothing seemed to alleviate his pain. It was as if the voices were driving him mad."

"What happened next?" Harris asked, his curiosity mingled with concern.

Clara sighed, her expression darkening. "One night, I was resting in my cabin, and Dr. Mallory was in his office, reviewing reports. The boy's condition seemed stable that evening, but something shifted."

Harris raised an eyebrow. "What do you mean?"

Clara's voice grew softer, as if recalling a dark secret. "The boy suddenly became violent. Out of nowhere, he started attacking everyone. The staff was caught off guard. He was stronger than we expected. It was as if the voices had taken over him completely."

Harris's eyes widened. "And that's when you called me?"

"Yes," Clara confirmed. "We were in desperate need of help. The situation was out of control. The boy was throwing things, screaming, and attacking anyone who came near. Dr. Mallory and I tried to subdue him, but it was futile. We needed someone who could handle the situation—someone with experience in dealing with extreme cases."

"Now I remember the rest," Harris said, breaking the silence. "We were able to capture the boy that night. It took a lot of effort, but we managed to restrain him. We tied him to a chair in one of the secure rooms. I remember the chaos—it was a nightmare."

Clara nodded, her face etched with a mix of sadness and dread. "Yes, it was horrific. The boy was beyond our control. I had never seen such strength and fury before. We struggled to keep him restrained."

Harris's expression hardened. "I even considered using lethal force to stop him. It was a moment of desperation. But Dr. Mallory, he insisted we find another way. He was adamant that killing the boy wasn't the solution."

Clara sighed, her gaze distant. "Dr. Mallory believed there was more to the situation, something that could be understood or treated. He was always driven by a desire to help, even in the face of overwhelming danger."

"Indeed," Harris said thoughtfully. "Mallory's refusal to resort to violence was a testament to his dedication. But now, I need to know more about the reports and the findings Mallory mentioned. I recall him saying that after diagnosing the boy, he discovered something abnormal—a defect in the boy's head, or perhaps something more. Can you provide any details on that?"

Clara took a deep breath and set her tea cup down on the table. "Have you ever heard of the *'Pineal Gland'*, Harris?" she asked.

Harris raised an eyebrow. "I've heard of it, but my knowledge is pretty basic. Why?"

Clara nodded, acknowledging his limited knowledge. "The pineal gland is an endocrine gland located deep within the brain, in the posterior aspect of the cranial fossa. Its primary role is to regulate our circadian cycles—sleep and wakefulness."

Harris listened carefully, intrigued by the connection. "And how does that relate to the boy's case?"

Clara continued, "The pineal gland is sometimes referred to as the 'third eye' because it's sensitive to light and darkness, similar to the way our eyes function. It contains cells that react to changes in light by releasing melatonin, which helps regulate our sleep patterns. But there's more to it than just that."

Harris leaned in, eager to hear more. "What more is there?"

Clara's eyes took on a distant look as she spoke. "In some spiritual traditions, the pineal gland is believed to act as a bridge between the physical and spiritual realms. Holistic practitioners suggest that activating the pineal gland can enhance intuition, clarity of thought, and a heightened sense of awareness. It's almost as if it's a conduit for something beyond our normal perception."

Harris absorbed this information, his mind racing with implications. "And what did Dr. Mallory conclude about the boy?"

Clara sighed, her face reflecting the weight of the past. "Mallory was convinced that the boy's condition was linked to an overactive pineal gland. He believed that the boy's heightened senses and the voices he heard were a result of this gland functioning beyond normal limits. Mallory and Mr. Hawthorne worked together to address this issue."

Harris's curiosity intensified. "What exactly did they do?"

Clara hesitated for a moment before continuing. "They decided to perform a procedure to remove the boy's memories and, more importantly, to 'close' his third eye. They aimed to suppress the overactive function of the pineal gland, hoping it would end the boy's distress and the supernatural phenomena associated with him."

Harris's eyes widened. "They actually performed a procedure to alter the boy's brain function? That sounds drastic."

Clara nodded solemnly. "Yes, it was a desperate measure. The boy's condition was deteriorating, and they felt it was the only option left. They hoped that by closing his third eye and removing the memories linked to the supernatural experiences, they could provide him with a chance at a normal life."

Harris took a moment to process this information. "And?"

Clara's face showed a mix of regret and uncertainty. "To some extent, yes. The boy's violent episodes and the voices ceased, but the procedure left him with gaps in his memory and a significant psychological burden. Dr. Mallory and Mr. Hawthorne hoped that the boy would find peace, but there were lingering questions about the long-term effects."

Harris nodded, understanding the gravity of the situation. "Thank you for sharing this, Clara. It's crucial to understand what happened back then. It might help us connect the past with the current events."

Clara gave a tired smile. "I hope it helps. If there's anything more you need, don't hesitate to ask."

As Harris was about to leave Clara's home, he turned back, a new question forming in his mind. "Clara, do you have any idea where the boy is now? Or any details about his current whereabouts?"

Clara's expression became thoughtful. "After everything happened, the boy was adopted by an orphanage. They promised to help him start a new life, giving him a new name and a fresh start."

Harris raised an eyebrow. "Do you have any documents or information about the adoption?"

Clara nodded and walked over to a drawer in her living room cabinet. She rummaged through it and pulled out a folder, handing it to Harris. "Here are the copies of the adoption papers. I kept them in case there was ever a need to trace the boy's history."

Harris took the folder with a sense of urgency. He carefully opened it and began examining the documents inside. The papers were yellowed with age but still legible. The adoption paperwork detailed the process and the new identity given to the boy.

Clara watched him closely, her expression a mixture of concern and curiosity. "What does it say?"

Harris scanned the documents, his eyes widening as he read the details. "The boy was 12 years old at the time of adoption. According to these papers, the orphanage gave him a new name... **David Hargrove**."

At Claire's living room the atmosphere was tense, everyone grappling with their own thoughts. The space was filled with a palpable unease as Claire, Sarah, and Tom sat quietly, each lost in their own world of worry. David, on the other hand, was positioned far from them at the dining table, his demeanor unsettlingly cold and distant. His eyes darted occasionally toward the others, but he remained otherwise still, as though brooding over some dark thought.

The sudden ringing of Hawthorne's phone cut through the silence. He glanced at the caller ID and saw Harris's name. Hawthorne answered with a steady, "Hello."

"Hawthorne!" Harris's voice crackled with frustration, "What the hell did you hide from me? Why the fuck didn't you tell me everything?"

Hawthorne's eyebrows furrowed in confusion. "Hid what? Harris, what are you talking about?"

Harris's voice was low, edged with anger. "You convinced me twenty years ago to keep that case under wraps. You said the boy was fine, that he'd be normal. But you didn't tell me about the third eye, the experiment you and Mallory did. Why the hell did you leave me in the dark?"

Hawthorne's face hardened. "Some things are better left unknown. But why the hell are you asking me this now?"

Harris's tone was grim. "Because I'm staring at him right now. That boy, the one you said was fine, is David. The twelve-year-old beast we faced is a man now, sitting right there in your presence. I've seen the adoption papers. *David Hargrove is the boy from St. Augustine.*"

Hawthorne's eyes widened in shock. "Are you sure? You're absolutely certain?"

Harris's response was unequivocal. "Yes, I'm sure. I've seen the documents. David— he's not just any man. There's something deeply wrong. He has that same energy, that same dark presence."

Hawthorne's mind raced as he tried to process the revelation. "So all this time, David was—"

"—The boy from the case," Harris cut him off. "And it gets worse. Whatever was done to him, whatever that 'third eye' experiment was, it hasn't gone away. It's grown, matured, and now it's affecting everyone around him."

Hawthorne's gaze shifted to David, who sat motionless at the dining table, his face a mask of eerie calmness. "Jesus Christ," Hawthorne muttered. "I had no idea it would come to this."

Harris's voice grew colder. "Well, now you know. And you need to act fast. We're running out of time, and whatever's happening here is only getting worse."

Hawthorne took a deep breath, his mind already racing through the possibilities. "I'll figure something out. Stay safe, Harris. I'll be in touch."

After ending the call, Hawthorne stood in silence, the weight of Harris's revelation sinking in. The house seemed to grow colder, and a sense of dread hung heavy in the air. He turned to face Claire, Sarah, and Tom, who had been watching him intently.

"Is everything okay?" Claire asked, her voice laced with concern.

Claire's house was suffused with an uneasy stillness as Hawthorne spoke in hushed tones, his face etched with concern. The shadows in the room seemed to grow darker, mirroring the gravity of the situation. Hawthorne turned to Claire, his voice a low whisper.

"Claire, we need to talk privately. Can you take us to another room where David won't hear us?"

Claire nodded quickly, her face pale with apprehension. "Of course. Follow me."

She led Hawthorne, Sarah, and Tom through the narrow hallway and into a small, dimly lit room at the back of the house. The room was sparsely furnished, with a few old chairs and a small table in the center. Claire closed the door softly behind them, ensuring David wouldn't overhear their conversation.

Hawthorne took a seat and motioned for the others to do the same. "Claire, we need to figure out what's been happening here. Do you remember anything unusual, anything that might have triggered these events, especially concerning David?"

Claire sat down, her eyes clouded with worry as she tried to recall the details. "Well… nothing really horrific comes to mind. But David did have an accident a while ago."

Hawthorne leaned forward, his interest piqued. "An accident? What happened?"

Claire's brow furrowed as she struggled to piece together her memories. "He fell down the stairs. It was a pretty nasty fall. His head hit the edge of the step, and he was unconscious for a while. We were all really worried."

Sarah's eyes widened. "That sounds serious. How long was he out?"

Claire took a deep breath. "He slept the entire day. It was unusual because he was usually so active. When he finally woke up, he seemed different. We attributed it to the shock, but..."

Hawthorne's mind raced. "And that's when everything started?"

Claire nodded. "Yes, after that accident, he began behaving strangely. He was more distant, and then the odd things started happening. The voices, the sensitivity to sounds—everything."

Tom, who had been silent until now, spoke up. "So, the accident was the catalyst for these changes?"

Claire nodded solemnly. "It seems that way. I thought it was just a concussion or something, but now… I'm not so sure."

Hawthorne's voice was steady but urgent. "Claire, the situation is more dire than we thought. The accident David had, it's not just a coincidence. It seems to have reactivated something that was suppressed twenty years ago."

Claire's hand trembled as she gripped the arm of her chair. "What are you saying, Hawthorne?"

Hawthorne looked each of them in the eye, his face grim. "The boy from the old case—David—is the same person who's been living here. The trauma from the fall has reawakened his abilities. His 'third eye' is active again."

Sarah's eyes darted nervously. "The third eye? What does that mean for us?"

Hawthorne took a deep breath. "The pineal gland, or the so-called 'third eye,' gives certain individuals the ability to perceive and communicate with the spiritual realm. David, as a child, had this ability suppressed after the events at St. Augustine Hospital. But the head injury reactivated it."

Tom leaned forward, his expression troubled. "So, what's happening now?"

Hawthorne's voice grew more intense. "With his third eye open again, David is able to see and communicate with spirits. The problem is that this communication has attracted them to him. Spirits can sense his presence and are drawn to him, and the more he interacts with them, the more vulnerable he becomes."

Claire's hands were now clasped tightly in her lap. "How many spirits are there?"

"More than a hundred," Hawthorne replied, his tone somber. "The house wasn't haunted before David's accident, but now it has become a beacon for these entities. They've started to invade the house, drawn to David's weakened state."

Sarah's voice quivered. "And you think David is possessed?"

Hawthorne nodded slowly. "Yes. It's highly likely that a powerful demon has taken hold of him. The spirits' collective energy has made it easier for a stronger, malevolent entity to possess him. David's body is now a battleground between these spirits and the demon."

The room seemed to grow colder as the gravity of Hawthorne's words settled in. Claire's voice broke the silence, barely above a whisper. "What do we do? How do we stop this?"

Hawthorne's face was etched with concern. "We need to act quickly. First, we need to keep David away from the spirits. We should strengthen the protective measures around the house and try to contain the influence of the spirits as much as possible."

Tom's voice was filled with urgency. "What about David? Is there a way to get him back to normal?"

Hawthorne shook his head. "It won't be easy. We might need to perform a ritual or seek out someone with experience in exorcisms. The priority now is to keep him safe and try to weaken the demon's hold on him."

Claire's eyes were filled with tears. "I never wanted any of this. How could I have known?"

Hawthorne reached out, placing a reassuring hand on Claire's shoulder. "It's not your fault, Claire. We'll do everything we can to help David. For now, we need to stay vigilant and act fast."

The room was filled with a tense silence, broken only by the occasional creak of the old house. Outside, the night was still, but within the walls, an ominous presence loomed. The team knew that the coming hours would be critical, and the shadows that had begun to gather around David were only a prelude to the horrors yet to come.

As Hawthorne, Claire, Sarah, and Tom prepared to confront the malevolent forces within the house, they were all acutely aware of the gravity of their situation. The house had become a prison, and the line between the living and the dead had blurred in the most terrifying way.

CHAPTER 19
AUGUST 12, 2005 – BEFORE THE RECKONING

The thunderstorm raged across the city, sending flashes of lightning through the heavy, rain-soaked clouds. Each crack of thunder echoed ominously as a car came to a halt in front of St. Augustine Hospital. The building, old and imposing, loomed in the storm, its windows dim and its structure creaking under the pressure of the wind. The entrance sign flickered, casting intermittent light over the wet pavement.

A man, tall and wrapped in a long, dark coat, stepped out of the car, his hat pulled low over his face to shield himself from the pounding rain. He stood for a moment, gazing at the hospital with a sense of unease. The entire scene felt like it belonged in a nightmare. The night's storm intensified the already eerie atmosphere of the hospital, making the shadows around the building stretch and flicker like ghostly figures.

The man adjusted his coat, the rain beating down on him as he made his way through the entrance. He pushed through the heavy wooden doors, which creaked as they opened, and entered the lobby. The hospital, quiet and dimly lit, had an unsettling stillness. It was as though the storm outside couldn't penetrate the oppressive silence within. A lone nurse at the reception desk looked up from her paperwork as the man approached, her tired eyes meeting his.

"Dr. Mallory's office," the man said, his voice calm but firm.

The nurse blinked, slightly startled by his presence. "Third floor, down the hall on the right," she replied, pointing toward the elevator. "You can't miss it."

He nodded in thanks, turning toward the elevator. His footsteps echoed through the empty halls, a haunting rhythm that matched the patter of the rain against the windows. As he entered the elevator and ascended, the fluorescent lights above flickered, casting the interior in and out of shadow. Each passing second felt stretched, as though time itself was wary of what lay ahead.

When the elevator doors opened with a soft chime, he stepped out into the hallway. The hospital lights seemed to dim further, casting long, foreboding shadows across the tiled floor. He walked to the right, his shoes tapping steadily on the ground, until he found the door with Dr. Richard Mallory's nameplate. The door looked worn, as though it had seen more than its share of troubled souls passing through.

He raised a gloved hand and knocked twice, the sound sharp in the stillness. From inside, a voice beckoned, "Come in."

The man entered, finding Dr. Mallory seated behind a cluttered desk, papers and medical files scattered everywhere. The doctor, a man in his late fifties, looked up from his documents, his expression tense yet relieved. His gray hair was disheveled, and his weary eyes reflected the weight of something dark and unsolved. Despite his professional appearance, the stress of whatever case was before him was evident.

"Hawthorne," Dr. Mallory said, standing up to greet the man. "Thank you for coming on such short notice."

Hawthorne removed his hat, revealing a face hardened by some years of experience but still youthful, with sharp, perceptive eyes that missed nothing. He shook the doctor's hand, his grip firm.

"Dr. Mallory," Hawthorne replied, taking a seat in the chair opposite the desk. "You said it was urgent."

Mallory nodded, settling back into his chair with a heavy sigh. He ran a hand through his hair, visibly wrestling with the right words.

"It is," the doctor confirmed. "I've seen many unusual cases over the years, but this one… This one's different. I can't quite figure it out."

Hawthorne raised an eyebrow, intrigued. "Different how?"

Mallory leaned forward, his voice lowering, as though sharing a dark secret. "It's a boy—a young boy. We found him abandoned in a house, in terrible condition. He doesn't speak much, but there's something off about him. The staff is on edge, and I can't put my finger on what's wrong. Physically, he's fine, but mentally..."

He trailed off, his eyes scanning the scattered papers on his desk. Hawthorne's sharp gaze never wavered, but a cold feeling began to creep up his spine.

"What do you need me for, Richard?" Hawthorne asked, his voice steady. "You've handled strange cases before."

Mallory leaned back, rubbing his temples as if warding off a headache. "This one's beyond medical expertise. I need someone who can see what's not obvious. Someone who can... understand things I might have missed."

Hawthorne frowned slightly, processing the cryptic nature of Mallory's words. "What exactly are we dealing with here?"

Mallory looked at him with an intensity that sent a chill through the room. "I don't know, but whatever it is—it's dangerous."

The storm outside rumbled in response, as if nature itself acknowledged the gravity of the situation.

Hawthorne adjusted his seat, crossing his arms as he leaned back slightly, his eyes locked on Dr. Mallory, who was still gathering his thoughts. The air in the room felt heavy, weighed down by the storm outside and the unsaid horrors that lingered between the two men.

"Start from the beginning," Hawthorne said, his voice calm yet commanding.

Dr. Mallory sighed deeply, pushing some of the files on his desk to the side. "The boy... he's about 12 years old. He was found in a horrifying condition—naked, abandoned, in the middle of an old, run-down place. Local people discovered him, huddled like some lost animal. They thought bringing him here would help, but they couldn't have known... they couldn't have imagined what was inside him."

Hawthorne furrowed his brow. "Inside him?"

Mallory nodded slowly, his eyes distant as if he were reliving the moment. "At first, everything seemed normal. He was quiet, cooperative even. But then things began to happen. Strange things."

"What kind of strange things?" Hawthorne's voice tightened.

"The kind that make you question reality itself. Lights flickering when he walked down hallways. Objects moving when no one was near. It was subtle at first, but as days passed, the atmosphere grew... unsettling. The boy would sit in his bed, murmuring things, talking to something that wasn't there."

Hawthorne leaned forward. "What did he say?"

Mallory's face paled. "He claimed there were voices in his head. He heard things—voices talking to him, instructing him. But it was more than that. He... he knew things, things he shouldn't have been able to know."

Hawthorne's eyes narrowed. "Like what?"

"He could hear conversations happening far away, down the hall, behind closed doors. One night, before the food was served, he described the exact meal being prepared in the kitchen. He even knew the ingredients."

Hawthorne's hand subconsciously tightened around the armrest. "Telepathy?"

Mallory shook his head. "No, it was something more insidious. Then came the night everything spiraled out of control. He changed—became violent. Completely unprovoked, he lashed out at the staff. His strength, Hawthorne... it wasn't natural. We had to call the police just to subdue him. Several staff members were injured, some badly."

"And now?" Hawthorne's voice was barely above a whisper.

"We have him locked up for now. But... I'm afraid it won't hold. There's something about him, something far beyond what I've ever encountered. He's not just a boy. There's something... or someone else within him."

Hawthorne leaned back slightly, taking in Dr. Mallory's words. His expression hardened. "If you want me to help, I'll need to meet the boy."

Mallory hesitated, shifting uncomfortably in his seat. "It's... not safe. You don't understand what we're dealing with here, Hawthorne. He's—"

"Not safe?" Hawthorne interrupted, his tone firm. "How does a doctor treat a patient without ever being near them? I need to see him, Mallory."

Mallory's lips thinned. He was about to argue, but then he exhaled, knowing Hawthorne was right. "Alright," he relented, standing up. "I'll take you to him. But—" he looked at Hawthorne with a warning gaze, "—don't say I didn't warn you."

The storm outside seemed to grow more intense, the wind howling like a warning as they made their way through the dimly lit corridors of the hospital. The overhead lights flickered occasionally, as if the very electricity was afraid of what lay ahead. Mallory walked in front, his long white coat swaying with every step, while Hawthorne followed, his eyes scanning the cold, sterile halls.

Eventually, they reached a heavy metal door with a small window near the top. A security guard stood nearby, his face pale, eyes downcast as though he was doing his best to avoid looking inside.

"This is it," Mallory said, nodding toward the door. "He's been kept restrained for the safety of everyone."

Hawthorne glanced at the window but couldn't make out much more than shadows. He turned back to Mallory. "Stay outside. I'll go in alone."

Mallory's eyes widened slightly. "Alone? You don't know what he's capable of—"

"I'll be fine," Hawthorne cut him off, already reaching for the door handle. "If it gets bad, you can pull me out."

With a reluctant nod, Mallory stepped aside. "Be careful."

The door creaked open, revealing a darkened room lit only by a single overhead light, casting long shadows that seemed to stretch unnaturally across the walls. In the center of the room, there was a boy—no more than twelve years old—tied securely to a chair. His head hung down, as though he was sleeping or in a deep, unnatural slumber.

Hawthorne stepped inside and closed the door behind him. The air in the room felt thick, almost oppressive, as though something unseen weighed heavily on everything. He could hear the faintest hum, like static electricity in the air. He moved closer, his boots echoing softly on the cold tiled floor, and pulled a chair across from the boy, sitting down.

"Hey there," Hawthorne said gently, his voice calm. "I'm Hawthorne. I'm here to help."

The boy didn't respond. His head remained tilted down, his hair falling in dark, damp strands over his face. Hawthorne leaned forward slightly, studying him. The boy's skin was pale, almost ghostly, and there was a thin sheen of sweat covering his forehead. His breathing was shallow, labored.

"Can you hear me?" Hawthorne asked, his voice steady but firm. "I know you're in there."

The boy's head slowly lifted, and when Hawthorne saw his face, he felt an involuntary chill run down his spine. The boy's eyes—once the bright, innocent eyes of a child—were now clouded, almost vacant. There was something terribly wrong behind those eyes, something dark, lurking just beneath the surface.

"I'm here to talk," Hawthorne said, watching the boy carefully. "Do you know where you are?"

The boy stared at him, unmoving, unblinking. Then, slowly, a voice emerged from his lips, soft, hollow. "They're coming."

Hawthorne raised an eyebrow. "Who's coming?"

The boy's head twitched slightly, as though he was fighting some invisible force. His voice grew quieter, but the words were still clear. "They talk to me. They're always talking. In my head."

"Who talks to you?" Hawthorne pressed, leaning closer. "Can you tell me their names?"

The boy's breath quickened, his eyes flicking around the room as though seeing things that weren't there. "They want me... they want to take me."

Hawthorne's brow furrowed. "Who wants to take you? Who are you talking about?"

Suddenly, the boy's body tensed, his wrists pulling violently against the restraints. His eyes rolled back for a moment, and then his head snapped forward again. When he spoke, his voice was deeper, unnatural. "They're already here."

Hawthorne felt a cold sweat forming on the back of his neck. "Who is here?"

The boy's face twisted into a disturbing grin, the kind no child should ever be able to make. His voice dropped to a low, rasping growl. "You'll see."

Before Hawthorne could react, the boy let out a blood-curdling scream, his entire body convulsing in the chair. The lights in the room flickered wildly, and the temperature dropped sharply, filling the air with a biting chill. Hawthorne jumped to his feet, his heart pounding as he instinctively backed away.

The boy thrashed violently, his eyes now completely black, devoid of any humanity. His voice, now layered with the whispers of countless others, echoed in the room. "They're coming for me... they're coming for all of us!"

Hawthorne turned toward the door and shouted, "Mallory, get in here!"

The door swung open as Dr. Mallory rushed in, his face pale with fear. "What the hell is happening?"

Hawthorne kept his eyes on the boy, who was still thrashing and screaming. "We need to sedate him, now!"

Mallory grabbed a syringe from his coat pocket and rushed to the boy's side. With shaking hands, he injected the sedative into the boy's arm. Slowly, the boy's thrashing subsided, and his head slumped forward again, his breathing returning to its shallow rhythm.

Mallory stepped back, wiping the sweat from his brow. "I told you it wasn't safe."

Hawthorne stood there, his mind racing. "This is more than just a disturbed kid. There's something inside him... something I've never seen before."

Mallory's office was dimly lit, with the storm outside casting shadows that danced across the walls. The sound of rain hammering against the window created an eerie backdrop to the unnerving events they had just witnessed. Hawthorne sat in the chair across from Mallory's desk, deep in thought, while the doctor poured them both a drink from a crystal decanter.

"So, what do you make of it?" Mallory asked, sliding a glass toward Hawthorne. His voice was steady, but there was an undeniable tremor beneath the surface. "I've seen strange cases, but nothing like this."

Hawthorne took the glass, swirling the amber liquid as he leaned back. His brow was furrowed, eyes distant, as if trying to piece together a puzzle with too many missing pieces. "It's beyond what we know," he said finally, his voice measured. "But nothing in this world exists without a scientific explanation."

Mallory's eyebrows shot up. "A scientific explanation?" he echoed, almost incredulously. "So, all the... horrific things we've seen—his voice, the way the temperature dropped, the way he spoke as if... as if there were others inside him—you're telling me that all of that has an explanation?"

Hawthorne took a slow sip of his drink, letting the warmth settle in his chest before responding. "There's always an explanation, Mallory. The universe doesn't operate on chaos. It's governed by laws, by rules. The problem is, we just don't understand them yet." He leaned forward, his eyes narrowing. "What we witnessed... it defies our current understanding of science, yes. But that doesn't mean it's magic. It just means our knowledge is incomplete."

Mallory sat back, clearly unnerved. "You're telling me this is all... what? Some phenomenon we haven't discovered yet?"

Hawthorne nodded. "Exactly. Even the supernatural has its roots in reality, whether we understand it or not. Fear of the unknown is what drives us to label things as supernatural. It's human nature to fear what we can't explain. But think about it—lightning was once considered the wrath of gods until we understood electricity. The same goes for this."

Mallory stared at him, trying to wrap his head around the concept. "So, the boy—what he said about spirits coming for him... you think he's possessed?"

Hawthorne's expression darkened. "Possessed... yes, but not in the way folklore would have us believe. He's not just a host for some malevolent entity. There's something more going on here. What he's seeing, what he's hearing... they're real. The spirits, as he calls them, want him—or more specifically, they want his body."

"His body?" Mallory asked, a chill creeping up his spine. "Why?"

"That's what we need to find out," Hawthorne replied, his voice low, almost as if he was speaking to himself. "The boy isn't just some random child. There's something about him, something that makes him... valuable to these entities."

Mallory sat back, rubbing his temples. "And how the hell are we supposed to figure that out?"

Hawthorne's eyes gleamed with a sharp intensity. "Start with the reports. Go through every detail. The medical history, psychological evaluations, anything that might give us a clue. Sometimes the answers lie in the minutiae. What's been dismissed as irrelevant could be the key to all of this."

Mallory hesitated for a moment before nodding. "I'll go over the boy's files tonight. But Hawthorne, you're talking about things that go beyond any medical training I've ever had. If this really is about spirits—"

"Spirits or not, they're bound by some law, some rule. They exist within our universe, even if they come from... somewhere else," Hawthorne said, cutting him off. He leaned forward, his voice growing softer, more intense. "You know, there's an old saying I keep coming back to: 'There's no terror in the bang, only in the anticipation of it.'"

Mallory frowned. "Hitchcock, wasn't it?"

Hawthorne nodded. "Exactly. Fear is driven by the unknown. The things we don't see, the things we don't understand. Once you can define it, explain it, that fear loses its power. That's what we need to do here, Mallory. Define it. Understand it."

Mallory shook his head, still trying to process everything. "But what if we can't? What if some things aren't meant to be understood?"

Hawthorne leaned back again, his eyes narrowing thoughtfully. "You know, a lot of people think science and the supernatural are opposites. But they're not. They're two sides of the same coin. Science is just the process of understanding the supernatural. The more we learn, the more we realize how little we know. It's like staring into an abyss. The deeper you go, the darker it gets, but eventually, you'll find the bottom."

Mallory let out a shaky breath. "That's a hell of a philosophy, Hawthorne."

Hawthorne chuckled darkly. "When you've seen what I've seen, you start to realize the lines between science and horror aren't as clear as people think. The real horror isn't the monsters or the spirits—it's the knowledge that there's something out there we can't yet explain. But that doesn't mean we won't, eventually."

Mallory's face was pale, his fingers drumming nervously on the desk. "So you're saying this boy... these spirits that want him... there's a reason for all of it. Something we haven't uncovered yet."

"Exactly," Hawthorne said. "And I have a feeling the answer is somewhere in his past. Maybe in those reports, maybe in something no one thought to consider. Whatever it is, we need to find it. Because if we don't, the next time those spirits come, they won't stop with just him."

Mallory stood, heading to the cabinet where the boy's files were kept. "I'll start going through everything we have tonight. If there's something we missed, I'll find it."

Hawthorne nodded, standing as well. He drained the last of his drink and placed the glass on Mallory's desk. "Good. But be careful, Mallory. You're dealing with forces that don't follow the rules we understand. Don't underestimate what's in that boy."

Mallory gave a grim nod, glancing toward the door. "I'll tread carefully."

Hawthorne turned to leave, his long coat trailing behind him. As he reached the door, he paused, looking back at Mallory. "One more thing," he said quietly.

"Sometimes the real horror isn't in what we find, but in what we already know... and have been ignoring."

The storm outside raged with relentless fury, battering the windows of the house. Thunder rumbled in the distance, its echoes rolling across the dark sky like the anger of some unseen force. The house creaked under the strain of the wind, as if it, too, was protesting the tension that had taken over inside.

In the dimly lit living room, Hawthorne sat with Sarah, Tom. They all huddled together, the soft glow of a single lamp casting long shadows across their faces. David, now grown and unknowingly at the center of a nightmare, sat in the other room, far from the conversation unfolding in whispers.

Sarah, her voice trembling with a mixture of fear and anticipation, leaned forward. "So... after you met the boy—what happened after that?" Her eyes were wide, the terror of everything they had learned weighing heavily on her.

Hawthorne remained silent, his gaze fixed on some distant point in the room, lost in the memories of that fateful night twenty years ago. The crackle of thunder interrupted the silence, startling them all, as if the storm outside were responding to the weight of the unspoken words hanging in the air.

Tom glanced at Sarah, then back at Hawthorne. "You said the boy was possessed. That the spirits were after him. But... how did it end?"

Hawthorne's jaw tightened, his fingers clasped together as he rested his elbows on his knees. His eyes were dark, filled with the haunting memories of the things he had tried so hard to forget. He took a deep breath, his voice low and measured when he finally spoke.

"After we figured out that the boy—David—wasn't just seeing spirits but communicating with them, things escalated," Hawthorne said, his voice thick with the weight of past horrors. "We knew the spirits weren't just passing through. They were... watching, waiting. They needed something from him, but at the time, we didn't understand what."

Thunder rolled again, and a flicker of lightning illuminated the room for a brief moment. The faces around him seemed even more pale and drawn in the flash of light.

Sarah shuddered, glancing toward the door that led to the room where David sat, oblivious to the discussion about his past. "And Mallory? What did he think?"

Hawthorne leaned back in his chair, rubbing a hand over his face. "Mallory was shaken. The reports, the tests, the medical evaluations—none of it made sense. Every scientific explanation failed us. The boy was being torn apart by forces we couldn't measure or explain. That's when I knew we had crossed a line. This wasn't just about medicine anymore."

Tom shifted in his seat, the tension between them thick. "So what did you do?"

Hawthorne's eyes flicked to the window, watching as rain lashed against the glass in heavy sheets. For a moment, he was silent, as if he wasn't sure he could bring himself to relive the moment again.

"I told Mallory I had to see the boy," he said slowly, his voice deep and steady. "I had to know for myself if this was just... a frightened child. Or something worse."

"And what did you find?" Tom asked, his voice barely above a whisper.

Hawthorne's gaze darkened, his lips pressed into a thin line. He took a long pause, his fingers tapping the arm of the chair. The storm outside seemed to swell, as if the world itself was holding its breath, waiting for his answer.

"Then... I saw it," he said quietly, his voice almost swallowed by the roar of the wind and the sharp crack of thunder that followed

CHAPTER 20
THE THIN VEIL BETWEEN WORLDS

The night outside was calm, with the occasional distant rumble of thunder. Hawthorne and his wife, Evelyn, lay in bed, the soft creaks of their old, spacious house blending with the rain tapping gently on the windows. The house, a Victorian-style residence with its dark wooden beams and heavy curtains, had a warmth to it despite its size. Its corridors were lined with old family portraits, and the wooden floors groaned under the weight of time.

Evelyn stirred from her sleep, hearing something. "Hawthorne..." she whispered, her voice barely cutting through the night. "Someone's at the door."

Hawthorne grumbled, still half-asleep, his body heavy with the weight of exhaustion. The doorbell rang again—this time more insistent.

"Who would be here at this hour?" Evelyn asked, worry creeping into her voice.

Hawthorne sat up, blinking into the darkness. The bell rang once more, more impatient this time, its sound reverberating through the quiet house. "I'll go check," he muttered, slipping out of bed and grabbing the robe draped over a chair.

Evelyn sat up, clutching the covers, her eyes wide with unease. "Be careful," she whispered as he padded out of the bedroom and into the long, dimly lit hallway.

The house felt different at night, the shadows stretching longer, the air colder. Hawthorne's bare feet tapped lightly on the wooden floor, the sound drowned by the rain and the continuous ringing of the bell. His hand reached for the banister as he descended the staircase, each step creaking louder in the silence.

At the front door, he paused, staring at it for a moment. Something felt off.

"Who is it?" he called out, his voice steady but with an edge of caution.

There was a pause, then a voice from the other side. "It's Dr. Mallory, Hawthorne. I need to speak with you."

Hawthorne frowned, glancing at the clock on the wall. It was well past midnight. "Dr. Mallory? At this time?" His thoughts raced, but the urgency in the voice was unmistakable.

Before he could open the door, his phone buzzed in his pocket. The shrill sound startled him. He pulled it out, the name "Dr. Mallory" flashing on the screen.

He froze.

For a moment, everything stopped—the bell, the rain, even the distant thunder seemed to hold its breath.

Confusion gripped him. He glanced at the door, his hand hovering over the handle. Then, slowly, he answered the call, bringing the phone to his ear.

"Hawthorne?" Mallory's voice crackled on the line, sounding weary. "I'm sorry to call so late, but I've gone through the boy's reports. There's something I need you to see. Can you come to the hospital?"

Hawthorne's blood ran cold. He glanced at the door again, the voice outside now eerily silent.

He swallowed hard, stepping back from the door. "Mallory..." he whispered into the phone, trying to keep his voice calm. "You're calling me right now... then... who's at my door?"

There was a long silence on the other end of the line. Then, Mallory spoke, his voice tight with confusion. "Hawthorne, I'm at the hospital. I haven't left. No one should be at your door."

Hawthorne's breath quickened as the air around him seemed to thicken. His eyes darted back to the door, but there was no shadow visible through the small window at the top.

The silence from the other side of the door was deafening now, as if whoever—or whatever—had been there, was no longer. His hand trembled slightly as he held the phone.

Evelyn's voice echoed from upstairs, breaking the tension. "Hawthorne? Is everything alright?"

He took a step back, his mind racing. "I think something's here." His voice dropped to a whisper, the sense of dread crawling up his spine.

Mallory's voice, now laced with concern, came through the phone. "Don't open the door, Hawthorne. I'll send someone. Just... don't."

Hawthorne nodded, his eyes fixed on the door. Something was watching. Something had come for him. He felt it.

Lightning flashed, illuminating the house in sharp, ghostly light. Hawthorne stood frozen, gripping his phone, his pulse quickening. The sense of unease that had quietly lurked around him all night was now full-blown dread.

He stared at the door, waiting for another sound, but there was only silence now. No footsteps, no voices—just the distant rumble of thunder.

Hawthorne's mind raced. The persistent ringing had been so real—loud, demanding, impossible to ignore. He glanced back at the door again, the handle just inches from his hand. The storm outside seemed to press against the walls of the house, as if trying to find a way in.

He could hear Evelyn moving upstairs, her footsteps soft and careful as she descended toward the hallway. Her voice carried from the top of the staircase, concerned but steady. "Is everything alright? Who's at the door?"

"Stay there, Evelyn," Hawthorne called up, his voice shaky. He didn't want her near the door. "I'm handling it."

The doorbell had stopped, but the atmosphere in the house had changed. It felt charged, like the air just before a strike of lightning. He looked at the door, its dark wood polished and untouched, but now it seemed more like a barrier between him and something unknown, rather than an entrance.

His phone buzzed in his hand again—another call coming through. It was Mallory's number again. He blinked in confusion. He was already on the phone with him, wasn't he?

He glanced at the screen. The same name flashed in front of him: "Dr. Mallory."

A chill ran down his spine. **Two calls?**

The voice on the other end of the phone—Mallory's voice—suddenly took on a more urgent tone. "Hawthorne! Who are you speaking to right now? Hang up! Hang up and answer the other call!"

Hawthorne felt his stomach twist. His instincts screamed at him to obey, but his hand hovered over the phone screen, unsure of what was real anymore. He ended the current call with shaking fingers and hesitantly swiped to accept the new one.

"Hawthorne, it's me, Mallory," came the familiar voice, now filled with panic. "I've been trying to reach you for the past five minutes. I don't know who or what you've been talking to, but I'm at the hospital. I haven't been anywhere near your house. You need to listen to me right now: **don't open that door.**"

Hawthorne's throat went dry. His eyes flicked back to the door, and this time, he felt the oppressive weight of something on the other side—something waiting, silent, patient. His fingers curled around the phone tightly, his knuckles turning white.

Hawthorne backed up slowly, his eyes never leaving the door, his heart pounding so loudly he thought it might burst from his chest. His breath came in short, shallow gasps.

From upstairs, Evelyn called again, her voice more concerned now. "Should I come down?"

"No!" he barked, more forcefully than he intended. "Stay upstairs. Lock the door."

Evelyn hesitated, clearly startled by the urgency in his voice. "What's going on?" she asked, her tone wavering.

"I'm not sure..." Hawthorne murmured, his gaze fixed on the door. His mind was spinning with questions, none of which had answers. What could mimic a voice so perfectly? What could be lurking in the dead of night, pretending to be Mallory, ringing the bell incessantly, wanting him to open the door?

He heard the faint creak of the front door hinge—a sound so soft it could've been mistaken for the wind. But Hawthorne knew better. He took another step back, his pulse racing as his eyes widened. The door was moving—just a fraction, but enough to see the edge of it sway.

"Hawthorne," Mallory's voice broke through the growing fear in his mind. "Get away from the door. Don't look at it. **Whatever it is, don't invite it in.**"

The words hit him like a slap to the face. His breath caught in his throat as he turned on his heel and bolted back toward the staircase. The door behind him creaked softly again, but he didn't dare look back.

"Hawthorne!" Evelyn's voice called out again, filled with confusion and growing panic.

He took the stairs two at a time, reaching her at the top. She stared at him, wide-eyed and pale. "What's going on? Who's at the door?"

He couldn't bring himself to explain. Instead, he wrapped his arms around her, pulling her close. "It's nothing," he whispered into her hair, lying more to himself than to her. "Nothing at all."

But deep down, he knew—something had come to their door that night, and it had left without entering. This time.

For now.

The morning dawned with a heavy mist clinging to the trees and rooftops, the storm from the night before still lingering in the air. Hawthorne stood by the front door, buttoning his long coat, his eyes scanning the quiet street beyond. His wife, standing in her robe by the staircase, watched him with concern.

"Are you sure you're okay to go?" she asked, her voice soft but edged with worry. "After what happened last night... maybe you should take a break."

Hawthorne forced a smile, though the tension of the night still hung over him like a dark cloud. "I need to go, Evelyn. The reports... I need to check."

She crossed her arms, looking unconvinced. "And what about that thing last night?

"I don't know yet," Hawthorne admitted, his tone somber. "But I'll find out. Just... whatever you do, don't open the door for anyone. Not even if it's me. Call me first."

Evelyn's eyes widened slightly, and she nodded, clearly unsettled by his insistence. "You're scaring me, you know that?"

Hawthorne stepped closer, resting his hands on her shoulders. "I'll be back by noon, I promise. Just stay inside. Keep the door locked. I'll call you if anything comes up."

With that, he gave her a brief kiss on the forehead, opened the door, and stepped out into the damp morning air. The rain had stopped, but the world still felt soaked and heavy. The drive to St. Augustine Hospital was quiet, the roads slick and gleaming under the pale morning light. The hospital loomed ahead, its old stone structure looking even more imposing in the mist

Hawthorne arrived at St. Augustine Hospital. The building loomed before him, its sterile façade barely hiding the horrors he knew lay within. Inside, the atmosphere was tense, the staff whispering in corners as though the hospital itself were holding its breath.

Dr. Mallory was already waiting, pacing in his office when Hawthorne entered.

"Hawthorne, I need to know what happened last night," he said as they walked inside and sat down.

Hawthorne took a moment, leaning back in his chair. "Whatever it is... it's playing with us," he said, voice low and controlled. "There was someone at my door last night claiming to be you, but when I answered, it wasn't. The real you was calling me on the phone at the same time. Something's not right."

Mallory's face darkened, his brows furrowed. "It's escalating. We need to figure this out before it's too late."

Hawthorne's gaze turned sharper. "I'm starting to think it's something we've never faced before. This isn't just a boy. It's far more dangerous than that."

Mallory nodded gravely. "The boy isn't just another violent case. There's something more to this, something deeper."

Hawthorne glanced at Mallory, his curiosity piqued. "Speaking of which, what did you find in those reports, Mallory? You said you found something last night."

Mallory stood up and walked over to his desk, pulling out a thick file with the boy's records. He laid it out on the table before them, flipping through pages of medical tests and observations. His voice lowered as he began, "I've been going through these reports again, looking for something—anything—that could explain what's happening."

He paused, his fingers tracing a line of data on the page. "There's an anomaly, something to do with the boy's brain. It's not like anything I've seen before..."

The room fell into silence as Mallory prepared to explain the findings. Hawthorne leaned in closer, sensing the gravity of what was coming next.

Mallory's fingers hovered over a particular page of the report, his brow furrowing. The quiet hum of the hospital outside the office seemed to fade as the weight of his discovery settled in.

"I ran some additional scans on the boy's brain after the last incident," Mallory began. "At first, I thought it was trauma or some form of neurological disorder, but..."

"But what?" Hawthorne urged, leaning forward in his chair, his eyes sharp with curiosity.

Mallory exhaled slowly. "There's something in his pineal gland—an irregularity. It's almost as if it's hyperactive, firing signals that... shouldn't exist. It's unusually large for a child his age. I can't figure out how this is connected to his violent behavior, though."

Hawthorne's face darkened with understanding. He looked straight at Mallory. "I know exactly what this is."

Mallory's eyebrows lifted. "You do?"

"The pineal gland," Hawthorne began, choosing his words carefully, "isn't just a small endocrine gland. In some ancient cultures, it's called the 'third eye.' You ever heard of it?"

Mallory blinked, a hint of skepticism in his eyes. "I've heard the term in spiritual circles, but I've never taken it seriously.

Hawthorne leaned forward, his voice low and deliberate. "Well, you should. The pineal gland has been associated with spiritual awareness for thousands of years. It's not just a biological remnant — some believe it's our gateway to dimensions we can't normally perceive. In cases like this boy's, it can be more than just theory. It can be deadly."

Mallory stared at him, brow furrowed. "Dimensions? What are you talking about?"

Hawthorne folded his hands on the desk. "The boy's pineal gland was somehow activated. You said it's enlarged? That's not just some anomaly. It's been stimulated, possibly by trauma or some external force, opening his so-called 'third eye.'"

Mallory shook his head, still trying to grasp the idea. "Are you saying this gland is what's causing his violent episodes?"

"It's more than that," Hawthorne said, lowering his voice, as if the walls themselves might listen. "That gland makes him a conduit. When the third eye is open, it's said you can see and communicate with entities from other planes — spirits, demons, whatever you want to call them. The boy, consciously or not, is communicating with them. He's been exposed."

Mallory's expression hardened. "That's impossible. How would a gland — a piece of anatomy — make someone do that?"

"It's not impossible. There have been documented cases, though most of them are buried in paranormal research. Look up the history of yogis, monks, even some modern-day psychics. The common link? Pineal gland activation. It's a sort of spiritual antenna, tuning in to realms that we are usually blind to. When the boy speaks of 'them coming for him,' he's not hallucinating, Mallory. They're real. There are documented cases, even in modern psychology, where people who claim to have their 'third eye' activated experience unusual phenomena—visions, interactions with entities that others can't perceive.

There was a case in India, about a man who suddenly started seeing apparitions after an accident. He described vivid encounters with spirits, and doctors discovered his pineal gland was damaged, forcing it to be hyperactive."

Mallory frowned, his skepticism still visible. "But we're talking about a 12-year-old boy. How could something like this happen to him?"

Hawthorne continued, "The boy's pineal gland was likely triggered by some kind of trauma—maybe physical, maybe psychological. If we think about the gland's location, it's deep in the brain, not easily affected unless something extreme happens. This kid… maybe he experienced something, or someone interfered with him, and that activated his gland. Now, he's not just seeing things, he's interacting with them. And these entities he's talking to—they've taken notice of him."

Mallory's eyes widened, but he still had questions. "So you're saying that what he's experiencing is real, in a way?"

Hawthorne nodded. "It's real enough to him, and to those spirits. They know he's vulnerable. It's like he's a beacon to them, a lighthouse in a storm, drawing them in. They want him, Mallory—they want his body."

Mallory's voice lowered, as if afraid someone might overhear them. "You really believe this?"

Hawthorne nodded gravely. "I do. There was another case I read about, back in the 1940s. A child in England, same age as this boy, started having visions after a head injury. They thought it was hallucinations at first, but the child became increasingly violent. His pineal gland had become overactive after the trauma, and it reached a point where he couldn't control his visions. The spirits he saw became stronger, more dangerous. They eventually drove him to hurt himself and others. The doctors didn't understand it at the time, but now… now I'm seeing the same thing in this boy."

Mallory leaned forward, a mix of fear and intrigue in his eyes. "So, what do we do? How do we stop this?"

Hawthorne's face darkened. "We have to sever his connection with those entities. We need to find a way to close his third eye, stop the spirits from using him as a conduit. But that's not going to be easy, especially if they're already inside him."

Mallory shook his head, his voice barely a whisper. "How can we do that? This isn't something we're trained for."

Hawthorne looked Mallory dead in the eyes. "It's not something anyone's trained for. But we don't have a choice. If we don't stop this now, the spirits won't stop with him. They'll spread, latch onto others, and this boy… he'll become their vessel."

A thick silence filled the room as Mallory absorbed the gravity of Hawthorne's words.

Finally, Mallory exhaled, rubbing his temples. "And here I thought I was just treating a traumatized kid."

Hawthorne's expression hardened. "This is beyond trauma. This is something ancient, something that's been waiting for an opportunity. And now, it's found one."

Mallory stopped pacing and faced Hawthorne, the gravity of the situation hitting him. "So what do we do?"

"We need to sever that connection, close the door. But that's going to take time, and we need to be careful. If the entities feel threatened, they may retaliate."

Mallory looked at the reports again, as if seeking answers in the inked words on paper. "And if we don't?"

Hawthorne's face was stony. "If we don't, they'll claim him. And trust me, when that happens, we won't just be dealing with a boy anymore. We'll be dealing with something far worse."

CHAPTER 21
A SHROUDED PACT

The silence of Dr. Mallory's office was almost suffocating, broken only by the distant rumble of thunder outside. Hawthorne stood by the window, peering out at the storm-riddled sky, his mind racing with what he knew had to be done—and the risks.

Mallory cleared his throat, shifting in his chair. "So…how are we going to do?" He ran a hand over his face, clearly exhausted and stricken with worry. "You've seen what that boy is capable of. How do we even… approach this?"

Hawthorne turned slowly, his eyes intense. "I need to deactivate his third eye."

Mallory looked at him, his face a mix of confusion and disbelief. "Deactivate…? I understand it's tied to something greater, but how can you just *turn off* something in his brain? Is that even possible?"

Hawthorne exhaled sharply. "This isn't typical science. This is where the realms of the spiritual and physical overlap—right here, in that boy. And his third eye, his pineal gland, is acting as a conduit, drawing these entities to him. But it's leaving him *vulnerable*… defenseless, really."

Mallory shook his head, clearly rattled. "But…there must be countless spirits flocking to him if that's true. You saw what he's capable of—those violent fits, the way he spoke… it was as if something else was speaking *through* him. How can we fight something like that?"

Hawthorne folded his arms, his jaw tight. "That's what I'm saying. It won't be simple. We don't know exactly how many entities are drawn to him, and the worst part…" He paused, his eyes narrowing as he considered his words. "The worst part is, I think there's *something else*. Something that's different from the others."

Mallory frowned. "Different how?"

Hawthorne hesitated, glancing back toward the closed door. "The one who… came to my house," he said quietly, almost as if saying it too loudly would invite it back. "It was powerful, intelligent. It wasn't just any spirit. I believe it's one that's been with the boy since the beginning, lying in wait. Possibly something far stronger than any of the others…something that's been guiding the rest."

Mallory's hand tightened around his pen. "So you're telling me we're dealing with a *leader* spirit? Something that's orchestrating this chaos?"

Hawthorne nodded slowly. "Exactly. And if we're going to calm the boy, to cut him off from them, we need to be ready to confront whatever this… *thing* is. Because if I'm right, it won't go easily."

Mallory took a deep breath, his face visibly pale. "Are we even…prepared for that?"

Hawthorne met his gaze firmly, his voice low and resolute. "We have no other choice, Doctor. If we don't act, that boy's mind—and possibly his life—are as good as lost. And the more these entities have him, the more they'll bleed over into our world. We either close his third eye or risk letting them *all* in."

Thunder rumbled again, almost on cue, as the weight of their decision settled heavily between them.

Hawthorne could see the terror in Mallory's eyes, his hesitation weighing heavily in the room. Mallory finally spoke, his voice a mere whisper. "If we go through with this… if we actually try to sever this connection…what do you think will happen to the boy?"

Hawthorne's face softened, and for a brief moment, his usual unshakable demeanor slipped. "I don't know for sure. But if we don't do this, we're leaving him at the mercy of these entities. This leader spirit won't stop until it's taken full control of him. The boy's only chance at peace is if we can sever that link."

Mallory looked down, his hands clenched into fists. "And how do you even deactivate something as mysterious as the third eye?"

Hawthorne began pacing slowly, as though every step helped him piece together a plan. "I'll have to put the boy in a deeply meditative state, first of all. That will calm him, make his mind still. And then… I'll guide him through a process of visualizing the closing of his third eye. It's a technique I've only read about, but if we can make him visualize the closing, it could break the connection."

Mallory shook his head. "So, you're relying on meditation to cut off something that's pulling in spirits like moths to a flame? Hawthorne…this isn't just risky—it sounds impossible."

"Everything impossible is just something we haven't figured out yet," Hawthorne replied. "You're right, it's dangerous. But I think there's more to that boy's mind than we realize. The way he spoke last night, the sheer will he showed—it's as though he's fighting to keep himself."

Mallory shifted uneasily. "But the entities won't just sit back and let this happen, will they?"

Hawthorne's expression darkened. "No. Maybe They'll resist. That's why I'm afraid we'll need…additional measures to protect him." He paused, lowering his voice to a cautious murmur. "I've heard of certain rituals, techniques that can create a temporary shield around the mind—a sort of psychic barrier, just enough to buy us time."

Mallory exhaled sharply, pushing back from his desk. "Rituals and psychic barriers… you're talking about something that goes beyond even the fringes of science. And you're asking me to believe that this will work against something we barely understand?"

Hawthorne fixed him with a steady gaze. "Dr. Mallory, if we approach this with the limits of science alone, we'll lose. We're dealing with forces that existed long before science could explain them, and I'm willing to try anything if it means saving that boy."

Mallory hesitated, glancing down at the boy's medical file with a mixture of fear and resolve. Finally, he looked up. "Fine. I'll follow your lead. But just know…if this backfires, if something goes wrong—"

Hawthorne interrupted, his voice grim but unwavering. "Then we'll take responsibility for it. But I won't let that boy suffer because we were too afraid to try."

A sudden knock on the door interrupted them, and both men startled slightly. Mallory frowned and opened the door cautiously. A nurse, visibly pale and shaken, stood outside.

"Dr. Mallory… something's wrong. The boy… he's…"

Hawthorne's jaw clenched, and he stepped forward. "What happened? Is he alright?"

The nurse swallowed hard, her voice trembling. "He's…laughing. Just laughing… but his voice, it's…not his own."

Mallory turned to Hawthorne, dread etched on his face. "It's already begun. Whatever entity is with him—it knows we're coming."

The air grew thick and oppressive, pressing down on Hawthorne and Mallory as they braced themselves against the malevolent force building within the boy. A sudden gust swept through the room, carrying a low, mocking laughter that bounced off the walls, seeming to come from every corner.

The boy's head lifted, his face twisted in a sinister grin that was unnervingly adult, something far removed from any child. His eyes blazed with unnatural light, and when he spoke, his voice had a twisted, taunting edge. "You think you're heroes, don't you? A doctor and a ghost hunter… coming to the rescue." The entity let out a harsh, mocking laugh. "Pathetic."

Hawthorne held his ground, his fists clenched. "Mock us all you want. We're not here to entertain you. We're here to end this."

The boy's face contorted with glee, the entity seeming to feed off Hawthorne's defiance. "End this?" it sneered. "You don't understand the first thing about what I am. I'm older than you can imagine. Stronger than you'll ever be." The boy's body surged forward, the restraints groaning under the strain.

"Do you need help, Hawthorne? Afraid to go it alone?"

As the words echoed in the room, the lights flickered violently, throwing long, shifting shadows across the walls. Each flicker seemed to distort the boy's features, warping him into something monstrous, his mouth stretched into an unnatural smile, his eyes hollow and black. Then, with terrifying suddenness, the boy's head whipped towards Mallory, his gaze boring into the doctor with an intensity that made Mallory recoil.

"Look at you," the entity hissed, its voice like nails scraping over glass. "You're nothing but a fucking coward, hiding behind your science. But there's no medicine for what I am." The boy's eyes flared. "And yet, you still dare to try…"

Without warning, the bed shook violently, rattling on its frame, and the restraints holding the boy began to strain and buckle as he laughed louder, the room filling with his sinister glee. Hawthorne and Mallory glanced at each other, realizing they had to act fast.

"Hold him down!" Hawthorne yelled, moving swiftly to the other side of the bed, pressing his hands down on the boy's shoulders. But the strength behind the entity's thrashing was otherworldly. The boy's body twisted and writhed, his limbs convulsing as he screamed—a blood-curdling wail that seemed to carry the rage of countless voices.

"Stop fighting it!" the entity roared, his voice laced with venom. "You're out of your league, Hawthorne!"

With a grim expression, Hawthorne leaned in, his voice unwavering. "You think so? Then why don't you face me yourself? Why keep hiding in a child's skin?"

The boy's body fell eerily still, the unnatural light in his eyes dimming as the entity's expression changed, shifting from arrogance to something that looked dangerously close to fear. "You... you don't know what you're inviting. Once I'm free... you're next."

Hawthorne's grip tightened; his voice steady. "Then come out and face me. Because right now, you're nothing but a shadow behind the eyes of an innocent boy."

The entity let out an enraged scream, the boy's body buckling in Hawthorne's grip, straining as if he might tear himself apart. A cold wind surged through the room, extinguishing every light, plunging them into darkness. In the pitch black, there were flashes of images—a gaunt, twisted face with hollow eyes, the entity's true form, flickering in and out of sight, watching them with a loathsome grin.

Suddenly, the lights burst back on, and the boy's face returned to normal for just a moment. He blinked, his eyes wide and terrified, and in a trembling voice, he whispered, "Please... help me."

Hawthorne held his gaze, his tone gentle but resolute. "I won't let it take you."

Just then, the boy's face twisted back into a sneer, the entity forcing itself forward again. "You'll regret this, Bitch!" it spat, its voice filled with venom. But Hawthorne kept his calm, placing his hand over the boy's forehead, focusing every ounce of his energy on closing off the boy's connection to the spirit world.

"You can't hold me back!" the entity shrieked, its voice cracking as Hawthorne's energy bore down on it. But Hawthorne's resolve was unbreakable, his focus unwavering. Bit by bit, he could feel the entity's grip weakening, its hold on the boy slipping.

Mallory, watching in tense silence, finally moved to help. He placed a calming hand on the boy's shoulder, speaking softly. "It's over. You're safe, son. Just hold on."

The entity let out one last scream, a wretched, furious sound that reverberated through the walls, shaking the room. And then, just as quickly as it had started, the thrashing stopped. The boy slumped forward, breathing heavily, his body limp and still.

Hawthorne released his grip, taking a step back and breathing a sigh of relief. The boy's eyes slowly fluttered open, filled with confusion but free from the malicious glint that had been there before.

Mallory reached out, checking the boy's pulse. "It's… it's back to normal," he whispered, his voice filled with awe.

The boy looked up, his voice soft and weak. "Is it… gone?"

Hawthorne nodded, exhaustion settling into his features. "For now. But we'll be keeping a close watch on you."

The boy gave a small, trembling nod, his face pale but grateful.

Some days later, Hawthorne received a call from Dr. Mallory. He leaned back in his chair, raising an eyebrow as he heard Mallory's voice, tinged with cautious optimism.

"Hawthorne," Mallory said, his tone almost relieved. "It's been… quiet. Almost too quiet."

Hawthorne straightened up. "What do you mean by 'quiet'?"

Mallory took a deep breath. "Ever since that night, the boy has shown no sign of the entity's influence. He's calm, lucid… almost as if nothing ever happened. No strange outbursts, no visions, no threats. The staff are even letting their guard down."

Hawthorne frowned, his mind racing. "That doesn't sound right. Spirits… they don't just let go, Mallory. Once they find a vulnerable host, they latch on, like leeches. Especially one as strong as that entity."

There was a brief silence on the other end of the line, and then Mallory spoke up again, his voice lower this time. "I knew you'd say that. But we've run every test we could think of—psychological evaluations, physical scans. There's not even a residual trace of trauma left in him. It's as if the boy's mind and body have been scrubbed clean."

Hawthorne's unease grew. "And the boy? Has he said anything?"

"No… he seems happy, almost carefree. He barely remembers any of the incidents." Mallory paused, as if hesitant to voice his next thought. "Hawthorne… is it possible the entity has left for good?"

Hawthorne's voice hardened. "It's possible, but it's not likely. Spirits, especially malevolent ones, don't just vanish without a trace. They're drawn to certain energies. And that boy… he's a beacon to them. No, Mallory, something doesn't feel right. This entity could still be lurking—waiting."

Mallory's voice dropped to a murmur, "But why would it leave so suddenly? After that struggle… after how it resisted, it doesn't make sense."

"That's exactly what worries me," Hawthorne replied, his tone darkening. "This entity wasn't just an ordinary spirit. There was a sense of… intelligence behind its actions. Like it had a plan."

Mallory was silent for a few moments, and when he spoke, his voice was tight. "Are you saying this thing might be waiting? Biding its time?"

"It could be," Hawthorne admitted reluctantly. "It's possible that it withdrew to wait for the right moment to strike again. Or, worse, it may have found another host."

There was a pause as Mallory absorbed Hawthorne's words. "But why leave the boy so abruptly if it wanted him so badly?"

Hawthorne hesitated, considering his answer. "Because that boy's third eye was open. Vulnerable as he was, he became aware of the entity, and that changed the balance. When the entity felt its grip slipping, it may have retreated in search of an easier target."

"Another target… are you suggesting it could come back? Through another person?" Mallory's voice had a newfound edge of urgency.

"Exactly," Hawthorne replied, his voice heavy with concern. "Entities like that… they're opportunists. If they can't fully control one host, they look for someone else close by. Someone susceptible."

There was silence on the other end of the line, and then Mallory exhaled slowly. "But there haven't been any other signs. The staff, myself, we're all fine. Nothing strange has happened since that night."

"For now," Hawthorne said, a warning in his tone. "But if it's lying dormant, it could resurface at any time. And when it does, it'll be stronger, more focused."

Mallory swallowed, the weight of Hawthorne's words settling over him. "So… what should we do?"

Hawthorne's voice softened. "Keep a close eye on the boy and everyone who's been in contact with him. Watch for any changes—subtle or otherwise. And, Mallory… if anything happens, call me immediately. We might not have a second chance to face this thing."

Mallory nodded, though Hawthorne couldn't see it. "Understood."

As they ended the call, a heavy sense of dread settled over Hawthorne. Hawthorne sat by the window, the faint rumble of thunder echoing through the distance. Mallory's news lingered in his mind, gnawing at him, each word underscoring the dread he felt in his gut. Quiet... almost too quiet. The entity's sudden retreat felt too convenient, as if it were merely giving them a false sense of security. He drummed his fingers on the arm of his chair, thinking back to the boy, the pale, terrified eyes that had stared into the unknown.

Then a thought struck him, simple but powerful—a solution that could sever the link permanently.

Hawthorne muttered to himself, "If he can't remember... if that part of his mind is closed, locked away for good…"

The phone rang again, startling him out of his thoughts. It was Mallory, calling back.

"Hawthorne," Mallory's voice came through, breathless. "You sound... intense. Have you thought of something?"

"Yes," Hawthorne replied, resolute. "This is the perfect time. We need to close that boy's third eye completely and remove every trace of memory associated with it."

There was a pause, as if Mallory were digesting the implications of such an action. "Close the third eye… and erase his memory?" he repeated, as though testing the weight of those words.

"Exactly," Hawthorne replied, his voice firm. "The boy's awareness of the entity—of any spirits at all—is like an open door, inviting them in. We've closed it temporarily, but as long as that door is even slightly ajar, they'll sense him, find him. If we want to break the connection, it has to be sealed shut."

"But… that's not an easy procedure," Mallory warned. "You're talking about tampering with both his consciousness and his memory. There's no guarantee we can do it safely."

Hawthorne took a steadying breath. "I understand the risks. But consider the alternative: that entity—or any other spirit—will continue to hunt him down. Without this, he'll never be free."

Mallory was silent for a moment, and then he spoke with a quiet intensity. "What do you propose? How do we even begin?"

"We'll need to induce a deep, almost hypnotic state," Hawthorne replied, his voice unwavering. "Using techniques that combine both spiritual barriers and neurological sedation. We'll isolate the part of his consciousness linked to the third eye, the one that's been awakened by the entity's influence. Then we'll repress it—bury it so deep that it'll be inaccessible, as though it never existed."

"...And the memories?"

"They'll have to be erased," Hawthorne continued. "The trauma, the visions, everything associated with the entity. If the memories are gone, there's nothing left for the spirits to hold onto. No awareness, no vulnerability."

Mallory let out a slow breath, a mixture of awe and anxiety. "It's... a drastic solution, Hawthorne. But... I agree. This may be our only chance to give him peace."

"Do you think he'll... remember anything? Ever?" Mallory asked, a note of concern creeping into his voice.

"No," Hawthorne replied, his voice softened. "With this, we'll be rewriting his future. He'll grow up without these shadows, without this fear. He'll be safe."

For the first time that evening, Hawthorne allowed himself a glimmer of hope. As he ended the call, he felt a fierce determination settle within him. Tomorrow, they would proceed with the ritual. And if it succeeded, the boy would finally be free from the dark forces that had haunted him—free to live a life without the ever-present shadow of spirits.

The night air was thick with silence as Hawthorne and Mallory prepared for the ritual. The room was dimly lit, a single candle flickering beside the boy's bed, casting trembling shadows on the walls. The boy lay still, his small body fragile and pale under the faint light, his breathing shallow but steady. Hawthorne knelt beside him, feeling the enormity of what they were about to do.

Mallory looked over at Hawthorne, his voice barely above a whisper. "Are you sure about this?"

Hawthorne nodded, his gaze fixed on the boy. "There's no other way."

Taking a deep breath, Hawthorne began to murmur softly, chanting words both ancient and powerful, his voice low and steady as he wove the spell. The boy's eyelids fluttered as he fell deeper into the hypnotic trance, his breathing slowing further. Hawthorne's voice held a rhythm, a cadence that seemed to reach into the boy's subconscious, pulling him into a place between dreams and reality.

Hawthorne placed his hand gently on the boy's forehead, his touch light but firm, as if grounding him to the moment. "You're safe," he whispered. "No one can hurt you here."

The boy's face softened, his features relaxing as Hawthorne continued, his words weaving a shield around him, layer by layer, like a cocoon.

"Imagine a door," Hawthorne said softly, his voice like a gentle lullaby. "A heavy door, solid and safe. Behind it lies everything you fear—all the shadows, all the whispers. But you're here, on this side. You're free from them."

The boy's fingers twitched slightly, his brow furrowing as if he sensed the weight of what Hawthorne was asking him to leave behind.

"You don't need to hold onto these things anymore," Hawthorne continued, his voice unwavering. "They are no longer yours to carry."

Mallory watched from the other side of the room, his face pale, his hands clenched tightly as he witnessed the delicate work unfolding before him.

With each phrase, Hawthorne drew the boy further away from the memories, gently closing the doors of his mind, one by one. He guided the boy through the fragments of terror, nudging them into shadows, binding each piece until it faded. As he spoke, he felt the faint echo of the boy's memories slipping away—the visions, the fear, the cold touch of spirits, dissolving into nothingness.

"There is a light," Hawthorne said, his tone gentle and protective. "A bright, warm light waiting for you on this side. It will guide you."

The boy's lips moved, barely a whisper. "The light…"

"Yes," Hawthorne murmured, his heart aching with a mixture of sorrow and hope. "Follow it. Let it wash over you. You'll be safe there."

The boy seemed to relax completely, his body almost sinking into the bed as he entered a place of calm, far from the shadows that had once tormented him. Hawthorne knew that this was his last chance to seal the door for good.

He lowered his voice, his words like a final benediction. "This place you're leaving behind—it's fading now, dissolving like mist in the morning sun. You will wake, and you will remember only peace, only light. The darkness will be gone. Forever."

With a deep breath, he pressed his fingers gently against the boy's temple, sealing the ritual with the weight of his intention. The boy exhaled, a slow, steady release, as if letting go of a burden he'd carried for far too long.

Mallory, overcome, placed a hand over his mouth, his eyes glistening. He could feel the shift in the room, a quietness, a stillness that hadn't been there before.

Hawthorne removed his hand, his own face drawn, exhausted yet resolute. He whispered one final word into the stillness, a blessing that only he and the boy would ever know.

"Rest."

The candle flickered one last time, then extinguished itself, leaving the room in darkness.

In that silence, Hawthorne and Mallory understood that they had not only closed the boy's third eye but had given him the chance at a life untouched by shadows—a life where he could walk freely in the light.

Mallory rubbed his temples, exhaustion visible in his eyes. "So, now what happens to him?" he asked, his voice a mix of relief and worry. "We've subdued the threat, but… what do we do with him? He's just a child, with his entire memory wiped clean."

Hawthorne's gaze grew intense. "This boy—he'll be given a new start. A life without the memories, without the burdens of what he's experienced. In his mind, he's a blank slate now." He paused, as if weighing every word. "That's why he has to be sent somewhere... safe. An orphanage will take him in, far from all of this. But it must be done carefully. No one must ever know what he was involved in."

Mallory nodded slowly, though his expression was far from calm. "I agree. But there's one concern," he continued. "Officer Harris... he knows about the boy. And he's seen enough to suspect more."

A flicker of frustration passed across Hawthorne's face. "Then he'll need to understand the stakes here. Call him—I'll explain this personally."

Mallory hesitated. "Do you really think he'll be on board? Harris is a man of principles; he's bound to have questions."

Hawthorne's jaw tightened. "Then I'll give him answers that make sense without revealing too much. We can't risk any leaks or outside investigations. This case has to disappear, along with the boy's memories. It's for everyone's sake—especially his."

After a tense pause, Mallory sighed and picked up the phone, dialing Harris's number. "I just hope he listens."

The next morning, Officer Harris arrived at St. Augustine Hospital, his brows furrowed with a look of quiet determination. Dr. Mallory greeted him at the entrance and led him through the hushed corridors to meet Hawthorne in his office.

Hawthorne rose as Harris entered, extending a firm hand. "Thank you for coming, Officer Harris."

Harris nodded, his gaze direct. "Dr. Mallory's message sounded serious. So tell me—what exactly are we dealing with here?"

Hawthorne took a measured breath, glancing briefly at Mallory before turning back to Harris. "The boy's condition was rooted in deep trauma. It manifested in a way that, admittedly, went beyond anything we could immediately rationalize. But with treatment, he's now in a stable, peaceful state."

Harris crossed his arms, his eyes narrowing. "I don't buy it just yet. That boy… whatever he went through—it wasn't something you just 'treat.' He wasn't just troubled. He was wild, dangerous."

Hawthorne nodded, prepared for the pushback. "I understand. Officer, the mind can unravel in ways that defy logic, especially when affected by trauma. The behavior we saw could look as if something else were at play, but I believe that now, he's at peace because the mind—when helped correctly—can heal."

"'Believe,'" Harris echoed, clearly unconvinced. "I need more than beliefs. I want to see for myself."

Mallory led them down the silent corridors to the boy's room. When they arrived, they found the boy sitting quietly, an open book on his lap, his eyes drifting across the pages with an innocent curiosity.

Harris cleared his throat and took a slow step forward. "Good morning," he said, watching the boy carefully. "Do you remember me?"

The boy looked up with a polite but puzzled expression. "No, sir," he replied. "Are you a doctor?"

Harris shook his head. "No, just a friend. Do you remember anything unusual… anything that happened here over the past few days?"

The boy's gaze shifted to the window, his eyes narrowing as he seemed to search his memory. Then he shook his head slowly. "No… I don't think so. It's been pretty quiet here."

Harris's jaw tightened as he observed the boy, glancing over at Hawthorne. "Pretty quiet…? And you feel… safe here?" he pressed.

The boy nodded. "Yes, sir. Everyone's been very nice." He looked up at Mallory with a soft smile. "Dr. Mallory especially."

Harris folded his arms, still visibly skeptical. He glanced sharply at Hawthorne. "Something about this still feels… too easy. You can't erase what he went through, no matter what treatment you used."

Hawthorne met his gaze steadily. "You're right, Officer. You can't erase trauma completely. But this boy's memory was altered in a way that lets him leave the past behind. His mind isn't plagued by memories he can't handle, and he's free from whatever… darkness held him."

Harris continued scrutinizing the boy, but then, a small detail caught his attention: the boy's calm, even breathing. His eyes were clear, without a trace of the wildness that had unnerved them all before. Harris's shoulders relaxed slightly, as if he were starting to accept the transformation, though still hesitant.

Finally, Harris turned back to Hawthorne. "Alright… maybe you did pull off a miracle here. I'll trust you. But I'll be keeping an eye on this, and if anything… out of the ordinary starts up again, I'm calling for backup."

Hawthorne nodded with a steady resolve. "Understood, Officer. But we believe the best place for him now is somewhere safe—somewhere he can truly start over. He has no family, no ties. An orphanage might be his best chance at a real future."

Harris sighed, looking at the boy, then back at the two men. "An orphanage, huh? So you think he'll be safe there?"

Mallory spoke up. "It's the best option, Officer. With the right guidance and a stable home, he can live a normal life."

Harris looked at the boy, then finally nodded. "Alright. But this doesn't sit well with me, you know. I don't want any more surprises. I'll do my part to keep this… quiet. For his sake."

Hawthorne extended his hand to Harris. "Thank you, Officer. The boy deserves peace, and sometimes, peace comes with silence."

Harris shook his hand, his expression softening. "You know, Hawthorne, I think I might just be curious enough to want to see what other strange cases you've handled."

Hawthorne chuckled, a rare smile crossing his usually serious face. "Well, I assure you, Officer, this isn't the last mystery I'll be facing. Something tells me our paths will cross again."

Harris laughed lightly. "I'll hold you to that. Keep me in the loop when you come across the next one."

With that, they exchanged a nod, a mutual understanding bridging the gap between their roles.

CHAPTER 22
TIPTOE THROUGH THE TULIPS

The room fell into a tense silence as the gravity of Hawthorne's revelation sank in. Shadows clung to the corners, distorted by the weak, flickering light filtering through the window blinds. Thunder rolled in the distance, but the soft patter of rain outside seemed inconsequential in the wake of what had just been disclosed.

Sarah, clutching her arms as though she could fend off the chill of the realization, leaned forward. "So... all of this, everything that's happened—it started that day when David fell?"

Hawthorne nodded grimly, his face etched with a seriousness that sent a shiver through the room. "Yes. The head injury likely disrupted whatever suppression Mallory and I managed to instill years ago. The third eye—the conduit that connects David to... them—was forced open again. Even though he wouldn't remember any of it consciously, his subconscious does. Each time he rested, his mind became vulnerable, reaching out to that other plane, unknowingly pulling them closer."

Clair's voice was barely a whisper, but the tremor was clear. "You mean... every time he closed his eyes, he's been contacting them? That they've... they've been with him all this time?"

Hawthorne looked into Clair's fearful eyes, his voice low and steady. "Yes, Clair. Every time he drifted into sleep, he unwittingly opened a door. And that entity, the one I encountered twenty years ago, never left. It waited. It fed off his vulnerability and has been lurking in the background, growing stronger with David's age and spirit."

Tom ran a hand through his hair, shaking his head in disbelief. "But why now? Why after all these years?"

"Because," Hawthorne said, his gaze hardening, "David isn't a child anymore. His soul, his energy, has matured. He's now at the peak of his life force—a far more tempting prize than he was back then. This entity wants him, and it's not just for revenge or cruelty."

Sarah, her voice a barely contained murmur, added, "It's for possession, isn't it?"

Hawthorne nodded. "Precisely. This entity has no corporeal form. It exists in a void between our world and theirs, unable to fully live or fully die. It wants to experience this world, to taste life in flesh. But it needs a powerful vessel. And in David, it's found just that. His open third eye, combined with his age and strength—it's everything it needs to bridge the gap."

Sarah's eyes went wide. "And you're saying there are others? Other spirits—hundreds of them, you mentioned?"

Hawthorne took a deep breath. "More than that, I suspect. You see, when the third eye is open, it's like a beacon in the spirit world. Most entities lack the power to do much more than observe, but those with stronger intent can manipulate, influence, and even possess."

"But why haunt this place? Why Serenity Grove?" Clair asked, her voice rising slightly, desperation evident. "We came here for peace."

"It wasn't haunted before," Hawthorne said solemnly, looking around the room as though the walls themselves were listening. "This place became haunted because of David. He brought them here—called to them, unknowingly. They followed his signal like moths to a flame. This house became a nexus, a focal point of spiritual energy drawn to his third eye's light."

Sarah's voice was a mixture of awe and horror. "So, what does that mean for David? Is he…is he possessed right now?"

A shadow flickered over Hawthorne's face. "Yes. The moment he opened that door again, they claimed him. His mind is a battlefield. He may not realize it yet, but he's losing control over his own will. The stronger ones—entities with more intense desires or power—are vying for his mind, each wanting a foothold in his life."

Tom exhaled sharply, pacing to the far side of the room. "So, what do we do? We can't just leave him to be taken over by some…some demon!"

Hawthorne looked each of them in the eye, his face grave. "We fight. But it won't be easy. This is no ordinary spirit. This is an entity with a grudge—a patience that's stretched across two decades. It waited for David to become the person he is today. And now, it's not going to let him go without a battle."

In that moment, a low, almost imperceptible whisper curled through the room, slithering around them like smoke. The lights flickered, casting sinister shadows across Hawthorne's face as the house seemed to shudder.

Clair's hand flew to her mouth. "Did...did anyone else hear that?"

Hawthorne's face was taut, his expression unyielding. "It knows we're onto it," he said, his voice barely above a murmur. "It knows... and it won't go quietly."

The room was heavy with silence as Hawthorne gathered his words. The storm outside had grown into a relentless symphony, casting eerie shadows across the faces in the room with each lightning strike.

"There's only one way left to save David," Hawthorne said, his voice steady but edged with a seriousness that seemed to chill the air. "But it's not going to be easy. It's risky…and if anything goes wrong, we may never get him back."

The gravity of his words settled over everyone, and for a moment, nobody dared to break the silence. Claire clutched her hands together, her face pale as she looked around, finding fear mirrored in the eyes of Sarah and Tom.

"But…there's no other way?" Claire finally asked, her voice breaking slightly.

Hawthorne shook his head. "No. The only way to sever David's connection with the spirit world is to perform a ritual that will close his third eye once and for all. It's a process that needs precision, strength, and—" he looked each of them in the eye, "—bravery."

Sarah's breath hitched, her gaze shifting to Tom, who was just as tense, visibly processing what Hawthorne was saying. "If this is the only way…then we do it," she finally said, nodding with a determination that almost surprised her.

Tom, feeling the weight of the decision, looked at Hawthorne. "But if this goes wrong…?"

Hawthorne's face remained unreadable. "If it goes wrong…then David could be lost to the other side. Forever." His words hung in the room, unsettling everyone in their finality. He took a deep breath, casting a cautious glance towards the hallway where David was resting. "Which is why someone needs to watch him. At all times. We can't risk him slipping into the spirit realm without us knowing."

An uneasy silence settled over them. Claire, her hands trembling, took a small step back, fear flooding her expression. "Do you mean…you want one of us to stay in there with him? Alone?" Her voice was barely a whisper.

"Yes, Claire. We need someone with him," Hawthorne replied gravely. "I'll be preparing the ritual with Tom, but someone needs to watch David closely." He looked at Sarah. "Sarah, would you be willing to do it?"

Sarah hesitated, her gaze falling to the floor for a brief moment. But then she raised her eyes, meeting Hawthorne's with a fierce resolve. "Yes…I'll do it." She gave a shaky breath, steeling herself. "I'll stay with David."

Claire, her hands instinctively wrapping around herself, looked at Sarah with a mixture of fear and respect. "Are…are you sure, Sarah?" Claire asked, her voice trembling.

Sarah forced a weak but brave smile, her gaze softening as she looked at Claire. "Yes. I have to do it."

Hawthorne placed a hand on Sarah's shoulder, his voice low and reassuring. "Thank you, Sarah. Just…keep a safe distance from him. And if you notice anything strange…anything at all, call us immediately."

Sarah nodded, gripping Hawthorne's hand briefly before releasing it.

Claire took a deep breath, forcing herself to nod. "Alright…please, just…be careful."

Hawthorne's voice was calm but intense. "Claire, take your daughters and lock yourselves in the room. Don't come out, no matter what happens. Whatever you hear… whatever you think might be happening out here, stay inside."

Claire's eyes widened, hands gripping her daughters' shoulders tightly. "Are you certain it'll be safe for us in there?"

"Yes, safer than staying out here," Hawthorne replied with certainty. "This spirit is growing bolder. It won't be long before it tries something drastic. I need you to be strong for them."

After a moment, Claire nodded, her voice barely above a whisper as she replied, "Alright… I'll do it. We'll stay locked in."

Hawthorne and Tom moved into a small room nearby, where Hawthorne began unpacking ritualistic items: candles, incense, a strange, gnarled piece of wood carved with unfamiliar symbols, and a ceremonial dagger with a curved, gleaming blade. Each item seemed to radiate an eerie energy, as though they held memories of other battles fought in shadowed places. Hawthorne laid them out meticulously, the tension in his hands betraying the calm he tried to project.

Tom glanced at the symbols, his face uncertain. "Hawthorne… this isn't just a ritual, is it?" he whispered, his eyes tracing the strange, haunting patterns on the wood and dagger.

Hawthorne's jaw tightened as he aligned the symbols in a specific arrangement. "No," he murmured, his voice barely audible. "This is a battle."

Tom swallowed hard, the realization settling heavily over him. He could almost feel the presence lingering just out of sight, watching, waiting. The shadows in the room seemed to deepen, and even the soft glow of the candles felt like it was fighting against something darker, something ancient.

Hawthorne's eyes didn't leave the altar he was building, his hands moving with purpose as he set each item in place. "This entity… it's waited for two decades. It's grown strong, patient. It's not going to let go easily."

A tremor ran through Tom's hands, but he steadied himself, nodding resolutely. "Then we'll make sure it doesn't get what it wants."

Hawthorne gave a tight, approving nod, his gaze never leaving the ritual setup.

The old clock in the hallway ticked steadily, a sound Sarah hadn't noticed before but now seemed deafening. She stood frozen at the entrance to the dining room, steeling herself before stepping into the unknown.

David sat at the table, hunched over, engrossed in the rustling pages of a newspaper. His figure seemed out of place, almost skeletal under the dim lighting. The sight of him sent a shiver down her spine. His hands, once strong and familiar, were now pale, veins bulging, with darkened nails that seemed too long. His lips were cracked, a dull purple hue, and his hair had turned nearly white, far greyer than it had been just days ago.

"David," she said softly, her voice wavering despite her effort to sound composed.

He didn't look up. "Sarah," he replied in a slow, deliberate tone, as though he had been expecting her.

She hesitated, her feet unwilling to carry her further into the room. "What are you doing?"

"Reading," he said simply, turning a page. "Keeping up with the world." His voice was calm, but something about its cadence unsettled her.

Summoning her courage, Sarah walked toward the table and took the seat opposite him. She studied his face, trying to find any trace of the man she knew, but his features seemed foreign—his eyes dull and sunken, the irises a strange shade that caught the light unnervingly.

"Anything interesting in there?" she asked, forcing a casual tone, hoping conversation would anchor the moment in normalcy.

He finally lifted his gaze, and the intensity of his stare made her breath hitch. It was as though he wasn't looking at her but through her, peeling back her layers to expose her very essence. "Old news," he said, a faint smirk playing on his cracked lips. "But the past always finds a way to the present, doesn't it?"

Sarah frowned, confused. "What do you mean?"

He leaned back in his chair, the movement making the wooden frame groan. "Everything has its time, Sarah. Some things are just... waiting for their moment."

The hairs on the back of her neck stood on end. She swallowed hard and glanced toward the doorway, instinctively mapping out her escape. "You're talking strangely," she said, trying to sound playful but failing miserably.

David tilted his head, as though pondering her words. "Am I? Or are you just hearing differently?"

Her heart pounded in her chest. "I-I'm not sure what you mean," she stammered, feeling as though she were tiptoeing on a crumbling ledge.

He leaned forward suddenly, his movements sharp, his eyes locking onto hers. "Tell me, Sarah, do you believe in inevitability?"

The question hung in the air like a storm cloud, heavy and ominous. She blinked, her mind scrambling for a response. "I... I don't know. Why do you ask?"

David smiled—a slow, deliberate smile that didn't reach his eyes. "Just curious," he said, leaning back again. "Curiosity is a powerful thing, isn't it? It's what drives us to the edge."

Sarah felt a chill creep down her spine. She reached for a distraction. "Maybe we should talk about something lighter."

David chuckled, a low, guttural sound that sent a jolt through her. "Lighter?" he repeated. "Alright, then. How about coffee?"

"Coffee?" she echoed, caught off guard.

"Yes," he said, rising from his seat with a sudden, almost theatrical flourish. "A warm cup of coffee. It's been ages since I made some. Don't you think it's the perfect night for it?"

Sarah hesitated, unsure how to respond. She nodded quickly, desperate to keep him occupied. "Sure. Coffee sounds good."

David's face lit up with an unsettling excitement. "Wonderful," he said, heading toward the kitchen.

The moment he disappeared, Sarah exhaled sharply, her trembling hands clutching the edge of the table. She considered running but dismissed the thought almost immediately. She had to stay. Hawthorne needed time, and she was the only one keeping David occupied.

From the kitchen, the sound of shuffling footsteps and clinking utensils drifted into the room. A moment later, a crackly tune began playing.

It was *Tiptoe Through the Tulips*.

The whimsical melody echoed eerily in the quiet house, its cheerful notes starkly out of place.

Sarah turned toward the kitchen doorway, her breath hitching as she caught sight of David. He was swaying slightly to the music, his movements oddly fluid yet mechanical, like a marionette on invisible strings.

He hummed along to the song, his voice low and uneven. He opened a cabinet, retrieving a can of coffee, then paused to sniff the air. "Ah," he murmured to himself, loud enough for her to hear. "The aroma. It's been so long since I've smelled this."

Sarah's pulse quickened as she watched him. He seemed lost in his own world, his fingers tapping rhythmically on the counter as he prepared the coffee.

Then, he began to dance.

It wasn't an elaborate dance, just small, shuffling steps that matched the beat of the music. He swayed his hips, nodded his head, and occasionally spun lightly on the spot.

Sarah's stomach churned as she watched, her mind screaming at her to do something—anything—but her body refused to move.

David glanced over his shoulder, catching her wide-eyed stare. "Music helps, doesn't it?" he said, his tone conversational, as though this were entirely normal.

Sarah forced a shaky smile. "Yeah," she managed to say. "It... it's nice."

David chuckled, turning back to the coffee machine. "Nice," he repeated. "Oh, Sarah, it's much more than nice. It's... timeless." He paused, then added, almost to himself, "Like a memory you can't escape."

The coffee machine beeped, and David turned off the music. He poured two cups with deliberate care, his hands steady despite the tremor that seemed to run through the rest of him.

He returned to the table, setting one cup in front of Sarah before taking his seat again.

Sarah stared at the steaming liquid, her hands trembling. "Thank you," she whispered.

David smiled again, that same unsettling smile. "Drink up," he said softly, his voice almost soothing. "You'll need your strength. The night is still young."

The dim light of the room where Hawthorne and Tom worked flickered occasionally, casting long, jittery shadows on the walls.

Hawthorne crouched near a large, circular chalk outline on the wooden floor, intricately drawn with symbols and runes that seemed to pulse faintly in the dim light. The symbols, though ancient, were precise, a culmination of his years of research into the paranormal and the occult. Tom stood behind him, holding a worn leather-bound book, his fingers trembling as he flipped through the brittle pages.

"We're almost done with the setup," Hawthorne muttered, his voice low and focused. He straightened up, his eyes scanning the circle to ensure there were no imperfections. "This ritual is our only chance to sever David's connection with the entity."

Tom swallowed hard, his eyes darting to the candles placed strategically around the room. "This... this will work, right?" he asked, his voice betraying his fear.

Hawthorne didn't answer immediately. He walked over to the table, where an assortment of items lay: a silver dagger, small vials of herbs and oils, and a pendant etched with a protective sigil. Picking up the pendant, he held it for a moment before turning to Tom. "It has to work," he said finally, his voice grim. "We don't have a second option."

Tom exhaled shakily. "And David? How are we going to get him in here? You've seen what he's become... he's not just going to sit quietly and let us do this."

Hawthorne placed the pendant around his neck and walked back to the circle. "That's the hardest part," he admitted. "The entity has taken a stronger hold on him now. It'll resist, fight back. But we have no choice. If we delay, it'll be too late."

Tom rubbed his forehead, his nerves visibly fraying. "Do you even know how many spirits are inside him right now? Or... what that thing is capable of?"

Hawthorne stopped, his expression darkening. "Not exactly," he confessed. "But there's one I'm certain of. The one from 20 years ago. The one that lingered even after we thought it was gone."

Tom let out a low whistle, pacing nervously. "So we're not just up against one spirit—we're dealing with an army, led by some ancient thing that's been planning this for years. Great."

Hawthorne glanced at him, his sharp gaze cutting through Tom's panic. "You knew what you were signing up for when you agreed to join me," he said firmly. "Fear won't help us now. Focus will."

Tom nodded reluctantly, taking a deep breath. "Alright," he said. "What else needs to be done?"

Hawthorne gestured to the table. "The herbs need to be burned in the brazier. Their smoke will weaken the entity's hold on David, make him more... manageable. The dagger will be our last resort. It's not for him, but for the tether that connects him to the spirit world. And the chanting has to be precise—any mistake, and it could backfire."

Tom's hands shook as he picked up the vials of herbs. "And what about Sarah?" he asked. "She's with him now. If he... changes, she could be in danger."

Hawthorne's jaw tightened. "Sarah knows what she's doing," he said, though his tone suggested he was trying to convince himself as much as Tom. "Her job is to keep him occupied until we're ready. We just have to move fast."

Tom nodded, pouring the herbs into a small brass brazier in the center of the circle. The pungent aroma filled the room as Hawthorne lit the mixture, the flames casting eerie, dancing shadows.

Hawthorne crouched beside the brazier, whispering an incantation under his breath. The words were guttural and strange, sending a chill down Tom's spine. As Hawthorne spoke, the smoke from the brazier thickened, curling unnaturally in the air and forming vague shapes that seemed to watch them.

"Are you ready?" Hawthorne asked, his gaze piercing.

Tom hesitated for a moment, then nodded. "Yeah," he said, his voice firmer now. "Let's do this."

Hawthorne stood, his presence commanding. "Good," he said.

"Because once we start, there's no turning back."

CHAPTER 23
THE GARDEN OF THE DAMNED

Sarah sat in the chair, her back stiff, eyes flickering nervously toward the door where Claire and the children were locked away. The house felt quieter than it ever had before, as if it were holding its breath. The storm outside had grown louder, the wind howling against the windows, but the oppressive silence inside was far worse. Tom and Hawthorne were busy in the other room, their muffled voices cutting through the stillness, but they didn't offer her any comfort.

David, who had been sitting across from her, reading the newspaper with an intensity that unnerved her, suddenly looked up. His eyes were wide, unblinking, as though he hadn't noticed her watching him for the last few minutes.

"I'm thirsty," Sarah said, her voice trembling slightly as she tried to break the silence, her hands gripping the edge of the table. "Could you... could you bring me some water?"

David didn't answer immediately. His lips curled into a slow, unnerving smile, one that didn't reach his eyes. The corners of his mouth twitched as though he were savoring something—something she couldn't see but *felt*.

"Of course," he whispered, his voice smooth but cold. There was something about the way he said it—too polite, too eager—it sent a shiver crawling up Sarah's spine.

As he got up to leave, Sarah noticed the way his body moved—unnaturally smooth, almost too precise. He walked away from her, each step measured, but there was something in the way his shoulders tensed that felt wrong, like a predator stalking its prey. His back was turned, but she couldn't shake the feeling that he was still watching her, his presence hanging in the air, thick and suffocating.

Her heart was racing. She had to distract herself—had to calm her nerves. Slowly, Sarah pushed herself out of the chair and walked toward the table where David had been sitting. Her eyes lingered on the newspaper he had left behind, the edges of the paper slightly crumpled, as though it had been handled far too many times.

With a hesitant breath, she picked it up, her fingers brushing against the cold, crinkled surface. The headline jumped out at her, jagged and violent:

"Husband Kills His Wife and Daughters, Along with Her Friends"

The words seemed to crawl off the page, scratching at her mind, sending a chill through her bones. She felt her pulse quicken as her eyes darted over the rest of the article. The photo beneath the headline was enough to stop her dead in her tracks.

It was a gruesome image. The bodies of the woman and her children lay sprawled across what looked like a living room, their faces contorted in unnatural stillness. And there, right in the center, was the unmistakable image of a man—*his face*—pale and lifeless, staring back at her from the page.

The room seemed to tilt, and Sarah's stomach churned as the air in the room grew thick. Her fingers trembled as she dropped the paper to the floor, her breath coming in short gasps. She backed away, her mind spinning, but her feet felt glued to the spot.

No. This can't be real. This can't be happening.

Her head spun, and she tried to steady herself, but the room was closing in. The shadows in the corners of the room seemed to grow longer, darker.

Then she heard the sound of footsteps—David's footsteps—slow, deliberate, getting closer. She turned, her chest tightening, and saw him standing in the doorway. He was holding the glass of water, but it wasn't the water that caught her attention—it was the look in his eyes.

His face was expressionless, but his eyes... His eyes were wide, too wide. They were fixed on her with an unnatural intensity, gleaming with something she couldn't name. A chill ran down her spine as she saw the twisted grin that slowly spread across his face.

"Here's your water," he said, his voice low, almost a whisper. His smile never wavered, but there was something about it, something hollow, that made Sarah's blood run cold. It was the kind of smile a predator gave right before it lunged.

She wanted to scream. She wanted to run. But all she could do was stare back at him, rooted to the spot.

David didn't move toward her right away. Instead, he just stood there, holding the glass of water out in front of him. His eyes never left hers, his grin stretching just a little wider, too wide, too knowing.

"Don't you want it?" he asked, his voice barely audible over the pounding of the storm outside. The glass of water trembled slightly in his hand.

But Sarah could barely focus on the water. Her eyes were glued to his face, to the sickening look in his eyes, the way his presence filled the room like a suffocating fog. It was as though he wasn't just standing there—he was *waiting* for something.

"David..." she whispered, her voice shaking, but she didn't know what to say, how to make sense of the terror bubbling inside her.

Sarah stumbled backward, her heart pounding so violently it felt as if it might burst.

David turned his head slowly, his gaze dropping to the newspaper on the table. His eyes gleamed with a strange, dark satisfaction. "Isn't the news... interesting?" he asked, his voice suddenly cold, sharp, and hollow.

Sarah froze, her breath hitching in her throat. "W-What?" she stammered, her voice barely above a whisper.

He chuckled softly, the sound low and guttural, like it didn't belong to him. "The husband. His wife. Their daughters... and her friends." His voice grew quieter, almost a hiss, as he leaned slightly closer, though his eyes remained on the paper. "All of them. Dead. Just like that."

Sarah's hand shot up to cover her mouth, stifling a gasp. She took another step back, her legs trembling. "That... that won't happen," she whispered, her voice quivering.

David's head snapped up at her words, his neck twisting at an unnatural angle. He stood perfectly still for a moment, his back straight, his shoulders unnaturally stiff. Then, in a voice that wasn't his—a deep, raspy growl that sounded like it was coming from the depths of something ancient and cruel—he said, "Oh, Sarah... but it *already has.*"

Before she could react, David turned his back to her. His body jerked and twitched, the sharp cracking of his bones echoing through the room as his shoulders began to move in ways they shouldn't. Sarah's stomach churned as she watched his form contort, his head tilting unnaturally to the side.

"David..." she whispered, her voice shaking as fear gripped her throat.

He suddenly spun back toward her, his face twisted in a grotesque smile, his eyes wide and almost glowing in the flickering light. Without warning, he flung the glass of water straight at her with alarming force.

The glass shattered against the wall behind her, narrowly missing her face. The shards rained down like jagged crystals, and Sarah let out a strangled scream as she instinctively ducked, her heart hammering in her chest. She scrambled backward, her hands fumbling for anything to steady herself.

David took a step toward her, his movements jerky and unnatural. "You can't stop it," he growled, his voice distorted, layered with something monstrous.

Panic overtook her, and Sarah turned and bolted, her screams piercing the heavy air. "Hawthorne! Tom! Help!" she cried, her voice cracking as she ran blindly down the hall, her shadow leaping and twisting on the walls around her.

From the other room, Hawthorne and Tom heard her screams. Hawthorne's head snapped up, his eyes narrowing. "Sarah!" he shouted, already rushing toward the noise.

Tom was close behind, his footsteps pounding against the floor as they ran toward the chaos. They burst into the room just as Sarah stumbled and fell against the wall, clutching her chest, her face pale and streaked with tears.

"Sarah!" Tom called out, reaching for her. "What happened?"

But before she could answer, a loud, sickening crack filled the room, freezing them all in place.

All eyes turned to David.

He stood in the center of the room, his body convulsing violently. His arms twitched, his fingers curling unnaturally as his head tilted back, a guttural growl escaping his throat. The cracking sound grew louder, more frequent, as his limbs began to bend in grotesque angles.

"Get back!" Hawthorne barked, pulling Sarah behind him as Tom moved to block her other side.

David's body jerked forward, his spine arching as his ribs seemed to shift beneath his skin. His face was no longer his own—it was distorted, twisted into something inhuman. His jaw stretched unnaturally wide, his teeth bared in a horrifying snarl as his eyes rolled back into his head.

The lights flickered violently, plunging the room into brief moments of darkness. Each time the light returned, David's form had changed further. His arms elongated, the bones snapping and shifting audibly. His hands grew claw-like, the skin stretching taut over his knuckles.

A final, bone-rattling crack echoed through the room as David's transformation reached its horrific peak. He let out a guttural, otherworldly scream that made the walls of the house tremble.

Hawthorne took a step forward, his jaw tight, his voice steady despite the terror in his eyes. "Tom, get Sarah out of here. Now!"

But David wasn't done. He turned his head sharply toward them, his face now a monstrous mask of rage and malice. His body heaved with every breath, his movements twitchy and erratic as he let out another low growl, the sound vibrating through the air.

This was no longer David. This was something else. Something terrifying.

Hawthorne stood frozen for a split second, his mind racing, trying to process the nightmare before him.

Tom stepped forward, his eyes wide with terror, but Hawthorne gripped his arm, stopping him. "Get Sarah out of here, now!" Hawthorne shouted, his voice sharp and commanding, despite the fear gnawing at him.

Tom didn't need to be told twice. He grabbed Sarah by the arm, pulling her behind him as they hurried toward the door. But before they could reach it, a hideous screech filled the room, deafening in its intensity. David—no, *it*—lunged at them with terrifying speed, the cracks in its body echoing as its limbs stretched unnaturally long, like spider legs reaching for them.

The room seemed to warp, the walls bending and warping with the force of the creature's movement.

Hawthorne instinctively shoved Tom and Sarah out of the way, barely avoiding David's claws that slashed through the air like blades.

"Get out!" Hawthorne shouted again, his voice hoarse, panic rising as the creature screeched again, thrashing violently. The very air felt thick, suffocating, as if something dark was pressing down on them all.

Tom and Sarah stumbled backward, their breaths ragged, heartbeats pounding in their chests. But they weren't fast enough. The creature's twisted form lunged at Hawthorne, its jagged teeth bared, its eyes wide and hungry.

Hawthorne dove out of the way, rolling to the side just in time, but David's claws raked across his jacket, leaving deep gashes in the fabric. A sharp, agonizing pain flared through his side, but he gritted his teeth, forcing himself to move.

"Tom, go!" Hawthorne shouted, his voice filled with urgency. "Don't look back!"

Tom didn't hesitate this time. He yanked Sarah toward the door, pushing her out of the way of the creature's grasping claws. She let out a strangled cry, her face pale, eyes wide with terror, but she kept moving, stumbling through the door and into the hallway.

As they reached the safety of the corridor, Sarah turned back, her breath catching in her throat. "Hawthorne!" she cried, her voice breaking. "Please!"

But Hawthorne was still fighting. He had managed to dodge the creature's strikes, but it was clear that it was only a matter of time before it overwhelmed him. Every movement David made was a grotesque distortion of the human body, his bones shifting and snapping with sickening regularity. It was as if the creature was in the throes of a violent, unholy transformation, one that made no sense, that defied nature itself.

Just as the creature lunged again, its jaws snapping at Hawthorne's throat, the air around them seemed to freeze. The house groaned, the very foundations shaking as a deep, guttural growl filled the space. The storm outside intensified, the wind howling so loudly it drowned out everything else.

What was happening?

A blinding flash of light erupted in the room, followed by an explosion of sound. The house seemed to tremble with the force of the blast, sending everyone crashing to the floor. For a split second, everything went still.

And then—David was gone.

Hawthorne slowly pushed himself up, his body aching, his heart pounding. The air was thick with smoke, and the dim light flickered weakly in the room. The creature—the abomination—had disappeared, leaving only the remnants of its presence in the air, a lingering feeling of dread that filled every corner of the room.

"What... what happened?" Tom whispered, his voice barely audible as he helped Sarah to her feet.

Hawthorne looked around, his eyes narrowing. "I don't know"

Without another word, he turned toward the door, motioning for them to follow. But as they stepped into the hallway, a cold, unnatural wind swept through the house, sending a shiver down their spines.

The house groaned again, louder this time, as if it were alive. And then, in the distance, they heard something—footsteps. Slow, deliberate, and heavy, echoing through the empty halls.

Hawthorne stopped, his instincts screaming. "Stay close," he ordered in a low voice.

The footsteps grew louder, closer, but they were coming from all directions now. They were surrounded.

David wasn't gone.

It was still here.

Claire sat on the edge of the bed, her daughters huddled close to her. The muffled sounds of screaming and crashing echoed through the house, seeping under the door like a sinister presence. Each thud made the walls tremble, and the faint light of the room flickered, casting unsettling shadows on the walls.

"Mommy, what's happening?" whispered Emma, her tiny voice trembling as she clung to Claire's arm.

"I don't know, sweetheart," Claire replied, trying to keep her voice steady, though her heart was racing. She smoothed Emma's hair, casting a worried glance at Lily, who was holding onto her sister tightly, her face pale. "It's going to be okay. I promise."

But even as she said the words, they felt hollow. The unease in the room was suffocating, and Claire's own fear was mounting. The air felt colder, heavier, as though something unseen was watching them.

Another loud crash echoed from somewhere in the house, making both girls yelp in fright. Claire hugged them closer. "Stay here," she whispered, her voice firm despite the panic bubbling inside her. "I need to check the door."

"Don't go, Mommy!" Emma pleaded, tears welling in her eyes.

"I'll just look," Claire assured her, her voice soft but urgent. She gently untangled herself from their grip, placing a trembling hand on the bedside table to steady herself as she stood.

The room felt eerily still as she approached the door, her footsteps unnaturally loud on the wooden floor. She pressed her ear to the door, straining to hear anything beyond the chaos.

"Please let this end," she whispered to herself.

But then, a soft sound caught her attention—a faint shuffling. Not from the hallway, but from somewhere closer. Claire's brow furrowed as her gaze shifted toward the window. The room grew colder, a chill spreading over her skin as she felt an inexplicable pull toward the glass.

She hesitated, her breath catching in her throat. Slowly, she turned her head, her eyes locking onto the window.

Her heart stopped.

Outside, in the dim light of the storm, she saw them.

At least a hundred figures stood in the garden, their outlines barely visible through the rain-streaked glass. Their stillness was unnatural, unnerving, as if they were waiting for something. The longer she stared, the more details emerged—rotting flesh, hollow eyes, tattered clothes hanging limply from skeletal frames.

"Mommy?" Emma's voice quivered, breaking the silence.

"Shh…" Claire whispered, holding up a trembling hand to quiet her daughters. She took a step closer to the window, her eyes locked on the horrifying sight outside.

The figures didn't move, but she could feel their attention on her, as though a hundred dead eyes were boring into her soul. Her breath fogged the glass as she leaned closer, her body trembling with fear.

And then, all at once, they smiled.

It wasn't a human smile. Their mouths stretched too wide, their teeth jagged and broken, some with gums where teeth should have been. The grotesque, collective grin sent a wave of nausea through Claire, and she stumbled back, her hand flying to her mouth to stifle a scream.

"Mommy, what is it?" Emma's voice was louder now, panicked.

Claire didn't answer. Her eyes were glued to the window as the figures began to move.

Slowly, unnaturally, each one raised a bony arm, their fingers pointing directly at her.

"No," she whispered, shaking her head. "This can't be happening."

The room seemed to darken further, the faint glow from the window casting distorted shadows that danced and writhed on the walls. The storm outside grew louder, the wind howling as if it carried the voices of the dead.

Claire turned to her daughters, her face pale, her eyes wide with horror. "Don't look," she said, her voice barely above a whisper. "Stay there. Don't come near the window."

But Emma, too curious for her own good, approached her mother. "What's out there?"

"No!" Claire grabbed her shoulders, pulling her back. "You don't want to see it, Emma! Stay with your sister!"

Just as she turned back toward the window, the figures outside moved again. This time, their movements were synchronized, jerky, and unnatural, as though controlled by invisible strings. They began to step forward, closer to the house, their smiles widening.

A loud, sharp knock on the window made Claire jump and scream, stumbling back into the bedside table. The girls shrieked in terror, clinging to each other as the knocking continued—faster, louder, relentless.

The figures were now pressed against the glass, their decayed faces inches from hers. Their hollow eyes stared straight at her, their mouths twisting into grotesque shapes as they began to chant, their voices low and guttural, blending with the storm.

"Claire…"

The sound of her name spoken in unison made her knees buckle. It was as if the house itself was alive, the very walls whispering her name.

"No, no, no…" she whispered, dragging herself toward her daughters, her hands shaking violently.

The glass cracked......

CHAPTER 24
THE BREACH

Crack...

It started low—just a soft tick.

Claire froze mid-step, her eyes snapping toward the window.

Then another sound—a second crack, sharper this time. The glass now had two long, splintering veins, branching outward from the center. And with it came a low, unnatural groan, like the walls of the house were holding their breath.

Claire's skin went cold.

She stepped backward—slow, careful—as if trying not to wake something already staring at her.

Behind her, Emma and Lily had gone completely silent. They were standing in the middle of the room, eyes wide, still in their pajamas. Emma clutched the sleeve of her sister's shirt.

"Girls," Claire said, her voice trembling, "come here. Now."

Another tick. The crack widened. Claire heard a faint tapping sound—dull, wet, unnatural.

It wasn't knuckles.

It was flesh.

From the other side of the glass.

Claire's stomach dropped.

"Emma. Lily. Now."

The wardrobe.

It stood tall in the corner—an old, gnarled piece of wood, once painted white but now aged and splintered, the handles rusted, its doors uneven from the years. It had gaps—thin wooden slats through which one could just barely see the outside. It wasn't safe. But it was the only place to hide.

Claire grabbed both her daughters by their wrists and dashed across the room.

The tapping turned to scratching.

Fingernails—or claws.

The wardrobe door creaked open like a tomb. The hinges shrieked softly, as if protesting their reawakening after years of stillness.

"In. Inside. Quickly."

Emma clambered in first, then Lily, and finally Claire. She pulled the door shut with both hands and pressed her back against the inside.

Darkness.

They were huddled close, the air stale and thick with the scent of old varnish, dried mothballs, and something earthy—the smell of dust that's lived in the shadows for decades.

Claire crouched low, arms around both girls, heart hammering against her ribs.

Through the wardrobe slats, she could still see the window. The glass was spreading with cracks, almost like cobweb.

Outside the glass, she could see them.

Figures.

At least a hundred—maybe more—pressing against the house.

Rotting. Swollen. Soaked.

Their skin sagged from their bones. Their eyes were black pits. Some had no jaws, just dark cavities filled with teeth that didn't fit. Others stared directly at the window—directly at the house—as if they knew where she was.

Claire couldn't breathe.

She clutched the girls tighter, her own breath shallow.

And then—

Lily shifted in her arms.

She tugged at Claire's sleeve gently. When Claire looked down, Lily was staring at her, eyes glassy with terror but still sharp enough to speak.

She raised one trembling hand and shaped her fingers.

The sign was small. Simple.

Scared.

Claire kissed the tops of their heads and whispered, "I'm here. I've got you. Just be still. Don't move."

The tapping stopped.

The glass trembled.

Everything fell quiet.

Claire kept her breath shallow, her arms wrapped tightly around Emma and Lily. The girls were still—tensed like frightened deer—as though even the sound of a heartbeat might give them away.

Outside, everything had gone still.

The tapping stopped.

No breath.

No footsteps.

No whispers.

Just... silence.

The cracked window—shimmering in fractured lines like a web of frozen lightning—stood suspended in tension.

Then—

BOOM.

The glass exploded inward, not in a rain of shards, but in a violent, sharp burst, as if punched through by something angry and inhuman. The sound tore through the silence like a scream. Bits of broken glass flew across the floor, embedding into the wood, the couch, the walls. The lamp flickered wildly before shorting out.

And then—silence again.

Not a sound.

Not even wind.

Claire's pulse thundered in her ears. Her eyes locked on the wardrobe slats, barely daring to blink.

Outside, the room was half-lit in a blue haze from the storm beyond.

Nothing moved.

Then—

A shadow passed over the shattered frame of the window.

And something stepped in.

Claire's breath caught in her throat.

It was a tiny foot.

Small. Pale. Bare. The toes curled delicately as it touched down on the wooden floor.

It made no sound. No print.

The foot was followed by a leg—short, thin, smudged with dirt and a faint red stain that wasn't paint.

Then, beside it, another matching tiny foot.

A second child.

Both barefoot.

Their skin looked cold, almost blue in the half-light.

Claire's stomach twisted into a knot as she clamped her hand over Emma's mouth. She could feel Lily shaking in her other arm.

And then—

Another foot stepped in.

But this one was not like the others.

It was longer.

Bonier.

The skin stretched tightly over tendons, blackened and cracked around the heel and toes. The nails were long—too long—and yellowed, curling slightly like talons.

It moved differently—not like walking, but like it was sliding forward, dragging itself.

Claire's heart stopped.

The foot was followed by a leg—covered in a torn white nightgown, stained dark with water and mud, clinging to thin, twisted calves.

Then, in the broken light, Claire saw the shadow of hair—long, matted, wet strands dragging across the floor behind the figure.

She didn't see a face.

Only the lower half.

But she knew—this wasn't human anymore.

The two children moved in silence, side by side, toward the center of the room. The woman behind them followed, her body jerking slightly with every step—like a puppet on tangled strings.

Claire couldn't stop staring.

She wanted to scream. To run.

But she couldn't move.

Couldn't blink.

Couldn't breathe.

Emma trembled in her arms.

Lily leaned forward again, her eyes locked on the figures.

Claire tightened her grip, barely whispering:

"Don't look. Don't move."

From the corner of her eye, through the wooden slats, Claire saw the three figures stop in the center of the room.

The two children raised their heads slightly—just enough for Claire to see their mouths—

Sewn shut.

And then, for the first time, she heard it.

A gurgling breath.

Not from the children.

From the woman behind them.

The breath came in short, wet gasps, like someone drowning while alive.

And then the breathing stopped—

And all three heads began to turn.

Toward the wardrobe.

The two tiny heads, stitched at the lips.
The taller one behind them—tilted unnaturally to the side, like her neck had forgotten how to hold her skull.

Their gaze—though hollow—locked on the wardrobe.

Claire didn't move.

Didn't blink.

The three figures took a step forward.

The wood creaked beneath their feet, but it wasn't like footsteps. It was heavier, as though gravity bent around them differently. Their limbs moved in slow, deliberate spasms, like old wind-up dolls fighting their gears.

Then the woman reached out.

Her arms were impossibly long.

She extended her bony, water-wrinkled fingers—and grabbed each child by the back of the neck.

Emma whimpered softly—Claire clutched her tighter.

But—

She wasn't holding Emma.

She was still staring through the slats when it happened.

The woman lifted the children—not as a mother would. Not with care. But with one sharp movement, yanking them both into the air by the necks. Their legs dangled like lifeless pendulums.

Claire's hands trembled.

The three of them—now one unit—began gliding across the floor.

Toward the wardrobe.

Closer.

Claire's heart pounded against her ribs so hard it felt like it might snap them.

Thud.

A footstep, just outside.

Thud.

Another. The wooden floor groaned.

The wardrobe door cast a thin line of light across Claire's face, and she dared to peek through the slats.

The woman was now right there—a few feet away. Her soaking nightgown dragged like seaweed behind her. Her fingers twitched around the necks of the babies like she was testing pressure points.

Then, silence.

Claire shut her eyes.

Tightly.

Arms wrapped around her daughters again.

Please don't open it.

Please don't open it.

Please don't—

Giggle.

Right in her ear.

A sound so close it made her skin crawl and her stomach lurch.

Claire's eyes snapped open.

It was dark inside the wardrobe.

She looked down.

And everything sank.

Emma and Lily were gone.

In her lap now were two tiny, pale figures, limp in her arms.

Their skin was ice-cold, damp like they had been pulled out of a lake.

Claire gasped—her breath caught in her throat.

She turned one of the faces toward her—

Button eyes. Hollow. Lips sewn shut.

A low growl came from the corner of the wardrobe.

Claire jerked her head around.

Something was breathing behind her.

But there wasn't room for anything else in here.

Was there?

Claire didn't scream.

She howled.

The moment she saw those lifeless dolls cradled in her arms—those cold, dead things with hollow sockets where her daughters should be—Claire screamed so violently it tore through the air like glass.

Her arms flung outward instinctively, throwing the two things off her. They hit the inside of the wardrobe with a dull, wet thud. One of their heads rolled sideways, the stitched lips still smiling.

Claire kicked her legs and scrambled backward, shoving against the wardrobe walls with her feet until the door flung open.

She tumbled out, falling face-first onto the cold floorboards.

The wind had knocked out of her lungs. She gasped, crawling forward on trembling limbs. Her palms burned on the splintered wood, knees bruising with each frantic movement.

Behind her—

Silence.

And then—

"Mommy?"

Claire's blood froze.

The voice was tiny. Familiar. Soft.

Emma.

Claire jerked her head back.

The wardrobe stood open now.

Inside—

Two small figures sat exactly where she had last seen them.

Emma on the left, Lily on the right.

Huddled.

Shivering.

Alive.

"Mommy," Emma said again, her voice cracking. "Mommy, we're scared,"

Claire blinked—disoriented, trembling.

"E-Emma...?"

She inched forward. "Lily...?"

They were really there. She could see their faces, pale but real. Their eyes wide and glistening.

Claire's heart surged. Relief flooded her chest like a wave crashing over panic.

And then—

A hand.

Pale. Veiny. Dead.

It slid out slowly from behind Emma—thin fingers curling over her small shoulder.

Another hand—equally lifeless and cold—slithered out from behind Lily, gripping her gently at first.

The girls didn't notice.

Claire's relief shattered.

She screamed, "NO!"

But she couldn't move.

Then—a face emerged from the shadows behind them.

Gaunt. Grinning. Missing half its lips.

Its eyes were too many—one normal, one gouged out, one just above the brow, milky and unblinking.

It leaned between the girls, resting its twisted chin between them, smiling straight at Claire through the wardrobe slats.

A smile that said—

You're next.

Claire let out a cry so broken it echoed through the walls.

And the thing's mouth—torn and stitched—opened wider than it should have, creaking with a sound like wet wood snapping.

"Shhhhhhh."
It pressed a long, blackened finger to its lip.

And then—

Creeeeeeak…

The wardrobe doors began to close.

Not fast.

Slow. Deliberate.

As if something inside was pulling them shut with careful intention—like a coffin lid sealing.

Claire's heart stopped.

"NO!" she screamed, launching forward with both arms.

She slid on the floor, knees burning, and slammed her shoulder into the door just as the crack narrowed.

"NO! Please!" she cried out, trying to wrench it open with both hands.

Inside, Emma and Lily had started crying, their tiny voices echoing from within.

"Mommy!"
"Don't let it take us!"

Claire dug her nails into the splintered wood, forcing the gap wider—inch by inch.

The grinning face behind them didn't move.
Didn't blink.

It just stared at her.

And smiled.

"I won't let you take them!" she shouted through her teeth.

Then—

A tap on her shoulder.

Soft.

Claire froze.

Slowly… she turned her head.

Standing right behind her were the two ghost-children again—the ones with button-black eyes, stitched mouths, and decaying pajamas.

Up close, they were worse than before. Their skin sagged like wet paper. Their fingers were twitching excitedly, like they had something to show her.

One of them tilted her head and spoke.

A wet, rasping voice forced its way through the stitches in her mouth, breaking some of the threads—

"L-look… what I l-learned…"

Claire could only stare.

Then—with a crack like dry bark snapping—the girl's head twisted sideways, all the way, until her chin touched her back.

One smooth rotation.

Unbroken.

Her mouth hung open, blood pooling from the ripped stitches, while the other ghost-child began giggling—a broken, glitching sound like a warped music box.

Claire screamed—a full, unrestrained scream—and threw herself backward, crashing into the nearby wall.

The wardrobe was still closing.

She turned just in time to see Emma's tiny fingers slipping through the gap, trying to reach for her.

"Mommy!"

Claire lunged forward again—

But the doors slammed shut.

BANG.

Everything went silent.

Claire pounded on the wardrobe doors with her fists, tears streaking down her face.

"My babies! OPEN!"

The doors wouldn't budge.

The room was still thick with that foul, coppery air—like wet rust and rotting milk. Behind her, the two ghost children still stood, twitching and swaying like dolls with broken necks.

And then—footsteps.

Fast. Urgent.

The door burst open, and Sarah ran in, panting, flashlight swinging wildly.

"Claire?! What the hell's happening!?"

Claire spun around, wide-eyed, pointing at the wardrobe. "They're in there! Help me! Please, help me get them out!"

Without hesitation, Sarah rushed forward and grabbed the wardrobe handles. Claire joined her. Together, they yanked with all their strength.

The doors creaked.

Groaned.

And then—burst open.

The wardrobe was—

Empty.

No Emma.

No Lily.

No shadows.

No sound.

Claire's breath caught in her throat; a scream locked behind it.

"Where—where did they go?" she gasped, backing away.

Sarah turned slowly.

And then—

"Claire..."

Claire followed her gaze.

Behind them—

A tall, soaked figure stood in the corner of the room. Her white nightgown clung to her twisted frame, dripping on the floor.

In her arms, she held Emma and Lily, limp—each cradled at her sides.

Their eyes were open, dazed—but alive.

Claire let out a strangled cry and took a step forward, but Sarah held her back.

The woman's head twitched. Her mouth opened, wide and trembling—like a wound splitting across her face.

Sarah's hand went to her jacket pocket.

"You creepy bitch."

She pulled out a small silver vial. Uncapped it.

The room filled instantly with the pungent scent of herbs and salt.

Holy water.

The spirit's face contorted in a silent shriek as Sarah lunged forward, flinging the liquid directly at her.

SIZZLE.

The water hit her chest and smoke erupted from her soaked gown.

She screamed—not with sound, but with the air itself. The windows rattled. The walls trembled.

Her hands snapped open.

The children fell.

Claire rushed forward, sliding on her knees to catch Emma and Lily, wrapping her arms around them as they burst into sobs.

"Mommy, Mommy!"

"I got you—I got you both!"

Sarah grabbed Claire's arm. "We have to go. NOW."

The spirit was twitching, shaking, her soaked hair lifting as if caught in invisible wind.

Claire scooped up the girls.

Sarah flung the rest of the holy water toward the spirit as a last defense, and they ran—bolting through the bedroom door, slamming it shut behind them just as a shadow struck it from the inside with a violent bang.

They didn't stop.

They couldn't.

Claire's footsteps echoed sharply off the wooden floor as she clutched Emma and Lily tightly in her arms, both still sobbing into her shoulders. The house around them creaked and groaned like it was breathing—like it was watching.

Sarah was behind her, panting, eyes darting everywhere.

"Claire," she said, grabbing her by the arm gently but firmly, "you need to go. Now. Take the girls. Get to the ritual room. Hawthorne must be there."

Claire's face was pale, streaked with tears, her arms still trembling from the adrenaline. "What about you?"

Sarah wiped the sweat from her brow with the back of her sleeve. "I—I came with Tom. He was right behind me before we split. But when I heard you scream, I ran to you. We... we got separated."

Claire swallowed, hard. "You're going alone?"

Sarah nodded, pulling out the empty silver vial from her pocket and muttering, "I just hope this wasn't my last bullet."

Claire's grip on her daughters tightened. "Be careful. That thing—she had them. She was inside the room with us."

"I know," Sarah whispered, glancing at the scorched holy water burns trailing along the floor behind them. "And whatever that was... she's not the only one."

They stood for a moment at the edge of the corridor, lit faintly by the swinging lightbulb above—a rhythm of flickers and shadows playing tricks on the walls.

Claire gave Sarah one last look. "Come find us. Please."

Sarah nodded once; jaw clenched. "Go."

Without another word, Claire took off down the hall, Emma and Lily buried in her arms.

Sarah turned and faced the darkness stretching ahead. Somewhere down that corridor, Tom was alone.

And in this house?

Alone meant hunted.

She took one shaky breath, pulled her flashlight from her side holster—and stepped into the shadows.

CHAPTER 25
HE WHO RECITES

The air was heavy.

Tom moved through the dark hallway with cautious steps, flashlight in one hand, a short iron rod in the other. His boots pressed against creaking floorboards; each step followed by the hollow echoes of the cursed house around him. He kept glancing back—hoping to see Sarah.

But she wasn't there.

"Sarah?" he called softly, voice trembling just under his breath.

Only silence.

He passed the cracked mirror near the corridor's bend. His own reflection looked ghostly pale. Sweat glistened on his brow, his pulse ticking like a bomb inside his ears.

He could still hear Claire's scream from earlier—echoing like a memory that refused to fade.

They were supposed to stay together. But this house… it knew how to separate people. To isolate them.

And then—

A sound.

Whistling.

Faint.

From somewhere ahead.

Tom froze.

The melody was not of a song he recognized. It didn't feel human. It was hollow, tuneless—almost as if someone were blowing air through cracked bone.

He turned off the flashlight.

Held his breath.

The whistling stopped.

Tom pressed himself against the wall, his ears straining. The hallway ahead was cloaked in darkness, but something moved in it—just beyond visibility. A shape. A slow, rhythmic thud, as if something large was walking barefoot on the old wooden floor.

Then—

He saw it.

Emerging slowly from the other end of the hallway.

Ten feet tall.

Massive. Towering.

It moved with a sickening, deliberate grace, each step booming softly as the floor strained beneath its weight.

Its skin—grayish, with a faint blue hue under the glow of the hallway light—looked smooth and wet, like polished stone freshly pulled from the ocean floor. Across its torso, it wore what looked like a leather jacket, but the material was too old, too tight, as if grown into its flesh rather than worn.

But what shook Tom—what rooted him to the floor—was the face.

The demon had no mouth at first glance.

Just two deeply set eyes, pitch black and pulsing ever so slightly, like they were breathing. They gleamed like oil slicks—dark, infinite.

Its face was oddly human in shape, but void of emotion, except for a faint twitch at the edge of its jaw.

And from somewhere deep within its body, that whistling returned.

Like wind through the hollow bones of a dying animal.

Tom's legs tensed. Every nerve screamed to run.

The thing stopped.

It tilted its head slowly—almost childlike.

Then—without a sound—its right arm rose.

In its hand: a massive axe.

The blade curved and chipped, stained with something old and dry. It dragged the weapon along the floor, scraping a metal-on-wood shriek into the silence.

Tom took a step back.

His boot hit something.

Clink.

A metal stand. It wobbled. Tipped.

CRASH!

The demon's head snapped toward him.

Its eyes widened—not in surprise, but hunger.

And then it moved.

No scream. No roar.

Just whistling.

Low.

Long.

Deadly.

Tom backed up fast, heart hammering, whispering to himself, "Shit shit shit shit shit—"

The hallway darkened behind him, the house shifting, as if walls were tightening to trap him in.

The demon raised its axe—

And Tom ran.

Tom dashed down the hallway, breath ragged, lungs burning. Behind him—

THUD. THUD. THUD.

The floor shook with each step the demon took.

The whistling didn't stop.

It stayed perfectly in rhythm—calm, detached—unnatural. As if the creature wasn't running, but gliding through space.

Tom turned a corner, slipping slightly on the polished wood. He crashed into the wall, pushed himself off it, and kept going.

Behind him—

A sharp WHOOSH.

Tom ducked instinctively—just in time.

CRAAAAAASH!

The demon's massive axe sliced through the hallway horizontally, burying itself deep into both walls at once—the blade wide enough to tear through two feet of plaster and wood like tissue paper.

Sparks flew. A pipe burst in the wall, spraying water like blood.

Tom stumbled forward, spun around a corner—and again—

WHOOSH—

He dove low.

BANG!

The axe sheared a wooden beam clean in half above his head. Splinters rained down on him like glass.

"Jesus f—" Tom coughed, rolling across the floor, just avoiding the next swing.

The demon moved with precision; its monstrous frame deceivingly fast. With every sweep of its weapon, the air trembled—walls shuddered, picture frames exploded off their hooks, and wooden panels splintered like cardboard.

Tom reached a narrow section of the corridor—too tight for a full swing.

Or so he thought.

He turned—just as the demon turned its body sideways and thrust the axe forward with both hands, trying to drive it through like a spear.

Tom threw himself against the wall, and the axe missed his chest by inches—tearing through the opposite side with a bone-snapping crack.

The whistle didn't stop.

It grew deeper.

Almost like it was… enjoying this.

Tom scrambled to his feet, heart trying to tear through his ribs, his shirt soaked in sweat.

He slid through an open doorway into what looked like a servant's pantry.

SLAM.

He shut the door. Bolted it.

Then backed away.

The sound of footsteps slowed.

The whistling, once rhythmic, now warped—slightly off-key. Unsettling.

Tom stood, iron rod shaking in his hand.

Silence.

No footsteps now.

No breathing.

Just—

Tap.

On the other side of the pantry door.

Tap. Tap.

Tom pressed his back against the far wall, trying to steady his breathing.

Tap.

Then—

WHOOSH—CRAAAACK!

The axe came through the door—cleaving it nearly in two.

The demon's axe tore through the wooden pantry door, cleaving it down the center with a force that sent shards flying across the room like glass shrapnel.

Tom didn't even get the chance to scream.

It stepped in.

Ten feet of nightmare.

Its massive frame filled the doorway, ducking slightly as it entered. The hallway light behind it flickered violently, casting its silhouette in twitching shadows on the far wall.

Tom stumbled backward, knocking over pots, broken shelves, a rusted chair.

He raised the iron rod—his only defense.

The demon stopped for a heartbeat.

And then—

It hurled the axe.

Not swung.

THREW.

A blur of black steel.

Tom screamed and lifted the rod just in time.

CLAAAAANG!

The rod snapped in half with a metallic shriek as the axe sliced clean through it—and in the same brutal motion— took his thumb with it.

"FUUUUUUUUUUCK!" Tom screamed, collapsing to his knees, clutching his hand.

Blood splattered across the pantry tiles.

The stub where his thumb used to be pulsed violently, crimson gushing between his trembling fingers. He fell back, chest heaving, eyes wide with pain and terror.

"SHIT! SHIT! YOU SON OF A BITCH!"

The demon stepped forward, retrieving the axe without bending.

The blade dripped.

With blood.

Tom looked up—tears mixing with sweat—as it raised the axe again.

Whistling.

That hollow, unbroken sound—so calm, so slow—like it wasn't just killing him, it was enjoying it.

He did the only thing he could.

He kicked the metal shelf beside him.

It collapsed into the demon's legs with a crash, enough to make it stumble for just a second.

Tom rolled under its arm—nearly slipping in his own blood—and bolted through the back door of the pantry.

CRASH!

The axe slammed into the frame just behind him, splitting the door in half.

Tom ran, hand clutched to his chest, screaming in pain.

"SHIT SHIT SHIT—SON OF A—!"

His vision blurred, his ears still ringing.

Behind him—

The whistle returned.

Faint.

And now…

Mocking.

The air still carried the metallic tang of fear.

Sarah was running—heart pounding, breath shallow—following the echoes of something violent. She had heard the sound: metal cleaving through wood, walls cracking, followed by a sharp cry. It wasn't just noise. It was a message—one of danger. And that danger, she feared, had found Tom.

The hallway was dim, bathed in sporadic flashes from the lightning outside. The storm had grown wild, hammering against the old house like an angry fist. As she turned a corner, her shoes slipping slightly on the wooden floor, she whispered, "Tom…?"

Only her own voice answered, bouncing back from the corridor walls.

Then she saw him.

A silhouette stood still ahead. A male figure—broad shouldered, soaked in dripping water, standing unnaturally still. At first, she thought—*Tom?*

But as she stepped forward, her stomach sank.

"Tom?" she called again, softer.

The figure turned slowly.

It was Mike.

But not the Mike she had known.

His skin was pale, like porcelain soaked too long in water. His hair, wet and clinging to his skull. His eyes were... hollow. And then she saw it—his lips were tinged with blue. His clothes were waterlogged, hanging from his body like a drowned corpse just pulled from the depths.

"Mike..." she gasped. Her feet froze in place.

He said nothing at first. Just stared.

Just took a slow, stiff step forward.

The sound of wet shoes squelching on the wooden floor made her heart drop.

Sarah stepped back instinctively, her pulse racing.

"You're not real," she muttered. "You're gone... I saw you—"

Another step.

Then his voice.

Soft.

"I called you."

Sarah blinked.

Mike's lips barely moved. The voice didn't even seem to come from his throat.

"I was screaming for you... while I drowned..."

Her chest tightened.

"No— you were gone before we even—"

"You didn't come."

His tone didn't change.

Just calm.

Just cold.

"I begged you. The water filled my lungs. I saw you standing there on the shore… You turned around."

Tears welled up in Sarah's eyes.

"I didn't… I didn't even know—"

"You knew."

Now his voice distorted, as if layered with something inhuman beneath it.

"You let me sink."

Drip. Drip. Drip.

The water from his body spread across the floor like oil. It crept slowly toward her boots.

Sarah backed up, lifting the holy water bottle in her hand.
"Don't come any closer. You're not him."

Mike tilted his head.

His skin peeled slightly at the cheek, as if his jaw had been sewn shut and then torn back open.

"I screamed until my throat tore… and then I sunk."

He smiled.

"Now it's your turn"

Sarah's eyes welled—not from guilt now, but fury.

"Fuck you!" she spat, her voice trembling with rage and fear.

She turned sharply—intending to run—

SNAP.

Something wrapped around her neck.

Tight. Cold. Rough.

A rope—thick and old, the kind used in gallows, coiled suddenly from above, catching her throat with a jerk so violent her feet lifted clean off the floor.

"Gaa—AHHH—!"

Her hands flew to her neck, trying desperately to dig beneath the rope, but it was already tightening—biting into her flesh like claws.

Her flashlight dropped with a clatter.

Her boots kicked helplessly in the air.

The hallway spun.

Then—

Mike stepped forward beneath her.

Still soaked. Still dead.

He looked up at her with those pale, milky eyes and whispered, almost lovingly—

"Now you understand…"

Sarah clawed at the rope, face flushing red, veins rising under her skin.

Mike tilted his head. His wet hair slid across his face like seaweed.

"That moment when your lungs… beg for air…"

He took another step.

"The pressure… in your chest…"

Sarah's eyes bulged. Her legs twitched, jerking violently. Her mouth opened, foam frothing at the edges, but no sound came—just a rasping.

Mike's voice grew colder.

"The panic. The darkness creeping in. That final second… when you realize… no one's coming."

Her hands trembled—weak now. Her vision started blurring. The light above flickered—casting her shadow swinging on the wall behind.

Mike smiled, softly.

Like a man watching an old friend.

"That's how it feels…" he whispered coldly. "The suffocation. The helplessness. I screamed your name. You never came."

Sarah's eyes welled, her body twitching as darkness crept into her vision. Her fingernails tore at the coarse fiber, drawing blood. She couldn't breathe. Her world began to blacken.

Then—

BANG!

The crack of a gun shattered the silence.

The rope snapped midair.

Sarah dropped like a ragdoll, crashing onto the floorboards with a sickening thud. Air tore into her lungs like fire. She coughed, choked, gasped.

The shadow that was Mike had vanished.

Her vision swam with tears, throat raw from the near-suffocation, but as she blinked through the blur, she saw the figure that had fired—standing a few feet away, a pipe gun in one hand, smoke still coiling from its mouth.

It was a man.

Not David. Not a ghost. A man.

Rugged. Worn. His coat was soaked, boots heavy with mud. A few flecks of blood stained the front of his shirt. His face was older, sharp-eyed, and tired—but alert. And not a stranger to this kind of horror.

He lowered the pipe gun slightly and took a step closer. "Are you alright?" His voice was steady, edged with concern, not panic.

Sarah scrambled back instinctively, her body trembling. "Who the hell are you?"

"Name's Harris. I'm… a friend of someone who's already in this house."

"I—I don't know you," she whispered, still gasping, her hands clutching her throat.

"No," he said gently. "But I know *him*. David. And I know Hawthorne."

"We worked a case together. Twenty years ago."

Sarah's blood ran cold.

Hawthorne had mentioned the past. The *boy*. The hospital.

"You… you're the officer," she breathed.

Harris nodded. "Didn't think I'd see this again. But I heard what was happening. Followed it. And now…" His eyes narrowed. "It's started again."

Sarah struggled to her feet, still shaking. "You don't understand… that thing… it *wasn't* Mike."

"I know what it was," he replied. "They take the ones we grieve. Wear them. Hurt us with them."

She looked him in the eyes now, breath still short. "We need to get to Hawthorne. They're preparing the ritual."

"Good," Harris said, standing tall and reloading his weapon with a click. "Then we better move before something else finds us."

The corridor twisted with long shadows as Sarah and Harris moved through the darkness, Harris leading cautiously with the pipe-gun cradled in his arms. The light from Sarah's flickering torch barely illuminated the peeling wallpaper and dust-clouded corners. The creaks of the house moaned like a distant growl.

Then—

Footsteps. Staggered. Fast. Approaching.

Harris snapped his weapon up in one swift motion, stepping in front of Sarah.

"Stop right there!" he barked.

Sarah froze.

From the end of the hallway, a figure emerged— limping, breathing hard, clutching his left hand tightly to his chest. Blood dripped in steady, crimson splashes on the wooden floor.

It was Tom.

His shirt was torn, one sleeve soaked in blood. His right thumb was gone, wrapped hastily in a strip of cloth and leaking red through the fabric. His face was pale, his lips trembling.

But Harris didn't know that.

He stepped forward, eyes narrowing. "Don't move another inch! Who the hell are you?"

Tom froze, gasping. "I—Sarah—where's Sarah—?!"

"Down!" Harris ordered, his voice sharp. "Now!"

"Wait!" Sarah shouted, darting forward, pushing Harris's weapon down. "He's with us! That's Tom! One of Hawthorne's team!"

Harris's eyes flicked between them—still suspicious, but reading the sincerity in Sarah's panic.

Tom nearly collapsed onto the wall, sliding down with a grunt. "It came at me... tall... it cut my thumb like it was nothing... I—I barely got out."

Harris's face softened—only slightly—but he slung the gun to his side and knelt beside him.

"Shit," he muttered. He pulled a folded, old handkerchief from his coat pocket and pushed it into Tom's trembling hand. "Press it tight. That's a lot of blood, son."

Tom nodded, teeth gritted, pressing the cloth to the wound. "I didn't think I was gonna make it…"

Sarah crouched beside him, eyes wide with worry. "You did. That's all that matters."

Tom looked up at her, then to Harris. "Who's this guy?"

"Harris," the officer answered. "Old friend of Hawthorne's."

Tom scoffed through the pain. "You always show up in haunted houses with a pipe gun?"

"Only on the fun nights," Harris replied dryly.

Sarah helped Tom to his feet. His face was pale, but his stance stronger now. The hallway was silent—but no one trusted that silence anymore.

"Let's go," Harris said, reloading with a practiced hand.

The ritual room buzzed with silence.

Candlelight danced across the ancient runes Hawthorne had etched into the wooden floor—glowing faint red now, like embers waiting for breath. The faint smell of burnt sage and salt hung in the air like a spiritual mist, thick and clinging.

Clair sat in the far corner; the twins huddled beside her. Emma was silent, wide-eyed. Lily buried her face in her mother's side, her trembling fingers gripping Clair's wrist tight.

Then—the door creaked.

Hawthorne stepped in, soaked in sweat and dirt, dark circles under his eyes, his coat flecked with ash and salt. He looked like a soldier returning from war.

Clair stood immediately. "Hawthorne—"

He raised a hand, tired but steady. "They're, okay?"

"Yes." Her voice cracked. "They haven't said a word since we ran here."

Hawthorne looked at the girls, his jaw tight. "Keep them close. No matter what happens."

Claire looked around nervously. "Where's Tom?"

"He'll come," Hawthorne replied, though he didn't sound sure.

Then—footsteps. Slow. Confident. From the hallway.

Clair's breath caught. "He's coming."

Hawthorne turned toward the doorway. "Stay calm. Let me talk."

David appeared.

He stepped through the door like he belonged there. But his eyes… they didn't belong to him. They were too still. Too knowing. His skin looked stretched thinner than before, the veins beneath dark like ink. His fingers twitched with unnatural rhythm.

He smiled. "Everyone's here. Lovely."

Clair's grip tightened around Emma and Lily.

Hawthorne took a step forward, his voice firm but gentle. "David."

David tilted his head. "You've been busy drawing on the floor like a madman."

Hawthorne nodded, keeping the calm. "Just a precaution. You know how unpredictable these old houses can be."

David's eyes roamed to the runes. "You think this can hold me?"

Hawthorne chuckled dryly, backing slowly toward the circle. "Oh, I don't know. I've always believed in tradition."

He stepped over the line—inside the circle—invitingly.

David watched him.

"You want to talk?" Hawthorne said softly. "Then talk to me here. Just us. Away from them."

David's smile widened, revealing teeth that looked slightly too sharp.

One step.

Two.

Then—he entered the circle.

The moment his foot crossed the final rune, a pulse exploded through the air like a shockwave. The sigils ignited—red, gold, white—blazing around him like a cage of ancient light.

David snarled. "Tricked me."

Hawthorne raised his hands, eyes glowing with cold purpose. "You stepped in on your own. The circle holds."

The thing inside David screamed—not with pain, but rage.

Hawthorne, finally, breathed a word that echoed like judgment:

"Now we begin."

Suddenly—a thud. Then hurried footsteps outside.

The door burst open.

Sarah stepped in first, chest rising, face still scratched and bruised from her near-hanging. Her eyes widened when she saw David inside the burning circle.

Tom stumbled in next, one hand wrapped tightly in a blood-soaked cloth, sweat glistening on his forehead.

And behind them—

"Jesus Christ," Harris growled as he entered.

The moment Hawthorne turned and saw him, something in his hardened face cracked with brief relief.

"Harris."

Harris strode toward him and they embraced quickly—like soldiers meeting at the battlefield after years apart.

"You son of a bitch," Harris muttered with a half-smile. "Twenty years, and it's this fucker again."

"Yeah," Hawthorne exhaled. "But this time we finish it."

"You better," Harris said, glaring at David through the shimmering circle. "Because if you freeze again, I swear to God—I'll put a bullet through his skull. This time I won't ask."

Tom groaned, leaning against the wall. "Let me know if you need backup."

"Sit your ass down before you bleed out," Harris snapped.

Sarah pulled Tom down gently into a chair, her eyes flicking nervously between the men and David.

Hawthorne turned, his voice low and urgent. "I need the book. The ritual incantation. The exorcism... It was right here."

He began digging through the small wooden chest on the far table. Candles fluttered as his movements grew more desperate.

Clair, still frozen in the corner, whispered: "Can't you just begin? Say what you remember?"

"I don't trust memory against something like this," Hawthorne said, yanking out drawer after drawer. "We only have one shot. If we say it wrong—"

"Maybe if you'd just let me shoot the bastard back then," Harris muttered, cocking the revolver, "we wouldn't be here again."

"Put that down," Hawthorne barked. "You shoot him now and whatever's inside him won't die—it'll just jump. You want that inside one of us?"

Harris glared but lowered the gun slowly. "Fine. But I swear, if he twitches—"

Then—a voice, soft and cold:

"Need help?"

Everyone turned to the circle.

David was smiling again.

"Looking for something?" he asked, eyes like cracked glass.

Hawthorne's spine stiffened.

David chuckled—deep and unnatural.

"I could help"

Everyone stared at David, who stood barefoot within the burning ritual circle. His body wasn't moving, but his grin widened, spreading almost too far, as if the skin on his face were loosening.

Then—

"In the name of the Father..."

His voice was low at first, barely audible.

"...and of the Son..."

Sarah froze, glancing sharply at Hawthorne.

"...and of the Holy Spirit..."

Hawthorne's mouth parted in disbelief. The words… they were verbatim. The same ancient invocation only found in the pages of the exorcism book—the one they hadn't yet located.

"Jesus," Tom muttered under his breath, clutching his injured hand. "He's reading the fucking ritual…"

"No," Hawthorne whispered. "He's not reading—he knows it."

David slowly tilted his head back, his neck cracking as it arched unnaturally. His arms hung limp at his sides, his fingers twitching.

"I call upon the light to cast away the shadows…"

"Stop it," Harris growled, lifting his gun. "I swear I'll—"

"No!" Hawthorne snapped. "He's provoking you."

David took a step forward inside the circle. The runes beneath his feet hissed, glowing with a deeper red, reacting to his movement.

"Purge this vessel. Break the binds of evil. In holy fire, I cleanse thee."

Then he stopped.

He looked straight at Hawthorne and smiled—a terrible, knowing smile.

"Isn't that the line you were supposed to say first, Bitch?"

Hawthorne's breath caught.

Clair pressed her daughters tightly into her chest, her eyes wide with dread. "How does he know the lines? How is this happening?"

"Because he isn't just possessed," Hawthorne muttered. "He's merged. That thing... it's inside and out now."

David slowly raised his arms. His fingers twitched like puppet strings.

"You left me once," he said, still speaking in that calm, ceremonial tone. "You tried to seal me. But the eye never closes forever."

Suddenly, his spine snapped backward. A bone-cracking jolt. His body arched like a contorted bridge, face pointed at the ceiling, his limbs trembling.

The circle glowed even brighter—but nothing was working.

"No reaction," Sarah whispered. "It's not affecting him."

"Because he's not resisting," Hawthorne said grimly. "He's—embracing it."

David's mouth opened again. But this time, his voice deepened—layered, doubled, as if another being was speaking through him in tandem.

"Domine, libera nos a malo…"
(*Lord, deliver us from evil…*)

Tom stepped back. "What the hell is going on? Isn't that Latin?"

"It is," Hawthorne said. "He's reciting the counter-prayer… the one we never finished writing."

David's arms suddenly flung outward, as if caught in a gust of wind no one else could feel. The candle flames bent inward, pulled toward him. The entire room began to shake.

Then David dropped to his knees—still grinning, eyes locked on Hawthorne.

"Need help?"

CHAPTER 26
THE COST OF SALVATION

The room was still echoing with David's last taunt: "Need help?"

Then—

A shift in the air.

It began as a low hum—the kind of tension that lives just beneath silence. The candle flames across the ritual circle began to quiver, bending inward like they were being pulled. The temperature dropped so sharply that Clair instinctively wrapped her arms around the girls, trying to shield them from something she couldn't see.

Suddenly—

The lights exploded.

Every bulb in the room blew out with a sharp, electrical pop, plunging everything into darkness except for the dying orange flicker of candlelight from the circle. That glow barely reached the walls.

Then came the footsteps.

Fast. Many. Some heavy. Some impossibly light, like bare feet brushing old wood. They came from every direction—the hallways, the stairs, the walls above. Hundreds of footsteps echoing in uneven, unnatural rhythm.

Tom froze, his bloodied hand gripping the arm of the chair. Sarah stood stone-still, her breath caught mid-inhale.

"Do you hear that?" she whispered.

"Yeah," Harris muttered, eyes fixed on the door. "Too many."

Then—all at once—silence.

Not just quiet. Dead silence.

Even the wind stopped outside.

Harris stepped forward.

His boots creaked on the floor as he approached the door. He raised a hand and pressed his ear to the wood, listening. The faint scent of rot seemed to waft in through the cracks.

No breathing. No whisper. No step.

He turned slightly to the group behind him and shook his head, lips parting to speak—

SLAM!

The door flung wide open.

And behind it—

Hell.

At least twenty figures.

Pale. Tattered. Their mouths stretched open, jaws unhinged as if silently screaming. Their skin hung off their bones, eyes black pits with no depth. Some hovered, some dragged themselves, others staggered like marionettes in mid-spasm.

But they all did one thing:

They pointed.

Twenty skeletal, shaking arms lifted in unison—all pointing to David inside the circle.

And then they began to scream.

No sound.

Just the motion—veins popping from their necks, spittle flying from their lips, and those mouths widening into grotesque holes as if trying to suck the very air from the room.

"Shit—!" Harris slammed his shoulder into the door. It barely budged—it was like the house wanted them inside.

"Help me!" he roared. "Sarah—NOW!"

Sarah snapped from her trance and rushed to the door, grabbing the edge and pressing with her full weight. Still, the door was buckling inward—the horde was forcing themselves in. Fingers slipped through the gap, gnarled and grey, scratching at the wood.

"They're not after us," Sarah gasped. "They want—David."

David didn't move. Inside the circle, he just sat there.

Smiling.

Tom's panting echoed off the stone-cold walls as he pressed his back against the wooden door, blood from his thumb soaking through the makeshift cloth Harris had handed him. His skin glistened with sweat, and his legs buckled slightly beneath him.

Then came a whisper.

No… not a whisper. A weight in the air.

A presence.

Thud.

He froze.

Another thud.

This time it came from inside the room.

Behind them.

He turned slowly, his eyes darting toward the shadows that flickered just beyond the reach of the candlelight.

"Did you hear that?" he whispered, voice tight with dread.

Hawthorne, glanced over his shoulder. "What?"

Thump…

The floorboards groaned behind the altar.

Tom's hand rose, pointing. "Something's in here. Already."

Hawthorne stepped forward, narrowing his eyes toward the darkened corner.

Then—

The shadow in the far wall began to shift—mass swell, limbs unfolding.

Ten feet tall, the figure stepped forward—its black, leathery skin glinting faintly in the flickering candlelight. It had no weapon this time, but it didn't need one. The force of its presence alone made the room feel like it was collapsing inward.

Then it lunged.

Before anyone could scream, its hand clamped around Hawthorne's neck. Effortless. Lifting him like a doll.

"Ghhh—!" Hawthorne choked, his boots leaving the ground, his papers scattering from his hand.

Then it threw him.

Hawthorne flew backward and crashed into the floor, his back smashing through one of the candle stands—his hand dragging through the salt line of the ritual circle as he landed.

The circle was broken.

"NO!" Sarah cried, seeing the breach.

Tom turned in horror, watching the demon step forward, its massive hoofed feet leaving ash-like burns on the wood.

David, inside the circle, opened his eyes.

He smiled.

And slowly—deliberately—began to rise.

Smoke-like shadows curled around David's ankles as he stepped beyond the shattered ritual boundary.

The room felt colder now—as if something had entered with him.

His steps were slow. Deliberate. Each one echoing louder than the last. Claire tightened her hold on Emma and Lily, backing against the far wall, eyes locked on the man she once called husband.

But this wasn't David anymore.

His eyes had lost all warmth—now dull pits of ink, void of thought or soul. His smile stretched unnaturally wide, skin cracking faintly at the corners of his lips.

Emma's voice, fragile and trembling, broke the silence.

"Daddy...?"

David paused.

He tilted his head slightly, mockingly—then slowly turned his gaze toward her.

His grin widened.

"Aww... look at you," he said, voice deep and layered with something else—a mocking rasp beneath the surface.

"*Daddy is getting raped in hell sweety,*" he whispered, his voice disturbingly gentle... but warped. "He's not coming back."

Claire stepped in front of her girls.

"Stay back!" she shouted, her voice trembling but defiant.

David took another step forward, dragging one foot slightly, like he enjoyed the sound.

He raised a finger and tapped the side of his temple. "You know what's funny, Claire?"

He chuckled—an empty, hollow sound.

"He watched it all. Everything. Screaming inside. And I just let him watch."

Lily whimpered, her fingers clinging to her mother's shirt.

Claire's eyes filled with tears.

David's face twitched violently—his grin breaking for a moment, replaced by something animal.

"Sweetheart…"

He leaned in closer.

"I'm what's left after your husband died screaming."

He took one more step toward them.

Claire braced herself—ready to shield her daughters with her own body.

Tom's boot bumped against the edge of a broken chair. He flinched, eyes darting for a weapon—anything.

Too late.

A massive hand grabbed his collar—and with a growl-like whistle, lifted him clean off the ground and slammed him against the wall.

BOOM!

Dust exploded from the wood as Tom's back cracked into the paneling. He cried out, fists pounding the monster's chest, but it didn't flinch.

The demon leaned closer.

Its breath was hot and foul, like rotting meat boiled in rusted metal. Its eyes were pure black, like oil slicks in the dark.

Then—it screamed.

Not a voice. A whistle.

Louder than before. Bone-deep and shrill, like a siren made of hate. Tom clutched his ears, gasping as his head rang. Then he saw it:

Its tongue.

Split down the middle. Shredded. Hanging in two twitching pieces.

No voice. No words.

Only whistles.

Tom whimpered, a laugh escaping him despite the fear.
"Can't even curse me properly, can you... freak?"

The demon responded with rage.

It raised its other hand—a clawed fist—and punched.

CRACK!

Tom was flung across the room, landing hard, skidding to the base of a pillar. Blood trickled from his mouth. His ribs screamed with pain.

He coughed, trying to crawl backward. The demon was still coming.

It didn't run.

It didn't need to.

It just approached...whistling.

"Poor Claire," David whispered.

"Still trying to protect them. Even now?"

He chuckled—a twisted, gravelly sound, like broken glass grinding against bone.

Then, leaning in slightly, his voice dropped. "You should've let them go. They'd have been safer... with me."

He turned toward the table, where a glass bottle—once used for ritual oil—sat innocently.

He grabbed it.

CRASH!

He smashed it against his own forehead.

Glass exploded—splinters scattering. Blood oozed down his face, soaking into the collar of his shirt. Yet he didn't flinch. He smiled wider.

Then he started walking.

Right toward Claire. And the kids.

Emma screamed.

Lily began to cry.

Claire pulled them behind her instinctively, eyes wide with frozen horror.

"David... please—" her voice cracked.

But David didn't answer. He just kept walking, his bare feet dragging through broken glass and chalk dust, crunching with every step.

Behind him, the demon turned slowly—almost protectively—as if guarding David's path.

Then—

"No—no—no..."

A groan from the floor.

Hawthorne stirred.

His ribs burned. His head throbbed. But when he turned and saw David stalking toward Claire and the girls, something inside him snapped back into clarity.

"Claire!" he shouted hoarsely, dragging himself up. "Take the kids—get back!"

Claire frozen—backed against the wall.

David was almost on them.

The door slammed against its hinges, spirits pressing, shrieking, clawing. Harris had turned his back on them, arms braced wide to hold it shut. His breath came in short bursts.

"I can't hold this much longer!" he shouted, voice hoarse from the pressure.

Then—he turned.

He had to act.

With a swift move, he lifted his pipe gun—arms steady, eyes locked on David, who was just feet away from Claire and the girls.

BOOM!

The shot exploded in the room, thundering like a cannon.

David's foot jerked backward, glass and blood scattering.

But—he didn't fall.

He didn't even flinch.

His head tilted slowly… and then he looked at Harris.

No pain. No rage. Just interest.

Like a predator realizing there's another meal.

And that's when Harris felt it.

His fingers.

They wouldn't let go of the gun.

"What the hell..."

He struggled—tried to loosen his grip.

But something unseen had hold of him. His arms trembled.

Then the gun moved.

On its own.

Slowly, surely...

Turning.

Away from David.

And toward—

"Harris—NO!"

BOOM!

The shot rang out again—closer this time.

Hawthorne screamed as the bullet tore through his left shoulder, flinging him backwards into the wall. Blood sprayed the air.

Claire shrieked.

Sarah shouted from across the room.

"What the fuck are you doing!?"

Harris staggered, eyes wide with shock. "I—I didn't... I didn't do that!"

But the gun was still smoking in his hands.

And David?

He smiled again.

As if he'd been the one holding the trigger all along.

Harris stumbled back, his hands trembling around the pipe gun. The heat of the shot that struck Hawthorne still pulsed through the barrel—his breathing turned shallow, panicked.

"I didn't mean—" he gasped. "I didn't pull—"

But the gun…

It moved again.

Slowly.

Deliberately.

His eyes widened in terror as the barrel turned—upward, rising toward his chin.

"No… no… NO!" he growled, trying to wrench it away.

His fingers wouldn't budge.

Veins bulged in his arms, muscles straining, but the grip held firm—as if someone else, something else, was in command.

David stood motionless, watching with calm, detached curiosity.

Claire screamed from the corner, clutching her daughters.
Sarah bolted forward—"Drop it, Harris! DROP IT!"

He tried.

God, he tried.

But the gun was already there—

Pressed under his jaw.

His face turned pale, soaked in sweat.

"Hawthorne—!" he cried out, one final time.

And then—

BOOM.

The shot echoed like thunder inside the chamber.

Blood.

Bone.

A mist of red burst up the wall like shattered paint.

Harris collapsed instantly.

His body dropped with a sickening thud, eyes wide open, mouth still parted mid-word.

Silence.

David turned.

His hand rose, trembling—not from pain, but from some unnatural frenzy. In his grip was the jagged neck of the broken bottle, edges still stained with his own blood.

And he was aiming it—

Right at Claire.

At the children.

His body hunched. His lips curled back.

Then he screamed.

A sound not human.

A guttural, gutted roar, like a hundred animals howling at once. It echoed in the walls, in the floor, in the bones of everyone in the room.

Claire shielded her daughters, frozen. "David, please..." she whispered, voice cracking.

But David lunged forward.

"DAVID!"

Hawthorne's voice boomed across the chamber.

Bleeding. Barely able to stand.

But he stood.

"David—listen to me!"

David stopped mid-stride.

His hand twitched, still raised.
His breathing grew ragged.

Hawthorne coughed, pain surging from his wounded shoulder—but he pressed on.

"This is not you. That thing inside you—it's using you. You can fight it."

David's eyes flicked toward him.

"It's too strong," he hissed, but his voice was layered now—two voices speaking as one. One human. One *not*.

"You're stronger."

Hawthorne took a shaky step forward, hands raised—not in threat, but in plea.

"You survived this once, David. You were just a boy—but you won. You were chosen not to be possessed—but to resist. That thing fears you. That's why it hides behind you. But you... you can end this."

David's hand trembled more violently now.

His smile was gone.

His face was flickering.

"I... I can't—"

"You can."

David stood frozen.

His chest rose and fell in violent spasms. His hands twitched, curling into claws and relaxing again.

His head dropped.
Then jerked.
His lips moved—silent muttering, unintelligible.

Darkness. Whispers. Cracks in reality.

But through the shadow—a light.

A flicker.

Laughter.
Not mocking, not twisted.

Pure. Sweet. Familiar.

Emma's voice, shrill and bubbly:
"Daddy, look! I drew you as a dinosaur!"

A flash—his daughters coloring on the floor, markers staining their fingers. Emma holding up a picture where he had a giant tail and teeth.

Claire's laughter from the kitchen.

"You're terrifying," she had giggled, kissing his temple.

Another memory surged—

David, holding Lily's tiny hands, helping her walk for the first time.

She looked up at him, giggling, falling against his legs. "Up, Daddy! Again!"

He had laughed, lifting her into the air.
The sky was blue that day. There were no demons in the sky.

Then the warm press of Claire's hand in his.
That night by the lake when they first found the house. She'd looked at him and whispered, "I feel like we belong here."

His throat caught.

The darkness twisted inside him—screaming, writhing.

But the memories pulsed brighter.

David let out a cry—deep, agonized.

"Claire..." he whispered, barely audible.

Claire rushed forward, but Hawthorne held her back screaming, wounded arm trembling.
"Let him fight."

David clutched his head, falling to his knees.

His hands beat the floor.
He was trying.

But his body trembled with unseen war.

And somewhere deep inside that war—

A voice growled.

"You are mine."

Then… his hands moved.

Slow. Reluctant.
But unyielding.

The broken bottle, lying beside him, scraped as he picked it up.

"David..." Claire's voice cracked, trembling. "No—don't—please."

His hand fought to stop—but it didn't.
His muscles trembled violently, but the entity within him was stronger.

The jagged glass trembled in his grip... and began to rise.

Hawthorne, barely able to stand, lunged forward.

"DAVID! NO!"

David turned toward them—his eyes clearing for a split second.
Just a second.

His gaze fell on Claire.

On Emma. On Lily.

They were clutching each other. Crying.

His face softened.
A tear slid down.

He smiled.

"I'm sorry," he whispered.

And then—

With one swift, brutal stroke—

The bottle slashed across his own throat.

Blood sprayed, hot and violent, hitting the floor like an explosion of ink.
His body staggered back, gurgling.

Claire screamed, collapsing forward.
"DAVID!!"

Hawthorne reached him, catching him as he fell.
His body twitching. His breath shallow. Eyes wide.

David's knees buckled.
He collapsed forward, clutching his neck.

His eyes went wide in pain… then blank.

No words. No sounds.
Just the gurgle of blood.
Just the thud of his body against the wood.

Claire screamed—raw, primal, shattering.

But it was too late.

David was dead.

A man broken. A father lost.
David's body lay still.

The broken bottle, slick with his blood, slipped from his lifeless fingers and rolled to a stop on the cold floor.

Claire held her daughters tight, trembling, eyes locked on him.

Hawthorne knelt beside David, one hand on his chest, eyes wide in disbelief.
No pulse. No breath. Nothing.

Then—
Everything changed.

The air, once thick with a suffocating darkness, cleared.

The vibrating tension in the room dissolved, like a weight lifting off their lungs.

The wind outside stopped.
The house was still.
No whispers. No voices.
No footsteps. No shadows.

Every spirit… was gone.

A holy silence spread through Serenity Grove.
Not peace—grief.
But also, a strange sense of freedom.

It was over.

Hawthorne sat back on the floor, eyes hollow.
Sarah collapsed against the wall, sobbing.
Tom, still bleeding, leaned into the doorway, shaking.

Claire slowly walked forward.
She looked down at David—her husband. The man who gave his life to save them.

She didn't scream this time.

She just knelt down and kissed his forehead.

"Thank you," she whispered.
Her voice was barely audible.

But the strength that had carried her through the terror broke.

A sob escaped her throat.

Then another.

Then the dam burst.

She collapsed onto his chest—clutching him tightly—

And cried like the world had ended.

Her tears soaked into the blood-stained shirt, her sobs echoing in the hollow room.

"You came back… you came back to me… and now you're gone…"

Emma and Lily stood behind her, too small to understand fully—but sensing everything.

They didn't cry loudly.

They just clung to each other.
Watching.
Frozen.

Sarah lowered her head. Even she couldn't hold her tears.

Tom, leaning on the wall, covered his mouth with his injured hand, eyes glassy.

Hawthorne remained kneeling… staring at the floor, broken.
No words.

Just grief.

And silence.

A house full of survivors.
But one of them didn't survive.

And the one who died… Had saved them all.

But the house—once cursed, once alive with things from beyond—
was still.

And for the first time in a long, long time…
it was just a house.

CHAPTER 27
ASHES AND ECHOES

The sky was overcast, heavy with unshed rain, as if the heavens themselves mourned the three souls being laid to rest.

Three coffins.

Three lives.

Three stories violently cut short.

The service was quiet—no grand speeches, no prayers shouted to the sky. Just the low rustle of wind through trees and the faint sobs that couldn't be held back any longer.

Hawthorne stood still near the front. His arm was in a sling, a dull plaster peeking from under the dark coat that couldn't hide his pain. The shoulder wound had stopped bleeding days ago, but something deeper inside him hadn't. He watched in silence as the priest whispered something, unheard by most. Maybe even by God.

Tom stood beside him. His hand heavily bandaged, the thumb gone forever. His jaw was clenched as if he feared the emotions behind it would pour out if he dared relax for even a second. He looked older now, not in age, but in soul.

A few steps behind them stood Claire, arms wrapped around her daughters, their small heads pressed into her waist. Her eyes were hollow, but not dry. The tears still came, especially when her gaze met the third coffin—the one with David's name etched into the polished wood.

Sarah stood close to them. She hadn't said much since that night. Neither had anyone, really. Some things leave you speechless, not just because they're horrifying—but because they're too vast to put into words.

Rain began to fall.

As the first drops hit the coffins, Claire finally broke. She let go of the girls and stumbled forward, falling to her knees before David's grave.

"Why did you do it?" she sobbed, clutching the edge of the casket. "Why couldn't you come back… come back to us…?"

No one moved to pull her back. This moment was hers.

The priest continued with the final words, and one by one, soil began to cover the wood. Hollow thuds echoed across the cemetery.

Sarah stepped beside Claire. No words—just a hand placed gently on her shoulder.

Tom looked up at the sky.

Hawthorne closed his eyes. "They saved us," he whispered. "All of them."

And as the wind picked up, just for a moment, it felt like a presence passed among them. Not malevolent. Not terrifying.

Just... a final goodbye.

The black cars arrived one by one along the gravel path that led up to Serenity Grove. The rain had stopped hours ago, but the ground still smelled of damp earth and dying leaves. The sky was clearing slowly—clouds breaking apart, letting streaks of gold pour through.

Claire stood at the front porch with Emma and Lily beside her, holding their hands tightly. Dressed in quiet colors—grays, browns, soft blacks—they looked like the ghosts of the pain they'd just walked through. But there was warmth, too. A kind of fragile strength.

Tom stepped forward first, his bandaged hand tucked carefully into his coat. He gave Claire a small, sincere nod. "You sure you'll be okay here?" he asked, voice rough from everything they'd seen.

Claire smiled gently. "Yes. It's quiet here. That's what the girls need now." She looked down at her daughters, who were staring at the visitors with tired but curious eyes.

Tom glanced at them, then knelt down slightly. "You two are the bravest kids I've ever met. And I've met some pretty strange people, believe me."

Emma gave a faint, polite smile. Lily clutched her mother tighter.

Hawthorne approached next, his left arm still in a sling. The fatigue in his eyes was impossible to miss, but there was calmness too—a strange, hard-earned peace.

"You can always call me," he said. "If anything feels wrong, off... or if you just need someone to talk to."

Claire nodded. "Thank you. For everything."

He hesitated, then added, "He fought hard. Till the very end."

Claire's eyes welled up, but she blinked the tears away before they could fall. "I know."

Sarah stood slightly apart from the group, hands folded in front of her, expression unreadable. When Claire finally turned to her, Sarah stepped forward and hugged her.

"Stay strong," she whispered. "Not for the world—but for yourself."

Claire held her a moment longer, and then let go. "Take care of each other," she said, looking at all of them. "Whatever this world throws at you next—promise me you'll stay in touch. Please."

Tom raised his bandaged hand like a vow. Hawthorne nodded. Sarah gave a faint smile.

Then, one by one, they said their last goodbyes and walked to their cars.

The gravel crunched beneath their feet. The wind whispered softly through the trees.

Claire stood on the porch until the last vehicle turned down the road and disappeared into the distance.

Only then did she take a deep breath, open the front door, and guide Emma and Lily inside.

The house creaked quietly as they stepped in. A silence fell around them—not an ominous one, not anymore. Just silence.

Claire locked the door behind them. The world outside had moved on.

Inside, life—somehow—had to begin again

The house was quiet.

Not the peaceful kind of quiet—but the kind that presses against your chest and makes you feel the weight of everything left unsaid.

A single dim lamp cast a golden glow across the living room. Hawthorne sat slouched on the old couch, a half-empty bottle of bourbon on the table in front of him, next to a chipped glass that hadn't been cleaned in days.

He didn't bother with the TV. No music. No distractions. Just silence, and the occasional creak of wood cooling in the frame of the house.

The framed photograph in his hand was weathered from years of touch—edges soft, color faded. It was of her.

A smile that lit up rooms. Eyes that saw through him like no one ever could. Her hair was tucked behind her ears, the way she always did when she was about to say something serious. He could almost hear her voice.

His thumb grazed the corner of the picture.

"I wish you were here," he muttered, the words slurred but sincere. "You always knew how to pull me out of this... darkness."

He took another sip—sharp, burning, but familiar.

"You'd laugh at me, wouldn't you? Still chasing ghosts, still trying to fix things I never could."

The room answered with silence.

He leaned back, closing his eyes, still clutching the photo like it anchored him. His shoulder throbbed under the bandages. His soul ached worse.

So many had died. So much had been lost. And yet—somehow—he was still here.

A whisper of wind passed through the cracked window.

He didn't move. Just sat there, watching shadows play across the wall as the bottle emptied and the night deepened.

Inside Serenity Grove, warm yellow lights glowed dimly from the old lamps Claire had managed to make work again. She moved around quietly, tidying the living space — not because it needed to be done, but because it gave her hands something to do.

There were shattered photo frames in one corner, a toppled bookshelf still half-unrestored. Pillows lay skewed across the couch. Blood had been scrubbed away from the floorboards, but in the cracks — she could still see memory.

Claire stood up from adjusting a rug and turned toward the mantle. There it was again — *his* picture. David. Smiling that crooked, confident smile like he could take on the world and win. Her eyes lingered.

She walked closer, wiping the dust off the frame that had begun to settle again as if time itself had grown tired.

"I hope you're at peace now," she murmured. Her voice broke on the last word.

From the hallway came the muffled shuffling of small feet. She glanced back.

Emma and Lilly were in their room. The door was half-open. Claire didn't need to see them to know they weren't playing. Not tonight. Their toys remained untouched. Emma sat curled in a corner of the bed, hugging her knees, whispering things to herself — perhaps to David, perhaps to the dark.

Lilly was by the window, chin resting on the wooden ledge, staring blankly into the backyard where the old swing still creaked in the wind.

Claire didn't disturb them. She couldn't bear to ask how they were. Their silence said enough.

She returned to the couch and sank into it, burying her face in her hands for a moment before leaning back. The cushion beside her was empty — had been for days — but still she placed her palm over it. As if David might reach out and hold it again.

The clock ticked faintly. Somewhere, a kettle began to whistle on its own.

But the house remained still. Grieving.

The whiskey glass in Hawthorne's hand had long since warmed in his palm. He hadn't sipped in a while — just stared. His gaze was locked on a framed photo on the wall — his wife, caught mid-laughter in a forgotten summer.

A sharp *DING-DONG* echoed through the quiet house.

Hawthorne flinched, the glass clinking softly against the side table as he placed it down and stood. His shoulder still ached under the plaster, and the suddenness of the doorbell made his gut tighten.

He approached the door cautiously and opened it.

"S-Sarah?"

She stepped in quickly, breathless, hair slightly disheveled as if she had come straight from the road. Her eyes darted behind her once before settling on him.

"Can I come in?" she asked, already halfway through the doorway.

"Yeah—of course," Hawthorne said, surprised. "Come in."

He gently shut the door behind her as she made her way to the living room and sat down on the edge of the couch. Her hands wrung together in her lap, and she didn't lean back.

"You okay?" Hawthorne asked, approaching her, concerned. "You look like you rushed your way here."

"I did," Sarah said quickly. "I had to come."

"What happened?" he asked, lowering himself into the armchair across from her. "You're not making sense. Why the hurry?"

Sarah opened her mouth to speak—

RIIINGGG.

The landline rang — sharp and loud in the stillness of the house.

Hawthorne looked toward it instinctively.

"I should get that," he muttered, beginning to rise.

"No—don't." Sarah's voice cut across the room, low and urgent.

Hawthorne paused halfway up, confused.

"Why not?" he asked, narrowing his eyes slightly.

Sarah didn't answer. Her gaze was fixed on the ringing phone, her face unreadable — somewhere between fear and dread.

Claire sat on the edge of the couch, arms wrapped around her knees, lost in thought. Her eyes wandered—first to the photo, then to the empty hallway where her daughters had gone some time ago. The silence in the house was beginning to feel unnaturally heavy.

She blinked herself back to the present.

"They haven't eaten," she murmured.

Rising slowly, she stepped toward the hallway and called gently, "Emma? Lilly?"

No answer.

She tried again, a little louder this time. "Girls? What do you want for dinner?"

Still, only silence.

Claire's brows furrowed slightly. She glanced toward the bedroom where the girls were supposed to be, waiting for even a giggle or footsteps—but nothing came.

Her voice grew slightly firmer, masking the small pinch of unease. "Come on, darlings. Tell me what you feel like eating."

Silence.

She stood still for a moment, then took a step toward the hallway.

Hawthorne looked at Sarah, confused, unsettled... and then slowly reached for the phone anyway.

Click.

"Tom?" he said.

The voice on the other end wasn't calm. It wasn't normal.

It was trembling, breathless—Tom, crying.

"H-Hawthorne—it's Sarah... her car—she... Oh God..." he choked, sobbing.

"What? What are you talking about?" Hawthorne's eyes darkened.

"She's dead, man. She's dead... The car crashed into a tree just outside the town border. A branch—God, it—it went straight through her chest—she died on the spot. We just got the news—she's gone, Hawthorne... Sarah's gone..."

Hawthorne's hand slowly lowered the phone from his ear.

His breath caught.

He turned, stiffly, like something inside him already knew what he'd see.

Sarah was still there.

Standing.

Right in front of him.

But now—she wasn't sitting anymore.

She wasn't panting.

She wasn't blinking.

She just stood there, still, solemn… her eyes glistening with a sadness deeper than words could express.

Hawthorne didn't speak.

Neither did she.

They simply stared at one another.

The hallway was dimly lit, shadows cast long and thin across the floor as Claire moved slowly, her hands wiping nervously against her skirt. The silence was unsettling. Not the calm kind—but the kind that makes your heartbeat sound too loud in your ears.

She reached the half-open door of her daughters' room.

"Lily?" she called softly.

No answer.

Claire pushed the door with trembling fingers. The hinges creaked open with a faint moan.

Inside, Lily stood frozen near the bed—small, shivering. Her arms were locked by her sides, and her eyes… wide, unblinking, terrified.

She wasn't crying. That was the most disturbing part. Just standing—staring at the far wall.

Claire stepped in, a whisper of panic rising in her throat.

"Lily… what are you—"

Then she followed Lily's gaze.

Her breath caught. Her feet stopped moving.

The world tilted.

The scream never came at first—just disbelief. Then the horror hit like a crashing wave.

She saw Emma.

Her little girl—her sweet, playful, full-of-life Emma—was nailed to the wall. Arms stretched unnaturally outward, legs bound tight, and her entire small body inverted in a mockery of crucifixion.

Blood trickled down her bare arms in lazy rivers. Her dress was torn. Her head drooped toward the floor, hair dangling like soaked threads. Her eyes were half-open, glazed, staring at nothing. Her lips parted slightly, as if caught mid-word.

Claire fell to her knees, her scream piercing the silence like glass shattering in a church.

"EMMA!"

The scream made Lily flinch, but she didn't move.

Claire crawled toward the wall, her hands trembling violently as she reached toward her daughter, not knowing what to do, what to touch, how to fix it—how to fix *any* of it.

Her sobs racked through the room. The crucifixion wasn't just a murder. It was a message.

A desecration.

And something far worse… had begun.

Printed in Dunstable, United Kingdom